W9-BUQ-871

ALSO BY GISH JEN

Who's Irish?: Stories

Mona in the Promised Land

Typical American

The Love Wife

The Love Wife

Gish Jen

ALFRED A. KNOPF NEW YORK 2004

THIS IS A BORZOI BOOK
PUBLISHED BY ALFRED A. KNOPF

www.aaknopf.com

Owing to limitations of space, all acknowledgments for permission to reprint previously published material may be found following the acknowledgments.

Library of Congress Cataloging-in-Publication Data
Jen, Gish.
The love wife : a novel / Gish Jen. — 1st ed.
p. cm.
ISBN 1-4000-4213-5
1. Chinese Americans—Fiction. 2. Chinese—United States—Fiction.
3. Interracial marriage—Fiction. 4. Adopted children—Fiction.
5. Married people—Fiction. I. Title.
PS3560.E474L685 2004
813'.54—DC22
2004040917

Manufactured in the United States of America
First Edition

For Paloma

Contents

PART I

1 / *Lan Arrives* 3

2 / *Beam Me Out* 24

3 / *Automatica* 39

4 / *A Family Is Born* 56

5 / *Nothing's Plenty for Me* 86

6 / *Wendy* 103

7 / *A Kind of Guest* 134

8 / *Carnegie Takes a Day Off* 151

9 / *Time* 177

PART II

10 / *Trying to Be Happy* 199

11 / *A Happy Family* 239

12 / *Blondie Takes a Day Off* 249

13 / *Blondie Quits* 261

14 / *Shang* 284

15 / *Independence Island* 317

16 / *Sue's Beach* 330

17 / *The Waiting Room* 353

Acknowledgments 381

PART I

I

Lan Arrives

BLONDIE / The day Lan came, you could still say whose family this was—Carnegie's and mine.

We had three children. Two beautiful Asian girls—or should I say Asian American—Wendy, age nine, and Lizzy, age fifteen, both adopted; and one bio boy, Bailey, age thirteen months. Carnegie's ancestry being Chinese, and mine European, Bailey was half half, as they say—or is there another term by now? With less mismatch in it—'half half' having always spoken to me more of socks than of our surprise child, come to warm the lap of our middle years.

Our family was, in any case, an improvisation. *The new American family*, our neighbor Mitchell once proclaimed, tottering drunk up our deck stairs. But for Carnegie and me, it was simply something we made. Something we chose.

His mother, Mama Wong, thought this unnatural.

The trouble with you people is not enough periods, she liked to say. *You can say I think like Chinese, but I tell you. A child should grow up, say this is my mother, period. This is my father, period. Otherwise that family look like not real.*

Always good about assigning blame, she blamed the family on me.

I know Blondie. Everything a nut do, she do too. She is not even a real nut, like her friend Gabriela. She is only try-to-be-nut.

To which my friend Gabriela would say: *Janie. Your name is Janie, I can't believe you let Mama Wong call you Blondie all these years. And Carnegie too! That is like the definition of low self-esteem.*

I tried to tell her that it was my choice—that I liked nicknames. I tried to tell her that she could think of Blondie as my married name, as if I'd changed my first name instead of my last. For that was the way I was—or thought I was, before Lan came. An open person. A flexible person. Had I not been voted Most Sympathetic to Others in high school?

CARNEGIE / Our very own Blondie had, in her day, held the Kleenex for the homecoming queen.

But, whatever. Gabriela minded the Blondie bit far more than she minded being called, herself, a nut. She being the first to admit that she had gone back to the earth two or three times, maybe more. Also that she had spent years finding herself without much progress.

BLONDIE / *At least you have your family,* Gabriela used to say, thumbing through the personals. She circled possibles in pink; her red hair looped out the back of her baseball cap.

At least I had my family.

I was forty-five when Gabriela last said that; Carnegie was thirty-nine. It was 1999. We lived in a nice town with good schools, outside of Boston—a town within easy driving distance, as we liked to say, of both city and ocean.

At least I had my family.

Every happy family has its innocence. I suppose, looking back, this was ours.

Back then, our bird feeder was the most popular in town. In the snow we could have a hundred birds or more. But squirrels came too sometimes, more and more squirrels as the years went on. I fixed a tin pie plate to the top of the pole from which the feeder hung; I greased the pole itself. Yet still the hungry birds huddled in the bushes, some days—too many days—twittering. Clumps of snow pitched themselves from the branches as the birds refined their positions. Meanwhile, the squirrels leapt at the feeder from the trees, often from two or three directions at once. They gyrated midair—hurtling, twisting, flailing—only to plummet, midflight, to the ground. It was only every so often that one would make it to the seed, tail twitching; but then how the feeder would shudder and swing! Seed flying in black sheets onto the white snow.

— Squirrels will triumph, said Carnegie, observing this. — It's only natural.

But the seeds, surprisingly, sprouted in the spring—and wasn't that natural too? I had assumed the seeds sterile. They ought to have been sterile. One day I noticed in the grass, though, a rosetta of sunflower seedlings—each topped with a little leaf bow tie—which were almost immediately no longer seedlings; which were daily, miraculously, larger and larger—until there they loomed, modestly hugeheaded, fantastic with a rightness I wanted to call beauty.

It was these that I saw when I sat up in bed, the early fall day that Lan came to us. Our house was an old house, with enormously wide floorboards and, between them, correspondingly wide cracks. I toed one of these and felt, for all our housekeeping, graininess. The children thumped hollering down the stairs; Carnegie called for reinforcements, meaning me. Still, for a half second more I enjoyed my flowers. In one way, they were all wrong—a sudden haphazard clump in the middle of the yard. And yet how I drank them in, through the window screen, and the sunlit fog—that awkward glory. So crowded; disorderly; addled. They looked as if they'd dropped their contact lenses, every one of them, and all at the same time. These were the homely, brown-faced kind of sunflowers—some twelve feet tall, single-stalked, scraggly-leaved. Their huge heads knocked into one another. How strange they were—that bird feeder still nestled among their knees, like something they might trip on. And yet how authentic, somehow. How blissfully undeterred; full of the triumph of having become, from the seed of themselves, themselves.

Would this Lan—her name was Lan, meaning 'orchid'—like them?

Back when I was a sophomore in college, I spent a summer in Hong Kong, studying Mandarin. A summer was not a long time. Still, I did learn, a little, about how the Chinese in general prized the cultured. The cultivated.

These sunflowers, meanwhile, were anything but.

Of course, Mainlanders were different than Hong Kongers. The younger generations were different than the older. The less educated were different than the more. Daoists were different. Lan herself could be different.

In this family, we do not generalize, my mother would say. *In this family, we keep an open mind.*

Still, in my heart of hearts, I wished that this Lan would never come to behold them at all. I wished not to have to explain their beauty.

Now I believed, please understand, in openness. In the importance of cultural exchange, especially what with globalization and whatnot. My family had always hosted exchange students. And whatever the circumstances under which this Lan came, she was, after all, a relative of Carnegie's. Family.

Yet if I could add a word to our language, it would be a word for this: the peace a grown woman feels on the days—the rare days—when she needs to consider no view but her own.

WENDY / Dad has the windshield wipers on but like no one can see on account of the fog. How can the plane even land, says Lizzy, but Dad says there are special instruments, no one has to be able to see anything.

— It's like jumping, he says, can't we land on the floor with our eyes closed?

— A plane doesn't have feet like ours, says Lizzy. That's reassuring but not true.

— Oh really, says Dad. And where did you learn that?

— Some things you know yourself if you're smart enough to realize it, she says.

— What's reassuring? I say.

— Oh, use your brain, says Lizzy.

— *Ah-ah-ah-choo!* says Bailey.

Baby Bailey is so little he still has this mirror in front of him in the car. Now he sneezes at the baby in the mirror again—*ah-ah-ah-chooo!*—and laughs and laughs, loving himself so much that he drools. Dad says he's like Narcissus making his own pool, but then doesn't tell us what that means. In the fullness of time you will get my jokes, he says. In the fullness of time.

— Maybe it will lift, Mom says. Let's hope for the best.

— Maybe it will lift, says Lizzy, imitating her. — Let's hope . . .

— Elizabeth Bailey Wong, says Dad. Stop now.

He twists his head clear around like an owl practically, so we can see how his neck skin always wrinkles in a kind of spiral when he does that. Dad's parents were Chinese Chinese, like from China, so he has the same kind of skin as me and Lizzy, soft smooth like a hill of snow nobody's walked on, only kind of tea-colored in the summer, and creased like in a couple of places, it makes you realize that every time he turns around he does the exact same thing. Over and over. But he keeps on doing it anyway, just like Lizzy keeps on being Lizzy, if she didn't we'd probably all float up to the ceiling with happiness and bang our heads.

Maybe it will lift, says Lizzy one more time, in her imitation-Mom voice, and then says, in her regular voice: — When I grow up will I also spout inanities out of nowhere?

No answer.

— And what if we don't like her? says Lizzy. Can we send her back to China?

— Can we send her back to China, sighs Mom.

Lizzy is wearing a nose ring and earrings, and henna tattoos in the shape of snakes. Thank god the tattoos at least wash off and that short short blond hair will grow out too, Mom says, but of course not in front of Lizzy, because she completely knows what Lizzy will say back. Namely, *Why shouldn't I bleach my hair, it's no different than you highlighting yours, and besides why shouldn't I be blond when my mother is blond?*

So instead Mom just says things like how she doesn't like that phrase, sending people back to China. Because people say that even to people who speak perfect English and have been here a long time, she says, and how are you going to like it if people say that to you?

— They aren't going to say that to me, says Lizzy.

— We hope, says Mom.

She doesn't twist around like Dad to talk to us, she just looks in the mirror on the back side of the car visor. Mom is like the complete opposite of Dad. Dad is muscle-y. If you threw him in the ocean he would sink plunk to the bottom, while Mom would bob right up, Dad calls her za-za vavoomy. And she's like colorful. We can see her in the mirror, those blue blue eyes and that blond blond hair and those pink pink lips. It's the complete farm girl look, Lizzy says, that being where her family is from originally, on her mom's side anyway, a farm in Wisconsin where people were real and not phony. Of course she herself grew up in Connecticut. Still who would've thought she'd end up in a place where people actually buy those black designer diaper bags? That's what she wants to know sometimes, I guess she always figured she'd kind of drift back to the farm someday.

But like here she is.

— We hope, says Mom. But even if they don't, in our family we don't talk about sending people back to China. Because some of the people who get told that aren't from China to begin with.

— Some of them are from New Jersey, says Dad.

— Some of them aren't even of Chinese origin, says Mom.

— You mean some of them are who-knows-what, says Lizzy. Right? Japanese, or Vietnamese.

— Right.

— Or mixed-up soup du jour, like me. Right?

— Right.

— You're too sensitive, says Lizzy.

Mom flips the visor back up, making that little light next to the mirror blink out. Which now that it's gone was the brightest thing I've seen all day, I see that's how gray it is out.

— And how is it that the honky in the family gets to explain this? Mom asks the air.

Dad puts the windshield wipers on high even though it isn't really raining.

— You are a superior being married to a quasi-Neanderthal who has yet to internalize the mores of the middle class, that's how, he says, turning to her. And when she doesn't turn back, he puts his eyebrows up and down, he has these big thick eyebrows like caterpillars. Then he says, quiet like: — I do beg your patience.

His cell phone rings, this week the tune is 'America the Beautiful,' which he says is for the benefit of Lizzy and me, he wants to make sure we know more than 'Afunga Alafia.' Not that he has anything against Swahili, Swahili is very nice, he says, a language spoken by many.

— Sounds great, he says now, into the phone, in his work voice. — Just make sure the visuals are in order and . . . exactly.

Bailey starts crying, so Lizzy plugs him up with a passy.

— Anyway, she's from a little town someplace between Shanghai and Beijing, Mom says. Which are cities in China.

— You told us that already, says Lizzy.

But Mom keeps going over the whole thing anyway like it's what to do in case of a fire or something.

— She's very nice and she's our relative, says Mom. She'll be here for a couple of years, helping with you guys, and we are all going to like her.

— That's reassuring but not necessarily true, says Lizzy.

— No one can say anything around here, says Dad.

— That's not true either, says Lizzy.

— So what is true? I say. If you're so smart.

LIZZY / — Parents are liars, I said. When they're worried they reassure you and they steal your Halloween candy if you're not careful.

— Nobody stole your Halloween candy, said Dad. If you're talking about last year.

— I was careful, I said.

WENDY / —Some was missing from mine, I say.

I look at the black back of Dad's head, and then at the blond back of Mom's.

— I don't even like Reese's peanut butter cups, says Dad.

— Oh, for heaven's sake, Carnegie, says Mom.

— Nor do I care for Kit Kats, he says.

— Honestly! says Mom. You are my fourth child.

— *So sue me, sue me, what can you do me,* sings Dad. *I . . . a-a-ate . . . them.*

His cell phone rings again, we can hear the words in our heads. *Ohh beau-ti-ful for spacious . . .*

— Will you put that thing on vibrate, says Mom. And when Dad doesn't answer: — Honey, please. Taking phone calls night and day is not going to help. If there are going to be layoffs, there are going to be layoffs.

— Thank you for that consoling insight, says Dad. It will bring me almost as much solace on a sleepless night as knowing the Great Greenspan saw this coming.

His phone rings again. *Ohh beau-ti-ful for . . .*

— And may I just point out that I turned mine off even though I have that board meeting tomorrow, says Mom.

—*Nobler than springtime, are you,* sings Dad then. *Sweeter than Kit Kats, are you . . .*

But he shuts his phone off and hands it to Mom. She puts it in the glove compartment, closing it up with kind of a bang because it doesn't work that great. Of course it falls back open again anyway, so she hits it again, only more gently, which works. There's that click. Then she looks over her shoulder and says: — Your dad is a joker.

— Better a joker than a joke, he says back.

— And all because his mother named him Carnegie, Mom says. Carnegie Wong.

— Who was Carnegie again? I ask.

But Mom says: — Who else but Mama Wong would do such a thing? Honestly.

Dad says his problem isn't just his problem.

— Don't you think at some point in life everyone has to ask, Whose joke is this?

— No, says Mom.

— That's because your family is from the Midwest where the eternal questions are, Is it going to snow? And, Is it going to rain? says Dad. Not to mention, Is it going to stop?

— The difference between us, says Mom, is that I can at least imagine a faith that's not laughable.

Road sign. Road sign. They pop out of the fog like out of nowhere, then get bigger and bigger until they're gone. Like *poof.*

— Whereas belief in the SATs generally lasts 1.0 generations, agrees Dad finally.

— Aren't the SATs that test Lizzy has to take? I ask.

The windshield wipers keep on wiping and wiping as if that's their homework and they just have to do it.

. . .

The airport is big and washable, that's what Lizzy says, every single surface is easy to clean because of all the people. People are dirty. They stick gum under the seats, they spill coffee, everything would get disgusting if it weren't for chemicals.

— Our Lizzy, truth teller, says Dad, cracking his knuckles. — Maybe you will be an investigative journalist.

— Journalists are liars, says Lizzy. All they are about is does it make a good story and the truth is not always a good story.

— Lizzy, says Mom. Please.

— No, don't stop, says Dad. Just try to say what you have to say in a way people can hear.

— You mean, in a way Mom can hear, says Lizzy.

— Mom and me.

— Hmm, she says. And then she surprises everybody by saying it again, louder: — Hmm.

There are no shadows in the middle part of the airport, and that makes everything sound funny.

Mom's bouncing Bailey and squinting at the writing on the screen. The diaper bag is swinging big and heavy behind her, it wouldn't be so heavy except for the bottles and ice packs she has to lug around now that Bailey weaned himself out of nowhere.

— Of course, I knew one day would be the last time, she told her friend Gabriela on the phone. Gabriela was in Italy, but still they talked and e-mailed all the time. — But I mean, for him to wean himself. A bottle's just a bottle. I wanted to keep him a little longer, that's all.

She was crying.

LIZZY / — Poor Mom, Wendy said.

But I said: — You see? She was never that close to us, even when we were babies. Not like she was to Bailey. Face facts, it was different.

WENDY / Though maybe Mom is going to be exactly the same with Bailey as us when he grows up, that's what I think. Maybe with Bailey she's going to be like, *We'll talk about it after supper, okay?* And, *I'm sorry, pumpkin, I know this was our special time, but this is the life of a working mother.* And maybe Dad is going to be like, *Tell me again, I'm listening, it just takes time to open a heart. Because first you have to stop. Like this.* And he'll take a big breath. *Whew. Now tell me again, no laughing. What is it?*

LIZZY / Or maybe they won't.

But anyway—the diaper bag.

WENDY / — Can't you lighten that thing up? Dad says.

But Mom says, squinting: — With what time? And you're welcome to clean out the refrigerator while you're at it.

So that Dad has only just taken the bag from Mom's shoulder and is still mushing it into the mesh thingy under the stroller when she starts hurrying. Bailey is bouncing and her boobs are bouncing, and her white shirt is flying all around her like there's a big wind, and she's turning pink in the face. It's like her lips and her skin are matching, so that her eyes are as blue as this special-effect laser beam.

— She's here already, Mom says. Early! In the fog! Whoever would have thought she would be early?

— Early! we yell. Early! Her plane must have special instruments!

And we are running down the halls, running and running.

CARNEGIE / Selected preconceptions, wholly inexcusable:

1. That she would have an unfortunate perm.
2. That she would cook better than Mama Wong but require education as to the horrors of cholesterol.
3. That she would be reliable.
4. That she would look half her age.
5. That she would mend.
6. That she would speak Chinese.
7. That she would eschew center stage.
8. That she would favor hot-water bottles.
9. That she would wear sweater vests.
10. That she would root for both sides of ball games.

She was indeed capable, as it turned out, of rooting for both sides of ball games.

And she did indeed speak Chinese. Mandarin, of course, as well as selected other dialects.

And she did indeed look half her age. No gray, and nary a wrinkle, thanks to that Asian predisposition toward subcutaneous fat. You could easily have taken her for a slightly older cousin of the girls, though I knew her to be forty-six. Seven years older than me, a year older than Blondie.

What a surprise, though, that she moved as arrestingly as she did. When we first spotted her—or what we at least thought was her, from her picture—she was proceeding along ho-hum with the stream of other passengers from California, headed past the arrival gates toward the public waiting area. A medium-tall figure in black, slim. Low ponytail, long neck, Modigliani-like shoulder slope.

There was a clog and ensuing backup; some geezer's shopping bag had lost its bottom. Sundry people helpfully chased down the surprising array of rolling items, while others looked on. Lan alone began then to disappear, then reappear, slipping calmly through the confusion. Let others mill; she wove and sidestepped with quiet aplomb. Accustomed to crowds, it appeared. Disappearing, reappearing, disappearing, reappearing. Stopping just once, disconcertingly, to spit into an open trash can. A quick, perfect little shot; compared to expectorations I'd seen in China, this was positively elegant.

She disappeared again.

Then materialized out past security, a few yards from us. A plainish woman, neither pleasing nor displeasing. Face on the long side, eyes on the large side, nose on the flat side, mouth on the full side. High cheekbones, one on either side. Haggard, and yet somehow on the alert, as if in a war zone. Nothing dangled from her. How dangly everyone around her by comparison, how idiotically overaccessorized. And how she held herself; with what sweetly intimidating posture. There was nothing Chinese about it. Only Lan held herself this way, as if bent on disconnecting her head from her feet.

— Lan! we called. Lan!

She suspended, briefly, her travel.

What was it that crossed her face then?

Maybe she was simply jet-lagged. Maybe she was taken aback by Lizzy's nose ring and tattoos, or by her blond hair. Or maybe it was the all-blond lineup of Blondie, Bailey, and Lizzy that surprised her. (It so happened that black-haired Wendy and I stood a little in back of the others.)

Later we learned too that though we'd sent her a picture of us, thanks to some semi-predictable postal vagrancy she hadn't received it. In any case, there ensued some manner of small-scale system failure. You could see her hit RESET.

— How do you do, she said, a moment later, recomposed.

She clutched her purse as if it was full of contraband she had managed to sneak through customs.

— Welcome to America! How was your flight? we said.

— Hello, she said again. Smiling a smile we would soon recognize, a certain lopsided half smile.

— Are you Lan? I asked, suddenly wondering.

— Nice meet you. She bobbed her head.

Blondie resurrected her Chinese: — *Nin shi bu shi jiao Lin Lan?*

Lan relaxed her grip slightly and said in Chinese: —*You speak Chinese!*

— *I do,* said Blondie.

— *You speak very well.*

— *I studied for several years in college,* said Blondie.

A long pause; Lan receded a bit. That half smile.

BLONDIE / Perhaps I was supposed to say, *Nali, nali*—meaning 'Where? where?'—when she said that about speaking well. That was the Chinese script, after all. Perhaps I should have denied being able to speak, or insisted I spoke badly, terribly, at most one or two words.

Or perhaps I should have said something that started with *you.* She had said something *you;* perhaps instead of starting with *I,* I should have answered, likewise, *You. You are too kind.*

CARNEGIE / — Don't forget the blond thing, I said. A blonde speaking Chinese. That might have thrown her. Or maybe she thought you were putting yourself above her.

BLONDIE / — Why in heaven's name would I do that? I said.

CARNEGIE / — I just know that's what my mother would have thought, I said. She was very binary in that way. Always looking down on someone, or else convinced someone was looking down on her. As if all the world was a ladder to her, and we but poor climbers on it.

BLONDIE / He said: — Lan might have wondered too whether she was a family member exactly—if by 'nanny' we didn't mean *ayi*. A servant. And what did it signify that she was being brought over on a student visa when she wasn't a student per se?

— But wasn't that just the easiest kind of visa to get? I said.

She was dressed, in any case, all in black, like Lizzy, yet with entirely different effect. Everything Lizzy wore was torn or altered in some way—in-your-face clothes. Lan's clothes, in contrast, seemed gotten together with care. Everything looked new—her thick nylons, and high-heeled, leatherette sandals; her narrow skirt, and V-neck sweater. The sweater was pointelle, with a flame-stitch bottom. The skirt matched. Neither fit very well. Even her undergarments seemed not quite hers—her bust preceding her in an odd way.

CARNEGIE / A distinctly cold-war affair, that brassiere, suggesting advanced industrial engineering and projectile menace.

BLONDIE / You could tell—even we could tell—that she was not exactly from Shanghai. You could tell that she was not even from a city proper, but from the outskirts of a city—the sort of town where people have more than they used to, but can hardly be called rich.

She appeared an inch or two taller than Lizzy, who was a good five-four. And yet how similar they seemed. All in black, as I've said, and willowy, though Lizzy was longer-waisted. Or no, maybe Lan looked more like Wendy—so I thought when Wendy walked up. Wendy hadn't started developing yet. You could see, though, what a slender thing she was always going to be—a wonder to someone of my shape. Though shorter than Lan, she had similar torso-to-leg proportions. They both had too that shiny black hair.

Wendy, thankfully, was not wearing black. Wendy still wore, then, what I bought her. A flowered shirt, and flowered shorts. Flowered sandals. One thing good about her being a somewhat shy child was that she was, at nine, still mine.

Still mine, I say. And yet from the first moment I saw the three of them together, I thought they seemed, despite their differences, a set. Was that racist? Like kitchen canisters, I thought. S-M-L.

Carnegie and Lan chatted awkwardly by the luggage carousel. Then no one said anything. Then Lizzy said something and, amazingly, Lan smiled and said something back—about Michael Jordan, of all things, and about somebody else—a Yao Ming?—her manner surprisingly warm. There was another exchange I didn't catch. How ringed, still, Lan's person with vigilance; and yet her face, as she began to relax, flickered with quiet life.

— Such beautiful skin, you have, she told Lizzy. You must know how to eat. Have good water too.

Lan said this smiling gently, gesturing gently. Her movements like a murmur—not making a big positive point, as Lizzy always claimed I did. Lizzy in turn beamed, tilting her head down shyly, so that a roll of fat appeared under her chin. I hadn't known she still had that roll of fat; suddenly I saw her, a toddler again, demanding I follow her around and around the patio. *I engine! You caboose!*

— How clever you are. I can see by your eyes, clever, she told Wendy, a little while later. — People should listen to you.

— I like to play chess, said Wendy, looking at the floor.

No fat roll under her chin. Though she had been a fat baby in China, she'd thinned out almost as soon as she got to America.

— Will you teach me to play? asked Lan.

— I'll teach you right away! said Wendy. I'm a good teacher! I take lessons! You can practice on the computer! At school I have to play with the boys because none of the girls will play, but on the computer there are these websites.

— You teach me, said Lan. I practice with you.

It was impossible not to like her. I tried to smile at her, and to gauge whether she was smiling back. And sometimes I thought so. Yet still, as the luggage snaked around, I remained outside the circle of her charm. Perhaps this was because I was occupied with walking Bailey. Hunched over him like some newfangled plant support, I helped him step step step his way to the stairs—Bailey loved stairs. He wore his brand-new white leather tie-up shoes; his hot fists gripped my fingers.

— Look what you can do! Lan cooed at Bailey as, on one tour, we slowly passed her way.

Right, left, right, left.

— Such a big big boy, said Lan on the next round.

She touched his cheek—her nails were beautifully groomed, oval and pink. Bailey, shy, motioned to be picked up. But once in my arms he cooed back, showing off his teeth. He batted his lashes and clobbered my upper arm, mysteriously emphatic.

— Why everybody talk to baby instead of talk to big girls? she asked Lizzy and Wendy. — Have you ever notice that?

Bailey's face crumpled then—at what no one could say. He wailed; the girls showed Lan his pacifier. They showed her the stroller too, and how it folded up. They let her try it once herself. She folded it perfectly, without coaching, the first try.

— In China, this kind cart, many people have it, she explained.

— Really? said the girls.

— How do you call it?

— Stroller, said Lizzy. Strol-ler.

— Stro-er, said Lan.

— Strol-ler. Strol-ler.

Her one suitcase arrived damaged. Lan squatted gracefully, placing the suitcase on the floor. The girls squatted beside her as if they did this every day. The suitcase had been wrapped in plastic. She opened this, not by tearing the wrapping, but by slicing it neatly on the diagonal, with a pair of fold-up scissors. Nothing seemed to be missing. Still Carnegie strode off, indignant, damaged bag on a luggage cart, to demand the airline do something. We trailed him like ducklings, gathering obediently outside the claims office until, triumphant, he reappeared, with the announcement that he had arranged for the bag to be replaced with a new one.

At this, Lan smiled her first full, true smile—a completely sweet, open, girlish smile, so guileless and lovely that Carnegie Wong, my husband of fourteen years, blushed.

WENDY / In the car she insists on sitting in the third seat, in the way back, so that Mom and Dad can sit together and we three kids can sit together too, in the middle seat, not that we want to. She doesn't talk at all in the beginning, but when we talk to her she turns around, and after a while she talks too.

— Do you have favorite color? she asks.

— Guess, says Lizzy.

And Lanlan—she makes us call her Lanlan—says: — Black.

Or at least sort of. She doesn't say 'black' exactly, really she says 'brack,' but we understand her because we like her.

— You knew because I'm wearing black! says Lizzy.

Lanlan nods. — Black very nice, she says. Do you like draw picture?

— Yes! says Lizzy. But how did you know that?

— Black very—how do you say?—artist, says Lanlan.

— You're wearing black! I say. You're wearing Lizzy's favorite color.

— Wow, she says. Or do you say Wow-wee.

— Wow, says Lizzy.

— I see, she says, though this frown like nests in her face. — How about Gee whiz? Or Gee, what. Gee willikers.

— Gee willikers? says Lizzy.

— Better stick with wow, I say.

— Wow, she says.

— Are you artistic? Lizzy asks.

— Me? Oh, no no, she says. Then she says: — I can see American fashion is not like Chinese fashion.

— We have bellbottoms, I tell her, and flower power!

— Not everybody wears that stuff, says Lizzy. Like I personally don't pay attention to fashion at all.

— In China, we have fashion too, says Lanlan. But I am like you. Do not pay too much attention.

— Not even a little? I say.

— Well, okay, she says, smiling. — A little. Last few weeks. Now I am—how to say—fashion victim.

— I pay a little attention too, says Lizzy.

— A little? I say. A lot! That's all she knows, is fashion! A lot of people dress like Lizzy. Like her friend Xanadu. Ask her about Xanadu, Xanadu is practically her twin!

— That is totally untrue, says Lizzy.

— Wow, says Lanlan calmly. And how about you, Wendy? Are you fashion victim?

She talks and talks to us, patting Bailey on the head every now and then even though he's asleep.

— My turn! My turn! Lizzy and I begin to shout at the same time, but when Lanlan puts her finger in the air, even Lizzy shuts up like magic.

— My English not so good, Lanlan keeps saying. I only know a few phrases.

— Like what? says Lizzy.

— 'Call 911,' says Lan. 'In case of emergency call 911.'

— Your English is fantastic! we tell her. Did you study in college?

She smiles a little, then says: — Not exactly college. But like college. Usually we say university.

Instead of 'usually' she says 'u-ally.'

— Like university? we say.

— In China, many people, maybe they not so rich, or have difficulty pass exam, try study by self, she says. See teacher every once a while.

— Wow, we say.

— Can get degree this way. Of course, take some time.

— Did you get a degree? we ask. Did you?

She doesn't answer but just smiles and sits there kind of ladylike with her back straight up and her knees pressed together, so that her lap is like a table.

— We are rich Americans, says Lizzy. Aren't we?

Lanlan looks out the window at the big mist, as if there's something to see. There's nothing to see but still you can see her eyes jerking back and forth, because of its going by so fast.

BLONDIE / Of course, she was amazed by our house. We ourselves were amazed by our house—a lovely old farmhouse, walking distance to town, with a porch, and a large rolling lawn, and a converted barn housing cars and, these days, a black-and-white pygmy goat—Gabriela's, actually, as you will hear. Even in the fog you could see how the house commanded its little knoll. The land settled in green swales around it, like a skirt. I had my eccentric sunflowers in back—you couldn't see them right away. But there, by the driveway, stood our small orchard of seven wide apple trees, planted in a circle so that their arms all but touched. Of course, individually those trees were awkward, as apple trees can be. They had that arthritic look. As a group, though, they appeared, charmingly, to be playing ring-around-the-rosy. And in the spring they formed a ceiling of blossoms. If from the front yard you made your way up the little incline—there were five or six stone steps—you ascended into a low sky of bloom—a heaven. Who could get enough of that magic? And in the fall! You could see the branches bending with fruit now—most of it edible, though we did not use pesticides. Soon the girls would be out apple picking, the old branches bending so low they all but dropped their fruit into the baskets. Both Lizzy and Wendy climbed on those branches when they were little, and pretended to be high in the air; both walked the branches like a circular balance beam when they were older. And both made it to the tops of the trees, one day, and yelled for Carnegie and me to come see.

CARNEGIE / The middle branches were squirrel diving boards; our Olympians sprang from them onto the driveway, that around the bikes and trikes, Rollerblades and roller skates, they might race. Overhead, the mockingbirds blithely popularized (okay, plagiarized) the more original songs of others.

Clouds drifted. The wind wafted.

Dew baubled the grass.

Altogether the house was a vision—the vision of my lovely wife, Blondie, whose extended description I here interject.

For Blondie, at forty-five, was herself a vision.

She had, it must be said, a dewlap. Lines patterned her forehead; she sported an asterisk on the bridge of her nose. Certain age spots, once indistinct, had found their proud round own. Her ears were both pinker and downier than they once were. Her in-truth lemon-lightened hair, once fluffy, now tended to go flat. How she would have been undone were it not for mousse! She sported a childbearing-related protuberance that disposed her toward rumpled linen jumpers. You would not call her limber anymore. The words Blondie brought to mind were all *lum* words: *lumber, lumbar* . . . I stop out of husbandly delicacy, but also because those words miss her paradoxical large lightness. A pufferfish, she was. A zeppelin buoyed by a certain singular gas.

She was not young. She complained of stress. She complained of short-term memory problems. She was perimenopausal. She took gingko, ginseng, echinacea during cold season. Huperzine A. Calcium with soy. Black cohash. She needed reading glasses and could not for the life of her remember names. Yet somehow, brilliantly, she managed to head marketing for a socially responsible investment firm she had helped found, even while imbuing her station-wagon life with the illusion of unharried ardency. This was non-trivial. It filled one with awe to see how she worked around her work haunted houses for Halloween (complete with dry-ice effects), not to say all manner of other wonders involving yogurt, cheesecloth, two-liter soda bottles. How enraptured she could manage to be (for the purposes of a school assignment) by the history of navigation, the idea of India, the point system of dog shows!

No one went in for homework like Blondie.

She had smooth, delicate, in places transparent, skin, through which her veins most touchingly showed. Her plump forearms tapered into surprisingly small, twinkly hands. Her fingers moved deftly, but in a slightly splayed way, as if she had just left a manicurist's table. Other small surprises: a surprisingly small nose, and small but round, lively eyes. The last time Blondie had gone to a hairdresser she had come back with a wayward crew; an anti-flop strategy. Now she looked like Laurie Anderson gone Smith & Hawken.

In short, in her broad middle age Blondie had retained a certain unforced sweetness and small-town spark. She could be shy, but she could surprise you. And she was sincere, my Blondie, a precious block of something pre-veneer.

Yet, inexplicably, she did resemble a Realtor as she showed Lan her new digs, an apartment in the garage-née-barn built especially for an au pair.

— This is your kitchenette, said Blondie.

She indicated with an open hand the wood-tone doors of the Pullman kitchen. She demonstrated the use of its apartment-sized electric stove. Next, the half-height refrigerator. All these things had been put in by the previous owners, who had in general abhorred the genuine and full-sized. She picked a hair off the butcher block–look counter.

— Ah! said Lan.

She was, I thought, at least semi-smiling. She nodded. She stepped into the main room, with its sculpted acrylic carpeting, then just stood there, pressing her fingers together. She contemplated the carpet.

BLONDIE / —We thought we'd provide the basics and let you do the decorating, I said. So you wouldn't have to live with someone else's taste.

— Ah! she said.

— If you don't like the white, we'd be happy to help you paint. The girls love that sort of thing.

— Ah! she said again.

CARNEGIE / The furniture was my mother's. Big boudoir-y mahogany we had no place to store. You could hear the goat bleating downstairs.

BLONDIE / Carnegie would have given her the guest room. He thought it would have made her feel more welcome to be in the house—part of the house.

But that was right below our bedroom, and the apartment was larger. It had a kitchenette, and a bath. It had skylights. There were windows on two walls, and a ceiling fan. Even in the fog you could see how airy it was. And you did not enter through the garage—there was a separate entrance opposite the house, behind the toolshed. You went down a little path, then up a spiral staircase.

CARNEGIE / — If I were her I'd want my own space, said Blondie. If I were her, I would want privacy.

One must consider one's chromosomes before speaking these days. Still, summoning my piddling male courage, I tendered a sensitive observation.

— Did you see how she looked down at her feet? First she looked at the carpet, and then at her feet. There was something she didn't want to say.

— I did see her bow her head, said Blondie, after a moment. — I thought it was after she saw my sunflowers out back. You know what a mess they are.

Lan had looked down at her feet, her eyebrows a little raised; she had stared at her big toes through her stockings, as if looking to them for advice or friendship. Then she had very slightly shifted her weight. I heard a squeak, and saw how new her high heels were, how synthetic, how cheaply made. They dug into her feet. I saw how she rocked back onto her heels, inching the balls of her feet up the ramps, out from under the front straps. It was a movement I'd seen many women make over the years, without seeing it. The female equivalent of loosening a tie. But never had I seen an instep as swollen as hers, nor welts so lurid. Her heels hung over the backs of the lasts; those shoes were too small. Maybe her feet had swollen up on the plane. That was possible. Still, Blondie would never have worn shoes like that. Today she was, in fact, wearing semi-orthopedic Danish clogs. When she walked she clopped.

Blondie would have rightly complained about how her feet hurt. Lan simply gazed, meditative, upon hers.

2

Beam Me Out

CARNEGIE / Lan. Of course we have started the story with Lan, on whose account so much eventually came to pass. But I hereby restart it to begin two years earlier, when my mother was still alive; for in the beginning, believe me, was Mama Wong.

Is this not allowed? Never mind.

We will return to Miss Fine Spine soon enough, never fear.

How soberly exhilarating the first four or five years of my mother's stay at the Evergreen Overlook Assisted Living Residence Home! Other residents of the Alzheimer's unit came and went; only Mama Wong survived, survived. For the next couple of years too we remained guiltily proud. She was beating the odds. She was outliving other people. She was proving, as she would have liked, a winner.

Such victory was expensive. I could not help but note, by the seventh year or so, that it cost $4,500 a month and was not covered by insurance; also that one could not say so. One was not permitted to recall that Mama Wong, then eighty-three, used to boast how in her family women often lived to be a hundred. That would be unfeeling.

— How often does she even recognize me? I said all the same, revealing my inner beast one fine suburban morning.

— But the times it does happen, said Blondie immediately. The times she's there.

Blondie held her hand to her belly as she spoke; she was then, at forty-three, to our most profound confoundment, pregnant. Before her thrashed the pygmy goat, its head stuck in a watering can. I was not too clear about the name of the goat; only that it belonged to Blondie's dear friend Gabriela, who had suffered a fencing failure such as had led to the destruction of her garden by deer. This had in turn led to her allowing a hunter on to her land, a man who shot with a bow and arrow, and dressed like a tree. He had donated the meat to a shelter. Nevertheless, Gabriela had been forced to recuperate in Italy.

This was how her goat had come to live (illegally) on our nice suburban property, where he butted our children and nibbled on their ice skates. He denuded our kousa dogwood. He made a mockery of our lawn.

His one charm: he could hold his ears out straight to either side, like a parody of a crucifixion.

Still Blondie doted on the creature because he belonged to Gabriela, and because he evoked, lucky quadraped, her sacred family-farm past.

— The goat butted Wendy again today, I said. She fell and knocked a tooth out.

Blondie absently left the goat to thrash, its balloon belly, like hers, heaving. The clanging of the watering can was loud.

— Was she upset? she asked.

— She ran off crying about how she was just glad she didn't live on a farm.

— And you said?

— I said she was right, she should be sure to remember this moment and stick to the suburbs all the days of her life. Also I asked if she wanted to eat the goat for dinner.

— Carnegie, said Blondie, putting a hand to her belly again.

I helped her free the goat, which in its eternal gratitude kicked me in the shin.

— He is not like your mother, said Blondie. He's only a goat.

I eyed its wattles.

— You have to forgive her, Carnegie, you do.

I looked the goat in the eye; it stared back with god-given indifference. Its rectangular pupils were like mail slots.

Across the street, our neighbor hauled a stuffed leaf bag out to the sidewalk. Mitchell, distinctly resembling the leaf bag, sported a new black leather jacket with his also new bifocals; there was, blessedly, nothing new in his wave. I waved back. Mitchell was on his third wife, a Norwegian minx given to sarongs. Was she a sign of vitality or of illness? Was she ridiculously sexy or just plain ridiculous? Blondie thought Mitch obsessed with death. He had, after all, gotten the wife post-prostate scare. I, though, thought Mitch obsessed with breasts, just like his brother Nick with his several Asian mistresses, about whom, through some obscure racial association, I heard about all the time: *I kid you not, they will do anything, singly or in groups.*

I, truth to tell, was the one obsessed with death.

Now Mitchell could be heard leaving, on his new motorcycle, for his new office. On a Sunday, no less. *Homo resurrectus.*

Leave it to me to have a dying mother who would not die.

Her slippers appeared magnetically attached to the carpet. Her arms appeared magnetically attached to her sides. Not all Alzheimer's patients were so infirm at first; but eventually they passed through Mama Wong's stage. It was just luck she had arrived there and stayed.

Once upon a time—long, long ago—she had been an anomalous woman, languid looks married to the manner of a fishmonger. I did not resemble her. Her absurdly long fingers were hers alone, that enormous reach. Her nose was too flat to be typically Sichuanese, but she had the large eyes and long face of her region; also the special skin people attributed to growing up in Chongqing. It was the gift of living in a steam bath; life was a continual facial. She had too the sloped shoulders of a Chinese immortal; whereas I, apparently, had inherited my father's block build along with his beetle brow. Barbarian looks, my mother said, *who know where you from.* That being the kind of sweet thing Mama Wong was given to say.

She liked to fish. This was something she had learned to do off a pier her first summer in America; and all her life she continued to love the long long lines that reached down toward the ocean floor. She loved the slippery mystery of the catch. She loved not knowing what was on the hook until it was out in the air—flipping madly, bigger or smaller or altogether different than what she had imagined. *Most people do not realize we are come from the sea,* she would say. *Those fish are our ancestor.* Sometimes she would laugh at herself as she said this. *Uncle dolphin, grandfather whale.* She was not above carrying, in her beautifully stitched pocketbooks, with their sleek calfskin sides and cunning gold-tone clasps, jars of bait. Mostly this was power bait or artificial bait, only sometimes was it live.

BLONDIE / How hard it was to diagnose her Alzheimer's! How hard to say what was inappropriate behavior for her. All her behavior was inappropriate.

CARNEGIE / To wit: she had, in her day, escaped from the Mainland by swimming across the harbor to Hong Kong. How appropriate was that? Given that there were sharks in the water; given that she couldn't even swim, exactly. Anyone else would have thought twice. But my mother, being my mother, simply snugged a basketball under each arm, kicked until she got there, then looked up a distant cousin.

Where there is will, there is way, she would explain, years later, if asked.

Or else: *I just don't like those Communists.*

Now she still said these things, her eyes blank.

— Where there is will.

— Those Communists.

— My cousin surprised, yes. Surprised.

Once I gave her a nightgown printed with fish for Mother's Day; she still wore it to bed at night. It had grown diaphanous with washing, so that you could see through the trout to her nipples, which sported the forlornly useful look of spare-the-counter stick-on appliance feet.

Worse, you could see her diaper, which she needed. She cried and cried while I tried to get her to drink juice.

— You are going to become dehydrated, I told her. Do you want to dry up?

Often, in her early years at the Overlook, she still had her English, having attended a primary school run by American missionaries. How lucky for us! Often too, she still joked. *What? You think you are white? You are Wong! Wong! Wong!* she would say, banging her hand on her mattress. Or else: *Two Wongs—two Wongs—two—don't make a white!* Those were the days I still hung on her words when she spoke. She had never liked talking about her past; now I waited, notebook at the ready, for whatever might emerge. And things did emerge, after a fashion, over time. A nun, a train, a girl who cried and cried. A dangerous place. A book. A bottle. But what place? What book? What bottle? Phrases emerged with more insistence than meaning. *Sounded like a cat. Like a cat. A cat sound.* My notebook stayed mostly blank—growing, it seemed, month by month, blanker—until finally I put it away.

As the years went on, more and more of her mumbling was in Chinese anyway. Sometimes Blondie could translate. Though Blondie had taken Chinese in college, and assiduously brushed up once Lizzy came to us, my mother used to insist she couldn't even tell what language Blondie was speaking when she spoke Mandarin. *Sound like something strange.* Now Mama Wong listened carefully. Responded earnestly, sometimes. But it was like a language lab with wiring problems; all the dialogs were scrambled. And what about the days—more and more all the time—when she had forgotten her Mandarin, and knew, apparently, only Sichuanese? How well we were coming to know the sound of it. That argumentative, sibilant sound, irregular and explosive, like firecrackers. I wished she had taught me to speak it. But she never did. Could she ever have said why?

In any case, she could no longer.

Some days she just stared. Some days she seemed to be trying to get me to remember things for her. *The river,* she would say. But when I said, *What river? Do you mean in Sichuan?* she would look as if she had no idea why I was talking about rivers. Some days she was liable to throw things; we kept glass and heavy objects out of her room. Other days she was sweet and childlike. Once she cradled a flower I gave her, stroking its petals. She compared her shadow with mine, and watched mesmerized as one disappeared into the other.

I put on a little shadow-puppet show for her.

— Then the crow said *caw caw caw!* I told her. And that was the signal for all the forest creatures to sneak down into the valley.

— Friendly crow very useful, she said. Whole forest look like empty without it.

Another day she asked if I would tickle her.

— I tickle you back, she suggested.

— Okay, I said; but then was surprised when the tickling turned into a kiss on the lips.

— Oh, Ma, I said. I'm your son. It's me. Carnegie.

She dropped her eyelids flirtatiously then, and pursed her mouth—for another kiss, I feared.

— That is your tough luck, she said.

BLONDIE / From time to time she recognized him. After staring or twitching for hours, she would suddenly cry, *Carnegie!* and ask him something. How many days he would be home over Christmas, perhaps. Or when he was going to learn no one cared what he thought? *Just shut up*, she would say. *Shut up. Just shut up*.

CARNEGIE / And what was the matter with my hair, it looked like even the barber couldn't stand to be in the same room with me, she would say. No wonder I was stuck marrying that old maid Blondie. *Next you are going have funny-looking kids, no one can even say what they are.*

BLONDIE / He cried.

CARNEGIE / I cried to see her there in her heartbreakingly individualized, climate-controlled room. I cried to see its shatterproof window and equally impenetrable pictures of my father, me, the children. (We spared her pictures of Blondie.) She squinted at them vacantly. The pleasure in picking up pictures was still there in her hands, but the rest of the experience was missing, as she seemed to know. She looked puzzled, like someone trying to remember what was delicious about chocolate.

Was it easier to walk her through the garden of the Evergreen Overlook Residence Home—fondly called the Overlook—even if amorous patients accosted me, clucking, *Handsome, so handsome* if not, *Fuck me, fuck me?* Sometimes I thought so. Other times the garden seemed so cheery I wanted to rip out its wagon wheel. This was not because I was a nice Chinese boy. It wasn't even because she was my mother, exactly. It was because I, alone of all the people left on earth, knew her. *Be mine!* people said on Valentine's Day. But of course they didn't mean it; no one would want another person to be his as Mama Wong was mine. No one would want to see her real self shimmering like a virtual reality beside her—bleating, banging, crying. *Beam me out, beam me out!* As if there had been a truly serious glitch. A grave, grave technical error.

Her younger self had not been easily confined. How much she risked, lived, made! A pioneer woman, alive to the real miracle of America; namely, mortgages. In the China of her youth, buildings were bought with cash. Meaning, as she pointed out, that the rich stayed rich. Only in America—O America!—were there mortgage loans open to all. She often recounted the thrill with which she discovered that she could buy a three-family house for just five thousand dollars down. How amazing that she and her little Carnegie could live in one apartment, and let the renters pay the mortgage payments. In just thirty years the building would be theirs.

Of course, people looked down on you. Mama Wong had been perfectly aware that none of our neighbors cared what she thought of them. That no one was ever going to come to her knowing that on her belt rattled certain keys. That she was always going to have to stand back and smile. *How humble!* people would say then. *How charming! How sweet!* She might as well have been a concubine.

On the other hand, what was a woman in China? There was a reason the wells of old were stuffed with bodies. More recently the fashion was for pesticides. Painless, people said, and what's more, they gave your body a sweet smell. And had not Mama Wong's mother been, after all, a real concubine? These days, there were women in Taipei and Hong Kong—businesswomen, wives of muckety-mucks—who were horrified by the idea of America. *Do you realize that in America everyone is treated the same?* they would ask. *Do you realize?*

But for my mother, well—America! Here, a widow could walk

into an office in Boston's Chinatown and receive help with her mortgage application just like that.

An aide did the legal work for free. It wasn't long before Mama Wong knew which areas to buy in, and which brokers to trust, and which sorts of triple-deckers brought in the most rent for the investment: 6-6-6es, because of the third bedroom in each unit. (*People pay more or less by bedroom,* she once explained to me. *Third bedroom mean you could rent to family, much less trouble than student.*) Sometimes Mama Wong credited my father for her success. If he hadn't left a *so-called nest egg*—imagine. How lucky that he had taken out an insurance policy and then died!

But the other hero of her story was America. *Only in America!* was probably her favorite saying. Where else could people come with nothing and end with whole blocks of real estate? She swaggered around in her fur coat and sneakers. She wore rings big as road reflectors. The restaurant owners in Chinatown all knew her, and claimed their fathers knew her father in China, or else that their cousins had been schoolmates with her uncle. Never mind that they were Cantonese. They claimed that their brothers belonged to the same fraternity as my father. She never ate off the regular menu; she parked wherever she wanted. Exciting, of course, the red-eye disease of others. Rumor stalked her: her business habits, her spending habits, her savings habits. What wasn't suspect? People scrutinized her cars, her clothes, her hair, her companions.

But if she was in love, it was with success. I tried to talk to her about balance. All she wanted, though, besides to expand, expand, was for me to agree success mattered.

— Otherwise, what? she said. Otherwise, you have to ride the subway, you know how people treat you there? Like a worm.

— I ride the subway all the time, I told her. It's not that bad.

And yet I knew what a tough was, it was true. I knew what a gang was, and a knuckle sandwich. I understood that going up meant getting out.

BLONDIE / Still he married me, Miss Make Your Own Meaning. Whenever Mama Wong thought of me, she bought herself a pair of shoes, or a pocketbook.

— Someday you will know what America is, she said.

CARNEGIE / The week before our wedding, she bought a Mercedes. She steeled herself for the event by reading over the owner's manual.

Ah, but those were the days, we saw now.

Mama Wong's younger self would have been the first to point out, with a certain grim glee, the price of the Alzheimer's unit of the Evergreen Overlook Assisted Living Residence Home. She loved to stand on the rock of no-nonsense.

What happen? In the end, you don't even take care of me? Since when you have to pay outside people take care of your mother? What is Blondie doing, tell me. Work outside for what? I can tell you, she is not work for money. She is work for herself! Make everybody suffer. Even her own kids, she do not take care of them. Your mother took care of you your whole life. Struggle so hard. For what, tell me. For what?

Was it indeed for this that she had scrimped and saved? Guestimating and maneuvering, bluffing and cajoling? Had she filed and complained, appealed and consolidated so that Blondie and I could buy our way out of our familial obligation? Whatever Mama Wong's other technical problems, her sound worked fine. *Ungrateful! Selfish! I work hard my whole life, for what?* Sometimes I was just glad she was past knowing that I really had squandered my inheritance on this, the poshest situation Blondie and I could find. Knowingly; we had done it knowingly. From day one we had been aware that this splendid situation with the wagon wheel in the garden, and the gnomes, and a Plexiglas-enclosed water feature, would eat up my after-tax inheritance in plus or minus ten years. Was it not a little noble that we had decided we did not care?

Throw mother out like garbage, waste money besides.

We knew how she felt. We knew.

BLONDIE / But then, Mama Wong had never had to witness herself, as Carnegie and I had. She had never discovered herself wandering out in a thunderstorm, calling for her husband, or trying to tell a telephone operator, in Chinese, that she had fallen. She tried to bait a fish hook with her own finger for a worm. She tried to remove her security bracelet with a cleaver. We'd kept after her hair and her nails, but she smelled. And then, of course, there were the questions.

Whose children are these? she'd ask, and one minute later: *Whose children are these?*

Who the mother?

Who the father?

CARNEGIE / We customized the house for her. Hired special help. Put in sound-absorbing materials. Edged the stairs and toilet seat with fluorescent tape. But still she would say, *I have no home. I have no home.*

BLONDIE / Perhaps we shouldn't have moved her—she did get so much worse, living with us. Perhaps we should have gotten around-the-clock help, but left her in her house.

CARNEGIE / Would-a, should-a, could-a. Anyway, it was too late.

Whose house is this? Whose house is this?

Is this your home? Is this your home?

It was hard not to suspect method in her madness.

BLONDIE / She frightened poor Lizzy. *That is not Mama Wong,* she would cry. *That is not her!*

One day Mama Wong wrestled Lizzy to the ground and tried to choke her.

CARNEGIE / It was everything we could do to find a facility that didn't smell.

BLONDIE / Carnegie did not care for the English hunting prints. Nor did he like the violet motif.

CARNEGIE / The decorator had a thing for sprigs.

BLONDIE / But there was light and air too, and a security door. The porch furniture was wicker-like. There was a bulletin board posting that day's activities—Sunshine breakfast, Morning Stretch 'n' Tone, All-Time Favorite Love Songs.

And not to forget the staff of saints.

CARNEGIE / Well, some saints, with an inevitable sprinkling of the ever-green. It was hard not to notice that their uniform patches read: THE EVERGREEN OVERLOOK—EVERYTHING YOU'D WANT IN A HOME AND MORE. There were aides who left when their shift was done, whether the new shift had shown up or not. There were aides who put the residents in one another's clothes. The six-month turnover was close to one hundred percent.

BLONDIE / Yet what about that aide who did morning exercises? That Caribbean man?

CARNEGIE / Ah, yes. How sweetly he woke the patients up if necessary. Straightened them into play position that he might bop a red balloon to each of them in turn while Margot, the lunch person, asked, *Chicken Cordon Bleu or Pasta Primavera, Mr. Marx?* four or five times. That was in between *Becky, please sit down* and *How about you, Eric, Chicken Cordon Bleu or Pasta Primavera? Becky, please sit down.* How diplomatically too the staff dealt with bouts of diarrhea among the residents! Cleaning, airing, disinfecting as necessary.

BLONDIE / Mama Wong had strawberries in season. She had a view.

CARNEGIE / There were patients who screamed. There were patients who slept in the public areas. They lined up on the benches, slumping like stuffed animals. One hugged a doll; her family had supplied her with a doll crib and bassinet. One welcomed visitors. *Are you my child? You'll be the death of me. Are you my child?*

The home seemed to attract a musical bunch over the years. Patients who sang opera, patients who sang show tunes, patients who just sang. Some of the songs stuck with you:

You can feed her all day with the vitamin A and the bromo-fizz
But the medicine never gets anywhere near where the trouble is.

There's a place for us. Somewhere a place for us.

Hello muddah. Hello faddah. Here I am in. Camp Granada.

All this talent was why the Musak had to be so loud.

One day we came in to find Mama Wong covered with bruises. She had been beaten up by another patient, who had thought Mama Wong a polar bear on the loose. *Get back in your cage!* he had yelled. Later he said that he never would have lifted a finger if the bear had moved. But the bear didn't move. It just stood there in the hallway as if it didn't speak English. He had had to hit it as a matter of public safety.

Mama Wong's cheek was bruised, her arm was bruised. Happily and unhappily, she did not remember being called a polar bear. She did remember the attendants attacking her with an iceberg, though. Was that the ice bag? We never knew.

It was a sad moment, in any case, when Mama Wong put her weightless hand in mine. Forgetting her lifelong disappointment in me, she cried.

— Look what happened to you, I said. This will never happen to you again as long as I live.

— You take care of me?

Her voice was as thin and shaky as her hand. She was wearing a man's sweater, Astroturf green, with a golf club and tee embroidered on it.

— I'll take care of you, I said.

— I pay you?

— No, you won't have to pay me.

— I give good tip anyway.

The trembling subsided.

— Seventeen percent, she said.

— Okay. Thanks.

I leaned across Mama Wong to draw the drape against the afternoon glare; Blondie stood to help. Mama Wong withdrew her skeletal hand into her grass-green sleeve. One of her orthopedic shoes was untied. Her hair was parted on one side toward the front half of her head, on the other side toward the back.

— Eighteen percent if you can make my son Carnegie get rid of that wife, she said.

— Okay.

— You know my son Carnegie?

— I do.

— Even as a baby he was pain in the neck, she said, her hand emerging suddenly. — Sometimes he cry cry, even I spank him, he do not stop.

— Well, I said, trying not to cry like my younger self all over again. — He survived you.

A short-haired attendant appeared in the doorway with a chart; I waved her away. Blondie rubbed my back sympathetically.

— How you know? Mama Wong demanded.

— I know.

— Oh really? She looked at me hard, hunching her back. Her eyes glittered as they rarely did anymore, being so dry.

— Really, I said.

— I know you, she said.

The attendant returned. Blondie waved her away as I had and, when she seemed disinclined to leave, politely shut the door in her face. A square of sun from the window popped up on the backside of the door.

— I know you.

— Yes, Ma, it's—

— You just want twenty percent.

— No, Ma, I—

— I know you, don't think I don't know who you are. That's why I give you nothing. You hear me? Nothing! Zero percent! Nothing!

She banged her open hand weakly on the bed.

BLONDIE / It did seem sometimes that if anyone was going to die, it was Carnegie. His angina flared up badly enough at the Overlook that twice he had to take some nitroglycerin.

Still, he visited every single day, and afterward did a little work.

CARNEGIE / Habit was habit.

BLONDIE / — Why don't you take a day off? I suggested one morning. — One day is not going to kill your mother.

I was having steel-cut oatmeal with brown sugar, my standard winter breakfast. On this I sprinkled pecans, and peach bits, and fresh blueberries while Carnegie fixed his All-Bran with 2%.

CARNEGIE / Call me perverse: I rather liked my breakfast to resemble a post-consumer recycled material.

— Carpe diem, I said. Memento mori.

— Exactly.

— Think how the kids feel that I take time for business trips but not them.

— Exactly.

— And the marriage. Think what it would mean to the marriage.

— You might think of it.

— I flunked my stress test.

— You flunked your stress test.

— So isn't it time to live? Should I not start living my own life before I die?

— Shouldn't you?

BLONDIE / He went back to processing the paper. Front page, op-ed, business. He never clipped anything.

I was the clipper in the family. I was fascinated by home-schoolers. Homesteaders. Ranchers. Recently I had clipped an article about a community of women in China who slept with men but did not live with them. The family was headed by a matriarch, possessions passed down through the daughters. Women took lovers as they liked. The Na, these were.

Carnegie had never heard of them.

Now he scratched his nose. When he was done with his cereal, I took his bowl but did not produce his coffee. This made him look up.

I waved.

CARNEGIE / From the far end of the great room came the whir of a rodent on its exercise wheel. Next to it hulked the treadmill, on which I defied my mortality, after careful stretching, watching my heart rate, once a week. Steel and rubber, with red plastic accents, it had that vaguely downtown, quasi-industrial look once associated with artists' lofts, now complete with training zone chart. Truly it filled one with despair, especially illuminated, as it was now, with the sort of vaporous morning light that could almost have been the precious downward glance of a normally distracted divinity.

What was man, that he had brought forth this apparatus to be shined upon? What was Sears?

BLONDIE / — Oh, Carnegie, I sighed finally, pouring. — Was it always this difficult to communicate? Tell me and I'll give you your coffee.

— Of course not, he said, moving on to the sports section. —You have to know someone very well to have this much trouble.

He put out his hand.

I closed my eyes.

Happiness. If every life embodied a great mistake, as Carnegie claimed, a defensive passion designed to distract its owner from the abyss, this was mine. I was like my mother that way. I desired to be happy, and that my children should be happy. I desired to be whatever it was given to me to be, and that my children should likewise have that chance. Carnegie, I tried to accept, was neither happy nor unhappy. For much more than he cared about happiness, Carnegie cared about a certain small vengeance. I had never tried to write a song for Carnegie such as my siblings and I used to write for one another, when we were growing up. But if I had time to write one about Carnegie now, in his middle years, I knew what its chorus would be.

> Right! Right! I, Carnegie Wong, am right!
> My mother is wrong.
> She'll never know how wrong.
> Whereas I am right, right, right.

3

Automatica

WENDY / Lanlan is in love with our bathrooms. So beautiful, she says, so clean and shiny and with no smell at all, there being no drain in the floor—I guess in China they have like these stinky drain holes. And so big! She thinks my parents' bathroom especially is the size of a living room. And how convenient that you can just drink the water right out of the faucet, and don't have to boil it.

LAN / *The towels were so thick and fluffy. There was a big open window with clean white curtains, just like in the American movies. There was even a wicker armchair in the corner, and flowers in a vase on a little table. A jar full of shells too, and a stack of magazines.*

WENDY / — Wow, she says.

Quiet like, she says it, and of course she wouldn't say it to Mom and Dad, she barely talks to Mom especially. But to me and Lizzy she does, especially me. *You are Chinese people,* she says sometimes, so I guess that's why, not that anything she says is so secret. She is amazed by how bright our lights are, and how much room there is everywhere, not just in the bathroom but in all the rooms, in our whole house, and our whole yard. Is this whole place really ours? Just for our family? *Wow.* She can't believe how empty the town is, how you can walk on the street and not see anybody at all. And those lawns everywhere! She can't get over how everybody has one, and how green and cushy they are in general, it's too bad ours got messed up by the goat. One day we find her a good patch and make her take off her shoes and Peds and walk barefoot in it.

— Wow, she says, wiggling her toes.

We take her to the grocery store.

LAN / *Of course, I had seen American everything in the movies, and there were supermarkets everywhere in China now. I was hardly so ignorant as to be amazed by a grocery store.*

WENDY / In a way the stores are not as beautiful as she thought, in the movies they're even more beautiful. Still she says it's like walking into a movie, and that's amazing, to be in a movie. Though how expensive everything is! Who can afford to pay such prices? American money amazes her, all those big bills—fifty-dollar bills, even hundred-dollar bills, and checks, and credit cards besides, she can't believe how everyone uses checks and credit cards, but now she sees why they need them. With everything so expensive! She goes up and down the aisles like she's doing an inspection. She doesn't stand right next to the counters like a lot of people, piling stuff into their plastic bags. She stands a little way off and reaches for the faraway fruit as if her arm is this very nice crane, or as if there's something about the fruit she doesn't trust, as if it looks like fruit but is actually something else.

LAN / *Of course, that kind of fruit was completely flavorless. If you picked up a peach, you noticed immediately that it had no smell.*

WENDY / She says she's from this place called Suzhou, but that she lives in Shandong Province, in a town near this city called Jinan, where I guess she got stuck because her great-aunt was from there or something.

LIZZY / For a long time she worked in a shoe factory. Like she used to have to sew the tops of the shoes onto the bottoms. Top to bottom, top to bottom. These were the ugliest shoes you ever saw, she said, just the sort of shoe you got when the state did the design. That's what she thought, and sure enough one day the world agreed.

LAN / *Then came the market economy and the factory got closed. Our whole production unit got put out of work. But we did all receive free shoes, three pairs each. You see? I showed them mine. Of course they were not as comfortable as the cloth shoes my great-aunt used to make. She made them with liners you could change if they got wet.*

WENDY / We thought she should wear those cloth shoes, why doesn't she wear them? But she says no, they're not appropriate. Too old-fashioned, she says.

Anyway, the factory closed.

LIZZY / After that she became a migrant worker with a job in this factory and that. For a while, she was the hostess of a karaoke bar in the city, which I thought sounded like fun. But Lan said it most definitely was not.

LAN / *It was no different than hanging around Friendship Stores, which lots of women did. There was no shame in it. What else were we going to do? We were* huang fei de yi dai*—the wasted generation—our lives wrecked by the Cultural Revolution. Once the state factories closed, we couldn't even get jobs as waitresses or saleswomen. Too old. For that sort of work it was better to be right out of high school.*

WENDY / We show Lanlan all the Chinese food our grocery store carries, and she is surprised how much there is. Bean curd, and bean sprouts, and ginger, and all kinds of noodles, and Chinese cabbage, and Chinese mushrooms, and bamboo shoots, and water chestnuts, and hoisin sauce, and soy sauce, and sesame oil. You can even get frozen dumplings, and frozen wonton, and frozen shao mai. There's sushi too we tell her, but she says she doesn't eat Japanese food, she's just not used to it.

LAN / *In China, we have frozen dumplings too.*

WENDY / Lanlan is proud that her family comes from this Suzhou, which is near Shanghai and has all these beautiful gardens. Her family once owned one of those gardens, she says, and she's proud of that, in fact that's why she was named Lan, which means orchid. Because her family had a greenhouse in their garden and grew all kinds of orchids in it. Which were very delicate and refined, she said, there was nothing common about them, they were not like the fruit in the grocery store. She inspects the mounds of fruit and asks if the supermarket is fuller during the harvest season.

— Now is the harvest season, she points out, as if she is teaching us something.

But of course we know that because of harvest festivals, pretty much our whole lives Mom's dragged us to press apples and watch sheep shearing, once she made us go in the pouring rain.

— No, we tell her. The grocery store is like that even in the winter.

— In the winter too! she says.

LIZZY / It's like she's surprised but embarrassed that she's surprised.

LAN / *I did not go to university, but I was not ignorant.*

WENDY / It's hard to explain how we always thought growing up in the countryside was great because of Mom, if we could we'd all go back to the farm. Lanlan doesn't think the countryside is so great. Of course it has some good points, she says, blue sky and clean air and no pollution. Also the government has less to say, she says. But there's no work, and isn't that a problem?

She looks at the fruit as if it could eat her, or make her sick. It's like if the food doesn't, the air around it will. She thinks you have to wear a sweater in the grocery store or else you will catch cold, also you have to be careful about catching cold through your feet. She believes in socks in general, but especially in the grocery store, and even for us, which is why Lizzy and I wear socks now, to make her feel better. And how powerful the cash registers, says Lanlan. *Wow.* She watches the scanner, how it sends out that little red line and *beep!* Her new big word is 'automatic,' which she pronounces 'awma-ic.'

— America should not be call 'America,' she says. It should be call 'Awma-ica.'

— Land of the free, and home of the beep! laughs Lizzy.

LIZZY / Lanlan discovered coupons, which she thought in the beginning meant you could buy something there wasn't enough of. Like cooking oil, she said, or sugar. How could there not be enough sugar? we asked, but she just said it was hard to explain. Like these coupons were hard for us to explain to her. She said she was sure there were coupons in China, in the big cities they had everything, but was it really free money? I told her it was all just a way for corporate America to get you to buy more of their brand, and Lanlan nodded and said she knew about American corporations.

LAN / *We heard about it on TV. How American companies wanted to control the whole world. How they sold everyone American things on purpose. It was actually a kind of weapon.*

WENDY / Still she goes looking for the coupons that come with the newspaper. She clips coupons for stuff she thinks we need, plus stuff she needs herself. Hand lotion, toothpaste. Her clippings are like beautiful, she never just tears stuff out. Mom gives her money for these things on top of money for books and stuff because she says she knows she would want to pick her personal products herself, if she were Lan. And Lanlan does pick, even though she says she does not need to pick everything like an American. Like she buys a kind of toothpaste that comes out of a pump instead of a tube. She is excited about the bonus toothbrush. Land of the free!

She gives the toothbrush to Lizzy, who loves it.

Lanlan is amazed by how much people throw out, like how many napkins they use in restaurants, and how they take ketchup packets they don't even use, but this is what's amazing to us, that Lizzy takes the toothbrush and smiles like she never had a toothbrush before, or like she's been dying her whole entire life for a blue one. When Lanlan walks with me or Lizzy she links her arm in ours. And Lizzy likes that too, no one can believe it.

How new everything is, says Lanlan, and no dust. She's amazed at how clean her shoes stay on account of everything being paved or grass, there's like no bare dirt anywhere. And is it true there's no dust even in the spring? Even in the spring, we say.

— But what about pollen, she says.

She says she heard that on TV, on an English conversation program, how there is a big problem with pollen, you have to wash your hair every day to get it out. Only in some places, we say, like down South, up here we have some pollen but not that much. And no garbage almost anywhere, she says, and where do people spit? We tell her nobody spits, and she's amazed. *Wow.* And how quiet it is! So peaceful and nice, she says, except for the goat.

LAN / *I was surprised there were no slums, like I saw on TV and in the movies. I asked the children where the slums were. But they said there were no slums near where they lived, only far away, in the city. I told them how in China we heard a lot about the slums, and they were surprised. The slums and the violence, I told them. But they said there was no violence in their town. They said people got shot, but only in the news. In their town, no one got shot.*

WENDY / She's amazed that instead of slums there are churches all over the place, I guess you don't realize from the movies how many of them there are. Do we go to church, she wants to know, and is amazed when we say we don't even though our mom does sometimes, because that's what we decided and our parents didn't make us. Like they said it was our choice.

LAN / *How could the parents let the child choose something so important? I could not understand it. Didn't American parents care enough to control their children?*

WENDY / — Not all parents do that, says Lizzy. Just some do. We're lucky.

Lanlan gets quiet like for a sec.

— People can do whatever they want, nobody has anything to say, she says. Wow.

— Freedom, we say. America is about freedom.

— Freedom, she says, wow.

But then she says she thinks too much freedom is no good either, and that individualism is terrible, she hopes we don't believe too much in individualism. I tell her I'm not sure what individualism even is, and she's glad.

She is surprised how there are no Thermoses, instead lots of computers. Four just in our house! That's because Dad's in high tech, we say, and Mom has a home machine hooked up to work too, and we have some extra machines left over from whatever. It's not typical.

— Wow, says Lanlan anyway.

We start to explain about the Internet, but it turns out she knows what that is already.

— In China, she begins.

And Lizzy says: — In China, big city have everything these days.

Then we all laugh. And how everyone crosses the street in the crosswalk downtown—Lanlan thinks that's amazing, that people don't just walk all over. Though how fast people walk here! Everyone in a hurry all the time.

LAN / *Chinese people were much more relaxed. Everything was so easy in America, so convenient. And yet people were tense.*

WENDY / And the bicyclists all wear helmets, and how many cars people had!

— In China, many people have car now, she says.

But still she is amazed that some families have two or three, and that even some kids have cars. And will Lizzy really be learning to drive soon? She is surprised that people drive one-handed, some of them, and talk on their cell phones at the same time, she thinks everyone in America talks and talks, especially the children are so curious. In China, kids do not ask *why why why,* she says. Then make everyone listen to them, as if they have something to say.

— At school, people say American children are very easy, she says.

People say you ask them one question they will talk, talk, talk. You ask them three questions they will love you.

— Like you ask us questions! I say.

She smiles her funny smile.

LAN / *At school, people say that when you talk to American children you have to ask,* You want this one or that one? The blue one or the red one? *Then they will be happy. If you simply say* Here is red one, I know you like red, *the children will not be happy. They don't want you to know what they like, they want to choose for themselves.*

WENDY / — That's kind of true, says Lizzy. Like I wanted to have blond hair, I didn't want my hair to be plain black until I died. Do you know what I mean?

Lanlan nods, but then she says: — Black hair very nice, nothing the matter with black hair. That is your natural hair.

She says she hopes we will not grow up *one hundred percent American.* First the children talk about themselves all day, she says, and then they think about themselves all day. All day long they think, What is my favorite this? What is my favorite that?

LAN / *Chinese people say Americans don't care about other people, they only care about themselves. Americans do not take care of even their own mothers and fathers. When their parents get old, Americans just put them in a nursing home. Their parents die by themselves. Chinese people say Americans have no feelings.*

WENDY / She says that in America, if you borrow money from somebody and *have some trouble,* people expect you to pay it back no matter what.

— Of course, these days, even in China, some people are like that, she says. Especially those people born in Cultural Revolution. But they are not real Chinese.

When her grandfather died, she says, he had a whole trunk full of IOUs from people he knew would pay him if they could, except that they couldn't, and it just went to show what a big heart he had, that he did not ask them. On his deathbed he just said that he wanted all the papers burned.

— That is how real Chinese think, she says.

— Wow, we say.

Lanlan is amazed that people in America drive and eat at the same time, eating in cars makes her shake her head. So dangerous, she says, really it should be illegal the way it is in China. Plus she thinks it must be bad for people's digestion, digestion being another thing she talks about a lot, besides catching cold. What is good for the stomach, what is bad for the stomach, what has heat, what is cool. She likes teaching us stuff, and Lizzy can tell you a lot of it already—that garlic and bananas have heat, and that pears are cooling, also lotus root. Forget that she barely knows what a lotus root is, even, Lizzy's like Elaine at school, she just says stuff if she feels like it. Lanlan thinks eating and driving must be bad for the stomach. She says she doesn't know how Americans can eat without stopping to eat, although obviously they do because look how many fat people there are! Many more than in the movies. She says she heard that once Chinese people come to America, they get fat too. Of course there are fat people in China now, more and more of them because of McDonald's, but still not as many as here, she cannot believe how people eat. How huge the sandwiches are, so big people can barely get their mouths open wide enough. And the drinks—so big people need two hands to lift them.

She does not want to eat at all, looking at them, she does not want to become fat like an American. Also the smell of people here makes her want to throw up. How people smell! That's one thing you don't realize from the movies.

LAN / *Chinese people do not smell.*

WENDY / She wants to know if people will smell less in the winter when they are wearing sweaters. She is surprised how hairy some of the people are too, she knew that from the movies, but still didn't realize how hairy, even some of the women, she says, and there are men who look *one hundred percent like monkey.*

LAN / *Even their backs are covered with hair.*

WENDY / And the way they sit, she says. The women not even covered with clothes some of them, and big as mountains and all over their chairs. She's surprised American chairs are not bigger. And she stares at the black people with that hair braided all different ways, or else loose like a big ball of seaweed, she wants to know if it has any use, like if they can cut it off and sell it for something. Scrub brushes maybe, or pillow stuffing. She's amazed at how different people look from each other, she knew it from the movies but still she's shocked by that, and by how complete strangers say hello on the street, even if they never saw you before. She says the first time that happened she ran away.

LAN / *Sometimes I saw men let women walk in front of them. Even open doors for them, as if they were important! Just like in the movies. I was amazed to see that.*

And nobody ate the squirrels, even in the countryside, that's what the girls said. There was so much food. People let whole trees full of fruit just fall to the ground.

LIZZY / It all made her want to throw up, which I understood. Because to be honest it all made me want to throw up too, sometimes.

WENDY / She can be warm and bright, full of funny songs and funny voices, but she can sink away like the sun, and come back as the moon. She is suddenly here and suddenly there, she knows lots of games. Sometimes we don't know what room she is even in. A lot of the time she is on the floor or on a stool, she likes stools. She does not need a chair to sit up straight, she sits up straight on a stool, in fact she doesn't even need a stool. She sits up straight even when she's squatting, and can squat a lot better than Lizzy. She rests her elbows on her knees like they are the most convenient thing, and she squats in this very light way, with her feet together, so that she looks like that kind of rice bowl that has a little built-in pedestal. Or like she could balance something on top of her head, and could stand up without knocking it over. She says she is comfortable anywhere. Americans need padding, she says, and we can see she is proud she does not. She likes to say what she does not need.

— I do not need more clothes, she says.

— I do not need more food.

— I do not need more room.

She says she can *chi ku*—eat bitter—and that makes her different than an American, she is just glad she is not staying here.

LAN / *Why was I brought here? Because Carnegie's mother wanted me to come, they said. But I wondered, what was the real reason? What did they want from me?*

WENDY / She says she is not like young people in China these days either, all they know is how to *wanr*—fool around. And how to *hui jin ru tu*—spend money like dirt.

— What is eat bitter? we say.

But when we say that, she looks at her feet.

— I see you are one hundred percent American, she says.

LAN / *What real Chinese would ever ask that question?*

WENDY / She says eat bitter is bad in one way but not so bad in another way. She says if you can eat bitter it will make you strong.

LAN / *Chinese people have a saying.* Chi de ku zhong ku, fang wei ren shang ren*—Eat the bitterest of the bitter, rise above other men. My father said that all the time.*

WENDY / She says Americans are rich but soft.

— You know why Chinese people survive such long time? she says. Because we are not soft.

She says: — Chinese people today, especially in the coastal area, like to have comfortable life. But real Chinese people think live easy life is like drink poison.

LAN / *My father, being a scholar, used to quote Mencius on this subject. Anxiety and distress lead to life, he used to say. Ease and comfort end in death.*

Of course, these are things Americans will never understand.

WENDY / When she says these things it doesn't really matter if you nod or not. Either way she looks at you then looks out the window like Lizzy, sometimes I wonder how old you have to be to look out the window like that. Her face is like the moon, there is nothing in it, she is done talking. When I look out the window I don't see anything there, I don't see what they see, and Lanlan looks at her feet too, that's another thing. How old do you have to be to do that? Lanlan looks at her feet to see how the veins are popping out even through her stockings, she says she didn't used to be able to see her veins at all. But luckily nobody knows except her. Even if they are in slippers and no one can see them, she says she always knows, and when she says that I can almost see them. I can almost see how she presses her toes together like she does with her fingers, her fingers keep to themselves.

— You can see everything in the feet, she says sometimes. You can see what that person's life is.

That's what she says, but when me and Lizzy look at our feet, we see nothing.

— Also you can hear everything, she says, if you listen.

But when we listen, all we hear is Tommy *naa*-ing downstairs.

— Do you hear it? Can you hear it? Of course you have to know how to listen, she says.

She mostly says these things to me and Lizzy. Mom only hears a little bit, but Mom loves it all, especially the part about needing nothing. It's like Lanlan is the best newspaper article she ever read.

— She is rich in spirit, Mom says. We have too much stuff.

Since Lanlan came Mom has been throwing stuff out, giving stuff away.

— We are choking on possessions, she says one day. Every day I am going to get rid of three things.

And another day she says: — These things have a life of their own. They have more life than I do.

Yesterday she gave a whole bunch of appliances to Goodwill. Like I think a toaster oven, and a pressure cooker she was always afraid was going to blow up, and a cappuccino machine that didn't foam that great. Today she is giving away a pair of ski boots, and an old watch, and a casserole, and a bunch of travel books. It's hard to stick to three things, she says, there is so much she wants to get rid of.

— Do you know what we do? she says. We consume to avoid living.

— That is like so true, says Lizzy.

She comes into the kitchen all of a sudden, who even knew she was listening, and instead of eating by herself because we bug her, the way she sometimes does, she gets a normal plate like a normal person because actually she likes Dad's French toast. Not that she would admit it. He makes the French toast with corn bread so he can say how corny it is, but nobody does think it's corny, everybody loves it. Even if it does sort of crumble all over.

The morning light is yellow, just like the kitchen Mom painted yellow so it would be warm and kitcheny even in the rain. So that everything now is yellow yellow yellow, even the plates, which are white.

Says Mom: — It helps us avoid questions like, Are we alive? And, Can we call this a life?

Mom says this because she was up half the night. The end of the quarter and you know how Porter is, she says. But Dad says that's not really the problem.

— Your problem, he says, is that you actually believe responsible investment will change the world.

— Absolutely it will, she says, cutting stuff up for Bailey. — Think of externalities such as the environment, and how much pressure . . .

— At the same time you wonder, Do you really believe it the way you used to?

Mom sips her coffee.

— Or does the spiel just come spieling out? says Dad.

Mom covers her nose with her mug. Then she uncovers it, which makes her nostrils flare just like this very little bit. Her nostrils are sort of oval, not round like Lizzy's and Daddy's and Lanlan's and mine, and usually sort of pink, but not today. Today the bottom of her mug is yellow, and her nails are yellow, and of course her hair, which was already yellow. Everything except her eyes.

— On the other hand, it's a job, says Dad. At least you're not laying people off, like my own dear Document Management Systems.

— Is getting laid off the same as getting fired? I say.

— Not exactly, says Dad. But of course you worry.

— You worry because you have a family to support, says Mom.

— You have a family to support. But here's the thing, says Dad. In one way you definitely, one hundred percent want to hang on to your job.

He turns around with a fresh delivery to dump on the plate in the middle of the table.

— But in another way you wonder if for all that work we're really that much happier than Lan.

— Of course we're happier than Lan, says Mom.

— We're more comfortable than Lan.

Me and Lizzy start putting on syrup.

— Please! says Mom. You can't seriously envy someone who's lived through the Cultural Revolution! Do you realize what life is like there?

— I'm not saying I'd change places with her.

Mom cuts up her own French toast.

— And yet, she says finally.

— And yet the last time I used the words 'endless possibility' it had to do with the myriad uses of a griddle.

He flips stuff over.

— You guys sound like you're sorry about your whole entire life, I say.

— A lot of things are written, and can't be rewritten, says Mom.

— Like what? says Lizzy. Like what would you write over, anyway?

— Our family would be the same, of course, says Mom.

LIZZY / She just said that because she had to.

— You can't exactly say you wish you hadn't adopted me, I said. Or Wendy. Not to our faces.

— I wouldn't say it, period. Because it isn't true.

— But you wish I was less dramatic and Wendy was less shy, and if we weren't adopted, maybe we wouldn't be like that. Maybe we'd be more like Bailey, and like you.

BLONDIE / — We've lived with you every day for fifteen years, I said. We couldn't begin to imagine life without you.

— Think of yourself as a body part, said Carnegie.

— Yeah, but what if you could do plastic surgery, said Lizzy. We're like the tummy flab you would fix.

WENDY / — Speak for yourself, I say. I'm not like tummy flab.

— I'm glad you realize that, says Mom.

— I'm more like a lung or something, I say.

Bailey rocks back and forth, meaning he wants more of something, but it must not be French toast, because when Mom gives him that, first he puts it on his head, syrup and all, and then he sends it flying.

— Bailey! Lizzy yells.

That's because a piece of French toast lands right between her boobs.

— Perhaps that blouse is a bit revealing, says Mom.

— Perhaps you should feel sorry for me instead of making sure to tell me what you don't like about the way I'm dressed! yells Lizzy. And anyway it's not a *blouse.* I wouldn't be caught dead in a *blouse.*

Lizzy stomps up the stairs so loud that even in the kitchen a bird flies away scared from our new bird feeder, which is stuck on the window with suction cups and supposed to be squirrelproof.

Even the bird feeder is yellow today, that's just the kind of morning it is.

— In my family, this was called overreacting, says Mom. Being too sensitive.

— We can call it that in this family too if you like, says Dad, finally sitting down. — She's being too sensitive.

— Perhaps I should quit work, she says. People say that the time to be home isn't the first couple of years, it's now, when you don't know when they'll want to talk.

— If someone quits it should be me, he says.

— Dearest, you're not going to get laid off.

— Dearest, this is America, says Dad. Anything is possible.

Later I report all this to Lizzy.

— Overreacting! she says. Sensitive! Of course I'm sensitive. I'm sensitive because I totally don't belong to this family!

Her room is like the most amazing place these days, completely empty and neat like a monk's cell. It's like she's too mad at the world to even have one single thing on the walls, all you see are CDs and headphones and a picture of her new boyfriend Russell the Musician, in the exact same spot that she used to have Derek the Normal. And there's her cell phone of course. She doesn't have a regular bed, all she has is a futon on this platform, which I guess I wouldn't mind having either, now that I lie down on it. It makes the room look so big, like the ceiling is so far away. Like you have all this room.

— You belong to this family, I say. You do.

— Someday I am going to go back to wherever and find my real mom.

— How're you going to do that?

— I'm just going to, she says.

She's sitting on her other piece of furniture, her beanbag chair.

Then she says: — At least you know where you come from. At least you can like go back to that orphanage in China.

— That's not true, I say. They don't even know my foster mother's name, forget about my real mother. Or my real father, you can like double forget about him.

— And why is that? says Lizzy. Have you ever wondered how come there are all these adopted girls from China where their parents at least know the foster mother and you don't?

— They're not supposed to, I say.

— But some do, says Lizzy. Like Lily does, and Mimi too. Don't you ever wonder how come?

She says that and looks out her big window, which you realize is the other thing in her room, like her third piece of furniture. A big big window she has, so big it's hard to open.

— I guess, I say.

— Because their parents made sure they knew, says Lizzy.

— But the foster mothers ask for money, I say. Lily's parents only know because her foster mother sewed a note into her clothes. Like over her heart, Lily said, in the very inside layer of all her clothes, it was just lucky her parents found it. Plus they could barely read the writing after it went through the wash.

Lizzy stares at me a little. Sometimes I wonder if she would stare like that if she went back to her old hair, it's like once she went blond nobody could stare at her anymore. Because they like so noticed her they had to try not to, and then she could stare at them.

— You don't get anything either, she says. I really, completely don't belong to this family.

— You do, I say.

— I do not, she says.

But she's sprawled out more on her chair, and like staring a little less.

— I'm like a visitor, like Lanlan, she says.

— What about me? I say.

— You can be whatever you want, she says. It's a free country.

— I like visitors, I say.

— Good for you, says Lizzy.

— I like Lanlan, I say.

— Good for you, says Lizzy.

— There is something about Lanlan that gets Mom and Dad to say the same thing the other one just said, I say.

— Hmmm, she says, and then is kind of quiet, which is practically the nicest thing she's ever said to me.

4

A Family Is Born

CARNEGIE / And again backward: to fifteen years ago, and the story of how Lizzy came to us.

BLONDIE / For this is how our family came together, Lizzy first. And is that not the start of the story?

CARNEGIE / I was a grad student back then, living in the Midwest, which I did not particularly like; and getting a master's in double e, which I did not particularly like. It so happened too that I had signed up for an opera class in the church annex with the copper beech tree. Did I like it, particularly?

My mother detested opera.

And so yes, I did like it most particularly. Yes.

I thought, what's more, that there might be interesting women in that class, women who would prove, surprise, unlike my mother. And should one of them prove particularly interesting, I knew what I would do: invite her to an opera. The local conservatory was always mounting something, so to speak. I warmed its shiny schedule in my pocket.

In the meantime, I passed and passed the smooth-barked beech tree. I looked up into that tree and thought about climbing it. But I was a man now; climbing the tree was like a question I did not have to answer. My life was full of new questions, questions so large I did not know what they were.

They preoccupied me with their vagueness.

BLONDIE / I like to think of Carnegie in that phase of his life—passing that tree, considering his life. Considering the tree—how huge it was, and what a room it made under itself. So rich and venerable, and yet like a prison, he said. Its lowest boughs, big as trunks themselves, grazed the ground, which was resplendent with moss. Years later Carnegie was still talking about that moss, and the way the roots rose out of it like a day of reckoning.

I didn't know any other men who stood back that way. Carnegie had big hands—like my father's, strong, but smoother and more delicate. He kept them in his pockets as though he was saving them. He might have been a surgeon, or a pianist.

CARNEGIE / My mother had considered me a sap on account of the things I did not do. *Forget about it!* was one of her maternal refrains because as a child I had refused to eat eggs, insisting they were baby chickens. As an adult I was bothered by raccoon traps.

Then there was the matter of evictions. It was just Mama Wong's luck to have her one child, her one son, her heir, turn out the type who was haunted by evictions. Several times I paid a tenant's rent rather than see a certain old couple or young mother or rascally codger out on the street.

The couple proved worthy of help. Even Mama Wong saw the point, in the end, of providing two old geezers in wheelchairs with a place to set their brakes. Also I made a good case for the single mother with twins. Anita went on, in fact, to become the best super we ever had; the twins grew up happy to cut our grass and shovel our snow. But what about the codger? Didn't he have two sons in sports cars who ought to have done their share?

— This is America. Nobody can count on a son, I argued once. Except, of course, you.

To this Mama Wong at first laughed appreciatively.

— You are the last real Chinese son in America, she agreed, her forefinger in the air. She crouched forward for emphasis, springing up at the end of the point like a conductor. Then she fetched her body back, her chin, her arm. Repacking herself, it seemed, in a kind of tai qi maneuver. — I know you will never forget what you are, she said. No one going to have to tell you.

But other days she waved her hand dismissively.

— For what can I count on you, you tell me? she said. Give money away to rich people, that's what. How can you be my son? I tell you honest way, I don't know who you are.

Her face then was resigned, and slack. Only her hands moved, dropping down to her desktop to rearrange the beautifully sharpened pencils. She watched some leaves, blown flat against her window; they lifted loose. Away they flipped, back out into the yard, flipping, flipping. Who cared? In her youth she had exuded a lovely suppressed animation. People had watched her, not because she was so beautiful, but because at any moment her face might break into something else. Something about her promised revelation.

Now, in her enfeeblement, she was becoming straightforward.

It was true that the codger, when he died, left half a million dollars to his favorite charity, the National Basketball Association. He left, in addition, one dime each to his sons. This was so they could each call a friend and cry. They wouldn't have had to do this, he wrote, if they had learned to hustle like even the lousiest substitute player in the National Basketball Association. Also he left a broadcloth shirt to me, writing,

> You would have given the shirt off your back to me. So I give the shirt off my back to you. You did touch me, you poor schmuck. But what kind of championship you ever going to win? You got this country all wrong, young man. You should listen to your mother. Rent is rent. Get rich, be happy. Isn't that what they say in China? It's the same here. Be poor, be miserable. Old world, new world, every world is still the world.

BLONDIE / Carnegie never wore the shirt.

CARNEGIE / I was in my poetry phase then; the phase in which I walked in the woods and considered myself working. I was entranced by the deathless morph of villanelles. And the compulsion of terza rima! Like a person with attachment problems. I owned an inkwell and a blotter and was never without a thesaurus.

Naturally all this was related to a lady friend who finally, finally slept with me, only to announce a half hour later that she wanted to be friends.

— Let's have a correspondence in verse, she said.

I switched to double e the next week.

BLONDIE / His mother was delighted.

CARNEGIE / She had a consolation girlfriend all picked out.

— Lily Lee, she said. Daughter of Filbert and Flora. Valedictorian in high school, now is medical doctor. But not just medical doctor. I'll tell you what her character is. Look like her mother have some trouble with her kidney, right? So what is her specialty? Kidney! Her mother never have to go see stranger, always get the best care. That's what kind of girl she is.

I declined to meet Miss Lee.

BLONDIE / Instead he stood by large trees with his hands in his pockets. Carnegie had left home; he had left his mother. He was awaiting something big and honest and potent.

We both had selves that were cresting some hill, then. Lives that before setting all four tires back on the road, could have said yes to almost anything.

CARNEGIE / To the opera. To the Midwest: to this sky, this wind, these grids. To these polite and helpful plain folk.

And, of course, to a most lissome, auburn-haired classmate who turned out, unfortunately, to be an anti–nuclear-arms activist and nun. Sister Mary Divine, she said her name was. I thought she must be joking. That really was her name, though, and she really was a nun, even if she seemed more of an anti-nun. To wit, she did not wear a habit or even a bra. She doodled. She carried a fanny pack. She swore. Not that she went so far as to take the Lord's name in vain, but she was heard to say, upon occasion, Dammit.

She didn't need a libretto, knowing every aria already, and one day came in with yet more amazing knowledge. A baby had been left on the steps of the church proper; an Oriental baby. She hoped she wasn't being racist, but was there any chance I knew where the baby had come from? She was sorry to ask. So far as she knew, though, I was the only adult Oriental in town. Did I have any thoughts about what would be best in terms of finding a home for the baby?

BLONDIE / Was he offended? I did wonder that, later.

For you see, I had gone to school in California, and majored for a while in East Asian Studies. I had had my consciousness raised.

CARNEGIE / Offended? No.

Would I follow her back to the church? she asked.

We left before class started, our rudeness forgiven by special dispensation. It was an enormous night. Dark enough to see the Milky Way, and how many colors the stars came in, actually: blue, green, citron yellow. No moon, just a summer breeze crackling as if with the waking stretch of night animals. We passed the old beech tree. The dark street glimmered with a recent rain, like a river.

If only I did not have allergies. But I did, hives. It was soybean-harvest season. My skin was dotted like op art.

Still I traveled the street river behind my guide, eyes on her fanny pack. My allergies, I knew, could not be racially linked, exactly. How many Asians, after all, could be given hives by soy harvesting? Yet they did seem linked to a certain proclivity to skin sensitivities; for example, an inability to wear wool. And these in turn seemed linked to my smooth and sparely hairy body. As I stood, itching, in the church hall, I wondered if there weren't indeed things I understood better about this bundle of swaddling than did, say, Sister Mary Divine.

I had never held a baby before, much less an abandoned baby.

The bundle was like a longish football, only warm and light. So tossable, yet untossable, what an idea! I felt what a civilized being I was. An enormous strength, stilled by defenselessness. Sister Mary Divine was saying, I thought, that from the umbilical cord she judged the baby to be a day or two old. This was not the receiving blanket the baby had come in, she said. That blanket was being fingerprinted by the police. I nodded, idiotic. Surprised by how close I felt to her. How intimate to be sharing this experience—of what? Of staring into this miniature face, like something out of a fairy tale. So red! So squashed. Circular. A gnome's baby, this seemed, with a white stocking cap on. The white cap was not even a real cap but a surgical stocking, knotted at the top. Fringed at the bottom by the baby's black hair.

Asleep.

— Where did you come from? How can you sleep at a time like this?

I wanted to count the baby's lashes. I put my face to the baby's face; that innocent breathing, breathing. Sweet, noisy, unpracticed. Its whole body heaved and collapsed. The abandon in its exhale! As if one part of its small spirit was bent on returning to the Old World, even as another said, *Stay.*

— You are the first to see her other than Sister Angela and myself. And of course the police.

A girl! I had forgotten to ask boy or girl. A girl. Of course! An abandoned Asian baby, even here, was most likely a girl. Again I felt it, a tug of connection like a hitch in my sweater. Healthy? Sister Mary Divine said so far as she knew. She had a doctor on the way.

— I don't think you have to clutch her like that. I think you can just rest her on your forearm.

I was indeed clutching it—her. My shoulder was raised way up into the air as if I were on a stage, and about to be yanked post-haste into the sky. Sister Mary Divine eased the baby from my wrist and hands into the crook of my arm. How loving her touch! I wanted to kiss her. She had exquisite hands, with surprisingly shiny nails, marred only by that ring. That ring was too big, witness the red indentations on the adjacent fingers.

— There, she said.

— Ahh, I said, or something like that. Then I said (or thought I said, or wanted to say): — Let's get married and have this baby.

— Thank goodness, the doctor's here!

Sister Mary Divine escaped to the door, that medievalish oak door, her auburn hair lifting behind her like a magic carpet. Her breasts were bouncing, her fanny pack unzipped. Later she left the convent, I heard. She ran for Congress as a Green Party candidate and married a dog-sled racer. In the meanwhile, the doctor was here! Another marvelously unswerving, sensibly shod, braless woman. She had a large bag in haul, and a friend, similarly jiggly.

— I am Dr. Pierce, the doctor announced calmly. Her voice was like a barge you could stand on. — This is my friend Jane from out of state.

— Thanks be to God, said Sister Mary Divine.

BLONDIE / I had just arrived at the airport when my old friend Nomie, now a pediatrician, announced, We have to go see this baby. And then there I was, in this church, with a man holding what might have been the Lord Jesus, except that in all the pictures Jesus was never crying, as this baby was. How panic-stricken that poor man! A Chinese- or Something-American. Explaining that a Sister Mary Somebody had gone to see about a bottle.

— Formula, I hope, said Nomie.

The man wasn't sure; and so off she went, leaving the man and me with the baby.

— Walk her. Give her your thumb, said Nomie as she left. Bounce her up and down.

— *Ehh, ehh, ehh*, the baby cried. *Ehh, ehh, ehh*.

Never had so tiny a sound seemed so loud. You could feel it pierce you—how it ran through you like a giant needle and thread. She was wrapped up like a papoose in a pilled flannel blanket with bears and bows printed on it.

CARNEGIE / — Your thumb will be too big. Try your pinkie, said the woman.

Why not hers? But she had just come from the airport; her pinkie was full of germs. So I advanced my finger toward the tiny mouth, and was startled by the mini-vac alacrity with which it was taken in. Electrolux, move over! And how quiet the vestibule now. I moved closer to the yellow lamplight, as if to a hearth. That hall was too big;

I felt distinctly anti-rafter. The baby sucked and sucked. I was glad the tip of my pinkie was so firmly affixed to my knuckle. I could feel her tongue work my fingertip, all wet focus.

— Thatagirl, I whispered to the baby. And to the woman: — It worked.

BLONDIE / I moved in closer then, sharing his triumph—touched by the shine of sweat on his smooth brow. How intently the baby sucked!—working even her eyelids and eyebrows. For a minute she seemed as though she had fallen asleep. Her cheeks stopped. Her breathing deepened. Then she opened her eyes and looked right at me—looked and looked.

— She's strong, he said. Someone left her on the steps.

I introduced myself.

— Carnegie, he said in return. What do you think?

— About?

— I think I'm going to have to adopt this young lady. Unless a better home can be found.

— That's a big decision.

— I'm a fool.

He leaned in closer to the baby's face. She was as profoundly asleep now as she had been awake a moment ago. Her hands moved mysteriously, as if she was dreaming. Or, no—as if her hands were themselves dreaming. Opening, closing, curling.

— You're not a fool, I said.

I massaged the bottom of the swaddling, expecting to feel a foot, but grasped only flannel.

— No, I'm not; I'm a wise, wise man.

He lifted his wrist a little, ever so slightly changing the angle of his pinkie.

— This is it.

— It?

He raised his eyebrows in a vaudevillian way I could almost have guessed would one day be familiar.

— Now don't go asking me what I mean, Jane, because I am too wise to know, he said. Jane.

He winked.

CARNEGIE / I might not have decided so easily had she not been there. Everything might have been different had I not had her to speak to. But I wanted to speak to her. People have always wanted to speak to her; everyone but Lan.

And so I said the words aloud, and—lo!—there they were.

A way, perhaps, of sabotaging my degree? suggested a therapist, with nudgy therapal delicacy, years later.

But how much more it seemed then, than that. A way of really living. Of living bigger. How I liked those words when I thought them; how I liked the hitching of my claptrap impulses to phrases of a certain gallop. *A way to meet life head-on. A way to live my own life.*

I stopped itching.

This baby was bringing us all into the world.

And may I point out that I did finish my degree in the end.

BLONDIE / I thought, *I am giving witness.*

I wanted to tell him how he had moved me. That I wanted to be like him, but would never be like him. How out of place, though, my small despair! I tucked it away—I had an expertise in certain fine folds, that's what it meant to be a plain Jane. Instead I moved in closer, into his circle. I drank in the baby—the redness of her, the sucking centeredness and level peace of her. What stillness a baby could bring. I had never known such stillness. Everything in the room, even the pictures and chairs, seemed to witness her—to attend. It seemed only fitting to be in a church. All the world was hush, and holiness.

It wasn't until I heard the door creak, the foot clicks, the greeting chatter of my old friend Nomie—take-charge Nomie—that I really looked at Carnegie.

A midheight man, Asian American, wearing blue jeans with no belt, and a T-shirt. No watch. An impressive chest—perhaps a weight lifter. His blotchy skin looked somehow related to his spiky hair. He wore black Keds with no socks. On the chair hung a leather aviator jacket, which looked somehow familiar.

CARNEGIE / Her ex, it turned out, had the exact same one, which he had proudly bought in SoHo, but then discovered for sale in an in-flight catalog.

BLONDIE / That was Christian—ever dismayed. Where his pockets were always empty, though, I saw in one of Carnegie's gaping breast pockets, three pairs of sunglasses. In the other, breath spray. I took in an open countenance; a warm glance; an expressive manner. He had large, fine, clean-nailed hands.

Nothing about him would have told you he could decide to adopt a baby in a moment.

I was sorry to see him give the baby up to Nomie. But Nomie had returned, sure enough, with a bottle she had sterilized in a convenience store microwave, and formula. It was time; the baby was hungry. Still, I was sorry to see Carnegie's finger leave that little mouth. The gesture had seemed so simple and natural, like something that went on in the tropics. I was sorry to see his wrist flip closed.

CARNEGIE / I took to visiting the baby, and in due time really did adopt her. Made her my Lizzy.

Mama Wong did not approve.

— You are crazy! she said. You do not even know what kind of family that child is come from. That child, her mother could be prostitute. Her mother could be drug addict. And her father!

Still I did it. Against the odds: though single men were not officially designated unfit to be parents, it was often judged not in a child's best interest to be placed with such low-life types. In this case, though, the church was handling the placement, and there was racial compatibility to consider. 'Matching,' they called it.

— Abandoned children speak to you, observed Blondie, years later.

She believed I would have adopted Lizzy even if she had been white. But of course no white newborn, not even a foundling, would have come to me. As it was, I could see the doubt on the face of the social worker doing the home visit until I told her that the baby in question was of Asian descent, and a foundling. That Sister Mary Divine supported the placement.

— I'll write 'unusual special circumstances,' she said then, talking to her clipboard. — Making this a natural fit.

In this fashion, I aced my home visit.

BLONDIE / — Lizzy was meant for you, I told him. She was your fate.

CARNEGIE / My mother had another view.

— Something the matter with you, need to do something crazy, she said. How you going to concentrate on your career? You do not know what baby is. Baby is lotta, lotta work. Lotta money too. I tell you, adoption can be big mistake. You are too young even to know what big mistake is. You do not know what life is, you think it is like college, everybody end up with degree, more or less the same. But I tell you, is not like college. Nobody love a man who is nobody.

Thus quoth Mama Wong.

Also: — Why you have to do such crazy things. As if people will love you for that!

But Blondie did. Blondie loved me *for that.*

BLONDIE / I loved him because he did not think of himself as particularly noble.

— I didn't have a choice, he said. Not like you.

CARNEGIE / We married at her family's place in northern Maine.

BLONDIE / Lizzy was eleven months at the time, an affectionate child—expert at shaking her head no, and just walking, though unsteady on the grass. For the wedding she wore a white bubble dress, like an upside-down crocus bulb with organdy sleeves. We fixed a circle of fresh flowers in her hair. But of course, she kept taking this off, losing a few petals each time. The dress was quickly green with grass stains where it wasn't brown with dirt—but still adorable, people said.

CARNEGIE / She wore a ruffled diaper cover, which wagged charmingly when she crawled.

BLONDIE / My father's family, the Baileys, were immigrants. This was the family of Grandpa the judge—Scotch-Irish city folk who didn't much care about land. Or at least not as much as the German side of the family—my mother's family, the Behnkes. So deeply attached were they to Wisconsin, where they had lived on a farm and kept a cabin on a lake up north, that the first thing my Grandma Dotie did when she married and moved east was to buy a good-sized neck of land on a good-sized pond. How the big fish and wild berries reminded her of her childhood!—though her family had never owned as much waterfront as she and Grandpa Werner bought here in Maine. A whole peninsula—really a skinny causeway broadening into a kind of island. There was a dock on one side, perfect for boats; and a sandy beach with a gradual dropoff on the other, perfect for children. It was so far north that she and Grandpa had no neighbors at first—so far north that it seemed a real retreat from all the getting and spending of the East Coast. Why ever had she moved?

Back home, her farm relatives struggled; they could barely survive on the milk they sold to the cheese factory. True, the ones who moved in—into town, that is—did better. Their boys worked in the cheese factory or became ministers; their girls worked in the cheese factory or became teachers. But in the end, no one stayed; no one could. In the end, everyone moved to Wasa, to work in the paper mill, or else to a bigger city still. Chicago, other places. Once the factory shut down, they had no choice. Yet still, as the years went on, Grandma Dotie wondered sometimes, Was life happier in Wisconsin? She did remember life on the farm—how they had no electricity, and no heat besides a woodstove in the kitchen. Still—the joy when the train brought oysters and oranges at Christmas! She could still taste her mom's oyster stew. And how she had loved huddling in the kitchen with her older brothers and sisters! All six of whom married the six kids of the farm next door; if the Voigtlands hadn't run out of kids, who knew whether she would have married Grandpa Werner with his lab books and specimens.

As she grew older, she began to talk about going back. She began to talk too about the lost past—about things disappearing. By the end, she was made anxious by anything missing, even for a short while—people, dishes, furniture. She would fret about threats she read about in the paper—to our country's waterways, to our country's forests. *This world, after all, can disappear like any other,* she would say. *I just pray for the health of the trees.*

WENDY / We still have these empty boxes in the attic that my Great-grandma Dotie saved, because that's like what girls got when they were twenty-five and not married yet, seeing as how that's what they were considered back in Germany. An old box. Never mind that Great-grandma Dotie did get married in the end, and anyway wasn't even all German. She was some other things too, like I think French.

Still German was what Great-grandma Dotie grew up praying, she said because prayers in German went to God faster than any other kind. And German was what she grew up eating—gross stuff like blood sausage and headcheese that they made on the farm. Also sauerkraut that Great-grandma Dotie kept on making herself in Maine, in these crocks Mom wants to teach Lizzy and me to use, forget about if we want to learn or not. She's set on it, Lizzy says, because she herself mostly ate SpaghettiOs and Spam and Twinkies growing up. Talk about gross, but that's what people ate because of the war, even after the war. Because they all just got used to it.

And that's why she talks about the farm like some people talk about movies too, Lizzy says—like she actually lived there or at least went there on vacation. She talks about stuff like how everybody back in Wisconsin knows what to do with a baby calf, nobody is grossed out by the newborns being covered with bloody gunk and the mama cow licking it all up, or is surprised by the mama cow lowing and pushing until that poor baby has to stand up either. My class saw that on a field trip once and we couldn't believe it, the way the mother was bullying that baby, pushing it all around the stall even though it was just born and kind of shocked. You know, by the outside world, it probably wasn't expecting so much hay. And to be pushed around first thing like that and expected to stand up. Everybody on the trip was shocked except Mom, who said that about Wisconsin. Quiet like of course, and not to make everyone else feel stupid. It was like she just wanted to tell me, because her mother told her.

LIZZY / And because she didn't want us to be so Chinese anymore. She wanted us to know we had relatives besides Mama Wong; she wanted us to know there was such a thing as too Chinese. Not that she would say so, of course.

BLONDIE / How Grandma Dotie had loved the property in Maine! The deep forest especially, with its cathedrals of evergreens. There were also, on a slight rise and small plateau, some buildings—summer-camp cabins that had been used for a time as a boys' school. She loved the cabins being so small, like her family's original lake cabin up north. She loved it that there was no heat besides a woodstove in the main building.

When we were little we called the camp our independence, as Grandma Dotie and Grandpa Werner had. Later, though, it became Independence Island.

CARNEGIE / The causeway to the mainland was wide enough for wedding guests to have driven over it. What with parking such a problem, though, we brought most people across the inlet via the old bicycle ferry. This contraption, involving a cable and a pulley and a bike seat with pedals, had been installed by the former owner, one Mr. Buck, who in his time had apparently been quite the honcho: locals still called the pond Buck's Pond, and the island Buck's Island. The road was Buck's Road. Only the beach carried a different designation: Sue's Beach, people called it, after Buck's great granddaughter, or somesuch.

BLONDIE / We set a tent up on the big lawn—not a rent-a-tent, but a billowy free-form yellow-and-white sail, designed by my arty sister Renata, and sewn by my obliging sister Ariela. This extended out from the beach pavilion, under which the ceremony was held.

CARNEGIE / Happily the proceedings were only drowned out by Jet Skis twice.

BLONDIE / The reception line was under the rose arbor, glorious with a repeat bloom almost as lovely as the first. The water beside us was blue and clear.

CARNEGIE / Blondie's brothers and cousins offered toasts. Sonnets, limericks.

BLONDIE / Friends played chamber music.

CARNEGIE / Blondie was the youngest of the family by a good bit; the epilogue, they called her. Her two sisters were the prologue; her two brothers, the main act. His and His Highness, Blondie's sisters had called them in their youth. Now they were jovial, articulate men, coming into the Bailey look. Bailey women were various; similar in height, but not noticeably of a type. Bailey men, in contrast, boasted a balanced heft in their youth that turned with age into a backsideless paunchiness. They looked as though they were being pushed through the tunnel of time by a firm hand situated at their lower backs: the more they resisted, the more they flattened in the rear and bulged in the front. Their pants rode low on their hips. The fabric of the seats bagged at the top of their thighs.

But how amiable they were! The cousins and brothers both. For Bailey men did not care in the least whether they bulged, or where. They did not care that they were all nearsighted, and wore metal-frame glasses. Their bow ties were undone long before the main course. They made hats out of the centerpieces. How the various brothers-in-law struggled to keep up! The Baileys critiqued the music and cracked obscure jokes. Should one of them shout, *Lillibolaro!* for example, the others would all jump up and shout, *Lillibolaro!* too—patiently explaining, if you asked, that this had been the battle cry of William of Orange's Ulster supporters. They played duets on their wineglasses.

Of course, what Mama Wong said later was true. None of the Bailey children owned anything like that neck of land themselves. For they were beyond real estate, those Baileys. Their capital was knowledge. Taste. And character, in Doc Bailey's generation. He and his siblings were outspoken, plainspoken folk. Blondie's generation, in contrast, placed more stock in their vocabularies, particularly their adjectives. *Pulchritudinous. Otiose. Restive.* They were chiefly defined by what they could not take seriously.

Blondie was the throwback, a plain Jane who seemed to have no part in certain family games.

All this was related to the second official reason Mama Wong had given, the night before the wedding, an hour before the rehearsal dinner, for wanting to call off the marriage. The first reason was that Blondie was old. Thirty-one, to be exact, six years older than me.

An old maid, said Mama Wong, a woman marrying while she still could. Who knew if she could even have babies? I was obviously not her first choice, who knew how many first choices there had been before me.

But the second reason Mama Wong did not like Blondie had to do with the Baileys.

— You watch, she said. In ten years they are all going to need your help. They are not go up. They are go down. You know why? Not because they are stupid. They are not stupid. They are go down because they do not want to go up. They are like children who do not know what they want for Christmas, that's how spoiled they are.

— They want to live in the moment, I explained. They don't believe in living for the future. It's a philosophical thing.

— You think I do not know what is philosophical thing, she said. But so happen I do know. They are like Buddhist monk. But who become Buddhist monk, you tell me? Not the success people. I tell you, in America people do not want anything, do not work hard, they are go down.

She said this in the cocktail area of the restaurant, the light from the street throwing her wrinkles in relief. She had had me late, and was now not young—almost seventy. Still, it was a shock to see her sidelit. She looked as if she had been sleeping, every night, with a plastic-net bag pressed to her face. Her jewelry, meanwhile, flashed cruelly—all the more brilliant, all the more unchanging—in the dramatic light. On one finger she was wearing two rings, one pearl with diamonds, one jade with diamonds. Something I had never seen her do before. Also she played with them in a way she would not have approved of, had she noticed it. *Why show everyone you are nervous?* Sitting by the window, she might easily have caught her own reflection in the window glass, or in the treacherous black ice of the lacquer snack table. But she did not. Only I watched her reflection, agitated as it was and, in the way of all reflections, strange.

— What time is it? she asked.

This was a new tactic. She sometimes asked me the time four or five times an hour, even if she was wearing a watch, as she was today. Two watches, actually, one on each wrist. That was a new thing too.

— Six o'clock, I said.

— Listen, she said. You break up engagement now, I give you one million dollars cash, spend however you like. Only you marry somebody else.

— Ma, I said.

— I tell you something. Lily Lee still not married. I just heard the other day. She almost married someone, but her parents say no. You want, I make introduction. Very nice girl.

— Ma.

— What's the matter with Lily Lee? You never even meet her.

— Exactly.

— So how you know you don't like her?

— Ma. I am not going to marry Lily Lee.

— Okay, okay. Listen. I give you one million dollars cash, even you marry somebody else. Not Lily Lee. Not medical doctor. But not Blondie. After marry, you can still go to movies with Blondie. You can still go out to dinner. But on the paper, name is somebody else. I find you nice Chinese girl, she is going to make everybody feel so nice. You like sports, she is going to watch sports. You like cars, she will like cars. She is going to cook some nice food, and one day, you watch, she is going to take care your old mommy too. You marry Blondie, you will be like servant to Blondie's family. They will look at you, say, Oh, but he cannot talk the way we do. And when you help them, you think they will appreciate your help? I make prediction, they will not appreciate.

I tried to cut in, to no avail. My mother had always been unswerving, but lately she seemed to have taken on new tonnage. She leaned toward me, her face bisected by shadow like a carnival mask.

— That's what those people are, she said. If other people look like them, more or less the same, they try to see, who is this person? But if they look at you, you are like mirror to them. All they see is how they themself look. You make their reflection look small, look weak, look not so smart, not so hardworking, they do not like you. Is that simple. You marry nice Chinese girl, she is like servant to you. If you want to look at her, fine. Otherwise, she hold up mirror for you to say, Oh, I am so handsome. Oh, I am so rich.

Despite another twenty minutes of this, I turned down the million dollars.

— Look, Ma, I said. I'm going to marry Jane. You can't stop us.

— Marry Blondie going to kill you.

— She is not going to kill me.

— Okay, then, she said. Blondie going to kill me.

I did not respond to that.

— You listen to me, she said. I offer you one million dollars. Cash.

She banged her open hand on the table in front of her for emphasis.

— I'm going to marry her if it kills us both, I said finally. Adding, preemptively: — You may disinherit whom you like.

The 'whom' felt funny in my mouth, like a largish pillow mint that had suddenly materialized on my tongue. Of course, we had always spoken in English. She had brought me up English-speaking. In general, though, I spoke in short sentences with her, employing a limited vocabulary. Eschewing subordinate phrases. Never before had I used this sort of English with her—English-major English. The mint was still there. Perhaps she had not noticed how I had thrown at her the fancy education for which she had paid?

In the next room, tables were being pushed together.

Finally she said: — What time is it?

I told her.

And in a voice so weak it seemed a kind of aftertaste, she said: — You are not my son. You can do whatever you want, I do not care.

— Ma.

— No heir, so what? Anyway, we are live in America now, right?

— Ma.

— When I come to this country, she began; then she stopped, as if forgetting what she had just said, and what came next. Then she started again: — When I come to this country, I did not know I end up here alone.

She asked yet once more what time it was.

— You're wearing a watch, I said. In fact, you're wearing two watches.

— What time is it? she asked, like a broken toy. —What time is it?

She did not stay for the dinner. When the Baileys came I explained that my mother was indisposed. Her place setting was discreetly removed.

The festivities proceeded according to plan. The restaurant chairs were over-designed, the hors d'oeuvres over-engineered. Still, people were laughing and jumping up and changing seats; the Baileys liked to change seats. There were limericks, replete with off-color off-rhyme. At one point, I danced with the chef. At another, my bride-to-be was set on a large platter on the table.

I drank as much as anybody, though I knew I was turning red. I told jokes. Then I left on the early side to check on my mother. Everyone understood; in fact, Janie—then she was still Janie—offered to come with me. I insisted she stay.

— The hero must face the dragon alone, I said.

One last swig of wine.

I found Mama Wong in her hotel room, darkly raiding the honor bar and snack basket.

— Are you drunk? she demanded.

There were opened cans and bottles and wrappers everywhere.

— No, I said.

I softened her up by ordering room service. Steak tartare, I began with, knowing she would be outraged and insist on sending it back.

She did.

I ordered a bowl of consommé; we sent that back too.

I ordered lobster eggrolls, figuring that though she would complain about what passed for Chinese cooking, she would eat them.

She ate them.

We ordered more eggrolls.

We admired the vase of carnations on the food cart.

I showed her how to work the safe in her room. I pillaged the bathroom amenities basket with her. I hid the honor bar price list and let her believe that all those snacks and drinks she had tried were indeed free (taking advantage of the fact that she rarely traveled and, if she did, always stayed in the cheapest joint she could find). When the turn-down lady came, I lobbied for extra chocolates.

— Free! I told my mother.

Still I could only convince her to come to the wedding by promising to start a family business once I was married.

— We'll be partners, I heard myself saying, my voice as soothing as the room lighting. — Blondie will be our property manager.

If only I were drunker than I was.

— You really think we can trust that Blondie?

Mama Wong's voice miraculously replumped, like an apparently dead plant that's finally been watered. Her face beamed. She flipped through a menu and ordered marbled cheesecake for dessert.

— Of course, I said. Of course we can trust Blondie.

It was the first time I'd called her that: *Blondie.* How odd it felt in my mouth, like a sound from another language.

I promised I would work out the details on my honeymoon.

BLONDIE / My mother's great-grandmother was a pacifist; she came to America rather than see her sons fight for Bismarck. My mother's great-uncle was an abolitionist; people said he installed false walls for anyone who wanted them. And my own great-aunt was a suffragette; we grew up hearing how her children had been excluded from birthday parties on account of her views.

Then there was my mother, an art preservationist/civil rights activist who, before she got sick, went door-to-door down South, registering people to vote.

Now our generation did soup kitchens. We did clothing drives, food drives, book drives. We sang carols in hospitals. We protested program cuts, development plans, the Gulf War.

Still we felt ourselves to be votive lights at best, if compared with the original bonfires.

CARNEGIE / The elder of Blondie's brothers, Gregory, made lawn art: big, suggestive sculptures that challenged community norms and ran gleefully afoul of local zoning laws. Her other brother, Peter, practically ran a summer music camp, the nominal director being a sot. This involved confrontations and crises, and hard stands taken for the sake of art.

Her older sisters, Renata and Ariela, filled the world with beauty. They were not thorny, like her brothers. They cooked and gardened; they made weavings, hangings, rubbings. They saw art retrospectives in previews. They did rubber-band balls, sing-alongs, capture the flag, leapfrog; they even devised their own fruitcakes—including, one might contend, their husbands, who affected a gentility so shabby as to verge on the ostentatious. One was a mapmaker. The other, a water diviner. How their beards blossomed! Their shorts bloomed with ink stains. If you talked to them about the Series, they would cock their heads and look at you attentively, awaiting further information.

Neither one of them knew the difference between the American League and the National League.

Blondie's father, Doc Bailey, was disgusted with them.

— Those boys are living inside a balloon, he said. One of these days it is going to go *pop!* The question is, Will they hear it?

Doc Bailey, an imposing man of intimidating health, liked me. He did not care that I came with a daughter. He thought that I reinfused their family with immigrant vigor; that I looked forward rather than backward, and that in this I was, not to mince words, more like himself than like his late wife, god bless her. Doc Bailey credited me with inspiring Blondie to grapple with life. (He had big hairy hands, and when he said the word 'grapple' he seized the air in front of him as if to squeeze out its excess molecules.) He thought this because I had coached Blondie in her move up the ladder from an art stringer to a full-time designer. This was in a high-tech firm doing handwriting recognition.

— Cutting-edge stuff, she would tell her sibs. — I'm working on the twenty-first century.

She would report to them about the future of technology.

— You wait and see, there will be computers in your shoe. There will be computers you can eat.

BLONDIE / No longer was I the baby, the afterthought, the least witty of the children. The child with the boring name—which my mother, even before I was born, had somehow thought appropriate. No more would everyone talk of how I had been the smallest at birth, a disaster at charades, in truth a touch shy.

Janie Runt of the Litter.

Janie Mommy's Girl.

Janie They're Picking on Me Again.

A listener, they called me. Agreeing on my strength with faint self-congratulation. How creative of them to have discovered a strong point!

A good listener.

Quite by accident I was making a most original marriage. My brothers and sisters approved. My father, too, approved heartily of everything about the match—even, apparently, Mama Wong.

CARNEGIE / How graciously he agreed with Mama Wong even when she announced that the Bailey family had *third-generation problem*.

— In China, this happen all the time, she said. One generation made it, second generation do nothing, third generation lost everything.

I pointed out that Blondie and her siblings were fourth-generation on her mother's side. Nor could you exactly call Doc Bailey *do nothing*. He was an upstanding and well-loved pediatrician who had seen many a low-income child for free and had, what's more, single-handedly established a number of clinics in underserved areas.

But Doc Bailey laughed modestly and insisted that Mama Wong was right. There had been a falling-off. How could there not be? Not everyone could pull himself up by the bootstraps the way his father had, fresh off the boat from Ulster. Grandpa Bailey had been remarkable even in his projects and hobbies. He had left behind silver brooches he had smithed. Leather items he had tooled. The younger Baileys were proud to be his descendants. Who wouldn't be?

Mama Wong left the get-together triumphant.

— You see! she chortled, banging her open hand on her pocketbook. — Even Doc Bailey admits. You see!

I adored the Baileys, though. It was true they cherished their own cleverness; Gregory in particular felt no need of facts to be knowing. *Russia expert turned armaments expert?* he would say. *I'll tell you why, there was no money in Russia anymore.* Or: *Japanese potter sues American author? Elementary, my dear Watson, some lawyer put him up to it.*

Still, they were more like than unlike the people I had gone to school with. People whose mothers did not carry fish bait in their handbags. People who were not strong-armed into managing rental buildings in the summer. People who were not summoned in the middle of midterms to come fix hot-water heaters. The Baileys made me feel as though I were still in college; as if life were full of electives, as if there would always be a cafeteria about which to complain. As if one's categorical imperative was to find oneself via the right seminar.

Nowhere was this sense stronger than here, at the family summer place. This had in fact at one point been Mr. Buck's sleep-over camp; but at another, a boys' day school. Besides Mr. Buck's own cabin, there was a library and a mess hall. The cabins all had blackboards; the Baileys were still finding compasses and ink bottles and pen nibs among the pine needles. What with Renata's husband the mapmaker ably charting where each artifact was found, this activity constituted one of the island's principal pleasures, surpassed only by the restoring of Mr. Buck's original abode. For Mr. Buck had been a Michelangelo of home improvements. His many windows opened via homemade crank-and-bicycle-chain mechanisms. The bathroom featured a chute for baby diapers, as well as a self-setting timer on the shower. (The water shut off when the timer ran out.) Was he not a kind of genius? So the Baileys agreed.

But every proper genius has limits, as the Baileys liked to point out, and so too did Mr. Buck. Exhibit A being the foundations of his cabins, for there were no foundations to speak of. He had simply built the cabins on wooden ties, placed directly on the ground; the Baileys would have given anything to know why. Or what to do about it, now that the water table was rising. The plateau sank a few inches every year.

— Have them replaced, I said when the subject first came up in my presence. — Jack up the buildings and have some footings poured.

— We hereby name you Sir Buildings and Grounds, intoned Gregory immediately. — Our Own Home Repair Counsel, whom we do love as we love ourself.

BLONDIE / Our place had become something of a headache. It was so far north, no one could get there very often. And it was assessed at so little that major repairs just didn't make sense. What's more, a developer had recently bought up twenty acres directly across the water from us.

CARNEGIE / An eighth of an acre each, his plots were going to be; his cockamamie plan was for, count 'em, one hundred sixty 'quality residences.' As if the market would support anything near that! We pictured tattered tarps, abandoned Dumpsters. Pits, rubble, wild dogs. Or worse, against our predictions, success: lane upon lane of cookie-cutter condos, in perky shades of aluminum cladding.

It was enough to make the Baileys think about selling. Not for the first time; a trailer park too was growing right smack at the base of their peninsula. But where else to buy? Downhill skiing had come to Maine, sending prices up. They could no longer begin to afford anything waterfront, other than where they had it. And hadn't Independence Island been in the family forever?

BLONDIE / I wore Grandma Dotie's dress. Neither of my sisters had worn it, but Gabriela had thought it blowsily marvelous enough that I had been moved to at least try it on. And then how could I not wear it? For it fit me perfectly—an old-fashioned, fairy-queen affair with a high neck, and long runs of covered buttons.

CARNEGIE / Not to say a bustle Peter called the apotheosis of the drape.

— No doubt it involves pulleys, he said.

Gregory said it put him in mind of various phenomena of the insect world, to wit, physogastric queen bees.

— Oh, be quiet, you bachelors, said Gabriela. Or I won't marry either one of you!

They were chastened then, and admitted the dress to be fun, a spoof of a pouf. For both of them were a little in love with Gabriela, indeed asked her two or three times a day if she would marry one or the other of them, her choice.

To this she would reply: — Oh, go marry your mama in heaven.

Or else: — I thought I married you already.

Back then Gabriela was a sexpot redhead, always in a flurry, who secretly longed to be serious, as everyone knew.

— But I am not serious, I am not! she would moan, while all around her men assured her: — No, you are! You are!

— About what? Tell me! she would demand.

— About something.

— Something, she would snort. Something is nothing. But you wait and see. One day I will find my true self.

She smiled dreamily.

— I imagine it will be through massage.

BLONDIE / People said I was the spitting image of my mother.

CARNEGIE / Maybe that was why she began talking, endlessly, about what her mother would have worn to the wedding (blue). What her mother read (nonfiction). How her mother died (cancer). She talked about her mother's painting restoration. How she had worked for the Boston Museum of Fine Arts at the end. How she had worked on a Turner. How this had involved many substances besides paint. How people had called her a genius.

— Is that so, I said.

I wondered how well I knew my fiancée.

Her lashes after the ceremony seemed longer than I had noticed; she felt like an alien in my arms. When I kissed her in the pavilion, her bustle forced me to support her waist in a new way. How beautifully her arched back fit my outspread hand; that was marvelous, I supposed, though did not those covered buttons dig into her back? I was glad, in any case, to see her hoist excited Lizzy up onto her hip, a familiar gesture, and to see Lizzy wrap her bare legs around Blondie's waist.

Mama Wong and her friends had been the only party to arrive by car, i.e., her new air-conditioned Mercedes, complete with chauffeur, from which they had to be coaxed out.

— We can see through the windshield, said Mama Wong. Mosquitoes have plenty to eat already.

Once out, though, she softened. The brothers Bailey fanned her and brought her drinks. They told her jokes. They made her teach them Chinese. They complimented her on her hairdo, so very like a beachball.

But Doc Bailey, more importantly, agreed with her.

— One thing I tell you: that trailer park no good for property value, she said.

He nodded.

— And that is foundation rot down there. Foundation rot mean big trouble.

He nodded.

— You know what this place is? This place is so-called white elephant.

He nodded.

The result: she seemed almost touched when, late in the afternoon, Blondie changed out of her mother's dress and into a red silk *qipao.* Also when Blondie knelt with me (this took some doing in that dress) and asked for her blessing. Never mind that this was a creative traditional touch straight out of *The Compleat Ethnic Wedding,* which Gabriela had given Blondie for a shower present. Mama Wong was moved.

— Okay, she said. She was seated in a baronial chair dug up in a flea market; the pillow behind her shone gold, with a deep braided fringe that could have come from a Gilbert and Sullivan admiral's uniform. — You are married now. Nothing anybody can do.

— Thank you, said Blondie, her hands clasped as if in prayer.

— Don't say anything, said Mama Wong. Let Carnegie say. Bride not supposed to talk too much.

My neck began to itch.

— Thank you, I said.

— And next time don't put white flower in your hair, she said. Chinese people consider that very bad luck, white is the color people wear when parents die.

— Do you at least like the dress? I asked.

— She found a good dressmaker, said Mama Wong. She is not easy to fit, I can see.

Blondie's eyes welled up, threatening her mascara; I thought I heard her dress rip as she stood. We turned toward the assembly.

How everyone clapped! The tear, happily, turned out to be minor. A septic-tank scare turned out to be just that, a scare. Neighbors from the trailer park came and ate cake; one man was heard to yell, *You leave our women alone!* but was quickly hushed by others. Anyway, I did and didn't hear him, having developed a mystery case of hives. This, happily, responded to an antihistamine in the medicine cabinet, though the expiration date on the box had long since passed.

Our local blue heron perched at the end of the dock—staring, with pencil-point attention, toward the moving water.

Meanwhile, every guest with a son or a cousin or a niece who had married in an unorthodox way proudly got out pictures of their new family members, and sometimes of the products of the union. They showed these to my mother. I held my breath, but Mama Wong generously oohed and aahed even over the mulatto babies, agreeing that they were unutterably precious and beautiful. The new face of America.

— You see what kind luck that baby bring you, she told one parent.

The parent beamed.

To another couple, she said: — Don't worry. Carnegie and Blondie's babies going to look even funnier than that.

How people laughed!

BLONDIE / How people danced! Even Mama Wong and her friends danced, their faces red—with one another, and with my family, and with other people too. The dancing spilled out of the tent, onto the lawn.

Outside the circle of our gathering, quiet gathered. The air cooled; the ground cooled. The mountains seemed to be assuming their rightful power as their shadows deepened; the drape of the willows was silhouetted by the sun. Still everyone bounced and swirled, magically unbothered by mosquitoes. But Mama Wong asked the time, and finally we pushed off in an old wooden rowboat—our ever-faithful Daedalus—with Lizzy in the stern, on the bench. She was bundled up in her bunny PJ's and asleep, amid many blankets.

A shower of clattering rice. Then, to the music of our oarlocks, we bid everyone good-bye and headed to a campsite across the way—the first place I had ever spent a night alone. The music resumed, but receded. We could see the crowd begin to thin. Loons crooned. There was a distant echo, and there were bats over the water—hundreds of bats. Every now and then one passed so close we thought we could feel, not so much its wing, as a push of air. My own thoughts then were flying too, circling. I wanted to give voice to one of them, but how to settle long enough on one, and not another, to speak? I hovered near Lizzy, trying to make sure she didn't get bitten; I had read once that a child could get bitten by a bat without anyone noticing. I crossed her bunny ears over her face, to protect her.

CARNEGIE / — Your mother seemed so happy, said my wife—my wife!—after a while.

— That red dress appears to have done the trick, I agreed.

— It's so tight I can hardly breathe. I shouldn't have eaten any cake. I was fine until I ate the cake.

Blondie was still wearing the Chinese dress. She had intended to change into a third outfit, as per Chinese tradition, for her leavetaking. But that involved spaghetti straps, which at the last minute she had thought too much for my mother and her friends.

— She's so crazy about you now, she's hoping you'll go into business with her, I said; trying out the idea in a joking manner.

Blondie laughed so loud she seemed to be startling the early stars out of the just-dark sky.

— I thought there would be some strings on that million dollars, she said.

Million dollars?

It seemed that after I had left Mama Wong, the night of the rehearsal dinner, she had summoned Blondie to her room. Blondie had responded to the summons, accepted a juice from the mini-bar, then sat as directed in the armchair. Mama Wong had offered her the million dollars not to get married; Blondie had accepted. Whereupon Mama Wong gave Blondie permission to marry me after all.

— You mean you agreed?

I stopped rowing. The boat rocked.

— I didn't agree, exactly. I just, you know.

— You know what?

She didn't answer.

I pushed the oar handles into my lap, so that the blades lifted like wings from the water, dripping. The boat rocked some more; the current nosed at it, nudging it clockwise. Lizzy woke and began to cry. Jane cuddled her.

— What if she had held you to your word? I asked. What if she hadn't relented? Would you have taken the money and married someone else?

— Of course not, she said.

— Then why did you agree?

— I'm an agreeable person.

— How can you not have told me?

— She said you knew.

Was that true?

You can't trust that Blondie.

I watched her jostle Lizzy and rummage in the diaper bag, and decided not to say more. Our wedding night, after all. The water; such stars as there were; the moon. I lowered the oars to the water and let go. The blades splashed and caught, my left handle driving in toward my waist, my right swinging away.

— I'll warm up the bottle, I offered.

We had a portable bottle warmer that recharged in the microwave, one of a panoply of nifty items that had recently filled our lives. All you had to do was crush it, to generate heat.

The warmth felt good. The air smelt of a campfire somewhere. From far away, across the water, came the surprisingly clear sound of people arguing.

The plan had been to leave Lizzy with her regular sitter, Zoren. But when Zoren, just our luck, developed an appendix, we decided not to leave Lizzy with her aunts. Seeing as how she knew them but not well, and was in the middle of stranger anxiety.

— We need to find someone we can trust her with besides Zoren, I said.

— We do. But first have a look at your daughter.

The moon shone on her sleeping face. Her face was not as perfectly circular as it had been that very first time I held her; still, her eyes seemed freshly inscribed. She had eyebrows, but no brow bone as of yet. Her chin too was more of a location than an actual feature. By day her cheeks were identifiable by their pinkness; at night they were yet one more idea we had about her face. Her bangs stuck up stick-like, softly bristly. Her mouth was still tiny—way too small for a grown-up spoon. How pure she was; it seemed to me that there was nothing left in the world that could be described as pure, only this child. These days when I picked her up, she still nestled her head into my shoulder and kissed me—*mmma!* And curled up her legs. How I loved that, the way she picked up her little legs, so high her knees approached her belly button. I loved the way she curled her feet up like shrimp and turned them in toward each other. A ball of life she was, still; more ball than forked stick. So much in life fell short of its billing—but a child, a child! How extraordinary her lashes! And what was her skin made of? In the moonlight it appeared a semisolid, something just poured. She was asleep again.

— Are you happy?

I volunteered that it felt odd to be wearing a ring.

— You know, this evening is not as romantic as it could be.

You really think you can trust that Blondie?

I rowed. My wife, settling Lizzy back in her Polarfleece nest, came and nestled herself in her own nest by my feet, amid our sleeping bags. She undid the frogs of her dress, revealing a distinctly bordello bra.

— Ah, she said. That's better. Don't stop rowing.

And so it was that she was half naked when we were set upon at the campsite by wild bears who turned out to be friends as well as Blondie's sibs and Gabriela.

Lizzy was up the rest of the night.

BLONDIE / Later, the gifts were of two sorts. There were practical items like cookie jars and toaster ovens, mostly from his side, and Asian selections, mostly from mine. There was a trivet made from the character for 'long life,' a Japanese lantern, an Asian-fusion cookbook; a feng shui manual, a set of rice bowls, two pairs of zebrawood chopsticks, and a bamboo desk fountain. I loved all of these. The Chinese things from his side were harder to be enthusiastic about—a pair of baroque jade carvings, complete with ornate rosewood stands, for example. An elaborately embroidered tablecloth, too big for any table we owned. Happily, there were more simply embroidered pillowcases too, and an amazing grain of rice, onto which had been inscribed an entire Tang Dynasty poem. This came with a stand and magnifying glass.

CARNEGIE / Mama Wong indeed gave us the million dollars she had promised Blondie, only with the new stipulation that it be used for an investment property we would manage and own jointly with her. But that wasn't the only surprise. Doc Bailey, with the blessing of the other Bailey children, was inspired to give us the summer house.

— No no no, we said. It's the family house. We can't accept it.

Doc Bailey, though, had real support.

— Don't worry, we'll all visit, said Peter cheerfully. We'll bring our dogs and expect to be fed and never leave. You'll just take care of it.

How to respond to such largesse?

5

Nothing's Plenty for Me

WENDY / She doesn't need much, but she does carry an umbrella if it's sunny, to make sure she doesn't get tan.

— In America it's good to be tan, we say.

But Lanlan wants to be pale anyway. This Indian summer starts almost as soon as she comes so that she does not put her umbrella away until practically October.

— I am not American, she says.

It's just a little beige fold-up umbrella, and she only uses it around lunchtime. Still we think it's weird.

— Would you want to be? says Lizzy. American, I mean.

— No no no no, says Lanlan, smiling. Too many beeps here. Other times she says: — This is not my home.

— But would you want it to be your home?

— Better to want nothing, she says. Then nothing means nothing.

She puts her finger up when she says stuff like that, it's like the finger is talking instead of her.

LAN / *In Chinese we say wu ai—without love. That it is better to be without attachment. Just as it is better to do things—wu wei—without effort.*

That is how my father used to talk. Like a Daoist monk.

WENDY / How can you do stuff without doing it? That's what we say in the beginning, but after a while we sort of get it or at least Lizzy does.

LIZZY / Because it was like so true! Like I could see that if I tried to get some guy, it just messed things up. It was better to go with the flow.

WENDY / — Better to want nothing, says Lanlan again, her finger up. — Ask for nothing. Expect nothing.

— But how can you want nothing, I say. I mean, how can you just decide?

— Of course you can decide, says Lanlan.

She tucks her hair behind her ear. We are sitting outside under the apple trees, me and Lizzy in the sun, and Lanlan in the shade. She has to wear a sweater because the ground is cold, and in the shade the air is cold too. It's not like being in the sun, where the air is warm.

Lanlan is in the shade but she stretches her neck up at the sky anyway, and closes her eyes. Her neck is long and beautiful, Lizzy says it's nice to be kissed on the neck, so probably if I were a man I'd kiss her there. But would she want to be kissed? Or would she decide to want nothing?

— Do you miss Shandong? I say.

— I miss Suzhou, she says.

Her eyes are still closed but not like she's sleeping, more like she's channeling some kind of message from the sky. Like she's reaching up to it and it's reaching down to her through the branches of the apple tree.

She says: —Suzhou is my *lao jia*—my hometown.

— But when you go back to China, won't you go back to Shandong? says Lizzy.

— Hard to say, she says. It all depend.

— Does that mean you'll go to Suzhou?

— Move to Suzhou very difficult.

She opens her eyes then, and I'm sorry we made her do that. Not that she acts bothered, but it's like we interrupted the sky, and now her neck is normal. I pull my own neck up to see if I can do that. Close my own eyes so my eyelids turn red, and straighten up my back.

— But why? says Lizzy. I think you should just go.

— Cannot just go, says Lanlan.

— But why not?

Lanlan tickles me under the chin, which is how it is that I open my eyes and see that the sky has gone away for her, and that there's this sadness coming down.

— First of all, I would need a job, she says. Not to say a *hukou*—sort of like a residency permit.

— So get one, says Lizzy.

— You have to know somebody, says Lanlan. Not just somebody. Somebody—how do you say?—have influence.

— To get a job?

Lanlan nods.

— You can't just apply?

Lanlan shakes her head.

— Do you know somebody with influence?

— I know no one, she says.

— So where will you go back to?

— It all depend, she says.

Her voice is all quiet like then, and wanting to want nothing.

BLONDIE / I loved Lan's simplicity, but some things drove me crazy.

The umbrella was one thing.

The other was that she hardly ate. She would not set a place for herself at the table—we had to do it every night.

WENDY / — Which is fine, Mom says.

But the way she says it we know Dad's going to have to say something soon.

— No wonder she is so thin, Mom says. I hope she eats at school. Or perhaps she eats at night?

And that's right, I've seen her. She eats putting the food near her mouth, then taking it away, then bringing it close to her mouth again and maybe finally beginning to chew. Sometimes she cries. Eating makes her cry, but very quietly, so you almost can't hear her, you can only see her cry and when she's finally chewed something, put her head in her arms. One day I ask her why she cries. But she says she doesn't cry.

— I saw you cry, I say. You were crying when I came in.

— How can you trust what you see, she says. You only have two eyes.

And I say: — Aren't two eyes enough?

But she says no, not enough, not nearly.

— Do you understand? she asks me.

And when she asks that her eyes fly away to the door as if she's making sure there's no one there, or as if that's where the other world is, in the hall, where it can hear us talking.

— I saw you, I say. I know I did. I did.

— All right, she says then. I cried. What does it matter?

— It does, I say. Because it means you're sad sometimes.

She looks at me.

— I think you are Chinese, she says. Very care about other people.

Then she tells me a story she says her *ayi* told her a long time ago, about this baby who got killed by accident by the servants.

— One day, you know, they are feeding her, and what happens? The *ayi* put the chopstick too far inside the baby's mouth, and poke a hole here.

She shows me by putting a finger inside her own mouth and poking in the way back.

— Of course, since all the way in back, nobody can see. And so the baby cry cry, but nobody know what is make the baby cry until one day the baby die.

— The baby died? I say.

— The baby die, and then the doctor look inside and find hole.

— Those chopsticks must have been pretty sharp, I say.

— Sharp, she agrees.

— I can't believe they didn't find the hole until the baby was dead.

— Hole is hard to see, says Lan.

— Are you going to die? I ask. Suddenly I think of that, I don't know how.

— No no, says Lanlan, and kind of half shakes her head.

— But you have a hole no one can see?

Lanlan smiles her smile.

— You are a real Chinese girl, she says. See not only with your eyes but with your heart.

Sometimes when it gets dark out we catch crickets. We hold a candle outside a cricket hole, and when the cricket comes out to see the light, we nab it quick. Lan hums. Nothing is baggy on her, her clothes looks like they're on a Barbie doll. Nothing wrinkles and she never has bare feet. Mom is the opposite, she loves bare feet and clothes she could sleep in. She would never in a million years wear Peds like Lanlan does, the beige kind that are like little stretchy stockings just for your feet. But that's what Lanlan wears, she's not the same as us. Just like the crickets all look the same to us but not to her, Lanlan sees things that we don't.

— See the legs, she says. How strong. See the lines on the head, how straight they are.

Or: — Look how beautiful this head here, that little gold in the middle.

She says every fall people used to travel from all over to Shandong where her great-aunt lived to buy fighting crickets, but that there are also beauty crickets and singing crickets. She looks over the crickets from our yard.

— This kind of cricket creep like a tiger, fight like a snake, she says. This kind charge like the wind.

Her favorite kind is the kind that *listens for sound, looks for the enemy.*

— That is smart cricket, she says. Ambush enemy instead of using brute force. That cricket is real Chinese.

We put the crickets in the cages and tickle them with those

skinny paintbrushes you use for crafts and stuff. But we can't get them to fight.

— Beep! Lanlan tells them. Beep!

I tell them too: — Beep!

But nothing happens.

— Typical American crickets, she says. Too much automatic make them lazy.

She teaches Bailey stuff too. Like she's trying to teach Bailey to walk by standing him up and clapping her hands and opening her arms to get him to walk to her. He mostly waves his arms and maybe takes a step but then falls down plop. She tries again anyway.

— You watch, she says. He will learn.

Some days we make kites, beautiful kites, with bamboo frames you can fold up, or that you can attach to each other. Flying them is like flying a pile of plates, except that they go up even when there's hardly any wind at all. Or else we do cat's cradle, which Lanlan says her *ayi* used to say brings rain. Lanlan knows how to do all kinds of things with string, like she loops it around her five fingers in a special way and says that's a snake, then pulls so that it comes off and says that's the snake's skin coming off. And we do paper play too, that's fun. Lanlan can make lanterns and all kinds of other things, like swans and goldfish and seals and flowers, she can even make balls out of paper, Bailey loves those. She blows them up and he shmushes them. If you give her scissors she can make your silhouette, or flowers, or a lantern, or a boat with a fisherman, or a house with animals and people playing instruments.

— Beep! she says when she's done. — Automatic! Wow.

Mom wants to get special paper for her to use, but Lanlan says she cannot use special paper. She likes scraps, wrappers we were going to throw away, pictures from magazines.

— It's part of her art, says Dad.

— Survivor art, says Mom. It has to be one part scrappiness.

— She doesn't pick and choose, says Dad. She makes.

— She makes you realize making do is a kind of making, says Mom.

— She needs nothing, says Dad.

Dad says he is going to make a movie of her hands, making these things.

— Her hands are amazing, he says. The way they move is so beautiful.

And that's true. Her fingers fly around, all except her pinkies, which she holds a little ways away—up in the air like, so you never forget how pretty her nails are.

Mom wants Lanlan to teach her something. Like how about embroidery, she says, Suzhou embroidery is so famous.

But Lanlan says embroidery is one thing she cannot do.

We teach Lanlan stuff too, like how to pick apples, and how to make apple crisp. Lanlan doesn't eat a lot of the crisp but she does eat some, and says that she likes it, forget that she spits out all the apple peels.

Mom says this is what cultural exchange is about, when we're older and don't have a baby in the house we're going to host some exchange students like her family did for sure.

BLONDIE / — I am happy anywhere, said Lan. I am not picky.

— *I got plenty of noth-ing,* she sang.

She seemed to have picked the singing business up from Carnegie, although she didn't make up words the way he did. Instead she learned them from tapes she played on her tape player; we had supplied her with a voltage converter. She sang Chinese songs, too, sometimes—so quietly you could barely hear her. And yet the girls were humming them now. For instance, this song about *moli hua*—jasmine.

CARNEGIE / The words were something like, How beautiful, how fragrant, I'd pick you except that I'd be pricked.

Also she sang this little number about road-building, and another called 'Rely on the Helmsman While Sailing the Seas.'

BLONDIE / Mostly she listened to tapes for school. She was taking English as a Second Language and studying very hard.

CARNEGIE / Ah, but her independent study: Broadway 101.

Not that she would ever go so far as to ask to borrow a cassette. But anything we left on her doorstep would disappear immediately and reappear a few days later. We thuswise introduced to her *The*

Sound of Music, South Pacific, Guys and Dolls. Porgy and Bess, Fiddler on the Roof. We begged her to tell us if we could get her something special, and one day, finally, she relented.

— Tchaikovsky, she said. *Swan Lake.*

She listened. We asked again.

— *La Traviata,* she said. *Aida.*

I unearthed my old opera-class tapes for her.

BLONDIE / — A good sign, he said.

He thought this even though Wendy said the sad songs made Lan cry so hard, it was scary.

— A sign of life, he said.

Sometimes he would hum a little of one thing or another. She would nod and look down.

CARNEGIE / Such was the sign of life.

BLONDIE / Eight weeks after moving in, she still had done nothing to decorate her room. She did use the refrigerator, but only for two or three items; they seemed to huddle together on the main shelf, as if in need of one another's company. She seemed reluctant too to take anything out of the family refrigerator.

— Thank you, she said when we told her yet once again to help herself. —You are too kind.

But when asked why she never did take anything, she sang softly, *Noth-ing's plenty for me.*

Her ESL course at the local community college was a full-time, intensive program, five nights a week. We had hoped she would make friends there.

But so far, nothing.

LAN / *All the jokes were in Spanish.*

BLONDIE / The Chinese community center was reopening after a renovation. We hoped that might be a source of friends for her too.

CARNEGIE / The center did picnics, newsletters, dragon-boat races. Calligraphy clinics. Karaoke fund-raisers. T-shirts, mugs, mouse pads.

You could tell the *echt* Chinese from the not-so-*echt* by how much they talked about self-esteem. Also by their piety level.

— You know what my mother used to say about customs inspectors in Hawaii? I said one day to one of the parents, who had just returned from Hong Kong. — She used to say, *Chinese inspectors are the worst. Only an idiot go through customs in Hawaii. Anybody with sense stop in Chicago or Denver.*

The parent clutched her flash cards for dear life.

BLONDIE / Still I loved belonging to the center, especially since the two couples who had traveled with us to China had both moved away—the Clarks to Maine after they inherited a house on the coast, and the Fonarovs to Ohio, to escape the East Coast rat race.

CARNEGIE / Owners, now, of a yoga franchise, the Fonarovs reported that their inner balance had come back.

BLONDIE / It didn't seem to matter, at the center, that we had two adopted children, and one half half—*hapa,* they tended to say there, thanks to the Hawaiian director. It didn't seem to matter that I was a *haole.* Some families had no Chinese connection at all. Some were only there because early language training was hard to find.

How excited they were to meet Lan. A native speaker! They begged her to teach a class. She politely refused, though. When she wasn't working, she wanted to study, she said.

Later it came out that she felt uncomfortable being the only one from the Mainland.

— Didn't you like Kelly? we asked. Didn't you like Michelle?

— I don't think they are real Chinese, said Lan.

There might have been more community in the city, but she didn't drive, and the T didn't make it out to our town.

CARNEGIE / Lan's primary attachment remained to her tape machine.

BLONDIE / She showed no interest in shopping, but was careful with the few clothes she had, most of which she had apparently bought on a shopping trip in Jinan, the capital of her province. Blue jean bellbottoms with a bleached-out stripe down the middle, for example. T-shirts, some of them with messages.

CARNEGIE / Our number one all-time favorite: ROCKS NEVER DIE.

BLONDIE / Yet no matter how casual the outfit, she did not treat it casually. She was reluctant to do anything that might get her clothes dirty, and she folded them as beautifully as she folded paper.

Our wash, too. She folded the shirts to exactly the size of a shirt cardboard.

I loved this.

CARNEGIE / Our recycling became an art form. Mitch and the minx made a point of routing their Sunday-evening walk by our curb, that they might behold it.

— What does it say? Mitchell would ask, stroking his new facial growth. — What does it mean?

BLONDIE / Her English was improving by leaps and bounds now.

CARNEGIE / We were unsurprised to learn, eventually, that she was a language teacher's daughter.

LAN / *My father was, before Liberation, an English and French and Russian teacher, as well as the principal of a small high school his parents had bought for him to run. My mother was a Communist who left him for an officer in the People's Army. After all, she was beautiful and young. Why should she stay with trouble? She left me then, too—like Lizzy's mother, and Wendy's. That's why I understand those girls. She left sorrowfully, my father always said, though she did not leave so much as a picture of herself. I never asked her name. There were so many stories like this, back then. It was not unusual at all, people breaking up because of their backgrounds, and prospects. Later she died, my father said, of a brain tumor.*

After she left, my father and I were forced to move from our beautiful Suzhou compound to a much smaller rental house we owned, in a town nearby. Then we moved to just one room of that house. He raised me with the help of an older woman who was not a servant—there were no servants anymore—but whose family had worked for our family for many years. Not that he even needed that much help from ayi. *He was good with children, as Suzhou men often were. He was a gentle man, like a woman, not abrupt like men in the North. I can still hear his voice. How he loved to quote from the ancient philosophers in his beautiful Chinese! His* Suzhouhua *was like music. When people said they'd rather listen to Suzhou people call each other names than to a Ningbonese singing, they were thinking of people like my father.*

It was not an altogether unhappy time. My father rode me around town on his bicycle. He taught me badminton. We watched the long lines of boats in the canals; we watched the fishermen on Lake Tai. We bought tang zhou*—a kind of sweet porridge—from the local peddlers; their stoves looked like camels. In the summer, we cooled watermelons in a well. There were thousands of wells in and around Suzhou, more than anywhere else. We lowered the melons in a net bag by day, hauling them up in the evening. How delicious they were after supper!*

— The Communists will never be able to take everything away, my father used to say. Always you will have nothing.

He liked to say that kind of thing and then laugh. He loved many Chinese things—crickets, for example. He would travel every fall to Shandong, where his maternal aunt lived, to get first-class fighters. Always he came back laughing at the way people talked up there, though in one way he liked them. So unpretentious, he said. So natural. Also he loved Chinese gardens, especially his own family garden, which was neglected but not physically destroyed during the Cultural Revolution; even the Red Guards stopped short of wrecking Suzhou. Seven families did move into our family house, though, destroying its serenity. What sort of painting could go on by a pond in which peasants washed their laundry? What kind of calligraphy? Our family garden had been a marvel, with all of nature—hills and water and trees—brought together within its walls. There were many viewing points and hiding places. My earliest memory was of climbing in and around the rock grottoes, with their endless twisting corridors and damp secret rooms. I remember the ancient trees too, planted long long ago, so full of beauty and spirit—so removed from everything petty and common. And, of course, there was a greenhouse. That's where the orchids grew.

Now the greenhouse flapped with shirts hung to dry.

We went back to visit, not so often, but every once in a while.

My father loved Chinese music. If he came upon a street musician playing the *erhu*, he'd often stop and sing along. The songs were mostly *pingtan*—folk songs in Suzhou dialect—or else songs from *Kunqu* opera, which are famous all over China—very graceful and slow and touching. Very gentle, very soft. Of course, all this was before the Cultural Revolution, when people still played these things.

It was true he loved Western music too, especially Tchaikovsky and Western opera. I grew up humming arias my father remembered, working them out on the violin. It gave him such pleasure to hear me play them on the violin. I grew up listening to the stories too, the big sad stories. Yet it was not fair to say my father worshipped Western ideas. Once when I criticized the father in *La Traviata*, saying that he had stood in the way of true love and wronged the heroine, my own father stiffened.

— She would have died anyway, he said. Those young people should have had more consideration for the father.

What's more, he was anti-imperialist. He completely believed that the West was out to destroy China. They talk so nice, he said, but does not every weasel standing at the gate of a farmyard talk nice? In the morning, he would go to the tiger kitchen in our alley to get hot water, but also to talk with the neighbors about how to strengthen China.

Still he was struggled against during the Cultural Revolution. For his laugh, I always felt. Also because he weakly applauded model Beijing operas like 'Taking Tiger Mountain by Strategy.' He claimed he was clapping loudly. Other members of his unit, though, maintained that his hands were not flat when he clapped, but loosely cupped. His hands were moving like summer ducks, they said. Sometimes his palms did not even meet. Neither was he looking at the cast as he moved his hands, but apparently at the sky.

— That was because I was contemplating the message of art, he said. So profound.

— There's nothing profound about it! yelled the Red Guards in *reply, and cut his throat to see if it had turned black with all the foreign words that had passed through it.*

This sort of thing had happened to so so many people. But when it happened to my father, I only wished they had killed me too. It was a pain as long as the Yellow River. You could only hope one day to empty into the ocean. They left him lying on the ground, covered with nothing but a straw mat, for two days. In the sun. I was not allowed to move him; no one was allowed to move him. His body was black with flies. His head swelled. Children ran to his body and back, daring each other to touch him with a stick.

Not long after that, I was sent down to the countryside to be reeducated. If my father had been alive, he might have been able to keep me home. Families were usually allowed to keep one child home. Sometimes a boy would be kept, and a girl sent. Often the girls wanted to be sent, to help the family. But usually families with only one child could keep that child, so though I was a girl, I might have been spared. For a short time too it seemed that I might be able to use my violin to escape my fate. How gratefully I would have played the very revolutionary operas my father abhorred. How enthusiastically I would have toured with a troupe. I know my father would not have minded at all, quite the contrary. He would have done anything to keep me from being sent down. The sound of those operas was Chinese, of course, but Western instruments were needed for volume and projection; and I could play thanks to a friend of my father's who had himself once studied with a White Russian. I got so far as to begin rehearsals in Shanghai.

But in the end a PLA soldier's daughter who could barely rosin a bow was deemed to play louder than I. Moreover, my overuse of vibrato, it was said, betrayed my rightist leanings. And so like many other young people who did not have the connections to join a music troupe or the army, or to produce a medical affidavit of ill health, I was sent down to live with the common folk.

Or rather up, I should say, and not to the Subei countryside, with the Suzhou youth, to live among peasants. Instead I was sent with the Shanghai youth to a decomissioned army unit in frigid Heilongjiang, near the Russian border. There we lived in barracks and trained to defend China against aggressors. In between exer-

cises, we also hacked at the frozen earth with pickaxes, sometimes, and of course denounced this one or that at mass rallies. That was hard for me. I shouted and leered like everyone else, but in my heart cried, still, for my father. How many of us were stuck there for six, eight, ten years? We cried to see the clouds drift in and out of sight, free. We cried to see buses come and go.

If I hadn't developed TB, I would never have been allowed to leave. But sick as I was, so pale and thin people said they could see through me, I was transferred to my father's aunt's work unit in the Shandong countryside. That was lucky. By then things had loosened up enough for me to get *bing tui*—sick leave. If I'd gotten sick earlier, I would probably have been left in Heilongjiang to die.

My great-aunt was a spinster, and very old. She knew nothing about nursing. She tried herbs randomly, sometimes. If she forgot what something was for, she tried it anyway, to see what happened.

Yet she was fearless. She did not try to avoid getting sick too. Rather she sat next to me, for hour after hour after hour. She said she was not afraid of dying. How should an old woman like her be afraid of dying? It was time for her to die anyway, she said. And how long had it been since she had someone to sit next to? Too long. So she sat close by me, proffering herbs, monitoring acupuncturists, until slowly I got better—perhaps, I thought later, out of terror. My great-aunt might not have been afraid of dying. I, though, was terrified of making her sick.

Once I was better, I was beaten up once a week. That was what it meant to be a 'class enemy'—the very worst category of social pests, worse even than being a 'stinking intellectual.' People eyed my bicycle enviously. Never mind that it had been my father's and, if he were alive, would be his still. Back then it was unusual for a young person to have her own bike. I stood out. People predicted flats, then proved themselves right. I did my repairs secretly, at night. They made fun of my umbrella too. I put it away. They made fun of the condition of my lips—so soft and kissable, said one older cadre. I allowed them to chap, that they not be kissed. Still they were, of course.

Every now and then, someone proved kind. At the end of the Cultural Revolution, a man even asked me to marry him. An old *man with a* VCR. *Later he got a* DVD *player. I used to go watch movies at his place, and probably I should have said yes. The neighbors, at least, agreed I had no choice. Who was I to be picky? Who was I to be proud? They said I was used up, spent—an arrow at the end of its flight. A worn shoe. Only my great-aunt said I should follow my heart. And in my heart, I felt he was too old and too short. Of course, many people feel there is nothing the matter with that, so long as he is rich. But anyway, in the end he married somebody else.*

Shandong was mantou *country—Northerners ate steamed buns with their vegetables. Such rice as my great-aunt and I got was gray and full of stones. I had to bring it outside, into the daylight, to pick the stones out. I ate in small mouthfuls, worried with every bite about cracking my teeth, not to say what were left of my great-aunt's teeth too. The air stank of night soil. Everywhere there were flies. Even in the winter there would be a few staggering around, looking drunk.*

Still, I was alive.

Besides work in the shoe factory, there were the neighbors, the chickens, the weather, and a set of English-language cassettes the Red Guards had somehow missed. Also my father's cassette deck. No batteries, though. Often I snuck into the factory early in the morning to use the electrical outlets.

*I studied, practiced, studied, practiced. I knew I would never be allowed to go to college. They called class enemies 'black families.' We would never be red revolutionaries. Still, I knew someone in another factory, a line worker, who had placed high enough on a provincial exam that she now gave factory tours. People said she came from a black family too. So I studied, practiced, studied, practiced. Not hoping, exactly, but listening to the English broadcasts on the radio anyway. People said no one was ever going to want to see our factory, but who knew where I might be one day reassigned. When '*Follow Me*' started on TV, I tried to find opportunities to watch.*

I was not reassigned. Instead the factory closed and I became a migrant worker. I stopped practicing my English then. It was everything I could do to find work enough to survive, and I had my great-aunt to take care of too, don't forget. I worked in all kinds of factories. Making toys, fertilizer, rubber mats. Anything. I was working as a karaoke xiaojie—a karaoke miss—when one day I heard that some distant relative had somehow heard of me.

An American relative! I had not known I had any such relative. And what could have moved this person to take an interest in me? My great-aunt looked me up and down. Then in the same voice she used for chickens she hoped would lay eggs, she said: — Fortune has come to you like a mother looking for her child.

Outside our one window, the squash vines flowered. The light outside was blinding, but inside it was dark and cool.

I had hung a few magazine pictures on the wall—mostly of movie stars, with big eyes and beautiful clothes—arranged in a little grouping. These were placed so that the morning sun shone on them. Of course the light only lasted for twenty minutes because of the building next door. But how beautiful the pictures at breakfast! There was another grouping, across the room, for supper. The light then didn't last quite as long, but almost, depending on the season. I particularly loved the moment when the pictures were losing their color and only one still glowed, a picture of a young girl with bright pink cheeks and laughing eyes. This was an old picture—the kind of picture you didn't see much anymore. But I liked it because it reminded me of simpler times, when a bumper harvest was something to celebrate and people were more genuine. It reminded me of the time before people started talking so much about money. Before anyone knew that the next generation would have opportunities we wouldn't, and that my generation had been left out of the new China.

Those old pictures usually looked completely fake. But in this light, for these few seconds, this picture seemed to be of a genuinely happy girl. Like myself! I was leaving! Of course I would have to come back unless I found someone to marry there, people said. They said, Watch, this time even if the man has no legs, she'll let him poke her. Do it right in his wheelchair.

Anyway, I thought there might be fewer flies in America, and less dust in the spring. All spring my hands and face and hair were gritty here. Shandong was terrible that way.

— Buy some clothes, said my great-aunt. Go to the city. I will give you money. Buy everything new. You don't want them to look down on you.

Of course. They would look down on me.

— You will be their ayi, *said my great-aunt. But you will be able to study too. And who knows? Maybe you will find someone to marry you. But first you must try to find out what they want from you. What are they trying to arrange?*

— Who will take care of you if I go? I asked.

The picture of the girl fell, like the others, into shadow. My great-aunt allowed a fly to walk clear across her wrinkled cheek. All her clothes were fastened with buttons and ties—she had never owned anything with a zipper. Her skin was thick and scarred and brown. Her toenails were thick too, and yellow with fungus.

— I will die, my great-aunt answered simply, when the fly took off.

And a week later, flat on her back, her arms by her sides, in her sleep, she did.

6

Wendy

CARNEGIE / — Baby crazy, said Mama Wong, if we boasted about Lizzy.

Of course, we did boast about her unconscionably, as you could with a child who was not yours biologically. She lines her animals up! She unscrews the dresser knobs! She knows absolutely all her animal sounds! Et cetera.

Said Mama Wong: — I am not baby-sitter.

And: — What's so special? A million babies like that. You go to China, can just pick one off the street.

When Mama Wong saw Lizzy, she softened and cooed and gave her nice things to eat. No sooner did Lizzy go down for a nap, though, than Mama Wong hardened.

— Lizzy think whole world revolve around her.

— Lizzy do not listen to reason.

— Lizzy temper no good, you wait and see.

Mama Wong had become more ornery than ever since I reneged on my promise to go into business with her.

— I'm sorry, I said. I promised more than I could deliver.

— I don't know what you talking, she insisted proudly. —I give a million dollars to Blondie? For what?

She said: — Why should I hire Blondie work for me? She have job already.

And: — As if I have a million dollars! A million headaches, that's what I have.

Being busy with Lizzy, we could not visit Mama Wong as often as we used to. And how sobering, when we did, to confront my mother alone in her house with her teacups everywhere; she seemed to pour and abandon them at the rate of one per hour. Sometimes I spent my entire visit on a cup hunt.

Of course, in time-honored fashion, I vowed every time to visit more often, like a proper filial son. But how could I? With a baby in the house?

The cups multiplied with each visit. They lay in wait; some with little pools of tea, some with the barest bit of sediment, the liquid having long since evaporated. Sometimes you could see, in the sediment, faint rings, irregularly spaced. Evidence of something, you felt. A record someone else could no doubt read about the temperature of the room, the rate of evaporation, the relative hope of the drinker. The relative length of the long, long day. As for me, though; how to begin to guess what went on in the house? And where did she get all those cups anyway? And wouldn't it have been only grandmotherly of her to come visit us?

BLONDIE / My mother would have come. My mother would have realized that a woman needs her mother all over again once there's a baby in the house.

Everywhere I looked there seemed to be a mother with a grandmother helping out.

CARNEGIE / — Since when mother go visit son, you tell me, said Mama Wong. Son should pay respect to mother. You pay me a million dollars, I'm not go.

She said: — If I had a million dollars to give somebody, I am give it to that National Basketball Association.

I sighed.

— Lizzy knows her whole alphabet, Ma, I said. You should come see. She is so amazing.

— Oh really. What time is it?

Blondie thought there might be something the matter with Mama Wong, but I thought my mother was just my mother. She did wear the two watches, and sometimes three or four rings to a finger now, but was there something the matter with Renata and Ariela, that they had made Lizzy seven hats and four sweaters between them?

— We're just woolly, they explained, laughing.

— Bitten by the big bad craft bug, commented Doc Bailey. Dedicated to keeping young women in glue sticks.

How we wished her sisters lived closer to us! Or at least visited more often. But the suburbs exhausted them. Lawn care exhausted them. Shopping bags, especially the bags made of coated stock, with ribbon handles, exhausted them. Excess packaging exhausted them. Lap dogs exhausted them.

They were always needing to go home. To see working barns again, to buy oilcloth at the cooperative. To buy yarn. Their whole lives were tied up, so to speak, with yarn. And babies, of course. Renata had five children, Ariela had four.

— Have more children, said Ariela, daisies in her graying braid.

BLONDIE / We tried and tried.

WENDY / Nobody wanted me exactly. Really they wanted their own baby, I was their second choice.

BLONDIE / Oh, but that's just not true!

CARNEGIE / Second choice didn't mean second best.

We were stupid. We were tired. Our strategy was to try things. Drugs, procedures, acupuncture. We tried to relax, as if it was possible for two people with jobs and a child and fertility issues to relax. We meditated. Accepted our fate. Got in touch with our anger. Embraced our helplessness. Moved past our disappointment.

Still no Wendy.

How many years did this go on?

By the time of the adoption, Mama Wong had been in assisted living for a goodish while. We tried to explain to her our game plan. The tremendous leap in the dark this was. The act of faith.

— Probably we are out of our minds, I said.

That at least occasioned some teeth grinding.

As did: — I won't be able to visit you for a couple of weeks.

Overall we had better luck with Lizzy, who was, confoundingly, six and a half already. Our newborn, six and a half!

BLONDIE / Old enough to bring to Wuji to meet her new sister. An exciting prospect and a chance to reconnect, we thought, with something important. Never mind that her heritage might not be Chinese.

CARNEGIE / Was she part Japanese? Part Korean? Part Vietnamese? Was she any part Chinese at all? Who knew?

— That baby is mutt, Mama Wong had genially announced, shortly after Lizzy's adoption. — You want to know who her father is? Her grandfather?

— No thank you, we said.

She did not look precisely Han, it was true, what with her long torso and short legs.

— You know why her mother give her away? said Mama Wong. I tell you why. Because you look at her, you see war.

Anyway, there was no harm, we thought, in Lizzy connecting with Asia.

BLONDIE / Or in knowing what adoption meant. We had tried to shelter her from my miscarrying and miscarrying. Still she had witnessed much too much. Now we wanted her to know something else—what a joy adoption was!

CARNEGIE / This was parenting, a mighty campaign.

BLONDIE / — Why did you keep going to the hospital for a baby then? Lizzy asked.

— We thought it would be more convenient to get a baby there, I said.

CARNEGIE / The spinmeisters, a-spinning.

— How come it didn't work? Lizzy asked.

Earnestly, creatively Blondie explained.

— But I saw lots of babies in the hospital, Lizzy said.

And: — Why did yours keep dying?

And: — I don't want to go to China.

BLONDIE / Lizzy was in on the adoption from the moment we knew we had a child. Uruguay was closed, Romania was closed, but China was open! Our first choice anyway—we'd heard such stories about those Eastern European orphanages. And how nice to have the children match.

CARNEGIE / A year later we would have had to take a child with a handicap, this being our second child. But in the pioneer days, before adopting from China became an industry, things were looser. Everything was case by case, practically do-it-yourself.

BLONDIE / We showed Lizzy the paperwork. The maps. An adoption video. We talked about the birth mother, and why she might have had to give the baby up. Was that why Lizzy's biological mother had given her up? We told her what the adoption guide said to tell her, that her biological mother gave her up out of love, that she might have the best life possible.

Not that we knew that, really. And of course later she would ask us why we said that, if we didn't know. But how could I tell her that I'd imagined her birth mother a thousand times; and that some of the thousand women were loving and heartbroken and desperate, but some of them were callous and uninterested in her. Some were career women; some were criminals. Some were raped; some surprised to find themselves in a family way. And how could I have told her that some of them, some of them, one day returned—to claim their children, or just watch them? Could I have, should I have told her that? Could I have told her—even worse, perhaps—that some did not?

CARNEGIE / No one thought much about that cad, the birth father, except Mama Wong.

BLONDIE / At least with babies from China, you knew the mother wanted to have the child. You could say that. For how very much easier for Chinese women to have an abortion than to go on with the pregnancy. You had to fight to go on with the pregnancy.

Lizzy and I talked about the difference between birthing and parenting—between having a baby and bringing it up. We talked about what it was going to be like, having a baby sister.

— What's so great about two children instead of one? she said. What's so great about company?

Were we adopting another child so that Lizzy would have a sibling? And what if we did not love the new baby as much as we loved Lizzy? Not that we wouldn't love her—we assumed it would be a her. We would love her. But as much as Lizzy? Our walls were covered with pictures of Lizzy splashing, swinging, running. Watering plants, hanging upside down, mummifying stuffed animals. Where was there space for more pictures?

Everyone worried about making a mistake. That's what the counselors said. It was normal.

CARNEGIE / When our phone call came, we jumped on a plane post-haste. In those days you didn't even get a picture, or a name, or a medical history.

BLONDIE / It was a new thing even for adoptive parents to stop in Beijing on the way to wherever—in our case, Wuji. The Forbidden Palace, the Temple of Heaven, the Great Wall! Fantastic places, hard to absorb—so enormous with history, so inconceivably ancient.

CARNEGIE / We had never been so jet-lagged.

BLONDIE / In an alleyway we bought a cage full of pigeons and released them, Buddhist-style, with a wish.

— I wish for health, I said. For all four of us.

CARNEGIE / That was code. Actually she hoped for a healthy baby but didn't want Lizzy to feel excluded from the proceedings.

— To health, I agreed reasonably. And to no surprises.

Blondie, I noticed, had an antiseptic hand wipe at the ready. Ever since we got off the plane she had been wiping Lizzy's hands several times an hour.

— I wish we would get to Wuji soon, said Lizzy.

Hear, hear!

BLONDIE / The birds crowded out of their bamboo-cage door—flapping, frantic, but then turning, in a wink, unutterably graceful—immediately forgetful, it seemed, of having ever been caged up. At once they separated from one other; at once they began to soar with joy—each beating its own strong way to heaven.

CARNEGIE / Or at least to the closest perch. Only one flapped about a bit, circling once or twice as if enjoying the use of its wings. The others were content with a hop of no great altitude. *Freedom!* we wanted to shout at them. *You have your freedom!* But they longed only, apparently, to roost.

Pigeons.

We knew what a pigeon was. And yet being, like them, irremediably ourselves, we stood there anyway, watching. Hoping. Cage full of pigeon feathers in one hand; hand wipes at the ready.

How enormous the specific gravity of Beijing! The center of the world, indeed, the middle of the Middle Kingdom. How insubstantial we felt there, with our plastic cameras. Three ephemera, under the spell of our autofocus.

We were headed, every moment, for Wuji.

It was hot.

It was noisy.

Everyone, everyone smoked.

Our hair smelled of smoke. Our clothes smelled of smoke. We worried about the baby in Wuji. Was she inhaling smoke?

BLONDIE / We saw what relatives of Carnegie's we could see. Carnegie had managed to contact a cousin of his father's, now living in Toronto, before we left; through him we were able to reach three other relatives, all male and living in Beijing.

CARNEGIE / One was a Party member interested in refrigerators.

BLONDIE / One was a student interested in Gandhi, and in talking about the Cultural Revolution. In remarkable English he told us how he had grown up in a building full of children and old people—with his parents, like the other parents, simply gone. As seemed normal enough, at the time. The only strange thing, he said—the thing that he still remembered—was that during lightning storms, when he could see down into the dark courtyard, there were often people being put into burlap bags. He remembered too that—their building being relatively tall—people jumped from the roof all the time.

Had not the people at the next table seemed to be openly listening, he might have said more. As it was, though, we never did discuss Gandhi. Instead we praised the Beijing duck, which was served with mini-*mantou* in place of the pancakes we were used to in the States. Was that typical?

Neither relative had ever met Carnegie's father or grandparents, though one did know Carnegie's grandfather's brother, and the other Carnegie's grandfather's stepson.

CARNEGIE / Both went through the ritual of trying to explain which generation they were, and what their generation names were, and who their fathers were, et cetera, all of which information glommed together in such a mass that if someone had scanned my brain after dinner, it would no doubt have appeared a mystery lumpen mash such as could be used to stuff mooncakes.

The third relative we met was a bourgeois intellectual who had spent twelve years in a labor camp either for translating William Burroughs or for practicing Catholicism; we could not ascertain which. A tiny man with a long wispy beard, he had an asymmetry to his neck motion such that he continually addressed his right. An old injury, he said, something to do with being hit with a shovel by a Red Guard. Happier to relate was how he had once met my grandparents. My grandfather, he said, in careful English, had been a scholar, and my grandmother a great beauty.

— In United States, you maybe call her Miss Sichuan, he said. But also she is smart. Your grandfather taught her to read and write many things.

— Was she a lot younger than him? I asked.

— Eh? Your grandmother can also sing and play instrument.

— What kind of instrument?

— Eh? She has just one child, that is your father. Unfortunately, then she die. But people say, at least she had a boy, she is good wife. Only your grandfather say he wish she had a girl, maybe a girl can look like her. Remind him of your grandma, he love her so much. That is true story. After that your grandfather have a couple more wives, but none of them he ever love so much. Every one of them has something wrong.

BLONDIE / Carnegie cried.

We vowed to come back another time.

The relatives were all amazed that Carnegie did not speak Chinese, and that I did, a little, though this seemed to explain his marrying a *da bizi*—a big nose. They all volunteered too that our children would be smart, because mixed children were smart. When we explained that Lizzy was adopted, and that we were about to adopt a second child, they laughed uncomfortably and asked if Lizzy was Japanese.

— What is Japanese? she asked. Why do people keep saying that?

— It's a compliment, we told her. Because they can see how well dressed you are. They think you must be rich.

But though that might have been true for an older person, we were not actually sure how to take it in this case.

Two of the relatives liked our gifts, but the Party member seemed disappointed we didn't bring something bigger. All three hinted that they wouldn't mind being sponsored to come to the United States for study. Or how about their son?

CARNEGIE / We took rolls and rolls of pictures, as if making images of ourselves meeting was the point of meeting. Which perhaps it was. Certainly the picture taking was the most natural part of our interaction, the ritual with the smoothest choreography. Everyone knew his part. It was like playing in a chamber group.

There was supposed to be one more relative, on my mother's side, a woman living in Shandong. My mother's father-in-law's sister-in-law's great-niece. We did not contact her, not knowing quite how. Also our Beijing window was so small; there simply wasn't time.

In the meanwhile, how omnivorous our Blondie! Always she had claimed herself a timorous creature, full of trepidation, compared to that fearless friend with whom she had trekked around Hong Kong in her student days. But now: move over, Linda!

BLONDIE / People said there were two types of visitors, forks and chopsticks. In college, I had proved a fork—truly. I wasn't as bad as the Clarks, who produced PB&J at every meal. But I was, unmistakably, a fork.

Now, though—how I hoped to prove better. How I hoped to prove, finally, truly, chopsticks.

CARNEGIE / She closed her eyes and bravely ate and only later discovered that she had eaten snake, or eel, or rabbit's ears. Things, in-truth, that I myself was not wild about. Were her efforts misguided?

Anyway, I applauded them.

How we all loved our adventure! Even if it was hot. How we all adored China, dammit.

BLONDIE / We were still in Wuji, still in Wuji, we had been there for weeks. We all had diarrhea. We were all on Lomotil, even Lizzy, from time to time; she cried so from the cramps. She was beginning to refuse tea. Dehydration, we explained. You have to drink. If only we were not out of Pedialyte! But we were; and we had stopped accepting the occasional precious ice cube, for who knew if it had been made with boiled water. That left only verifiably boiled water, which could be cooled but was never cold. And of course tea; and soda, also warm.

Should we have taken prophylactic Pepto-Bismol, even if it made your tongue turn black? Anyway, it was too late. We stayed close to the hotel; the public squat toilets just made us feel sicker.

Making the best of our situation, I found two Chinese tutors—one to work with me, one with Carnegie and Lizzy. Both came for a few hours each afternoon, giving us something to do.

We made surprising progress.

CARNEGIE / And their rates; such a bargain.

BLONDIE / What was happening with the baby? Nothing was clear except why the rich Chinese of old used to build their compounds behind walls.

CARNEGIE / People, people, people. Dust, heat, dirt, heat. There was a reason the natives did their strolling at night. They squatted in the alleys in their underclothes, fanning themselves.

BLONDIE / Everything needed cleaning.

CARNEGIE / We had seen all the sights.

BLONDIE / I dreamed of Independence Island—that cool pond water. I used to swim right out to its middle, and float there—tilting my head back until I could see the upside-down mountains. Now in the afternoons I rested with my head back too, a cold compress on my forehead—my upside-down view of the barred windows.

Carnegie and Lizzy did not overheat the way I did. They were bothered instead by the mosquitoes.

The mosquitoes left me alone—too tough, apparently.

I translated more and more when we were out. My translating was two parts guessing to every one part knowledge. Still it felt good.

— Never before, said Carnegie, have I so completely understood the word 'respite.'

— Do you mean you hate it here? asked Lizzy.

CARNEGIE / Such a charming walk we were on, at the time. The path was broken concrete; the air, muggy and fetid. The lakewater beside us shone opaque as one-coat-covers-all paint.

BLONDIE / But at least there was shade. At least there were trees, and a trickle of slow-pedaled bicycles, as opposed to a sea.

CARNEGIE / — You hate it, said Lizzy.

— Please do not put words in my mouth, I said. They don't taste good.

BLONDIE / He opened and shut his lips like a fish.

— But you hate a lot of it, said Lizzy.

— I don't hate any of it, he said. It's just nice to have a break. One needs a break from everything, after a while. From work. From friends. From family.

I gave him a warning look.

— In this family, we take a dim view of complaining, I observed. You know how some people do nothing but complain?

CARNEGIE / — It's hot, Lizzy complained.

— We have an air-conditioned room and an air-conditioned car, young lady, said Blondie, strolling on. —Those are great luxuries around here.

— Yeah, but it doesn't get cold.

— It does, I said; supporting Blondie, she would say, for once.

— I am, like, *hot* hot, Lizzy said. I'm *burning.* I hate China.

She stopped short. A bicyclist *brrring!*ed and swerved by, so close his handlebar caught a strand of Lizzy's hair and sent it flying. She nonchalantly caught it back.

— Didn't you like the Great Wall? asked Blondie.

— The Great Wall was cool. But everything else is boring.

— Boring! I said.

— Boring! she shouted. Boring!

On the lake, the rowboaters looked up.

— Waiting like this is hard, said Blondie then, stopping.

A familiar small bewilderment came over me, as I tried to fathom why she had changed tacks.

— I'm hot hot, said Lizzy, sticking her tongue out at the rowboaters. — I'm like a volcano that can melt everything in the whole wide world.

Said Blondie: — I'm hot too.

— Didn't you like anything besides the Great Wall? I asked stupidly. There must have been something else.

— It's lonely here, said Lizzy.

— Even with us here, it's lonely? said Blondie.

— And hot.

— Of course it's hot, it's China, I said. Also you need to learn how to deal with boredom, if you are bored, which you shouldn't be. Ever to be bored means you have no inner resources; remember that. You're lucky to be here.

— Why, because you adopted me?

— Not just that, but you are definitely lucky. As are we.

— If you're so lucky, how come you had to come here to get another kid? If you're so lucky, how come I do nothing but complain?

— You do things besides complain, said Blondie.

— No I don't! shouted Lizzy, stomping off. — I'm hot and all I do is complain! She started to cry. — And I mean it!

BLONDIE / The baby was sick; that was our guess. Why else the unexplained delay? At the welcoming banquet Director Wu had looked at two other couples in our group and said, *Your baby looks like you.* Only to us had she said, *Your baby is waiting.*

What did that mean?

— Don't fret, she is thinking of you already, said Director Wu.

CARNEGIE / Director Wu was a dedicated woman shaped like a haystack. She had short hair and glasses, and referred to her charges as sprogs.

BLONDIE / The Clarks, short and round, were matched with the fattest baby imaginable. The Fonarovs, tall and thin, were matched with a red wiry thing.

Everyone cried. The enormity of the moment! Whole lives joined together by luck, and fate. What faith to have taken this step, to have allowed—to have willed—lives to change, just like that. Such were the enormities that Carnegie and Lizzy and I cried too, overwhelmed for our friends—reliving what it was to take Lizzy into our lives.

How frustrating to still be waiting!

CARNEGIE / Unlike the Clarks and the Fonarovs, who had been put in a local university, we had been inexplicably parked, first in an Overseas Chinese Hotel (an experience), and then, thankfully, in a foreigners' hotel with private baths and sit-down toilets and cleaning personnel. All along we had listened with envy to our friends'

Belgian-professor stories, the university being for some reason popular with Belgian professors. And how friendly the Chinese on campus too! Knocking on the doors of the Americans at all hours, to practice English and to bring gifts. The Clarks and Fonarovs had made rafts of friends. They had never known such goodwill.

But when we inquired as to whether we might move to the campus now that our friends had left, the answer was a decided, *We'll see.* As for the reason: *Not convenient.*

BLONDIE / Everywhere people gawked at me. Even in Beijing, I had aroused interest. In Wuji, I had to keep moving if I didn't want to find myself mobbed. Carnegie and Lizzy had to walk on ahead, pretending not to know me.

Was it possible to have people stare all day, and not see oneself differently at night? In bed, by the fluorescent ceiling light, I stared too, sometimes. At myself, in the mirror. At Carnegie. At my hand touching his hand, at my feet touching his feet.

The mosquito coil dropped its ash. The table fan rotated toward us, away, toward us, away. It was far enough from the mosquito coil not to disturb the ash, but close enough to make the tip of the coil flare and darken, flare and darken.

Carnegie, normally so sensitive, looked perfectly comfortable on the coarse sheets. He was wearing boxer shorts he had bought here—more comfortable in the heat, he said. He had powdered under his arms and behind his knees, as had Lizzy and I. What a great invention, talcum powder, we agreed.

I got up to check on Lizzy—gingerly inserting my sticky feet into the hotel plastic sandals. I did not like these but wore them to avoid stepping on the mildewed rug.

Carnegie, when I returned, was exactly the same. His smooth-skinned self, relaxed and sweat-free.

— We're going to look so different when we're old, I said. You're going to age so beautifully, and I'm going to look so wrinkly. My upper lip is going to look like a vertical blind.

— Not true, he said.

— I see these women on the street, and not one of them is baggy. They're like gymnasts. Even the old ones are like gymnasts.

— I've seen fat ones.

— But none of them is voluminous.

How foreign that polysyllabic word, after weeks of Chinese. How amorphous itself. Even when speaking English, I realized, we had taken to speaking in a more succinct way than we did at home.

— What about Director Wu?

— We're going to look even less natural together than we do now, I said. I'm going to look ten years your senior and pasty. Like your third-grade teacher, following you around.

— Is all this because people stare at you?

— No, I said.

— I'll hold your hand so people stare at me too, offered Carnegie, reaching and squeezing, as if in demonstration.

— All right, I said.

Holding hands, sure enough, produced a stir everywhere, but was worth it.

— We might as well be a person married to a camel, I said.

— I always wanted to marry a camel, said Carnegie.

CARNEGIE / We broached with Director Wu the minor matter that was our employment. Vacation policies, we explained. Deadlines. No iron rice bowl, we said. We could get fired. Americans were rich, we explained, except for Americans without jobs.

We waved in the air such faxes as we'd been able to arrange to receive. The thin coated paper curled around our hands.

— Also my mother, I said. Alone all this time. And sick. Very sick. Her mind is not right. Her head—you understand.

— You have bloody work to do, said Director Wu, amiably taking off her glasses. — And your bloody mother's waiting.

She nodded sympathetically, then put her glasses back on.

BLONDIE / We went to an acrobatic show involving feats of great daring. There were human ladders, contortionists, balancing acts. But the most amazing moment of all came when a performer began to throw candies and favors into the audience.

CARNEGIE / One boy lunged so far over the edge of the balcony that he had to be caught by his feet; we almost thought him part of the act, dangling there, his shirt in his armpits, on the verge of plunging headfirst to the floor.

— What is the matter with these people? complained Lizzy, fanning herself.

— People say the accident rate here is phenomenal, I said.

— In this family, we do not use the expression 'these people,' said Blondie.

BLONDIE / Lizzy complained more and more. Carnegie complained, too. But that didn't turn them into forks.

Only I could be a fork.

When I was in college, I did a summer of intensive Chinese in Hong Kong—the same summer Gabriela was studying in Florence. What grand adventures we were both on! Mine the more exotic, perhaps. But as the letters accumulated, I began to feel that while Hong Kong was dramatic, Florence was superb. How disloyal! In my letters, of course, I wrote of the food and shops and discos my friend Linda and I were loving. It was easy. For I did love parts of it. The temples, the markets. The views, the boats, the energy. The fruit—I had never eaten so much fresh fruit. And so many kinds! I did love that. But I could not revel in the rest the way Linda did—with a shiny, bright love undimmed by the heat, the smog, the traffic. The humidity. I had never seen so many people. It was like a subway at rush hour, only you never got off. At night you could see right into people's apartments; you could see how whole families squeezed into a single room. To think that wasn't even crowded for Asia! How much worse the conditions in places like Bangladesh. Linda and I both felt for the hordes living this way.

Yet only I shrank from them. Linda traipsed everywhere in her embroidered Chinese shirt, its high collar unfrogged. She wore old silver peasant earrings, with a bat-and-cloud design and wires so thick her ears bled. When there was a typhoon, she insisted on experiencing it live, in the streets; she almost got hit by a flying street sign. She made friends with people and went to visit them in their rooms. And how she loved the night market! Dismayed as she was by the slitting of live snakes right before her eyes, she loved its authenticity.

— Don't you see, it's so real, she said. That's so rare these days. Don't you see?

Linda had grown up in a suburb where wall-to-wall carpet muffled every sound and every meal came out of the freezer. The land of pink and green, she called it.

— Don't you see? Don't you see?

As the summer went on, Linda ate more and more daringly. She would ask to sit as close to the air conditioner as possible, and then, minidictionary in hand, she would order squab, sea cucumber, gooey duck. Things with XO sauce. One night she ordered a turtle soup that came with the turtle in its shell. Of course the turtle's head was still on—the Chinese liked everything whole.

— Delicious! she cried.

The turtle had not been declawed. The curved nails looked as though they might fan out in another moment, as the turtle's feet found the bottom of the bowl, and the turtle began to crawl.

— Try closing your eyes, said Linda. Think of it changing shape, like something Daoist. You have to bypass your mind.

I closed my eyes.

— You can use the air conditioner. I find the noise of the air conditioner helps.

I tried using the air conditioner, and did get down a mouthful. But when I opened my eyes and looked past the turtle—I had to look past the turtle—all I saw in the blue fluorescent light were stains on the tablecloth, three of them. Deep brown in the center, with light brown halos.

How I wished I had not grown up putting the tablecloth in to soak right after Thanksgiving dinner! But this was my heritage, if I was honest about it. The Chinese had special strokes for painting pine trees and rocks; I had a faith in household order.

Bus dread. I did not write to Gabriela how I suffered from rush-hour bus dread. Before I went to Asia I did not understand why tranquillity was so prized—in painting, in poetry, in architecture.

Now I knew the meaning of peace.

I loved the ferry.

I loved the hotel lobbies.

I loved the mountains ringing the city; I went hiking as often as I could. I loved taking trips out to the islands. The seafood markets there! How gorgeous the shells of the flowered crabs, so extravagantly patterned; there was nothing like them at home. And how artistically bound up, those crabs, with red twine. I loved the knots. I wrote to Gabriela about the knots.

What I did not write even in my own journal was that I thought I had the wrong skin for the climate—too fair. Too delicate.

When I got home I switched my major to graphic design. My Chinese teacher tried to dissuade me; I'd picked up the tones so easily, she said. I had an ear. I was a natural. Still, I switched. Gabriela became my best friend; I more or less lost touch with Linda, though I did hear, years later, that she too adopted two girls, both from Asia. Of course, she was ecstatic. She took teaching jobs abroad whenever she could. I saw her picture several times in the alumni magazine—in each her face was more radiant. She was always wearing indigenous clothes of one kind or another; her girls were fluent in Mandarin.

CARNEGIE / Finally, finally we had her! Wendy was ten months old—or so we were told—when she was placed in our arms. Or dumped, actually; such being the emotional state of her conveyor. Wendy herself was the picture of calm. With what perfect wondering composure she stared up at us! For a full moment.

Then she started bawling too.

Still—bawling ourselves—we adored her every particular.

How she could touch the soles of her feet together without bending her knees, for example, and how full of intelligence her feet were, still, like hands. She had a black buzz cut tied up in a red bow; a fat face; bright slit eyes; four teeth; and many chins, past which we hypothesized a neck.

BLONDIE / We tried to comfort her. This was tricky as, despite the heat, she was dressed in several layers of slippery acetate. She was surprisingly heavy, too; her thighs were like hams. And how she arched her back! With such strength. It was everything I could do to hold on to her.

The foster mother touched her several times, and each time she stopped crying. But when the foster mother took her hand away, Wendy started crying again. It was hard not to wonder whether we were doing the right thing—if the natural thing wasn't to leave her with the foster mother. Send money for her support, if we were so concerned about her welfare. Were we adopting this child for her good or for ours?

Full of doubt, I gave Wendy my pinkie to suck, as Carnegie had once done with Lizzy. She made a face—the taste of the hand wipes, I guessed—but then accepted it.

We all relaxed a little.

— Do you want to hold her? we asked Lizzy.

Lizzy clutched a stuffed panda she was supposed to give to her new sister.

— No, she said, but then changed her mind.

We traded bundles. Carefully—Carnegie and I standing ready to rescue Wendy should Lizzy drop her. But Lizzy did not drop her. And when I gingerly removed my pinkie from Wendy's mouth—look! She smiled!

— She loves me! shouted Lizzy.

We thanked and thanked the foster mother.

— *All my life, I've taken care of children, but this one really got inside my heart,* she said, covering her mouth as she spoke. — *My Mandarin is no good.*

Her cheeks were ruddy, her skin tight and dry. One of her eyes had a sty. She began to cry again.

— *Your Mandarin is perfectly clear,* I said. *We understand you fine.*

I could not tell whether she understood or not. Neither could the woman be coaxed to say anything more to us, except in dialect through Director Wu.

— The baby likes bean curd, and needs quiet for a proper nap, said Director Wu.

— What's her name? we asked, clutching the panda.

— You can name her what you like, said Director Wu.

— But what do you call her?

— We call her Little Seven, said Director Wu. Seven or Eight?

She turned to ask the foster mother, but the woman was crying so hard she had to leave the room.

— Wait—a picture! we said, or tried to say.

How could anyone have taken a picture, though, of someone crying like that?

The foster mother shuffled out; the room without her seemed bright and empty. The walls were half green, half bisque, and peeling.

— Can we get her name and address? we asked. Someday our little girl will want to come back and find her.

— Not necessary, said Director Wu.

Later we kicked ourselves that we had not pushed her harder to give us something. But at the time it just didn't seem possible.

— You see? said Director Wu. This baby looks like you.

What did she mean? Carnegie and I agreed later that, if anything, the baby looked like the foster mother.

That should have been the big moment of our trip. We drove away in a hired car, undressing her—imagining her to be hot, thinking that she might cry less if she was more comfortable. Her pants were slit, the way Chinese children's pants were, but she was wearing a too-big disposable diaper. A luxury, we'd heard. A way of dressing her up for her big trip. We were in the process of replacing her acetate with an all-cotton onesie, when something bumped the car. It was dusk—still light on the larger streets, but getting to be night in the lanes and alleys. I might not have even registered the bump except that I was in such a protective frame of mind. No seat belt with which to strap in a car seat, Carnegie had commented as we got in. We had had to put the car seat in the trunk.

CARNEGIE / How we all enjoyed the sensation of straplessness. Lizzy particularly, having never experienced it before we got to China. And in this car, an interesting small freedom: no logo on the horn. It was, at least on the interior, a no-name small car, with a springy ride and torn brown seats. The whole contraption stank of smoke. Still we asked the driver to please put out his cigarette.

— The baby, we explained.

A truth self-evident, yet he continued smoking until our guide, the humorless Mr. Qian, told him again to put his butt out. With a laugh the driver then sidearmed it out the window, still lit.

Something hit the side of the car.

BLONDIE / — Was that a rock? I asked.

— Something on the road maybe, said Carnegie.

The car slowed; the street grew crowded. People gawked in the windows—at all of us, but especially, I felt, at me. Or was it at Wendy? For she was still crying when she wasn't sucking; I rummaged around for a pacifier.

How large I felt—larger than ever.

I found a passy. She took it.

I had snugged Wendy in the sweaty valley between my thighs; my hands cradled her small head, which was tied up in a red bow. Buzz cut, no soft spot—her fontanel had closed up. A bud mouth, with lips so red I rubbed them with a finger to see if they had been rouged. Shiny, shiny eyes—all those tears. They caught the light blackly. Her long eyelashes, clumping, gleamed too. We mostly registered the bump because it caused me to move my forearms in closer to Wendy's small body. Keep her from rolling.

— Bump! I said softly, playfully, moving my nose in toward hers as the car stopped. I was trying to establish contact without excluding Lizzy. — Look, I said. That's Lizzy. That's your big sister.

Wendy blinked and spat our her passy, which tumbled, before we could catch it, onto the car floor.

— She's going to stick her tongue out! said Lizzy.

And Lizzy was right! Thrillingly, Wendy opened and closed her mouth, several times, just as some last sun bounced in the window. I could see clear back, for a moment, to her tonsils. Hungry? I wished I could nurse Wendy; Gabriela knew someone who had managed to nurse her adopted child by stimulating her breasts with a breast pump for some months. (An amazing machine, that pump, reported Gabriela, no different than what they use on cows.) The friend's milk supply was never much—but the bonding!

Wendy began crying again. I rummaged in the diaper bag for some formula and a bottle as Carnegie leaned toward us. He peered between the front seats, down the notch between the driver and Mr. Qian.

CARNEGIE / The driver had hit someone—a tiny, wiry man in one of those ubiquitous saggy undershirts, his blue pants cinched around his nothing waist via an overlong black belt. His baskets and shoulder pole had fallen to the ground. Now he crouched beside them, whether out of pain or concern for his goods was hard to tell. I started to get out of the car to help him.

— Please stop, said Mr. Qian. We don't want to have incident. Number one important point is to avoid incident. Bring a lot of trouble.

— To hell with that, I said, getting out of the car.

The driver also got out—to check the car, it turned out. Squatting, he ran his hand over the bumper. He spit on one spot and rubbed it, then examined it again.

With characteristic alacrity, Mr. Qian got out last.

BLONDIE / The slamming doors shook the car.

— This car is made of tin, I told Wendy, even as I tried to see how badly the man was hurt. —Yes it is! This car could be a cat-food can.

Wendy cried.

— You're hungry, aren't you, I said. I can tell. Mommies know everything, you know.

— They do not, said Lizzy in a stage whisper, already in league with her sister. —They do not know everything. She's just saying that.

People stopped to stare, at the accident and at us. I caught an occasional Mandarin sentence through my open window.

Sile ren ma?—Did anyone die?

An argument began.

I jiggled Wendy, looking for another pacifier. How fat she was! What with the extra creases on her upper and lower arms, she looked to have three elbows on each arm. And the texture of that fat—so silken.

I rolled my window up and told Lizzy to do the same.

— Also the front windows, I said. And lock the doors, please.

I worried she was going to complain that it was too hot to close the windows, but thankfully she just dove into the front seat and then back again.

People began to press their faces to our window glass. Wendy cried. In the half dark I could hardly make out more than the gleam of eyes and teeth, but Lizzy seemed able to see fine.

— What are you staring at? she demanded, making faces at the people. She hit the glass with her hands, scaring a few away. — You are so nosy!

I found another pacifier. A different type than the first, but Wendy took this one, too.

Mostly the argument involved Mr. Qian and the driver. I couldn't follow exactly what was being said, especially with the windows up, but stiff Mr. Qian seemed to be blaming the seething driver, who in turn, between shouts, jabbed wildly in Carnegie's direction. The argument was in dialect. I wished I were not upset; my comprehension of dialect was at best a guess, but my guesses were better when I wasn't distracted.

I opened a Thermos to mix some formula, just glad that there were raised markings on the baby bottle so I could tell how many ounces of water I was pouring. Was I right to try the soy-based powder first? So many Chinese babies were lactose-intolerant. Milk-based formula, though, was closer to what they were used to, people said, and less constipating. I had brought both, in any case, and a selection of nipples—traditional and natural with both cross-cut and regular openings—all of which fit the special no-air-bubble bottle. The moment of truth. Wendy took a suck, then spat the nipple. Did it taste funny? Did she not like that nipple? I was considering adjustments when, funny-tasting or not, she tried again and began to drink. Happy, I watched her gulp. I stroked her fat legs.

— Good for you! I cooed; then began to piece together the picture, somehow, beginning with the cigarette butt. Apparently it had hit someone, who had hurled a retaliatory melon at the car. The car had slowed; a crowd had formed. It was in an effort to get past them that the driver had hit this man. This something or another, he had apparently said. Perhaps he had called the man a turtle's egg or one of the other odd things the Chinese found so offensive.

Of course, we had not had our headlights on. Even in the dead of night, the drivers drove without lights then, to save the bulbs.

Was the man hurt? It was hard to see past all the faces pressed against our window. Carnegie, too, had disappeared from view. Kneeling down, I guessed. Then he stood, sure enough—there he was, for an instant. How substantial he looked beside the other men, even in the near dark. How tall, how well fed, how well clothed. Commanding a spot of his own—people stood back from him a little. Of course, he was the same race as they were, but he seemed a different race; if I had been walking by, I might have thought him white. In the hotel, his button-down shirt had looked less than fresh. Out in the street, though, he looked crisp, rich, young, lucky. American. He stood with authority, hands on his hips. Gestured, then took off his beautiful shirt.

With no particular flourish—not bothering with the buttons. Carnegie simply grabbed the back of the collar and pulled his shirt off over his head in a motion as familiar to me as the feel of his back. Now he was naked to the waist—a pale, smooth expanse of shock. Many people stared; others continued to yell. What did those men want? There were more of them now—a hundred of them, maybe. Or maybe more—a mob. No women. The accident had become a man's business—possibly because of Carnegie's naked chest? As most of the men wore those thin undershirts, with deep armholes, I could make out their sharp ribs heaving as they shouted, pointed, glowered. I made out their scrawny necks and wiry arms.

CARNEGIE / — Could we not at least give the man a ride to the hospital? I asked. Having run him over, after all.

But it was no go. Mr. Qian and the driver, suddenly a team, adamantly opposed even this basic humanitarian action, never mind that the man's leg was bleeding badly. I had no choice but to remove my shirt to serve as a tourniquet.

BLONDIE / — Should I go see what's going on? I asked the air. Try to help translate?

Giving out a reassuring air, I rummaged coolly through the diaper bag again, this time for a cloth diaper so I could burp Wendy. Wendy could hold her head up easily. All the same, I supported her neck with my left hand.

The engine was still running—galumphing unhealthily, sending a message about itself that the driver or Carnegie could receive, but that I could not. Fan belt? Engine mounts?

— Lizzy, I said. Do me a favor and climb into the front seat again, would you?

— Why are these people staring at us? Why are they yelling?

— I want you to turn the engine off, please. Now.

— Aren't you going to say I shouldn't say 'these people'?

— Now.

Lizzy grumbled but dove into the front seat a second time, her skinny legs midair, one sandal dangling. She kicked over the bag into which we'd stuffed Wendy's orphanage clothes.

Wendy burped—a loud, solid, whole-body burp.

— Good girl! I told her, feeling the warm wet through the diaper on my shoulder.

It had been a long time since I'd burped a baby; I'd forgotten what a satisfaction it was. I'd forgotten too how surprised the baby always seemed, and yet how instantly ready for whatever the next moment might bring.

She began to cry again. Should we have left her with the foster mother? What were we doing?

How the car stank of cigarette smoke! It was in the fabric of the seats.

— Which way do you turn it, anyway? Lizzy asked.

I settled Wendy back down for another few ounces of formula, stuffing her orphanage clothes back into their bag. Those precious clothes, after all. I knew how much they would mean to her one day.

Unfortunately, as Lizzy pushed away from the steering wheel, levering her body over the seat back, she hit the horn. A long beep, unbelievably loud. Wendy startled just at the point she might have fallen asleep, and began to cry yet again. People pressed even closer to the glass now—faces, body parts. The car began to rock. Not so much because anyone was pushing it, exactly—it was more the sea motion of the mob. Or so it seemed. Where was Carnegie? Someone banged on the roof.

— This car is a tin can, I told Wendy, offering her the bottle again.

She was too upset, though, to take it. Long past the newborn whimper stage, she had a good strong wail.

— What is going on anyway? demanded Lizzy, banging some more on the window.

The car stopped rocking, then began again. *Luan.* I remembered a professor lecturing at the front of a classroom. Chaos. *Luan.*

That smoke smell.

If only we had not turned off the engine! The running engine had kept people back, I now realized.

The formula sloshed. Wendy was still crying.

— Dad! Lizzy called, starting to cry, too. — Dad!

For there was bare-chested Carnegie, waving his arms, engulfed. I held on to our wailing Wendy, trying not to panic. The car was rocked so hard that it heeled like a sailboat, the seat tilting at a thirty-degree angle; I braced myself with one hand in order to avoid sliding into Lizzy.

— This is like sailing, I said calmly. We ought to hike out.

— Are we going to tip over? Lizzy sounded terrified. — I don't know how to sail.

The car thudded back to the ground, bouncing. Where was Carnegie?

— I can't see Daddy, yelled Lizzy. And will that baby ever shut up?

— In this family, we do not use the phrase 'that baby,' I said.

— That baby! That baby!

I tried the bottle yet again. Wendy, thankfully, took it. Quieted.

— They're hurting Dad! shouted Lizzy. I know it. We have to go help Dad!

— Lizzy. You cannot get out of the car. Do you hear me?

The car began to rock again. We were set back down and heaved back up, set back down and heaved back up. The pitch was so steep now we could not keep from sliding.

Still Wendy, amazingly, drank.

— We're going to go over! shrieked Lizzy. We're going to tip over!

Was she right?

The wildness in the theater, that boy who almost fell out of the balcony.

— Calm down, I said. Then: — Lizzy!

I grabbed her forearm just as the whole car really did tip over.

The baby!

The car landed on its side, so that Wendy and I were heaped on top of Lizzy, who screamed. Our belongings avalanched down on us; Wendy's head hit the glass. I dropped the bottle. Bodies thumped against the window glass above us—much yelling. We appeared to be at the bottom of a pile of people.

— My arm! Lizzy cried.

Wendy shrieked, her whole body clenched.

— Are you all right? It's all right, it's all right, I cooed at Wendy, trying to right myself.

— You're stepping on my hair! cried Lizzy.

I managed a kind of half crouch, standing on a side window, which cracked but, to my surprise, held. Wendy by a miracle was still on my arm. One of my feet was on the diaper bag; the other on the panda. Was Lizzy hurt? Dampness—Wendy needed a new diaper.

— Lizzy. Lizzy. Can you straighten up? Here, try to sit up.

CARNEGIE / Lizzy sat up only, apparently, to see calm Blondie keel over. I slogged my way through the crowd to find Lizzy popped up through a window as if from the hatch of a submarine, cradling the baby with her good arm.

— She's making my arm hot! she cried.

For her part, Wendy, astoundingly, had fallen asleep. Her hair bow was askew but still affixed to her fuzzy head.

The police dispersed the crowd, wielding their sticks with the delicacy of mad apes.

Meanwhile, Mr. Qian, reinforced now by a Chinese Frankenstein, continued to insist that we foreigners be removed from the scene immediately. Before the injured man was seen to; before the injured man—who had lost a lot of blood but was conscious enough to swear—was taken anywhere.

And so it was that by the time Blondie came to, we were being grandly escorted in a brand-new, air-conditioned Toyota van to the hotel, where we could at last let Blondie lie down; see about Lizzy's swollen arm (a sprain); and liberate the baby from her distinctly gooey diaper.

BLONDIE / There was poop on everything.

Wendy cried all night.

Her orphanage clothes were lost.

CARNEGIE / As for myself, I had been shoved a few times but, lo and behold, had escaped with my life, I reported. Though of course my shirt was history.

Later we discovered that—just our luck—a local textile factory had shut its fair doors that very afternoon. One of those gloriously inefficient, state-run enterprises, this was, to which one could only say good riddance in the long run. But in the short run, how were people supposed to live? And what about their pensions? Et cetera. In the process of closing, the factory leaders had conveniently blamed American quotas for what was happening. Never mind their fantastic mismanagement, they kept anger at bay with rumors: that America set quotas because it could not compete with China. That America was afraid of China. That America was determined to keep China weak.

Or so we understood via a chance dinner, once we got back, with Peanut Butter Clark, as we called him. Who, it turned out, was in textiles himself, and had, what's more, learned much from the Belgian professors. Over peach cobbler he argued that the mob was about nationalistic resentment.

Did the crowd even realize we were American, though? we wondered as we did the dishes. Maybe any car, any sign of privilege, would have drawn ire.

How lucky, in any case, that we'd lived to analyze the tale.

BLONDIE / I wanted to report the incident, but Carnegie just wanted to get home. We'd been in China too long already, he said, and what good would it do? The man was okay, or at least that's what the guide said. In fact, we would never know.

— Do you realize we've been gone for five weeks? he said.

And: — Please remember they haven't signed off on the adoption yet.

CARNEGIE / Shots—poor Wendy. Papers papers papers.

BLONDIE / What artwork we brought back!

— Look at the workmanship, I said. The detail. The colors.

My sisters framed every last paper cutting. My brothers wore their fur-lined vests all winter.

CARNEGIE / Making fine use of gravity, Doc Bailey parked Chinese boxes on every available horizontal surface. I.e., his home desk, his work desk, the cocktail table, the hall table. Anywhere there wasn't a box, there was a bowl. He dusted his cork carving with the puffer cleaner for his camera lens.

Still Lizzy insisted she was never ever going back to China. Nothing traumatic could be recounted without Lizzy putting in, *You think that's bad, you won't believe what happened in China.* At least the memory was sometimes comforting: the day she fell out of a tree and broke her arm, for example, she did tell the doctor, *It wasn't as scary as what happened to me in China.*

BLONDIE / Of course, we did not respond to these comments. Naturally.

This infuriated her.

— Why don't you ever say anything when I talk about what happened in China? she demanded.

— The accident was upsetting, I said sometimes, when Lizzy brought it up.

Other times, I said: — You know, what happened to us was very unusual. Most people go to China and have a perfectly nice time. Think how you would feel if we'd left after the Great Wall.

But Lizzy began to elaborate on what was the matter with the trip, in addition to the accident.

— It was really crowded, she would say. All these people pushing. And it was so hot! Like an oven! Only hotter. And the mosquitoes—once I got fifty bites in one day. I am never ever going back there.

Later the conventional wisdom held that it was important to bring children to China before they were nine—that after nine they sometimes developed negativity. Lizzy was six. It should have worked out.

> do you really want to shut down lizzy's real self, that's the question, e-mailed Gabriela. do you really want her to grow up saying the nice thing until she herself doesn't know what she thinks?
>
> Of course not, I wrote back. But what am I going to do?
>
> have you tried aromatherapy? i know it sounds flaky. but you might try lavender spray. lavender is calming.

CARNEGIE / Whose house was this? Smelling like a country-home outlet store. I was half afraid, walking in, that I was about to behold a trunk show of faux naïvery, the sort of folk junk with which corporate America has thoughtfully sought to homeify our mobile society. Heart and goose dish towels, picket-fence napkin holders. Items meant to stop us mid–rat race, that we might pay homage to the stencil.

What a relief to find Blondie laboring with Lizzy instead, on a photo album of good memories. Freeing the birds! The Great Wall! First days with Wendy! (After the accident, that was.) Sprawled on the great-room rug, obscuring at least six of its cabbage roses, Blondie and Lizzy were ringed by acid-free mounting supplies. (Thanks to her art-restorer mother, Blondie had a horror of the non-archival.) That Lizzy might help write the captions, Blondie was giving her a choice of markers. The passion purple? The flamingo pink? Lest I fail to recognize this as a mother-daughter moment, the sun obligingly backlit them, gently suffusing the scene with something peachy rosy. The exact color you would imagine called Sunset.

But already in school Lizzy had learned that there could be many different versions of a fairy tale. Using the legend of the gingerbread man, for example, she had done exercises where she filled in the parts of the story that seemed to be missing in a particular version. Now she brilliantly applied what she had learned to the China photo album. She wrote:

> What you don't see in this story is how crowded it was, and how people pushed, and how hot it was, like an oven.

Blondie frowned at her pen assortment.

BLONDIE / Any mother would have been dismayed, yet I was particularly so. How had I ended up an outsider in my own family? The person who could never admit how hard she herself had found China—who had to be more careful than everyone else. Who felt, I suppose, a kind of guest.

When I strolled Wendy through town now I was reminded of the days when having a child of another race was simply a matter of fending off ignorance. How simple that was—how easy to know what was right. When people asked, *Is she yours?* or, *Where did you get her?* I could laugh and feel proud—of myself, of my family. It was a species of vanity. I had struggled against it when Lizzy was a baby. But now, I sometimes brought Wendy out into the world to feel that challenge, and my own fine resistance. I had always drawn strength from the fact that my hair next to Lizzy's should be a picture that challenged the heart. Now I drew on it purposefully, the way other women drew on the knowledge that they were intelligent or thin. I had had the heart to take these children in, after all. Had I not loved them deeply and well, as if they were from the beginning my own?

7

A Kind of Guest

CARNEGIE / Still, confoundingly, Lan refused to set a place for herself at the dinner table. Still, patiently, we set a place for her. She had proven herself knife-and-fork competent; still, hospitably, we provided chopsticks every day, and a cup of hot tea, so she wouldn't feel she had to drink our cold water.

The water business—I understood that much, my mother having drunk everything room temperature.

Gently, sensitively we inquired, did she like the food? Serve yourself, we said, please. Serve yourself. But though she half-smiled back and did eat, it was nibblingly. One bite, two.

Several evenings Blondie left food out for Lan at the base of her stairs. An after-school snack, in case she was hungry when she came home.

She never touched it.

BLONDIE / Wrote Gabriela:

> you know what she is? she is chopsticks.

I e-mailed back:

> Isn't it more understandable, though? For her to be chopsticks than for us to be forks? I think it is more understandable.

She replied:

> it's more understandable if you understand it.

WENDY / She has no place in America, that's what she says late at night in her apartment. Or that's what she means. 'No any place' is what she actually says.

— America is cold, she says. In China, many more people help you.

— Help you? says Lizzy. I thought people were mostly out to get you.

— Help you too, insists Lanlan.

Sometimes Lizzy and I go over to her apartment after she gets back from class, when we are supposed to be asleep. We eat snacks. Nothing tastes right in America, she has no appetite, but she still likes eating with us, we find out. And so we come, so she'll eat and not starve, most of the time we boil up some of those frozen dumplings that she said from the beginning were just like the ones you can get in China. We eat chicken ones, and pork ones, and vegetable ones.

LAN / *Why make believe I belonged in the dining room? What use was it? Anyone could see it was* bu heshi*—inappropriate.*

WENDY / She says she's the servant, really, and that's why it isn't fitting, since when does a servant belong at the table? I tell her that she isn't a servant, I don't think we even have servants in America.

LIZZY / In America, we have cleaning women, which is different.

LAN / *And who is given the leftovers to eat? Is that not the servant?*

Wendy / Lanlan says if she were a real family member she would live inside the house. We try to tell her that we'll help her if she wants and that she can definitely live in the house if she wants and that Mom just has the idea Lanlan wants to clean and stuff and can't really be stopped.

Still she insists she is the servant to the rich Americans, meaning us.

LAN / *For did not Blondie decide I should live in the barn with the goat instead of in the guest room? Could anyone deny this?*

BLONDIE / We served her as if we were at a banquet. We heaped her plate with food while she protested. We treated her as if she were an honored guest, with that exaggerated politeness the Chinese love.

She seemed to view all this as so much insincerity.

LAN / *Was it not completely fake? I never saw them treat anybody else that way.*

Of course, Blondie talked so nice. But I felt xiao li cang dao*—that her smile hid a knife.*

Sometimes I sat in my room and thought about my great-aunt's house. Who was living in it now? And what was I going to do when I went back? Carnegie had relatives in Beijing. I wondered if they could help me.

America did not want me. But could I say that the new China wanted me either?

The only people who really wanted me were little Wendy and Lizzy—girls with no mothers, like me. Sometimes Bailey too. I was getting used to Bailey, strange as he was.

BLONDIE / Outside, the days grew shorter. Colder. I knew this mostly by continuing to drive to work with my windows down long after others had stopped. I did this so that I could feel how the summer sun, which had shone on my elbow on the way home, did so no longer. How I began to need a sweater, and then to bundle up. How I began to become aware of my legs—that they were cold though my torso was warm. The day came when I welcomed the soft blow of heat on my toes, when the *sssshh* of the heat fan simply belonged to my day.

By that time the trees were well into dropping their leaves. I tracked certain trees on my route—for example, a stand of birches like the ones we had at home, only so much more massive, so much more extensive, that I could not behold it without making that comparison—without thinking of our stand. And vice versa. The difference in scale so bordered on a difference in kind as to fascinate me. Of course, the stand by the parkway went by so quickly; that explained some of my seeing it in the way that I did. But I was generally less occupied when I beheld the birch stand at home; and yet I could not see that stand in relation to other stands either, only in relation to the stand by the parkway. I could not see it in a way that was not already my habit.

That was all right with me sometimes.

But there were other times when I felt I would like to know whether I was capable of disengaging the two stands from each other.

I tried to tell Carnegie about this once. He listened politely enough, head bent—a sign he was trying to focus. He cracked his knuckles.

I rubbed his back to reward him.

Yet he didn't understand, in the end.

There was also an old maple on a knoll by my office that I watched. That tree had had an enormous hole hacked into its branches by the telephone company—because it was obstructing the wires, they said. Yet still it put on a show with what it had left. For was that not the nature of nature, to carry on? I always slowed as I passed that tree. Once I expected that, with its leaves down, its mutilation would be less glaring.

But no, it was not.

Or so I remembered from last year. Now here it was again—more glaring, as I recalled.

My sunflowers, of course, were long cut down by now.

The maple, bare. Then, many trees. Then, all the trees. The giant street cleaners with their huge round brushes and second-story drivers actually seemed to be doing something for a change. People raked and raked their yards. Only a few people hired those backpack blowers, thank goodness—most being more considerate of the neighborhood peace. Stuffed leaf bags lined the streets on Mondays.

I was sorry to see the leaves go. Yet I loved watching the structure of the trees emerge too. Those branches—so brave and forthright. Straightforward. Comprehensible. I loved being able to see, now, where the birdsnests were.

We were ready for Lan to help herself. To make herself at home.

She appeared to be losing weight.

E-mailed Gabriela: did you try chinese food?

But of course we had. Maybe it wasn't the right kind of Chinese, though; we only had two Chinese restaurants in town, one Cantonese, one nouvelle. And to be honest, we did not try the restaurants in other towns. Honestly, we were preoccupied, when we walked in the door, with connecting with the children. What with only two hours before their bedtime, we did not want to lose a minute.

I thought we should bring Lan to a therapist. I thought she had an eating disorder. But Carnegie didn't want her to think we thought her crazy.

CARNEGIE / She had an antipathy for outdoor labor; no doubt associating yard work and suchlike with peasants. But indoors, what a dynamo! She not only watched the children and handled the laundry, she also did a good bit of cleaning. Nothing heavy-duty; that remained our housecleaner Damiana's job. But Lan kept after the kitchen, and the playroom, and the kids' bedrooms. She organized the sports rack, the gift wrap, the front hall closet, and the linen closet—all without being asked. She seemed to anticipate things we might ask and do them before we could—a preemptive strategy—thereby avoiding the indignity of being ordered about. She was not, she said several times, like Damiana. She did not need things pointed out. We tried to stop her, but it was like trying to get her to eat, more challenging than it would seem. And so we settled for fulsome expressions of appreciation and awe.

The only subject we ever had to raise with Lan was goat care. Blondie brought this up. Sounding Lan out, she said later. Proposing nothing.

Should Blondie have realized that Lan would feel forced to say yes?

WENDY / Lanlan says Tommy doesn't listen to anybody. She says the goat is above her in the household, she thinks the goat is like a feudal boss, and we are its oppressed workers. What are oppressed workers? I ask, and she says it is like what I would be if I had a job and my boss was Elaine.

— You mean like a slave, I say.

And she says: — Right! Like a slave. We are all slave to the goat. How should a goat be so precious?

— Taking care of a goat doesn't make you a slave, I tell her. It doesn't make you anything. It's just something you have to do, like math.

Still she hates it that she has to feed Tommy. She says that in Shandong she was always being butted by her neighbor's goat, especially when she went to pee in the fields, once she was knocked right over.

BLONDIE / We had to spell out every single thing. It was not enough to tell Lan the goat needed water every day. You had to tell her that the water should be in a bucket. You had to tell her that a large puddle after a rainstorm was not enough. You had to tell her to refill the bucket if Tommy drank it all. You had to tell her to change the water every day even if Tommy didn't drink it all. You had to tell her to tell us if the bucket was leaking.

It was the same with the feed bucket. You had to tell her to change the food every day. You had to tell her to tell us when the food was running low.

LAN / *Everything I did, Blondie criticized.*

Blondie / Then there was cleaning out the stall.

Honestly, we would've taken this job back, if we knew how. We told the girls to go help. But the more they tried to help, the more Lan insisted on doing it herself.

WENDY / She can't understand what the goat is for.

— For fun? How is a goat fun? she says.

CARNEGIE / The goat would levitate, plant its hooves on the barn wall such that it was well nigh horizontal, then push off. Landing neatly on the driveway a moment later, free! Its furry wattles swinging.

Said Lan, the first time she saw this: — Your goat can fly.

The next time: — Maybe it will run away.

But goats generally stayed close to home.

— No, no, the goat is ours until our friend returns from sunny Italy, I explained. Or until one of our neighbors reports us to Animal Control. Whichever comes first.

— What is Animal Control? she asked.

— Don't give her ideas, said Blondie.

WENDY / She doesn't think it fair that a goat should have such an easy life. Every day Chinese people eat bitter, she says, every day real people suffer.

BLONDIE / Sometimes I wanted to say, *You see, I have my goat, and Carnegie, well, has his.*

— You can cut him, said Lan, indicating an ankle tendon. —Then he will not fly anymore.

— We don't do that here, I said.

CARNEGIE / We explained that Americans in general adored things farmy. That it wasn't just Blondie. That it had to do with our agrarian past.

Of course I regretted the word 'agrarian' even as it emanated pretentiously from my lips. But naturally, she knew full well what it meant.

— I understand, she said. Before capitalism you were feudal landlords.

WENDY / One day when Tommy butts her, she throws a pail at his head.

— In this country, we do not throw pails at animals, says Mom. And when was the last time this stall was cleaned out?

BLONDIE / When would she start eating? E-mailed Gabriela:

healing. lan needs healing. what about a sweat lodge?

This, it seemed, was a kind of retreat where the participants huddled in a sauna for days, then burst out naked into the cold outdoors, reborn. I e-mailed back:

> I don't think so. To begin with, Lan is horrified by sweat.

Gabriela:

> didn't she sweat in the countryside? or did she carry her umbrella around with her then too?

I tried to explain, ending with:

> Honestly, we are just too busy for this nonsense. It is too much to spend the day running from meeting to meeting to meeting to meeting to meeting—for half of which I am underprepared—only to have to psychoanalyze our nanny when I come home. Does not our attention at the end of the day rightly belong to our children?

To which Gabriela replied:

> of course it does. take back your life!

I handed over the place-setting to Carnegie that night, saying I had other things to think about—for example, the workplace-diversity initiative.

— If we're going to include that among our investment criteria, we are going to have to make our case, I said.

CARNEGIE / That was the same evening she took the lid off our largest casserole and announced: — My life is too short for this nonsense. I value my moments and choose to spend them otherwise.

Gabriela-speak, this was.

BLONDIE / Still—I meant it.

CARNEGIE / I took over general Lan management. Beginning with the next day, Saturday morning, which found Lan on the kitchen floor, diligently and of her own accord ruining with Ajax our authentic Mexican tile.

I watched her from the doorway. With what grace she moved! She might have been playing a servant in a ballet—Cinderella, about to look up and behold her fairy godmother. Partly this was the way she held herself, but partly too it was the way she used her arms; not working her forearm back and forth like a windshield wiper, but rather engaging her whole arm, sometimes her whole upper body, in a kind of sweeping motion that began and ended with her sitting neatly on her heels. How sweetly she tucked stray hairs behind her pale ears. She even wrung her sponge with unwarranted delicacy—holding her rubber-gloved pinkies aloft, as if handling an antique sugar bowl. Around her, the wet floor shone so brightly in the morning sun that it lit her face when she leaned over, bathed it in an evanescence I would not have thought possible in our mall-rat world. How beautiful she was! I had not realized; maybe it was just the lighting. Though I had noticed, recently, how others noticed her. How she had become attractive to crossing guards, repairmen, delivery boys, as she began to dress a little better. Wear a little makeup. It seemed she had done something fetching with her hair. But I was fetched by something else—some promise of simplicity. Clarity. The purity of her skin, the naturalness of her movements. I wanted to touch her. To take the sponge from her hand; to raise her to her rubber-booted feet. This was not an impulse I generally experienced with adults. Lan, though, seemed singularly registered in my amygdala. Was it because she lived in my house? Did feeling her day-in, day-out intimacy with the children—with my children—make me feel a proxy intimacy?

First, in any case, to stop her. For what was Blondie going to say? To Lan, and to me too. For was I not the person who had bought the Ajax? Was I not the caveman who had summarily dismissed our sweet-smelling collection of lovely organic cleaners? Who had argued, all too successfully, that households all over America had found ways to keep harsh chemical abrasives away from unscrupulous scrubbers of vulnerable porcelain sinks?

But now, two hours before Wendy's soccer match (we were pushing soccer, an anti-shyness strategy): Voilà! Our floor, diligently definished.

Lan looked up expectantly, her face aglow with modest pride.

— How clean the floor looks, I said.

— Not done yet, she said, renewing her attack.

— Stop, I said weakly. Please. I think you are done.

— Of course, she said then.

She sat back on her heels, bright light all around her. Brushed her loose hair back over her ear with her shoulder. Did not squint. She was wearing a blue sweatshirt and yellow rubber gloves. And on her feet, yellow galoshes, apparently Lizzy's. These were not an ordinary yellow, like her gloves, but a safety yellow such as was used for rescue operations at sea. In our earthtone kitchen, they pulsed technology; yet her natural dignity was undiminished by the aesthetic clash. With aristocratic simplicity she lay her hands, palms up, on her knees.

I had not thought myself unhappily married. But as she knelt there, awaiting direction, I knew Blondie too had awaited something. That the husband Blondie had hoped for did *such crazy things.* That the husband she had hoped for surged with a life force that put her wacky siblings to shame. How interesting the husband she had hoped for. The last time I saw Doc Bailey, he asked if I planned on staying in my job forever. How to tell him that I might indeed be moving on soon?

What they want from you?

I worked too hard for the Baileys.

What they want from you?

I bored them.

In truth we bored ourselves, hauling out our calendars night after night, comparing schedules. *What do we want?* Blondie asked sometimes. *Do we even know what we want?*

I gazed now upon Lan's bent head. At the smooth nape of her naked neck.

Wendy bounced in, announcing that she was going to be the Great Wall for Halloween. This was a change of plan; originally she had planned to be a teenager.

— Just part of it, I mean, she said. A tower.

— Great idea! said Lan.

Her rubber-covered hands flew up. From her attitude of quiet suspension, she seemed to spring full blown into the very picture of Halloween costume support.

— Very original, I agreed. Not to forget the barbarian invaders.

Wendy rolled her eyes and, in concert with them, her besocked feet, such that her soles faced each other and her ankles grazed the floor.

— Is there a contest at school? Lan asked.

Wendy nodded.

— You will win! Lan predicted.

Wendy beamed, straightening her feet up.

I beamed too. Though I knew Blondie, had she been there, would have said, *Life is not about winning and losing*—and of course I agreed—still I was happy to see Wendy so ebullient. To see how Lan was bringing her out.

— Of course people will probably think I'm a rook, said Wendy.

— No one will think you're a rook, I said.

— But how will they know? That I'm a Chinese wall, and not just any wall?

— You'll have to tell them.

— Elaine is going to say you can't tell.

— Who is this Elaine anyway, who gives you so much grief? I said. Tell her to go to hell.

Wendy hung her head.

— I can't, she said plaintively, her spunk gone. — You don't understand.

Her nose quivered as though she was about to start sobbing.

— I'm sorry, I said then. Your father just doesn't know what to say, does he? He doesn't know how to act. He's not like Lan. He doesn't understand anything.

— That's right! You don't!

— Of course he knows how to act, said Lan soothingly.

— He doesn't! said Wendy. He acts however he wants!

And with that she departed, leaving tracks on the wet floor. Lan watched her. Still kneeling—beautifully—she eyed the tracks, the first indication I had ever seen that she registered her work as work, and minded having to do it over. Up to now she had seemed an inexhaustible source of energy that would do things two, three times if necessary, so long as they did not involve goat care.

— You know how to act, I said quietly.

— No no no no, said Lan, pressing her fingers together.

I wanted to kneel beside her, and might have done so if I could have with poise. If I would not have appeared some patron saint of tile men, tardily come to bless the grout.

I sat down instead.

— Lan, I said.

I placed my elbows on my knees and clasped my hands together. I lowered my head so that it was on the same level as hers. I feared that even on a chair I seemed a parody of sincerity.

— Lan.

It came out as a near-whisper. Husky, urgent.

With what clarity each of her dark hairs emanated from her pale scalp. How wonderfully they stood clear of one another, even as they fell together, a simple multitude of strong strands. And how they shone in the early light; I could not believe how unabashedly they shone.

— You don't have to—how to say?—whisper, she whispered back.

— Of course not, I breathed.

She laughed then—a lovely, rippling, low laugh with something private about it. She did not send it out into the open air, for anyone to hear. It was like her performance, addressed. *You,* she seemed to say. *You. You.*

I performed too, of course, in a great many ways. And yet for no one in particular; Wendy was right. Where was my community, who was my audience? As for Blondie, did she not perform, still, after all these years, for her family?

You, Lan seemed to say, *You.*

— Lan.

— Yes?

— Stand up please.

Up she sprang, sponge in hand.

I stood then as well, so that I would not be eye level with her breasts. Her blue sweatshirt read LANDER'S ART SUPPLY in cracking red letters. A hand-me-up from Lizzy, apparently.

— I want to talk to you about dinner, I said; my voice near normal and yet not normal.

I observed the part in her hair—a side part—and, again, the many black hairs starting resolutely out of their roots. There were a few strands crossing the part, strands that belonged on the left side of her head but that had fallen, somehow, to the right. How hard not to take those strands and flip them the other way. How they begged to be set straight. She would have thought the same, I knew, if she could have seen them. I nobly succeeded in restraining my hand. But when she turned her head, I did blow gently at the errant hairs, stirring a few of the shorter strands into their proper place.

She looked up, unsurprised. It was if she had believed all along that behind the front stage of our lives lay a back stage; as if she had been waiting to learn the way there.

LAN / ***Finally I was inside the house. Everyone knows in America, girls have no morals. How can you expect the men to be better?***

CARNEGIE / — I want to talk to you, I said. About not setting a place for yourself at the table.

She backed away a step. But only a step; she seemed poised to run away, yet able to consider how to act. She wrung her natural sponge into the recycled-plastic pail, deciding.

Drop. Drop.

Run, or stay?

An inexplicable calm settled over me.

— Forgive me, I said.

— I'm sorry?

— Forgive me for asking, I said. But if you would please set a place for yourself. At the table. At dinner.

She did not say anything.

Then I asked, surprising myself:—Will you be taking the TOEFL exam?

If she was taken aback by the change of subject, she gave no indication. The Test of English as a Foreign Language? She shook her head no. It was as if she knew we were going to have this conversation; as if we both knew.

— Because?

— Because it is no use.

— You are never going to college.

She nodded.

— But if you could go to college. Would you take it then?

— Do you know how old I am?

— Not that old.

Silence.

— Here in America, there are people who go back to school in their sixties, I said. Of course, I can't promise anything. But who knows.

— Would I get a degree?

She shifted her weight; her rain boots squeaked on the wet floor. A surprisingly bright sound, as somehow befit their color.

— I'd have to talk to Blondie, I said.

LAN / *How happy I was, and yet how unhappy. For even if I could get a degree—a degree!—it was too late. Women in China retired at fifty, fifty-five at the latest. Who would hire someone like me?*

So much shi qu ji hui*—missed opportunity—in one life.*

CARNEGIE / She dropped her gaze to the pail. Reading her fate, it seemed, in the suds. She wrung her rough sponge.

— Why am I here? she asked finally, her eyes full of tears. — Why do you help me?

I explained about my mother's will.

She dug her gloved thumb into one of the craters of the sponge, then asked: — But why your mother want me to come here?

I thought.

— I guess she wanted the family to be more Chinese. Like her. She wanted us to be Wongs.

We observed each other in the rippling water. Though we stood some distance apart, our reflections appeared to touch.

She dropped the sponge in the water. Then slowly and deliberately, still gazing at the water, she began to slip off her gloves, one long finger at a time. I watched. The first glove she let fall into our reflection with a soft disturbing splash. It replaced our image with a floating severed hand, bobbing cheerfully alongside the sponge.

The second glove she handed to me.

That night, miracle of miracles, Lan set a place for herself. I saw her doing it and winked at her—as much, I suppose, to make myself feel that I knew what I had begun, as anything else. If in fact I had begun something.

— She set a place for herself, marveled Blondie after dinner, loading the dishwasher.

— How do you like that, I said.

I helped clear the table.

— Did you speak to her?

— What makes you ask?

— Well, she set a place for herself, and when I asked her why today, she said you told her to.

— I did.

I set a last pile of dishes on the counter with a clatter.

— But you weren't going to tell me you did, said Blondie. You were going to let me think she had decided to do it herself. Also you spoke to her when you knew I had already.

Blondie's tone was more tired than confrontational. No-nonsense, and yet somehow mild and good-natured.

— And you asked me if I had spoken to her or not, when you knew that I had, I said. You were testing me.

— You wanted to know if you could sway her. If you had some power over her I didn't.

She poured soap into the soap dispenser, then pushed the energy-saver button. The machine, ever reliable, came on.

I beheld her then, my wife. Today she was wearing a wrap dress and, unusually, a turquoise necklace. An experiment, I guessed. An allowing, to see how it made her feel. How alert she was for revelation; Mama Wong would laugh.

Forget about inner truth. You know what life is about? Life is about survive. That's it.

— I don't know that that's untrue, I said. But I don't know that I wanted to sway her either. If I come to know, I will tell you.

— Thank you, she said simply.

— I wanted Lan to stop washing the floor, I said. I did know that. I'm sorry about the floor. She was using Ajax.

— On the floor?

— I threw it away.

Blondie's mouth tightened in the corners. The dishwasher churned.

— I did notice the tiles looked dull, she said.

— Maybe the floor can be waxed?

I did not actually know if anyone used wax anymore; my last experience with floor wax had involved an appliance with two revolving heads and a distinctive smell, at a friend's house, in first or second grade. Still I raised the idea, effective penitence in our household having a practical aspect.

— Perhaps, she sighed. We have the goat to ruin our lawn, Lan to ruin our floor. That's what it means to have these things at all. Where did that VCR come from?

— I dug it out of the attic, I answered truthfully. — So Lan could watch movies. And that's my old TV, from graduate school. I hooked it up for her.

— How helpful, said Blondie.

She seemed unmoved by my contrition.

— Also I suggested we might think about college for her. So she could get a degree.

— How interesting, said Blondie, that you would raise such a subject without consulting me.

— I'm sorry. Let me at least put forth that it was wholly unpremeditated. If that constitutes a mitigating circumstance.

— As my mother used to say, How extraordinary.

She said what her mother used to say as her mother used to say it, crisply. With pointed restraint. But the moment after the delivery was all Blondie: grave and, though she would not have admitted it, shaken. She folded her arms in front of herself, playing with her necklace.

— Scout's honor, I said. It was spur of the moment.

And with that I slid my hand across her waist, found the end of her wrap-dress tie, and pulled.

— Carnegie! she said. Honestly!

But she followed me into our bedroom, and herself took off

the necklace, placing it carefully on a side table even as her back was arching, and her dress falling, her breathing plangent, like mine, with worried desire. It seemed then that the light was too bright—something. And was that Bailey? We checked to see; the bed, when we returned, was cold.

But a moment later we were old married ease—bored then not bored, us and us and us.

8

Carnegie Takes a Day Off

BLONDIE / Everyone was amazed back when I got pregnant at forty-three. On my own, the doctors said.

CARNEGIE / Though I, excuse me, begged to differ.

BLONDIE / No one dared hope that the bip bip bip on the ultrasound would turn into eyes and ears and nose; I refused to buy maternity clothes. For what were the chances of my going to term? At my age. With my history. Still I grew larger and larger—amazing myself. Was this self always hidden in my other self? And were there other selves like this one, secreted within plain view? How accidental my old self began to feel, how partial. How ignorant.

In Art, Wendy made a clay statue of me with my arms akimbo, like chicken wings; I laughed. For that was me all right, my hands glued to my lower back by the end, for balance. Lizzy dubbed me Mount Mama. Led by Carnegie, their choirmaster, they sang me lullabies at bedtime. *Lullaby, and good night—so your figure's a fright / May you lay down and rest / We still lo-ve you the best . . .* Every night there were different lyrics. *You people!* I said usually. Happy to be able to laugh, if not to sleep—there being no sleeping position, no pillow configuration that worked. As for the daytime: — *Does anyone need to use the bathroom before we go?* Wendy would ask before we got into the car. And Lizzy would join in: — *It could be a ways before the first rest stop.*

On hot days I thought nothing of parking myself in front of an air conditioner. And how I sat! Legs apart, like a benched basketball player.

CARNEGIE / Only what jersey would fit her? And what sort of player could this be? With the basketball stuck to her lap.

As per the advice of others (fair-haired women being problem-prone), she was trying to toughen her nipples for breastfeeding, which mostly involved roughing herself up with sisal bath sponges and oatmeal scrubs. I volunteered to help, of course; but how disconcerting when my nibbling brought leakage. And to be slapped away, that was strange too. To be barred from the dairy bar.

BLONDIE / Month nine came and went.

CARNEGIE / A lucky thing, as I was hugely pregnant at work as well. That baby being release one of the document-management server and, like Blondie's baby, overdue. Every day marketing screamed and screamed, as if we development people didn't realize how important it was to stay in synch. As if we didn't want to see the product launched too.

Truly: it was twins.

BLONDIE / Month ten brought ultrasounds, stress tests, talk of inducing. Then suddenly it was all happening—the breathing, the talk of a C-section—my age, my age—but in the end an episiotomy, crowning—I felt it with my hand, a head emerging—hair!

CARNEGIE / A boy!

— Fresh from the factory, said the OB, holding him up for view.

How unreasonably happy I was to have, in the family, another pecker.

BLONDIE / A boy. We were happy enough to hear it. But how that fact paled beside the not-there, then there-ness of him! This strange, wailing creature, waxy bloody goldeny, to cuddle briefly—look, how already nuzzling! How already trying to nurse!

CARNEGIE / But first: time to wash up. How in touch with his outrage, our little man! That whole-body wail. And such emotive toes—splayed out like the spokes of a wheel I'd say, except that they were hardly spoke-like. Rather scrawny through the mid-section and bulb-like at their ends, like the toes of tree frogs. Had they extruded something sticky, I would not have been altogether surprised.

And of course, those toes were but one part of a package with deeper adhesive qualities. You didn't have to be a hormone-drunk woman to feel immediately, irremediably bonded, as he was returned to us. To the toes, the ankles, the knees of this being. To his nostrils, to his eyelashes, to his fingernails. To his pecker.

BLONDIE / Now, the afterbirth.

— Fresh from the factory, said the OB again.

Then she failed to say more. If she was smiling, you couldn't tell because of her surgical mask. And of course her hair was hidden too, in that blue shower cap doctors wear.

She failed to say congratulations, or that he was beautiful.

Fresh from the factory.

My heart did still bloom, as I cradled for keeps now our child—how he was looking about! Looking and looking at everything. After such a big pregnancy, such a surprisingly small human.

— Where are you? You're in the world, I told him. Welcome. Welcome.

I held my hand over his eyes, shielding him from the too bright light. And sure enough, he liked that—opened his eyes wider.

Carnegie extended the visor with his hands.

— Hello there, he whispered. I am your captain. This is planet Earth.

Yet in the midst of all this happy welcoming, I noticed it. The silence. Of the doctor, and of the nurses, too. I would not have thought to look up except for their silence.

But I did. And so it was that I saw how they were focused, oddly, on Carnegie.

CARNEGIE / Between their masks and bouffant caps, they were bug-eyed, like some exotic species of crab. Reading me even as I read their guesses, the upshot of which was that I was not necessarily Bailey's father. Could I, right there, in their very own delivery room, before their eyes, be experiencing a largish doubt? Indeed they appeared to be hoping, poor bored souls, for a moment of soap opera. How they would have loved for me to denounce my wife, right there. Slut! Slapping her as she cried and pleaded, thrusting her innocent babe before her.

I was sorry to disappoint those nosy professionals. Stuck as they were with the mere miracle of life.

At the same time: the ever-inventive workings of biology!

— I'm not going to even ask, I whispered to Blondie.

— Ask what?

All this because my son—and I did believe that I had begat him with my own one-two—was not just on the fair side. He was not one of those brownish-haired, somewhere-in-between-y kids you see around everywhere these days. This child—my child—was blond blond. He was bright, brassy King-Midas-couldn't-have-made-him-blonder blond.

And his eyes: Virgin Mary blue.

— Ask what? said Blondie; though later she too admitted surprise.

It was good to have witnessed the delivery. Had this been the fifties, I might well have stumbled off to a lawyer, mumbling *something something Switched at Birth!*

Instead we developed, Blondie and I, a marital dislike of the obstetrician. She was not even our own doctor, but a member of an OB group whose doctors cross-covered. We decried this practice at dinner parties. And there, look, on his bottom, at the top of his sweet bum. Was that not a Mongolian spot? A faint bluish bruise-ish indelible shadow, proof of some Asian connection.

Or so people said on the Internet, in a chat room I found on the subject.

BLONDIE / The books say men have more trouble than women when it comes to bonding with children who don't look like them. But Carnegie did fine. He was not relieved that Bailey eventually turned brown-eyed like him. Or dismayed that Bailey stayed fair-haired during the year, turning even blonder in the summer. Carnegie was not chagrined that Bailey had pale skin, like mine, though seal sleek, like Carnegie's.

People at first glance thought Bailey white. They asked Carnegie if Bailey was his.

CARNEGIE / — No, I would say, he's a rental.

BLONDIE / Of course, those kinds of questions only went on up to a certain age. I knew because I used to get the same question, strolling the girls around—were they mine and so on.

CARNEGIE / That went with, *Oh look, how cute! Don't they look like dolls?* And: *Oh! That straight black hair!*

No wonder Lizzy dyed hers.

BLONDIE / Still Carnegie thought Bailey looked like him. He pointed out Bailey's eyes. Didn't they have a telltale tilt?

CARNEGIE / And his nose. Not as flat as some, but still: didn't he look as if he'd walked into a door?

BLONDIE / Actually our baby's name was Ellison. Ellison Bailey Wong. But we called him Bailey, after my family, and that was perfectly all right. More than all right, really. Here in this airiest of spaces I can confess that I loved it more than I would have said that my genes were not swallowed up by Carnegie's. I had assumed that they would be, somehow—that dark would trump fair. A reasonable assumption, given what I knew from paint boxes and markers.

But that was wrong—and I was surprised what it meant to me, not to find my blood, my side, myself drowned out.

Some would say that the point of raising children is of course self-replication. How hopelessly idealistic, to imagine love and values might count more than genes! But truly, I did. I was honestly chagrined to find in this child anything like a new order of experience.

And yet; and yet. To have held his soft skull as it emerged from my body; to have felt him tugging at my breast; to have ached for him in turn, sleeping when he slept. What a unit we were! I had never known anything like it.

I watched him in a different way than I had watched the girls. Maybe I would have seen him more clearly anyway, having watched other children grow up—being more practiced. Better understanding his wants, for example, I saw how, even at four or five months, he pushed other people away from my breasts—something I might not have caught in Lizzy or Wendy even if I had nursed them.

But also I watched Bailey for bits of Carnegie and myself and our families—that was new. He looked like me. He had Carnegie's tilt eyes, and bridgeless nose, and perfect ears. From birth, though, he had my light hair and, for a while, my blue eyes—things that somehow mattered more. He was left-handed like my father and, like my father, from birth a full sail. The more I looked at him, the more I saw bits of my grandparents and parents, and all my brothers and sisters.

Of course, he was Carnegie's son, too—no one forgot that. And we completely loved the girls just the same.

CARNEGIE / Most people didn't notice he was soup du jour. The people who noticed, though, did a double take, some of them. Thinking he meant something. But what?

The future, most of them would have said, probably—the kindest way of putting their thoughts.

No one except for me would have said, *The disappearing past*.

I looked forward to doing guy stuff with Bailey. Building forts. Shooting baskets. Rooting for the Red Sox. I worried about the usual things. That he would turn out a drug dealer. A bozo. A stiff.

But also I worried that he would marry a white woman, like his daddy. I worried that no one in the delivery room would even be shocked if his child was born blond.

BLONDIE / I held him closest because he would let me—and because, of all our children, he seemed the most vulnerable. The girls had had their share of unwanted attention. But Bailey people peered at, sideways—as if it was one thing to be a kind of Asian, like Lizzy, and another to be a kind of white.

— This is what's happening, said a lady at the mall to her friend. — I'm telling you.

And said our dear neighbor Mitchell, one day: — When I look at that boy, all I can think is, Is this the new face of America?

CARNEGIE / Thus spoke Mitch to Blondie. To me he said: — My brother Nick's going to have himself one just like yours, you watch and see. What do you want to bet that one of his China dolls doesn't get herself knocked up first thing?

BLONDIE / Who cared what people said? To me, he was Bailey—in so many ways a Bailey—my Bailey. Our one Bailey. Was I wrong for wanting to keep him that way?

CARNEGIE / How could there be trouble at the summer house now? With a new baby at home, his umbilical cord yet to fall off. And not to forget the new baby at work too, with complications no less. For here we'd finally shipped the server, only to have our biggest, baddest client find a bug.

Should not the remainder of the world have had the courtesy to stop?

But there was trouble indeed at the summer house, the alarm going off so often that the local police called to complain.

— We have a goddamned county to take care of, said Sergeant Reilly. We're not your personal security guard.

And: — We country types don't go in much for alarms.

I related all this to Blondie as she nursed. She glided in her glider, half dressed, happy, Bailey on her good side, as opposed to the side with the crack. She held a special bone-shaped pillow in her lap, across which he lay, becapped, in a state of private transport.

— It sounds to me like we have to do something about that alarm of yours, she said.

That alarm of mine. The alarm having been undeniably my idea, my response to the new caretaker sweetly quitting last year.

BLONDIE / For years and years before that, we had had Larry, a gentle guy with bad teeth who never complained about anything. But after he died, his son Billy took over. We paid him more than we had paid his dad. Yet he was less satisfied, perhaps because he'd gone to college for a couple of years—had lived in the city, and gotten ideas. We made him mad. If we asked him to open up the cabins for the season, but then never came, for example—that made him mad. Even if we paid him extra for opening up, and extra for closing back down, he got mad.

CARNEGIE / Said we wasted his time. Said that even if a man had nothing better to do, he didn't like having his time wasted. Said working for us was the very definition of shitwork.

BLONDIE / He didn't like being in charge of the beach. As it became more of a challenge, we offered him extra; but that made him mad too.

CARNEGIE / Said he was a caretaker, not a guard. Said he felt like a whore, being paid more than other caretakers. Not that there were so many on our lake, but there were on other lakes. Said people treated him like a whore too. Asked him things like why did he work for a family that had to pay that much, if he wasn't being bought.

BLONDIE / We thought perhaps people were jealous. And perhaps they were. When he quit, in any case, he said no one in town would take our job, and no one did. Had working for us somehow come to seem like working for the devil? Or did Billy's job remain, somehow, Billy's job—a job other people were afraid to take without his say-so? We never knew.

And how had our beach become, by then, the town beach? We never knew that either. Would it've happened in any case? Or did Billy let it happen? Billy was an intimidating guy—big, and tattooed. We had not wanted to hire him, but as Larry was dying he had begged us to take Billy on.

— It's a dog's life, he had said, but it's a living.

And so upset had we been by that comment that we had promised not only to hire Billy, but to send him to school if he wanted to go. As we did. Billy was a smart guy, active in campus politics. We encouraged him to finish, and to move somewhere with more jobs. But he moved back—said he couldn't be paid to leave the land of his father, and that if we thought we owned everything, we were wrong.

CARNEGIE / We posted NO TRESPASSING signs. We put up a gate at the end of the causeway, a joke.

BLONDIE / Carnegie's alarm had at least provided several months' peace of mind about the main cabin.

Now, though, someone was tripping it. Apparently without breaking in, the police said, though who knew. Possibly the locals were just having fun.

CARNEGIE / —An alarm does reflect a territorial mind-set, Blondie said. An us-and-them mind-set.

—If I were them, she said, I'd be offended too.

—I'm not saying it was a bad decision, she said. I'm only saying that I can see their point of view.

You help them you think they are going to say thank you?

I was tempted to point out how her sibs still availed themselves of the place, from time to time, when they felt like it. How they left their stuff there, and how everyone had a key, though the maintenance fell entirely to me. But she was nursing so beautifully; I watched Bailey drift straight from the most avid sucking to the most profound sleep. His cap had lifted from his head, but kept the shape of his skull.

—Someone has to go up there, said Blondie.

—I don't know if you realize, I said. There's a bug in the server. I need to be in touch with Ruth, Hsiao, the client, the product manager. Hold some hands, you know. It is not going to look good for me to be off someplace with no cell service, even. If the house phone were on, that'd be a different story. But as it isn't, I can't go.

So I argued.

Blondie rocked in response. There was a new thick carpet on the floor, sea green; Blondie hadn't wanted to start the gender thing from day one. Also there was a beach scene complete with sand chairs and crabs and seashells on the lower part of the walls; on the upper walls and ceiling, there was blue sky. Clouds. Bailey's crib was like a ship, a-bob in all this. His changing table was like a dinghy.

— Please, she said.

Rocking rocking, as if on the waves. There in their private sea. How little he was, a bit of flotsam. I waded in to give him a kiss, reseating his warm hat on his small head.

Still as I left it was lifting and settling again, lifting and settling. Flashing like a lighthouse: blond, blond, blond.

Day off! Day off!

Leaving the city, I did think that. Being the first to admit I had a complex, the man who mistook a personal day for a crime. But mostly I thought, Bailey. Blondie. The girls. Did I have a map? Did I need one? Also I thought about our broken radio/cassette deck, its repair obviously insufficiently prioritized.

The traffic its own circle of hell. If only Dante could do an update from the grave, surely this was material: the wavy air, the exhaust, the construction dust, the heat. The stop and go, stop and go, stop and go. Brake job coming up, I thought. And the noise! Finally I put on the AC. Why did I even delay? Some misguided masochistic concern for the ozone. But anyway, I did turn it on, as much to shut out the noise as to cool the car down. Also to claim some silical remove from those concrete barriers lining every lane; and beyond them, the strip malls. Could the Founding Fathers have foreseen this? That the pursuit of wealth would take the form of restaurants for eight hundred, with bulls big as the Trojan horse out front, grinning?

How far I was from home already—from the world of breast pumps and nursing bras and bag balm. For all her sisal and oatmeal, Blondie's left nipple had still cracked; leave it to Gabriela to meet this eventuality with the very ointment that vets used on cow udders. Which came in a green tin from whose side beamed an udderly (okay, okay) happy cow ringed by red roses. Who knew if it was safe for humans. In the meantime the milk ran bloody; not that Bailey seemed to mind, but Blondie had to do breathing exercises as if still in labor. In, out. Knotting her toes, watching the clock. Of course there were going to be psycho consequences, a good-breast/bad-breast split. But the bonding, and how he was gaining. La Leche said they'd never seen a baby so perfectly able to latch on from day one. Even before Blondie had milk yet, even when she was engorged, two bowling balls, he latched, he latched. My son, the best nurser in the nursery! How proud I was already, how convinced this would prove a stable personality trait that would serve him in his later years. It did not say so in any of the baby books, but even as I sat in traffic, I knew it was true. This was a predictor of great things. Call it my own great-man theory.

Brake jobs these days could run six hundred dollars; honestly, you had to wonder.

Of course the girls were jealous. How could they not be? Blondie trying to help them work through their whatever, while I managed to react with, *Well, life isn't fair.* Infuriating Blondie. *You forget you forget,* she said, *how you drive her into the arms of that horny Derek.* Whom we did discover entangled with Lizzy one night, in a state of engrossing undress. A nice boy otherwise, but still: was it time to buy a shotgun?

Though hadn't I had my own days as a horny beast, what about that Esther What's-Her-Name? The first girl to vulvate against my manhood on the dance floor. Whatever Lizzy was doing, I hoped she did not vulvate. *In this family, we let sleeping logs lie.*

A shotgun, a shotgun.

And when was Blondie returning to duty?

Ah—but now, finally, two whole lanes to choose from. You could drive in one and consider the other and feel free.

What a shame Mama Wong had no idea about Bailey. I had tried to tell her:

—*Your grandson, Mom. Your grandson.*

— *We call him Bailey, but he's a Wong, you know. Until the day he dies, a Wong.*

— *The Wong heir, even if with the wong hair.*

But all she did was grind her teeth.

Of course, what she would have said, if she did understand: *What's the matter with his hair? What's the matter with his eyes? That child is mutt.*

The office. While still in cell-phone range, I called the office. What? The bug already found, and on its way to heaven?

— Good! Great! Yes yes, do tell Marketing.

So it was okay to leave town after all; Blondie was right.

I'm so glad, sweetie. Does this mean you're surviving your day off?

Trees.

Rest stop.

Should I have married Blondie?

Trees.

And what to say to Mitchell's brother Nick? Wanting to go into business together, wanting to do up some—what? Content-management software, large-scale web-server database-type stuff. Bring some sweet access to the reams upon reams that, say, courts or Congress churned out; it'd be easy as pie, and then let the sunshine laws shine on us, right? He'd do marketing, I'd do development, Nick knew a funder. The key being your outside-the-box story, you had to learn a thing or two from these kids who had no idea how to tell a hope and a prayer from a business. For look how it paid off! All that fresh-faced ignorance, those baggy-panted skateboarders pitching VCs with their underwear showing. Think anyone'd give them a dime if they wore real pants?

Thus quoth Nick, and as I headed into the state of Maine I could almost picture myself in a loft office. Mine that high-ceilinged chaos. Mine those industrial windows. Mine those temporary partitions and half-erased white boards; mine those junk-food stockpiles, and ad hoc phones, and community futons. I was young, I wore funny pants, I let my underwear show. I never worried. For I was the future! The future was mine! Creativity! Revolution! Out-of-the-box thinking! All mine!

Trees.

I headed into the state of Maine proper.

Trees.

Distance learning, Nick was doing now, English as a Second Language. Meaning that every get-together began with pics. I did this one, I did that one. Of course he went to other countries, but truly there was no country like China. He thought I would be especially interested to hear. This one in Shanghai, this one in Xiamen.

These girls, you do not know. Truly you have not lived. Are they not beautiful?

Trees.

I kid you not.

Trees.

You would be so at home.

Trees.

They will do anything.

Could I really stand to be in business with Nick?

Truly you have not lived.

My foot tiring of the pedal. My arms tiring of the wheel. My back tiring of the seat.

The sun pulling its long foot out through the passenger window, slowly.

How much farther this drive by myself. Farther than any plane ride, which you made with fellow passengers, after all, and with certain certainties. From whence you were departing, to whence heading, at how many miles per hour, hence your estimated arrival time barring weather. How long the charge on your computer battery. No lull into which unproductive realizations might seep.

For example: *My mother slaved her whole life so that she could pay her own bill at the Overlook.*

Slaved her whole life.

Trees.

The first time I went to Maine with Blondie, her brothers dared me to swim across the pond—technically a great pond, i.e., practically a lake. And of course I accepted, could not but accept. For anyway, what was it, a mile. I'd swum a mile before, definitely. And so I plunged in. But halfway across, the wind picked up—a sudden Canadian event—the surface swells more and more monstrous until I could hardly see over them. Which was the opposite shore? On land it had been perfectly clear; but now—what a circle the pond. My goggles fogged up, yet I couldn't take them off—my contacts—the swells now waves; in fact, whitecaps. When did I realize that I was not swimming straight—that I veered to the left on my crawl? What I would have done then for lane markers! Some nice nylon rope with intermittent lozenge buoys. Had I really gone, as it seemed, in a semicircle? I tried to compensate, veering right, then switched to the breaststroke, though I barely knew how to breaststroke. So as to be able to see. No, I did not know how to breaststroke, in fact was hardly a swimmer, in fact had failed the swim test in college, almost drowned; being too embarrassed to say that I had not learned as a child. Swim lessons! What an idea. *Who need to know anything, all you need are some nice basketballs. New ones.* And of course I did not exactly spend a lot of time around pools. Until college, that is, where I finally learned. Looked at some books. Tried stuff out.

But what use the breaststroke? Why wouldn't the crawl be enough? Beware people good at the butterfly, I'd always felt. Show-offs. Now, though—here I was, heaving myself over the waves. Trying to breaststroke. Trying to stay calm. The whipped-up rhythm of the water being nothing like my rhythm; what pattern its pattern? The lake at odds, what with, was it me? How to breathe? In the sometimes air sometimes water. I battled. Resting, sometimes, on my back. Trying not to think how deep the water was.

Once upon a time my mother braved ocean and sharks, hell-bent for Hong Kong. Now her son struggled in—what?—a pond. And could I even say where I was headed, if indeed I was headed there? Gasping, wheezing, wishing I had had swim lessons. Swallowing water.

Where was the shore?

How the Baileys laughed when finally I struggled onto somebody's dock, who knew whose. From which I had to be rescued.

— What a course! We thought you were headed to Canada! they said. Or else writing something, *J* for Janie, maybe. Or maybe drawing a heart, except that somewhere around the aorta you bagged it.

And what a funny heave-ho I gave, it seemed, coming up for air. Launching myself out of the water like an orca at Sea World. Bonus points they gave me, for entertaiment. What a guy Janie'd found! Just marvelous!

Trees.

BLONDIE / I cried, years later, to hear the truth.

CARNEGIE / Blondie used to say there were fields of lupine in Maine. That one of these days we were going to go up when the lupine were in bloom.

The lupine!

More trees.

My father had been a Christian; he had had his lupine too. But for me: the trees, the trees. In the hard slant of the afternoon light, the many many trunks. So close together, they couldn't be closer. And yet—such shadows between them.

The pond!

At last, at last, the pond; the fantastical pond. It sparkled so brightly that the inside of the car shimmered and jumped with shards of reflected light. Pond genies, Blondie's sibs had called these dancing lights. They lit the car; they lit the woods. I slowed to see how far back into the woods they danced, hitting several rocks in the dirt road as a result. My car jounced hard enough to make me think, *flat*. Way back when, the Baileys had had gravel spread on the shore road, at their own expense. But the gravel had long ago washed away; now there were ruts of a scale that could not but intimidate the owner of a two-wheel-drive vehicle, especially as the drop from the road to the water was steep. Happily, the road was at least dry. Still my car tipped and lurched and bounced disconcertingly.

Half the shore from which our peninsula stemmed was undeveloped, being precipitous; the other half was now a trailer park. The trailers all had awnings, and decks with flowers on their railings; some were double-wides. A crowd of them nosed the pond, their cinder blocks set so as to cantilever them over the rocks, right to the edge of the water. I wound through the settlement, then stopped to unlock the gate to the causeway. The gate had been festooned with junk-food wrappings and empty beer cans, all ingeniously affixed with twisties and string to the metal grid. Folk art. As for what the gate blocked, other than my car—clearly nothing. I drove farther only to behold whole encampments of people and beach towels clustered on the Baileys' beach. No children today; mostly teenagers Lizzy's age and up. Gregory always claimed even the ten-year-olds around here sniffed glue; the evidence before me suggested a continued interest in chemical entertainment. A number of the kids had boom boxes, all tuned to the same loud station. That spoke to some spirit of cooperation, as did a general fondness for tattoos. Some of them leaned against the NO TRESPASSING signs. Others were casually entwined.

I honked as I drove in, more to warn them of my intrusion than to intrude on them. Lackadaisically they began to scatter, like concertgoers done with their ovation but still hearing music. Some waved. I waved back. A few gave me the finger. Others made slant eyes. One skinhead felt compelled to cup his girlfriend's near-naked breasts from behind and shake them at me; she slapped him, but still he yelled: — Eat your heart out, chink boy.

Chink boy.

This was the sort of moment when I took refuge in ownership. Shielding myself, mostly, the way my mother taught me: with the knowledge that I had a net worth several times my tormentor's. *Eat your own heart out. Let's see your tax return,* I wanted to say. Also, though, privately, I used another knowledge: that I had a white wife, with breasts many times more beautiful than the pair being flaunted.

I would have preferred not to have thought this.

Was one of these kids the jerk setting off the alarm? One guy in particular seemed to eye me with special interest—a burly dude, his entire chest and back blue-black with tattoos. He had the fantastic ears and eyebrows of a pirate; his eyes bulged bold.

BLONDIE / Billy.

CARNEGIE / For the record, I did not actually blame the locals for enjoying the beach when we weren't there. They might take their empties with them, though; and if only they would betake themselves elsewhere too, when we came to town. But how to negotiate such an arrangement?

The main cabin was dark, the alarm on RESET.

The entrance-hall walls were covered with photos of the Baileys sailing, playing tennis, building things. How many construction projects there had been over the years! The dock, the wooden canoe, the beach pavilion, the boathouse. And there I appeared, with Lizzy and Blondie, on our wedding day. How splendid a scene; I could see why the Baileys had time and again been unable to bring themselves to sell. I myself straightened a few frames up. Of course the Baileys had made relentless fun of the downtown when it got its first cappuccino machine. But how sad when the gentrification stalled! The upscale café looking emptier and emptier; the bottles of Italian syrup less and less Italian. Every year the property assessment dropped.

That was good for taxes, anyway.

How dark the living room. How empty, how cold. I started—was that somebody lurking in the corner? My chest tightened.

Still, profile in courage that I was, I turned on the lights.

BLONDIE / Of course it happened when Carnegie was gone.

I had not been to the Overlook for a while. But I had told Carnegie I would go, and so I did, Bailey and all.

Mama Wong was in bed, half covered. Asleep. She had one orthopedic shoe still on, its lace untied.

I sat down heavily. My first solo excursion since Bailey was born—already I felt drained. How was I going to get home? I peeked at Bailey. He had a snap-out car seat, but I carried him in a sling—a kind of hammock across my chest—not wanting him to become overly attached, as Wendy had, to his seat. He was not smiling yet, but he did make a smilelike face. Gas, I knew. Still I cooed, and admired his eyelashes, and marveled at his eyes. That baby stare—that measureless openness. How it opened all it fell upon; I returned its wonder wholeheartedly, then placed on Mama Wong's rolling tray a bowl full of wonton. Gingerly—my stitches. I had brought the wonton from a restaurant, and warmed them in some soup in the kitchen microwave. Of course they were not in soup now—hot soup in the room? No. But I hoped she would like the wonton themselves. Carnegie thought Mama Wong might be forgetting how to eat; Alzheimer's patients did, toward the end. If so, these might help her remember—the smell might help.

And indeed—because of the smell?—she seemed to stir. Her eyelids fluttered. Between her black lashes a crescent of white eyeball seemed to push forward, bulging yet dry. Her mouth opened; that was dry, too. Yellow teeth, dry lips. Even her gums looked dry. A rasp to her breathing. Where was the humidifier we had bought her? We had bought one, I knew. The cool-mist type, believing that the safest.

She fell back asleep, snoring. A patch of light on her shoulder grew and shrank, grew and shrank.

I closed the curtain.

My mother, when she was dying, had had old friends visit every day. They baby-sat for us kids. They made up casseroles. They brought in books, then books on tape. No one, in contrast, came to see Mama Wong. All the people who had so envied her rise now ignored her fall. There was no church service with special prayers for her, no hairdresser to make a special trip in. No son of a friend, now bigger than his mom and wearing a white coat, to offer a second opinon. Would things have been different if Mama Wong had been part of a community? If she had had more family? If she hadn't been so successful? Her first year in the home, a few people came. Some of the same people who had come to our wedding.

Now it was just Carnegie.

I was glad to be here. I was glad for this chance to care for Carnegie's mother in a way I had been unable to care for my own. I was ten when my mother died; often I wished I had been older. All I had been able to do was help brush her hair sometimes, and pick the stray hairs off her blankets and sheets. Her hair was falling out in clumps, so the picking up was a job. Which she appreciated having done, having always been fastidious—one of the reasons she had been so good at her work. *Thank you, Miss Jane,* she would say through her oxygen mask, holding my hand with both of hers. Though mine was much smaller, it seemed equal, somehow, to her two—having so much more substance. *My elf,* she said.

Now, a voice in the hall: — Help! Help! it cried. I'm stuck! I'm stuck! Help! Help!

Leaning over Bailey, I peeked out into the living room. None of the attendants had so much as glanced up. The woman had been calling this way for months—at breakfast, at lunch, at dinner.

— Help! Help! Get me out! Get me out!

Eventually she would stop. Eventually she would see rescue. Thanks to Mama Wong's longevity, Carnegie and I had seen the pattern again and again—how the shouters stopped shouting, the singers stopped singing. They missed story hour. They missed meals. Generally, they were moved then to a nursing home. You could only stay as long as one attendant, alone, could handle you. Once you needed two you had to go.

Only occasionally did a resident stay, and have hospice come. Before Corinne, Mama Wong's suite mate Ronnie had died in her room. How grateful the family had been that there were no IV tubes in the end, no extraordinary measures—that they were able to watch Ronnie waste away. Carnegie and I watched, too, as Ronnie grew thinner and thinner—shrinking to the size of premodern man, Carnegie said later. She slept all the time; her breathing became more and more labored. Her eyes opened but didn't focus, then didn't open at all. Her eyeballs rolled back into her head. Her jaw hung slack. The days were marked by the quickening and slowing of her breathing. The family gave her morphine under the tongue; the drug ran red from the corners of her mouth. Hospice turned her expertly, often; she was on a vibrating air mattress, but still wanted turning. Her fingers turned blue. Still she hung on and hung on, in a coma. Her family slept in chairs, eating candy and chips—swabbing her mouth with water. They reported on the night scene.

— There's only two people on at night, said her son Angelo. If there was a fire, there's no way they'd ever get everybody out. No way.

We shook our heads. Something we hadn't thought of.

— And that Mary Lou, you have to watch out for her, said Angelo. She wanders around at night. They found her rifling through the office files. She goes through people's pocketbooks. They found big bucks in her undies.

We shook our heads again.

Then came the changing of the nameplates. The nameplates were made of brass and hung outside the residents' room—a sign that the Overlook saw its residents as individuals, that people's loved ones were in good hands. Never mind that the plates were more substantial than the residents, and sure to outlast them.

For a while there had been no nameplate outside Ronnie's room. Then it became Corinne's room. Corinne only stayed a few months. Now her plate was gone too, and the room was empty again—the bed stripped, Corinne's walker gone. Corinne's bulletin board gone. Corinne's rocker.

— That was the rocker in which she nursed all seven of us kids, her daughter Crissy used to say. If she remembers anything, it's that rocker.

Crissy had brought it in after a workshop on stimulating the memory. That was after the workshop on safety and before the one on grieving.

Now there was a new workshop series. I cooed at Bailey as I glanced over the schedule. Its layout was cheery as an aerobics schedule at a health club.

Mama Wong opened her eyes suddenly, sat up, and said something in Sichuanese. Even over the course of a single sentence she could look alternately blank and agitated. She ground her teeth.

— I brought you some wonton, I said.

I said their name in Mandarin—*huntun.* How many times in the past Mama Wong had made shriveling fun of my Chinese. But now she seemed to be listening, trying to understand.

— *Huntun,* I said again.

— *Huntun,* she said.

There it was—a familiar edge of correction in the repetition. Then the teeth grinding. It was not clear she understood me.

— Would you like some?

No response.

— Would you like some? I asked again.

This time I crossed my hands as I asked—as best I could, with Bailey in front of me. I didn't know any Sichuanese, but Carnegie had once told me that the word for 'wonton' sounded like crossed hands in that dialect, that as a boy he had crossed his hands when he wanted wonton. He had called it a kind of Chinese sign language.

And sure enough, Mama Wong crossed her hands back, even smiled in response.

— Would you like some?

She nodded.

A smile! A nod! I was surprised how elated I felt.

I stood, helped her sit up, then pushed her tray cart in front of her, arranging the bowl and chopsticks on it. A napkin. All with Bailey hanging in front of me like a kangaroo joey. Then I sank back down, admiring him—examining the peeling skin on his hands, the hobbit hair on his ears. Both were perfectly normal, according to the doctor. How seriously Bailey studied my face. At home he could already track a black-and-white toy moved slowly across his bassinet; now he seemed to be able to track my face, too. I smiled.

— They're warm, I said. I warmed them in the microwave.

— Cold no good, Mama Wong said.

So lucid! Ignoring the chopsticks, she lifted a dumpling to her lips with her fingers.

— *Hao chi ma?* Good?

— *Hao chi,* Mama Wong answered.

She reached for another, then began to cry.

— Carnegie should bring you Chinese food more often, I said, tearing a little, too. — He should bring people to speak Chinese to you. I'll tell him when he gets home.

— Carnegie, said Mama Wong.

Her arm rested on the bed rail. Absently she swung, very slightly, her sensibly shod foot; the plastic ends of the shoelaces clicked softly as they hit the bed frame.

She dropped her dumpling. I hated to leave it on the carpet, but the thought of bending to retrieve it—impossible. Why had I boiled the wonton in soup? They'd picked up a sheen of fat, making them that much more slippery.

— Where is Carnegie?

— He had something to do. *Ta you shiqing.*

— Not coming today?

— Not today.

I placed a fresh wonton in her bowl.

— Eat, I said. Delicious.

She ignored it.

— Not coming! His old mother stuck in hotel, he is not coming to pay the bill?

— No, no, don't worry. He pays the bill.

— How much? Expensive. How much?

Her shoe stopped swinging.

— Five thousand dollars, I said.

— Five thousand dollar! Highway robbery! For one night!

— No, no. Not for one night. For one month. Or no—forty-five hundred, I think.

— Five thousand dollar! Who can afford that kind money? Nobody! Highway robbery! Who can afford that kind money?

— Have another *huntun,* I said.

Bailey was beginning to smack his lips and butt his cheek against me.

— Are you thinking about eating too? I asked him.

Settling in the chair, I prepared to nurse.

— We lived in a tall house, said Mama Wong suddenly. Way up in sky.

I thought for a moment. — A stilt house? I guessed.

— We throw things down. All kind things. Down down, into river.

— That must have been fun. What kind of things? Do you remember?

She ground her teeth and scowled. — Who can afford that kind money?

— Nobody, I sighed.

— Nobody!

An attendant appeared.

— And how are you today, Madam Wong?

Ranginna parted her hair exactly and drew it back severely, but was cheerfully flexible as she opened the curtain.

— Too sunny for you?

She closed it again with perfect equanimity.

— Look, Mama Wong, did you see? You have a new grandchild.

I lifted Bailey quickly out of his sling—just for a moment, knowing he was hungry. Supporting his head. Spittle foamed at the corners of his mouth; his onesie rode up under his tiny arms. But Mama Wong was not distracted.

— Crazy money! Crazy! Who can afford that kind money?

— Nobody.

— Nobody! Especially he marry that Blondie, all she know is spend money.

— Another *huntun*?

I started Bailey as we talked. Thanks to the cracked nipple, the left breast was not producing as well as the right; I therefore began on that side, to stimulate it with Bailey's first, hungriest sucks. But the pain—I could barely keep myself from crying out.

— Went to bathroom, said Mama Wong.

Her voice dropped suddenly—so faint, now, I could barely hear her.

— Wheelchair, she said.

— Mouth, she said.

— Not coming, she said.

— Not coming, I echoed, watching the clock.

Bailey sucked. Mama Wong grew agitated again.

— Five thousand dollar! Carnegie not coming! I know you! I know you!

She edged out of bed, picking up a *huntun* as if it were a snowball she was going to throw.

— I know you! she shouted. You are not Carnegie!

— No, I'm not Carnegie.

— Carnegie not coming! Who can afford that kind money? Nobody! Nobody! I know you! You cannot fool me. That is a doll.

She began to stand, steadying herself with the tray cart.

— Sit down, I said. Calm down. And be careful, that cart rolls. Do you want a glass of water?

— You are Blondie! yelled Mama Wong, throwing the *huntun*.

The wonton flew over my shoulder, landing on the dresser.

— Where is Carnegie? she went on. You are Blondie! Blondie! You are not Carnegie! You are Blondie!

Three more minutes. Bailey sucked.

— My name is Janie, I said, in case you've forgotten.

— I did forget.

Mama Wong did not sit down.

— Blondie, she said, short for Jane.

I almost cried.

— Thank you, I said. This is your new grandchild. Bailey.

I opened the sling a bit, so she could see. She was still standing, leaning on the tray cart.

— My name is not Mama Wong, she went on calmly. My English name is call Lucille. I am Lucille, mother of Carnegie. Next time I make sure he do his homework on time.

— Thank you, Lucille, I said.

— Is that a baby?

— This is your grandchild. Bailey.

— Bailey. *Hen ke ai,* she said—very cute.

— Your grandchild, Mama Wong, I said. Carnegie's son. He is going to carry on the Wong name.

What her reaction would have been before she got sick! But all she said now was: — Good girl. Beautiful.

Bailey sucked; I watched the clock.

— This is your grandchild. He's ten days old. His whole name is Ellison Bailey Wong. But we're calling him Bailey.

— Bailey, Mama Wong said again. Hungry.

— Yes, I said. The baby's hungry.

— What's the matter with her hair?

— He was born that way.

— Ah, said Mama Wong. Another Blondie.

— Another Blondie.

Mama Wong craned her neck to see better. She took a step, using the tray cart as a walker; her bowl and chopsticks shone in the sun.

— Beautiful, she said. Strong.

— Thank you, I said. He is strong.

— Adopted?

A surprise there.

— No, I said. He's real. Your real grandchild.

I didn't like saying it that way, but there it was. I had said it. One more minute.

— Be careful, don't lose her, she said.

— Don't worry, I won't.

— I gave babies the bottle, she said. Warm up in a pan of hot water.

— Breast milk is always the perfect temperature, I said. It's very convenient.

— Where Carnegie? Is he dead? He have bad heart, you know. Big trouble. He told me.

Such sentences! If only Carnegie were here to hear them!

— No, no, he's fine, I said. He just took a day off to—

— Day off!

— He hasn't had a day off in years, and—

— Because of you!

— That's not quite true. He took the day off—

— Who can afford that kind money?

— Nobody.

— Day off!

— He hasn't had a day off in years, and—

— You going to be the death of me!

— No one's going to be the death of anyone, I said. Sit down. Calm down. Have a *huntun*. Very delicious.

I switched Bailey to the other breast—hooray—closing up my bra flap and slipping in a nursing pad just as, instead of eating the *huntun,* or hurling it at me either, Mama Wong simply dropped it. Its white folds spread like a nun's wimple on the blue carpet as Mama Wong put one hand to her chest and slowly, heavily crumpled, knocking aside the tray cart and toppling sideways into a half-sitting heap on the bed. Her hand was not splayed, the way it is in the movies, but curled, as if she was pressing something to herself.

— Mama Wong!

I grabbed her knee with my free hand.

She rocked. Her hand left her chest; there was nothing in it. Using the bed rail, she pulled herself upright, surprising me.

— I am not your mama, she said clearly. Why is my child not here? All my life, I do everything alone. Now still I am alone.

— He's coming back, I said. Soon. In a couple of days at most.

— I am alone woman, she said. You tell the doctor. Very hard to cure, even the doctor is number one in his class.

She tried to stand up again.

— Day off! she cried. Day off!

— Mama Wong, I said. Don't stand. Sit.

I tried to pat her knee but with Bailey nursing, couldn't quite reach. She stood, unsteady, her bare foot on her loose shoelace.

— Day off!

Bailey was slowing, his body relaxing. Soon he would be asleep— as I would be too, if we were home. Having trained myself to sleep when he slept; having not slept more than four hours at a stretch in days. How heavy my body. I closed my eyes.

— I am very hard to cure even the doctor is number one in his class, Harvard Medical School, she said.

Then she fell. I opened my eyes in time to see her topple without trying to stop herself—hitting her tray cart as she crashed to the carpet. Sending her bowl sliding. I stood to help her—Bailey still nursing, with renewed interest, in the sling between us—but something was wrong. Her eyes and mouth were open; she was not breathing; she had no pulse. I pulled the emergency cord for help, but by the time I knelt again her skin was already turning cool.

Bailey left off.

Cradling him with one hand, I put my other on her heart—nothing. I kissed her on the cheek, half expecting that some reflexive indignation would jolt her back to life.

She accepted my kiss.

I stood to pull the cord again.

No one came.

Bailey fell asleep in the sling, unburped, his little chest filling, collapsing, filling, collapsing—unnaturally, it seemed. As if he were on a respirator.

Carnegie was right, I thought idly. The staff was overloaded. Overworked. Underpaid.

I ducked out of the sling, settling Bailey in a nest of pillows at the foot of the bed. Then I picked Mama Wong up—how heavy she was, weighing nothing though she did. I laid her out on her bed, above Bailey, as I hoped someone had laid my mother out. I took off her orthopedic shoe, and closed her eyes, and watched her cheeks sink—pulling the emergency cord one more time. Carnegie, Carnegie, Carnegie. Where are our cell phones when we need them? Is it really possible to die without saying good-bye to your children? I knew I should go out into the hall to get help. But instead I lay down beside Mama Wong. How bony she was—nothing but bones.

An alone woman.

I needed to rest.

Outside her live silence, the hall noise grew and grew.

9

Time

CARNEGIE /

What time is it?
What time is it?
What time is it?

I washed the body with a hospice worker. Turning, sponging, turning, sponging. The hospice worker, Cleopatra, was a short, strong woman, with a nose like her namesake but a conquering disposition of a different sort. She knew how to plant her feet and lift with her knees, glowing with a competence so equal to death that my mother, by contrast, looked deader. Her skin had no color. Her jaw hung open and would not stay shut, affording a fine view of her dental work. At least Blondie had managed to close her eyes; I was grateful for that. I was surprised how loose my mother's skin was, like a body bag that did not come in her size. I was surprised too how thin she was, and yet how heavy, being dead weight. And how little hair she had, and how little that hair covered. What a large word, 'mother'; how puny its incorporation. Like the words 'her family,' meaning me. It was at times like this that I missed having a father, but not only for myself. I missed my mother having a husband—someone for whom her body would have been a long-loved familiar, not a conglomeration of body functions in need of management until they ceased.

When I come to this country, I did not know I end up alone.

She smelled.

Apparently she had broken a rib as she fell, and punctured a lung. Everyone agreed that Blondie was in no way responsible.

— I missed her, Blondie said anyway. Why didn't I tie that shoelace? I should have put Bailey somewhere out of the way. So I could bend down.

Said Blondie: — I was the death of her.

But that honor, I believed, fell to me.

Mama Wong always claimed to have buried my father in style; I chose for her a top-of-the-line package the funeral home called The Ultimate.

How did Mama Wong's suite mate's daughter come to hear about the wake? I'd barely talked to Crissy back when she used to visit Corinne; yet how overwhelmed I was now to see her, a woman who had witnessed at least one part of my mother's decline. Distractedly, of course; she was preoccupied too, back then. Still I greeted her with excessive warmth, which she either failed to notice or graciously overlooked. I examined her too, as if she were a loved one. Taking stock, noting minor changes. I thought she looked more diminutive than she had in the Overlook, as if she'd lost weight. More elegant. She wore a dry line of corrugated lipstick and a cross complete with suffering Jesus such as you didn't much see anymore; but most notably, despite her best efforts, she radiated a somber joy. For Corinne was still alive, it turned out.

Alive!

I was glad for the news yet could not forgive Crissy for it.

— My ma started having seizures in the hospital, Crissy said. That's when they discovered she didn't have Alzheimer's after all. She had a tumor. Now they've operated, and she's better.

So someone had outlived Mama Wong. Mama Wong had not won.

— Of course, we wish there hadn't been a misdiagnosis to begin with. But Alzheimer's is tricky, as you know. There are mistakes all the time. She's coming home soon.

Did Mama Wong have a tumor too? Was that why she lasted so long? Had there been a mistake?

— I'm so sorry about your mother, said Crissy. How old was she?

— Eighty-four.

— Eighty-four. I'm so sorry. She was in the Overlook a long time.

— Nine years.

— So she went in when she was seventy-five. That's how old my mom is now. I'm so sorry.

— Thank you for coming, I said, and meant it.

Still I hated her little French suit, as she turned away. I hated her little waist and little hips, and her faith in her little gold cross—the whole little unbroken package of her. *Corinne daughter Prissy,* my mother had called her once.

I had a more reasonable reaction to my work colleagues.

— Yes, there are relatives in China, but frankly, even if we knew how to contact them, she would not have approved of their coming, I said. That is, if it meant taking time off.

My direct-reports laughed.

— Don't worry, boss, we have our laptops out in the car, they said.

And of course I laughed too. Glad they had come, even as I heard my mother's voice: *How many people care if work get done, so long as they get paycheck?*

— Just promise me one thing, Blondie had said the night before. — Promise me you won't embrace everything you once rejected now that she's dead.

— Let me guess. Gabriela read that in a book, I said. Or no. She e-mailed you an article from *Mindful Dying* magazine.

— I hope you're not going to stay this way, said Blondie.

— What way?

But of course I knew, and tried to make up for it now by squeezing her hand when she squeezed mine. I was trying in general to share my grief, even as I heard: *You watch, the day I die she is going to say, Why don't you take a workshop?*

Blondie did not suggest a workshop. However, she did scatter *Mindful Living* catalogs around the house, with the 'Living with Dying' seminars circled.

— I'm so sorry about your mother, said someone.

— Alzheimer's is the pits.

— I'm so sorry.

— You know, your mother very smart in business, never once lost money.

— Are you the son never learned one word Chinese?

— I'm so sorry.

— You think that you'd said good-bye years ago. That you'd given up years ago. Then she goes.

— I'm so sorry.

— Ah, but will your mother's death kill you? That's the question.

— Thank you, I said. Thanks for coming. It was a blessing, really. Alzheimer's is indeed the worst. Did you see the picture board? You're so right. I never did learn Chinese, it's true. Yes, I should've become a doctor. She was a hard act to follow, no doubt about it. Thanks for coming. Thank you. Did you see the baby? Bailey, yes, almost two weeks old. Yes, how wonderful she at least got to see him. Yes, blond like his mother. Thank you. Thanks for coming. Yes, we were surprised too. Thank you.

— Dad, you already thanked that person, said Lizzy, wearing, for once, a dress. — Thanking them twice is weird.

— I'm glad the coffin is closed, said Wendy. And I don't want to look in the morning, I don't care if it is our last chance ever.

— You're going to be sorry, said Lizzy. You are. Because even if we were adopted, she's still our grandmother.

— Thanks so much for coming, I said. Thank you. Thank you.

— No she isn't, said Wendy. She's not anything, she's a corpse.

The last guests to appear were our beloved neighbors Mitchell and Sonja.

— It's tough, said Mitch.

Not content to put his arm around Sonja's waist, he had his fingers tucked deep inside the twisted chiffon scarf she wore for a belt.

— My parents went one two, left me my inheritance just in time to get it eaten by the divorce, he said. Crunch, crunch. Worst period of my life.

— Thanks for coming, I said.

Mitch was wearing an earring—a little gold hoop that looked as though it ought to be hanging down, but instead was flipped up oddly.

Crissy wearing that cross; Mitch wearing that earring. What did it mean? Why was everyone wearing new jewelry? And what were we going to do with Mama Wong's? Bury it or keep it?

What should we bury? What should we keep?

What bury?

What keep?

What time is it?

It was time to stand up and speak, it was time to bow my head, my heavy head, it was time to throw the dirt. How I wished the ground was warmer; I could not believe my mother's body was being put into that cold ground. Actually that was only temporary. Her coffin was to be removed after the ceremony, and embedded in a concrete 'surround.' To ensure that the ground above the grave wouldn't buckle as the coffin rotted.

I had nodded at this information, delivered by a man with a crew cut. His hair suggesting how perfectly even the grass over the grave would be. Of course. Of course. I agreed, submitting to his aesthetic, though in truth the idea made me feel claustrophobic for Mama Wong. As if her spirit would be unable to escape. What had happened to From dust to dust?

O brave new world, that hath so much concrete in it.

Lucille, the minister kept calling her. Lucille. At the end of the service his assistant began pulling roses out of the largest of the flower arrangements, distributing them to the assembled to toss onto the lowered coffin. Blondie and Lizzy and Wendy each threw one, as did Bailey, with Blondie's help; and as did I, though I detested this scripting of my last moments by the grave. Had we asked for this? I wanted to complain to the manager: *I did not appreciate having some extra bit of mourning squeezed out of us.* I detested too the look produced: roses on shiny coffin, how Hollywood. How phony the whole thing. How I hated knowing they were going to take the coffin back out of the ground, roses and all. But this was my mother's funeral; I did not want to make a fuss.

Why you let them throw flowers? Next time tell them go to hell.

Concrete surround very useful, lawn mower can go right across. When you come visit, look all nice and neat.

Good-bye, Mama Wong.

Good-bye, Evergreen Overlook. We moved her furniture out the next day, but donated the clothes in her drawers. Both those that were hers, and those that were not hers, including the Astroturf green golf sweater. The rest of her effects fit into one box.

For some time we continued to notice funeral arrangements.

— That's The Supreme, we'd say as we passed the funeral home.

Or: — That must be the standard-package casket, really it doesn't look bad. The Value was probably indeed the best value.

— That hearse looks newer than the one we got.

— I like the gray. Mournful but fresh.

It surprised me that the world was still what it was, busy, even as it was nothing like it was. How thin daily life seemed now, like the earth's crust floating on an unfathomable ocean of magma. How fragile; I cried for its fragility. I cried for the privilege of saying, Nice day out.

— Nice day out!

— Have a good day!

— How's the family?

— What time is it?

My mother did not have many friends, but some did write:

> What a smart cookie your mother was, number two in our whole class.
>
> How proud she was when she moved into that big house.
>
> How lucky you are to get her for a mother, and not somebody else.
>
> Of course, she was rich, but still she loved plain food.

They wrote on paper I would never have thought to use myself. Massively substantial, expensive paper suitable for proclamations. Coated note cards with pine and bird motifs. Memo-pad paper.

Acquaintances wrote too, people I had never particularly noticed. A neighbor who lived, I thought, around the corner, in the house with the solar panels. The local dry cleaner. Her gynecologist. I tried to imagine myself writing to one of them about the death of a loved one, but couldn't. It was hard enough to know how to respond on the subject of my mother.

> Your mother was such a sweet and gentle woman. Her laugh was so clear and bell-like that I always wondered if she was musical. Was she musical? Did she sing in her youth?

We had boxed up Mama Wong's accumulated effects when we moved her into the Overlook, but had not actually gone through them. Seeing as she was still alive, we had simply stockpiled her stuff in one corner of the attic, as if preparing for the day she might want it again. Now we felt freer to sort and rummage and begin to reduce the pile. The attic was warm; we pored idly. Trying, as much as anything, to get used to the idea that we could. I had friends who had made discoveries when their parents died—that their parents weren't married, that their brother wasn't their brother, that their father had applied to law school ten years in a row before getting in. Mama Wong was not a writer, though. Neither, it seemed, did people write much to her; and what notebooks and letters she did have were not only in Chinese, of course, but in complicated characters, and in script. Blondie, who had learned simplified characters, could not decipher one line.

— We could find someone to translate them, she said. If you want.

That's when I announced: — I'm going to learn Chinese and read them myself someday.

— Well, who am I to say you won't, said Blondie, fluffing up her hair.

— I am, I said. I am.

I found a list of the colleges I had applied to, with a checkmark beside the ones that had accepted me. Also I found a notebook in which she had recorded her daily temperature. For birth control, maybe? It covered a number of years with not one missed day. And here were pictures of my father I'd never seen. Nothing that revealed anything I didn't already know; still I studied them. The pictures were black-and-white with wavy white margins, and mostly featured him with famous landmarks—the Statue of Liberty, the Golden Gate Bridge—looking as if he were on an all-expense-paid trip to America. He did not look like he missed his homeland and worked ungodly hours and was going to die in a senseless accident. He looked like a lucky man. A smart man, a worldly man. In several photographs he was not even looking at the camera, but at the famous landmark, appraisingly. My mother used to say he had the best English of all the Chinese students; it was just too bad he was in physics, where people could barely tell. He had longish hair, carefully Brylcreemed to resemble a car hood, or an ocean swell; a high, wide forehead that seemed an extension of that swell; and a brow almost as heavy as mine. In one picture, he stood in front of a blackboard, pointing at an equation with a bamboo backscratcher. In another, he held me, beaming as if I had just been handed to him from behind curtain number three. *Just what you've been waiting for—a brand-new baby boy!* In yet another, he stood arm in arm with my mother; how naturally the ripples of her permed hair seemed to emanate from his grander heave.

I wished now more than ever that I had known him. He was not a desperate refugee like my mother; he was also from Sichuan, but he had come to America in the forties, before the war, for graduate work. On a fellowship. He had, in fact, had his choice of fellowships, my mother used to say, offers from all the number-one schools. If he had lived, I might have grown up a faculty brat; as I tried to imagine sometimes. Sometimes I tried to imagine a whole different life—the grad-student baby-sitters, the department scandals, everyone knowing your name and IQ.

Instead I grew up my mother's son. *Of course I was worry about those sharks,* she admitted. *But in my heart, I know they will leave me alone.* She was just lucky that both her basketballs kept their air until the end of her swim, and that she happened to have that cousin to help her once she reached Hong Kong. As for why she had to leave: *I ate so many chili peppers when I was little. Make me too spicy for those Communists. A spicy girl.*

Was she too spicy for my father? Was he too bland for her?

— Your father had Ph.D., she told me once. He was scholar. Also he was citizen.

— Is that why you married him? I asked.

— I could see he was going to be success, she said. Many man are citizens, but not all are the success type.

— And what did he think about that?

— He didn't care why I loved him, she laughed. So long as I married him and not someone else.

— Was there someone else?

— He wanted me to marry him, she said. That's all.

— He loved you.

— He loved me, yes. It was as if he opened a book, and there was my name. Period. He liked my cooking. Remind him of home.

— And you? Did you have a book like that?

She laughed again.

— Me! I never care too much about what is inside book. If you ask me, a book is just someone make joke. Write everything one way. In fact, life is all kind of way. Not just one way. If you ask me, did I marry him, sure. But can I marry someone else? If you ask me, my answer is again, sure.

Now I studied the pictures and thought I could see, in that picture of the two of them, how he was pulling her arm in toward him. Maybe it meant nothing that he not only clenched his right elbow to his side, locking her forearm against his body, but grasped her wrist with his free hand as if to make absolutely sure she would not slip away. Her arm, caught though it was below the elbow, was hardly bent; her body too swung away from him, as did the wrinkly mass of her hair, and her gaze. She looked as though she was trying to glimpse something just around the corner. Maybe it meant nothing. Still I could not help but notice that this was the one picture in which my father did not look as if triumph was once again his.

— I wouldn't make too much of it, said Blondie. It's only one picture.

But she also said: — It really is too bad you don't have a brother or a sister or an aunt or uncle to ask.

And: — You never trusted her, did you.

— No, no, I did, I said. Of course I did.

But another day I had something else to show her—how many new clothes my mother had bought but never worn. Slacks, shirts, cashmere sweaters. As if she was saving them for something, or thinking about returning them. She typically pinned the receipt to the inside of the garment.

— I felt that way sometimes, I said. Like something that might just get returned.

— And here I feel that way too, said Blondie. What a coincidence.

BLONDIE / In the beginning he received much sympathy. Is there a word for the satisfaction of a pain people understand? His misery connected him, in the beginning, to others.

As the months wore on, though, he was more and more alone.

CARNEGIE / The world buzzed; deals were struck; other people died. I became a death bore. Mr. Memento Mori. *You too,* I wanted to say. *You, and I, and everyone. Everyone.* The world, which not long ago had seemed divided between those who had kids and those who did not, was now obviously divided between those who had lost a parent and those who had not. And what had I to say, really, to those who had not? I could not converse with them.

You don't know. You don't know.

You can't know.

You, and I, and everyone.

I took more family time now. I helped Wendy build an igloo, a wigwam. I learned to distinguish between butterflies and moths, alligators and crocodiles, sea lions and seals. I went on a camping trip with her class and pulled a kid out of a stream.

I helped Lizzy memorize Shakespeare. *The quality of mercy is not strained.* We went bowling. Took up Rollerblading. Looked up countries in the news in an atlas. How far off China seemed! Much farther than I'd realized. How I wished I had gone back to China with my mother while she could go; I vowed to at least take the kids again sometime.

I spent time with Bailey. Getting up with him at night, so that Blondie could sleep. Playing earthquake with him. Taking him for walks in his Snugli. I gave him massages. Brushed up on my lullabies. Kept Kodak in business. Every day he seemed to do something new.

Learned to hold his head up. Reared up on his arms like a lion. Rolled over from his back to his stomach. Babbled, babbled, babbled.

How much we had to say to each other!

I tried to live so I would have no more regrets. Daily, I asked myself, *Is this living? Am I alive?*

Outside of the nursery, I ceased singing. To the relief of all around me.

I agreed to go into couples therapy. One might not think it would cost one hundred dollars an hour to rid me of the idea that I had killed my mother by taking a day off. However, it did. My other theory was that I had killed her by sending Blondie. That was expensive too, as was Blondie's idea that she'd killed my mother by closing her eyes.

— I miss things, she said. It runs in the family.

I took up Chinese. I didn't have the wherewithal to take a class, but I did locate some great software. I vowed to memorize five characters a night, beginning with my name: *Guangfu*—Vast Riches. Blondie helped me copy the characters when I had questions about the stroke order and, though it wasn't my focus, insisted I learn to pronounce the words I was learning. *Tian*—sky. *Da*—big.

— Let's get a tutor. We can study together, she said. You can learn, I can review.

We embarked on a search. In the meanwhile I began checking in with a number of sites on the Internet, and was surprised how Chinese this made me feel.

— There's Han Chinese, I said. Hong Kong Chinese. Mainland Chinese. Overseas Chinese. And now, ladies and gentlemen: Internet Chinese.

— Dad, said Lizzy, replenishing the printer paper. — There is not!

— Ah, but look at me, I said. Exhibit A. Descended from the noble Hypertext family, which dates back—scout's honor—to the late twentieth century.

— You're hogging the computer, complained Wendy.

— You're being funny, complained Lizzy.

— I'm getting in touch with my heritage, I said. The question is, How does anyone get in touch with himself without the computer?

— I hope that's rhetorical, said Lizzy.

I pulled Chinese poems off a poetry site:

> And after you're gone, nothing left to do,
> I go back and sweep the fishing pier.

I was surprised by the purity and beauty of the lines and considered putting some on Mama Wong's tombstone:

> Spring now green, you lie in empty woods,
> still sound asleep under a midday sun.

My mother, though, was not Internet Chinese. She was a Sichuanese businesswoman who always got a good return on her dollar. I decided not to put poetry on her gravestone, given that she'd probably have preferred a copy of her tax return from the year of her highest net income.

Poetry has no use, that I can tell you.

Still I felt a connection to the Chinese words I found hard to express. All that suggestion. All that reticence, and economy, and melancholy.

What kind of person look like suddenly China-crazy? Not Chinese people. Not real Chinese.

I pulled poems up all the same. Western poetry too, poems I remembered from my romantic youth:

> Mother, your master-bedroom
> Looked away from the ocean.

And:

> It happens that I am tired of my feet and my nails
> and my hair and my shadow.

And:

> so many things seem filled with the intent
> to be lost that their loss is no disaster.

But it was the Chinese poetry that spoke to me, somehow.

As if read Chinese poetry make you Chinese!

BLONDIE / How I loved seeing him interested in poetry again! As at odds as it seemed with his ironic grown-up self.

A replacement for his singing, perhaps?

He read me things sometimes.

— Beautiful, I would say. Beautiful. Read me more.

Then one day I said: — I feel a kinship to it, too.

— Do you, he said.

— I love how it makes you slow down. How it puts you in the moment.

— How it puts you in the moment, he said.

— I know that sounds New Age.

— It may put you in the moment, he said. But I know this whole way of thinking. I recognize it.

CARNEGIE / I could hear my voice rise with an impatience and insistence that surprised me.

Said Blondie slowly, then: — It's in your blood.

— Yes.

— Well, she said. And suddenly she sounded like her father: — So then what does this mean? In your view?

I found a new batch of photos one day. The people in these pictures mostly wore Chinese dress, but a few of the younger men wore Western. They had shiny hair and shiny faces, and a certain swagger. Who was who? I tried to remember things my mother had said over the years, but all I could recall was that most of her family was dead. That she had lost all three of her brothers—or were they half brothers?—in the War Against the Japanese. Were they the swaggerers? I recalled too that her father had died early—was he one of the older, gowned men?—and that though the women in her mother's family used to live to be a hundred, her own mother—one of the women?—had died young too, of grief and poverty. She was not even my grandfather's wife, exactly, but a love wife—a concubine—his favorite. I remembered too that my grandfather was a scholar turned chile merchant, and that once he died his family turned my grandmother out of the house. But more than that I could not remember.

Blondie said that if I had been a girl, I would know everything, and who knew but that she was right. Much as I hated all things New Age, I began in any case to meditate, at her suggestion, to see if that would help my recall. I kept a small notebook by the side of the bed at night, and carried another around in the daytime, in case things came back to me.

Omm. Omm.

This did seem to help, slightly. Only what came back were not stories about my family in China so much as images of my childhood here: Of my mother, young and preoccupied. Of the powdered milk we drank, not being able to afford fresh. I remembered the peaches my mother brought home for us one day—two beautiful, enormous peaches, not one for her and one for me, but both to share, one that day and one the next. One had a bruise; she insisted on eating that part. I remembered the taut give of their fuzzy skin; I remembered their thick smell and their juicy flesh and, inside, those strange red-ridged cups that had held the rutted pits. So close had they grown, the pits and the flesh, so completely had they fit themselves to each other; and yet look how they came apart, just like that, there on our melamine cup saucers. The saucers my mother had bought cheap to use as small plates, and were still in good shape. They weren't like our larger plates which, having doubled as cutting boards, sported dark brown cross-hatching in their centers. Across the table our gray metal fan turned and turned its head, like the radar on a warship. How hot the apartment we lived in! In the summer of course, but in the winter too. It was because we lived on the top floor, my mother always said. Anyway, it was better to be too hot than too cold, and how lucky we were to have a window. We left it open until the heat was turned off in the spring, never imagining how cold a house we would someday live in, when finally we were rich enough to buy a house, but not rich enough to take our eye off the gas meter.

Every day was full of struggle, but it was struggle with a purpose. My mother beat me, it was true—with rulers or with belts, she was flexible that way—but that too gave a meaning to things. Made me part of the plan.

Or so I tried to explain to Blondie. I tried to convey to her the long days into evenings my mother worked keeping books—she had to, having two jobs. I tried to convey how anxiously I waited, alone in the apartment after school. How I leapt to my feet when I heard her marching up the steps. Even at eleven o'clock at night she would march up as if she were just starting her day; and then it was time for one more accounting. She beat me if I had dropped by a certain friend's house, say, and lied about it. She beat me if I had been caught stealing candy. She beat me if I had handed my homework in late, or gotten a B in math.

— Oh, honey, said Blondie.

My mother never talked about her day, or her past, or my father, I explained. We never wondered what life was, or if we were happy. The apartment was too hot; that's what we knew. We were tired of listening to our neighbors fight. We desired a whole peach each.

— Of course you did, said Blondie.

— In a way we were lucky, though. *This is a big life,* my mother once said, after we moved. She walked around the house counting the windows, and said, *So many people have no story; we have a story. A big life, a big story. Every day going up up up! In a way we are very lucky.*

Blondie was quiet a moment, then said: — Those were holy days.

— Not to romanticize, I said.

— Still. They were holy.

— We were making money.

— It can't have been fun, being that poor.

— No.

— But life was simpler. Harder but simpler. Like life on a farm.

— Exactly. It was our Wisconsin, I laughed. We didn't need voluntary simplicity, seeing as how we had involuntary simplicity. Speaking of which, I've been meaning to tell you. There was a woman living in one of the cabins in Maine. Did I tell you?

— Really, said Blondie, drawing back.

— Her name was Sue.

— Not Mr. Buck's great-granddaughter?

— You knew, I said.

— The famous Sue, said Blondie. Is that Bailey?

I filled her in as we headed for the nursery.

— A sighting! she said, tugging on the shade; light flooded in. — And a daughter. Living in our house, no less. Well well well. What's this?

Bailey was rocking on his hands and knees, banging his head against his crib bumper.

— Are you crawling? she cooed. Did you crawl all the way up the crib?

BLONDIE / How proud we were! But worried, of course, about the head banging.

CARNEGIE / Through a condolence note I discovered that the legendary relative who had once welcomed my wet mother to Hong Kong was still alive. I wrote back for contact info, and received in time the man's every coordinate, including an e-mail address. Enabling me to notify him of my mother's death.

BLONDIE / This was how, months after the funeral, Carnegie suddenly discovered that his mother had left a will.

— I thought all her money went to her Overlook bill, I said.

— She didn't leave money, said Carnegie.

The family book, it seemed, was a family history, all in Chinese, which Mama Wong had somehow sent to this cousin in Hong Kong.

CARNEGIE / Chinese families kept these kinds of records, I knew. In the olden days, the very first thing a man did, if he became rich, was commission an update to his family book. Some of these went back for dynasties; some of them were a thousand pages or more. I knew it, and yet: For my family to have such a book! I couldn't believe it. I thought of the notebooks I'd been trying to fill for years. I thought of the pictures I'd pored over. All that was fine. But now this; this was something else.

— It's going to be in Chinese, warned Blondie.

— I don't care if it's in Lithuanian, I said. Do you realize what this is?

The will, we found out, was written some five years ago.

— But five years ago, your mother already had Alzheimer's, said Blondie. Is it valid?

A good point. The will was not a valid legal instrument. Mama Wong was, after all, officially demented when she wrote it. Mama Wong had, what's more, not had it witnessed. Mama Wong had simply written down her wishes, half in Chinese and half in English, and sent them, via sea mail, to this relative in Hong Kong.

But legality, as it happened, was not the issue. Legal or illegal, the fact remained that Mama Wong had left the family book to Wendy—the only real Chinese in the family, as she called her—

BLONDIE / So Mama Wong had understood Wendy came from China!

CARNEGIE / —on one condition: that the children be brought up by a relative of mine.

BLONDIE / The one we didn't meet, from Shandong—Mama Wong's father-in-law's sister-in-law's great-niece. How had Mama Wong even come to know of her existence? Never mind. Her last name was Lin. Her father was from Suzhou.

CARNEGIE / We were instructed to sponsor said relative, apparently an orphan, to come live with us as a nanny for an unspecified number of years. Wrote my dear mother:

> That way the children will at least speak Chinese, not like Carnegie.

— Do we even know this orphan wants to come? asked Blondie. And: — Isn't there some way around this?

We probed and queried, but our stalwart Hong Kong relative was, in his e-mails, quite adamant. He wrote:

> I myself am an attractive widower who nonetheless never remarried subsequent to a vow I made to my wife on her deathbed. As she died, I promised her I would never lay eyes on another woman, and I haven't. Eyes, or anything else, I might add. Moreover, I gave up beer and ice cream subsequent to a vow I made to my mother, on her deathbed. You may think this

> strange, but I do not mind at all. It gave her peace of mind to have a guarantee I would take care of my health in her absence. People always like guarantees, don't you find? It's human nature. Whenever I see people drinking I think of that guarantee and feel a kind of peace in my heart myself.

We wrote back. In another long e-mail Mr. Peace-in-His-Heart explained that he did not care whether Mama Wong was demented or not.

> Her brilliant mind was obviously clear as a bell when she wrote the will. If you were to behold the writing, you would be astounded; it is so perfectly intelligible. I would be happy to fax you a copy. And behold the fact that she managed to get the letter posted. Behold the fact that she to all appearances recalled the address from memory, making only one small mistake, on the apartment number. Instead of 726, she wrote 762. Now are you not mightily impressed? I myself was mightily impressed.

— We could use someone new, I said.

BLONDIE / Our present live-out, Leesa, was completely unreliable, it was true. Bailey liked her, but she called in sick when her cat disappeared. She called in sick when her boyfriend came to town. She called in sick when she had a headache.

On the other hand, the live-in stories! We had a friend who hadn't cooked a thing since her dear Lucy came. And we ourselves had had an absolutely perfect Chinese sitter one year, when the girls were young—Ying, her name was. All our friends said how present she was.

But there was also the nanny who stole the baby's clothes. There was the nanny whose ex-boyfriend stalked her. There was the nanny who hid booze everywhere.

Of course, Lan—her name was Lan—wouldn't be a regular nanny. As for how to sponsor her, Carnegie said that we could bring her in as a student.

— It can be arranged, he said.

I wished I could say no. But even now, when I closed my eyes, I sometimes saw Mama Wong falling, falling.

— A second wife, I said. Only your mother.

— What second wife?

— Only your mother, I said, would send us, from her grave, the wife you should have married.

PART II

10

Trying to Be Happy

BLONDIE / How could a collection of pages have meant so much? Not even an actual book, but the promise of one—a promise sent by e-mail. Who even knew if there was such a book? And this Mr. Peace-in-His-Heart! Sometimes I pictured Mama Wong fresh from her harbor swim. I pictured her dripping wet, her basketballs still in her arms, buzzing her relative's apartment from downstairs. What sort of person would simply say, *Come up?* And would not such a person be capable of other help? Of even agreeing, perhaps, to contact her son after her death—promising him this family book though there was, in fact, no book? Though there was, in fact, only her determination, fierce as the determination that got her off the Mainland, to replace her daughter-in-law with someone more to her liking?

— I believe this is called paranoia, said Carnegie.

Never mind the million-dollar incident. Never mind the promise that turned into *What million dollars? As if I had a million dollars.* He believed what he wanted to believe.

Of course, there could be a book. I believed that, too. But

Carnegie would believe nothing else. He believed not only that there was such a book, but that he had an obligation to get hold of it—that it would be unnatural to keep such a book from being passed from generation to generation.

I understood this, in one way.

And yet I asked: — What if it is simply a list of names you cannot read?

He admitted that some of these books said a bit about each family member, but that some did not—that some were simply genealogies.

And if his was simply a genealogy he could not read—would that not make him feel, more than anything, plain American?

I tried to ask this gently, but still Carnegie was upset.

— Is that how your family keepsakes make you feel? he demanded. Plain American? How about your Grandma Dotie's empty boxes?

— I'm sure I would feel differently about them if we had to have some German relative move in with us for years.

— It's all I have, he said. I have no sisters, no brothers, no uncles, no aunts. I am as on a darkling plain. Of course the book matters to me. I have no family.

— What about your children? What about me? Aren't we your family?

He paused, then said: — I hazard you know what I mean.

And, of course, I did.

He kissed my neck.

— Don't worry, he murmured. I'm sure this woman will remind me of my mother. And think what it will mean one day to the *bambini*. Bailey especially, but the girls too. To know where they might have come from. Trust me. This book, this nanny will have zilch effect on our marriage.

But already they were affecting our marriage—already I felt his unwillingness to defend us against his mother's scheming. And the intensity of his desire—already he seemed to have half left us. He might as well have been having an affair.

Leave it to Mama Wong, to prove more powerful dead than alive!

Wrote Gabriela in an e-mail:

i would feel abandoned too, but maybe you should give him time. maybe he's still in mourning, that's all. i think i read somewhere how being in mourning and being in love are a lot more alike than you'd expect.

To which I responded:

What about the second wife? Should I let her come?

Gabriela:

do you have a choice? i'm not sure you have a choice.

The will did seem to have precipitated some new phase of mourning. Carnegie was more closed off now than when his mother first died.

— All I wanted, you know, when my mother was alive, was to get away from her, he said one day. — All I wanted was to be free.

— And now that you're free . . .

— I freely chain myself to her.

He laughed at the irony of it—a hopeful sign. Still he spent hours, now, chatting on the Internet with people who had family books.

CARNEGIE / How many volumes would it be? What color? And what would the pages be like? Would they be rice paper? Would they be conventional pages bound into a conventional book? Or those horizontal scroll-like sheets I had heard about, folded in half and bound with silk thread? Would it need restoration? Would I understand its dating? Apparently the Chinese used a Byzantine system involving intersecting ten- and twelve-year cycles, which began anew with each emperor. Or so said one chat-room buddy. Luckily another volunteered that there were tables converting the Chinese system into ours, which you could buy easily enough in Chinatown.

BLONDIE / How long this obsession hung over us!

Eventually, though, he began to obsess less. Eventually he became more peacefully convinced that the book would be his—developing, finally, some of the focused ease of faith. This was in one way lovely. In another, it was disconcerting. His certainty was so substantial that he could almost have stood it, in place of the book to come, on the bookshelf. He had only, he believed, to be patient.

CARNEGIE / And, of course, to secure the iffy cooperation of my wife.

BLONDIE / — Our family will always be our family, he reassured me.

— Will it?

— And you will always be my Blondie.

We made love that night, and again at dawn—having fallen asleep naked, without brushing our teeth, curled up together like newlyweds. We were, miraculously for our age, not tired. Still we kissed ourselves back to sleep for a while before the alarm rang—how loudly! And in the bathroom mirror, there we were—flushed rose, still. How mottled, I. How even-toned, he. Happy.

Was this not love?

Our family will always be our family.

I thought of his words some months later as I e-mailed Gabriela:

The girls are no longer quite mine.

and why do you say that? she replied.

Last night Wendy said, "Lanlan is like us. She just is, I can't explain it. Lanlan understands everything, even if you don't tell her. She can read our minds."

and lizzy?

Lizzy says she honestly would not be surprised to find out Lan was her real mother. "Lanlan gets things," she says. "Like she always asks what the other kids think, and doesn't say things like why do you care. Plus she knows a fake when she sees one."

i can see why you're worried.

WENDY / Lanlan teaches us Chinese, starting with *Ni you mei you Zhonguo pengyou?*—Do you have any Chinese friends? That's weird.

But pretty soon she figures out what works. She gives us all Chinese names, to begin with, which we sort of had already, Dad says, I guess his mom gave us some. Except nobody can remember what they are, that's why Lanlan has to give us new ones, and why she has to teach us to write them. So we won't forget. I am *Wenli,* meaning culture strength. Lizzy is *Zili,* meaning self strength—independent. Bailey is *Baili,* white strength. Also she figures out all about us. Like she asks whether or not I like Ping-Pong. And do I like to draw pictures? And do I like to sing songs? I like learning to grind Chinese ink with an inkstone, and to paint bamboo with a Chinese brush, and I can make a bunch of paper animals myself now, like a panda bear, and a frog, and a phoenix. Sometimes I teach Lanlan chess while Lanlan teaches me Chinese, we can talk about the Sicilian defense for like hours.

I like hearing Chinese versions of stories we know. Like 'Little Red Riding Hood,' only with a soldier hero who gets the grandma back out of the wolf's stomach, and who doesn't shoot the wolf but tames him instead, so that by the end everyone is friends. And there are Chinese versions of songs we know too. Like 'Frère Jacques' turned into

> Two-oo tigers, two-oo tigers.
> How fast they run,
> How fast they run.
> O-ne has no ea-rs,
> O-ne has no tail.
> Ver-y strange. Ver-y strange.

Mom doesn't like that song because it calls the tigers strange, she says she doesn't like all the talk about strangeness.

BLONDIE / The Chinese had so many charming expressions involving the word 'strange.' For example, *guai wu,* 'strange animals'—meaning foreigners.

WENDY / But Dad doesn't care, he's just glad that whatever Lanlan's teaching, it's Chinese. He thinks it's good for us, Bailey especially, not that it's not important for me and Lizzy too. But it's like he wants everybody to be at least a little Chinese, and me and Lizzy have the black hair. He doesn't have to worry as much about us, we're not in danger of turning total Baileys.

— I want Bailey to be Bailey Wong, he says. Not Bailey Bailey.

Still Mom says she doesn't like that song, she doesn't like calling things strange. Not that Mom doesn't find as many things strange as Lanlan does, Lizzy says, she just doesn't think it's nice to say so.

— And which is worse? says Lizzy.

Lizzy is all excited because of her boyfriend Russell who's into music too, although not exactly Chinese music, obviously. He's more into stuff like Korn, and Creed, and Rage Against the Machine, and Lenny Kravitz. He's a senior and plays the guitar—like seriously, Lizzy says. Also he fades his own jeans instead of paying like two hundred dollars for somebody else to fade them, and he can borrow his parents' car whenever he wants, because they have three. Lizzy says Russell wants to live in a cabin and catch his own food and not see anyone he doesn't want to. Meaning like he just wants to see Lizzy, and the guys in his band, and maybe Lizzy's best friend, Xanadu, who's going out with the drummer.

— I don't think you'd like catching your own food, I say.

Of course that just makes Lizzy roll up her sleeves to look at her henna tattoos as if my saying that is making them smudge or something.

But then she says: — I could never gut a fish.

She's shivering a little. It's getting cold out.

— You'd probably have to eat squirrels, I say.

And for a while we sit there and watch the goat run across the yard. It's misty down near the woods, there are these cold pockets, so all you can see is hooves going kick kick kick in the fog. Of course he's not supposed to be out but there he is anyway, oh well. We let him run. And that makes us feel like sisters in a way—that we both sit there and see that and just sit some more. Because we know he'll come back, Tommy always comes back.

— Squirrels, ugh, says Lizzy.

We laugh.

I like the Chinese songs because it's like doing everything I did when I was little, only different. It's like growing up again, only someplace like Russell is talking about, where there is no Elaine.

— You're Chinese! says Elaine when I come to school. —You're Chinese!

— I'm Chinese American, what are you? I say.

That's what my mom says I should say, first of all because plain Chinese means you don't really live here, like Lanlan, and of course I live here. Also I think it's supposed to confuse the other person a little and make them not sure what to say back.

But Elaine doesn't get confused.

— I'm real American, she says.

We're supposed to talk about our roots in school so the first thing she says when she raises her hand in circle time is: — Wendy is from China.

— Thank you, Elaine, please allow Wendy to tell us where she is from herself, says Miss Tobey. And then she says: — Wendy. Where are you from?

But I don't say anything, it's just like they say on my report card, sometimes I don't say anything.

— She isn't saying anything! says Elaine. She knows how to talk but she doesn't talk! She's shy!

— Thank you, Elaine, that's enough, says Miss Tobey.

— I'm not shy! says Elaine. I'm outgoing!

— Thank you, Elaine, says Miss Tobey again, and this time you can see how her head twitches to the side when she's mad.

— I'm outgoing and that's a good thing in America because if you don't get yours nobody is going to get it for you! says Elaine.

— If I have to thank you one more time, says Miss Tobey, you are headed to Think Tank.

Miss Tobey told Mom we're going to do a whole unit on China soon, everybody's excited except me.

BLONDIE / — You're not proud? I asked her.

She shook her head no.

— It's that Elaine, isn't it, I said.

She looked at her knees.

— I'm going to talk to Miss Tobey.

— Don't, she begged then. I mean it.

We sat in her bedroom surrounded by Chinese slippers, Chinese paper cuts, Chinese dolls, Chinese brush paintings. She had a Chinese birdcage and a Chinese cricket cage. She had a Chinese silk quilt embroidered with bats.

CARNEGIE / Concentrating the chinoiserie in the adopted children's bedrooms: a classic mistake.

BLONDIE / But Lizzy in a fit one day had bequeathed her Chinese everything to Wendy. So there it all was in her room.

CARNEGIE / A veritable Chinatown tchotchke shop.

BLONDIE / Of course, there were non-Asian items also. Besides the stuffed panda, there were many other stuffed animals. Books. Wendy's upstairs chessboard, on which she was playing a game against herself. That being the sort of thing Wendy could do—take both sides of something, and play it right out.

How unlike her sister Lizzy!

— I'm sorry you're not excited, I said.

She shrugged.

I wanted to cry. How could she not be excited?

CARNEGIE / Had we not, after all, done Chinese lanterns and Chinese dragon races and Chinese dumplings since she was two? Chinese culture camp? The Chinese Community Center? We subscribed to the *Families with Children from China* newsletter. And how mightily we had strived to build her self-esteem, to give her 'tools for her tool kit.' Did we not balance our checkbook on the abacus? Find the girls Asian dolls? Provide them with multiracial crayons?

BLONDIE / We had not gone so far as to move to Chinatown, the way some people had. But I wasn't the one who resisted that idea. It was Carnegie who laughed and claimed to hear the voice of his mother.

China-crazy those people are.

CARNEGIE / What one week with Mama Wong would have done to them.

BLONDIE / And yet we had seriously talked about moving, way back when—wanting to do something, anything for this child who cried all night in her sleep. We could never have imagined that, before Wendy—that a child could sob as she slept. It went on for months. If we had believed Chinatown would feel like China to her, we would have moved.

Sometimes at night I still woke up, thinking I heard crying. Sometimes I still entered her bedroom, and put my hand on her warm bony back, thankful for the even peace of its rise and fall. I was thankful it no longer heaved and shuddered as it once did, night after endless night. Wendy's window looked out onto the yard—slightly bowed, the land glowed in the dimmest moonlight like something rising. How thankful I was for that, too. What a blessing to have something to gaze on, in those long hours.

— You're not going to have to speak Chinese in front of your classmates, I said now. If that's what you're worried about.

She arranged some dark polished stones on her desk, placing them, one at a time, in a shiny line.

— Though I bet they've never known anyone their age who spoke Chinese, I said.

— I knew you were going to say that.

She messed up her arrangement.

— I'm sorry. You don't have to. I mean it.

Wendy stared at the stones. In their shiny curved surfaces I could see her thin face reflected over and over.

I had not meant to push her. Yet I hadn't wanted to reinforce her shyness, either. It was hard to follow my instincts with Wendy. For example, my instinct now was to hug her. Yet I did not, as she had never really liked hugging, just as she had not, when she first came to us, liked being held in our arms and gazed at. I had anticipated attachment problems—I had read that I should carry her all day in a Snugli, facing in. But I had also read that I should follow the baby's lead; and she so strongly preferred to be laid down in her crib. Or better yet, to be strapped into her car seat, the molded part of which snapped out and rocked. This sort of seat was really designed for infants—I never intended for her to spend hours in it. But apparently it felt familiar to her. And gaining weight as slowly as she did, once she came to the States, she fit in it longer than most children.

Back in the Chinese orphanage, in an unsupervised moment, we had glimpsed a brown room full of green plastic chairs with straps. Could our Wendy really have been strapped into such a chair? We told ourselves that the children were probably strapped into the chairs to keep them from crawling on the floors, which were broken tile and concrete. Why would they have done that to our Wendy? Who, though supposedly ten months when we adopted her, was not yet crawling. We told ourselves, too, that though the foster mother worked in the orphanage, Wendy, theoretically, had not lived there. Our Wendy, theoretically, had lived in the foster mother's home.

Yet Wendy loved the rocker seat, and plastic seats in general.

That changed once she was vertical. *My third leg,* I called her then. How she clung to me! And how happy we were about that—how relieved. So much so that I sometimes wondered if we didn't in small ways encourage the clinging—wanting to fill her with the warmth we felt she had missed.

Did that make her shyer than she would have been anyway?

I gently touched, now, her knee.

— I mean it, I said again.

She took her knee back for herself—staring, still, at the stones. Her hair curtained her face. Her back curved, as if she was trying to make herself into a stone, too.

— I hate doing stuff in class, she said. I hate even raising my hand.

— I know, I said, resisting the impulse to draw aside the curtain. I talked through it instead, as if to a priest in a confessional. — If you'd like, I'd love to come into class and do something.

— And do what? she said. Talk about that car accident?

— How about Chinese New Year? I said. And how do you even know about the accident?

WENDY / — Lizzy told me, I say. Was it a secret? Lizzy says a lot of things are secret in this house.

— It is not a secret, says Mom. We just try not to dwell on unpleasant things.

— How come?

— We are trying to be happy, says Mom.

— Lizzy says you talk about all kinds of things behind our backs, I say. She says you talk about us.

— Of course we talk about you, says Mom. We talk about how you're doing. What your teacher had to say and so on.

— But what do you say?

— Next time I'll write it down, says Mom. Okay?

— You're going to forget.

— You know I might, she sighs. I forget a lot of things these days, that's why I take this herb, you know, this gingko? For my memory. Also I'm pretty busy. But I'll try.

— That's not why you'll forget, I say.

BLONDIE / I heard Lizzy then, in Wendy. Second children were double-voiced that way.

— In the past, I said, I would have just said I won't forget. I wouldn't have burdened you with how hard it will be for me to remember. How many things I'm juggling. Whether I get enough sleep. That's the kind of thing we keep from you. Do you understand?

She clicked her stones against one another while I tried to forget some of the things I was juggling. For example, her little brother's ear infections—how many ear infections he had! And that interview with—what—some business magazine, in which I was asked three times whether our firm wasn't first and foremost about profit. Could I deny that the social-responsibility angle was just a way of differentiating ourselves from other funds? Could I deny that it was just marketing?

Could I?

— It isn't exactly being phony, I said.

— But there's other stuff, too, right? That you don't say?

It was chess, too, that taught her to lay traps.

— Yes, I said. I suppose there is.

— Hmm, she said. Here.

She dropped some stones then, still warm from her hand, into mine. I caught them with surprise. At closer range, by different light, I could see that the stones bore fingerprints—Wendy's or my own, or both. How soft they felt, too, I was surprised how soft. Perhaps because they were warm?

WENDY / Mom rubs my knee the way she likes to for some reason, it's like she's polishing a doorknob.

— Thanks, she says. She tucks my hair around my ears so it's out of my face, then says: — Do you want Lan to come to your class instead? Lan can come instead.

— No, I say.

That makes her look so relieved I feel sorry for her.

— Lanlan says nobody in China does the New Year's plate like we do, I say. She says they don't do hot pot either, or at least not like we do, where everything means something.

— Well, that's what they did in Dad's family.

— Lanlan says no one in China eats fortune cookies.

— We can forget about the whole thing if you like.

— Okay, I say.

— Fine, she says, playing with the stones I gave her.

— Okay, I say again.

But while Mom can forget about it, Elaine never will.

— We're going to do a China unit! she says. Every time she sees me she says: — We're going to do a China unit! Are you going to talk Chinese for everybody? Everybody's waiting for you to talk Chinese!

I'm picking up Chinese like gangbusters just like Mom says, already I can speak better than Lizzy and Mom too, and of course Bailey, who can't talk. Mom says half the time she can't even understand what Lanlan and me are laughing about, she says it's because I heard all that Chinese as a baby.

Now Lizzy's jealous.

— No speaking Chinese! she yells sometimes, and grabs Lanlan's arm and pulls her real close. — No private jokes! No speaking Chinese!

But when we don't talk Chinese, Mom's as upset as Lizzy. Because sometimes we hang around and don't even have to talk. It's like Lanlan knows what I'm thinking anyway, and like I can feel how she's feeling too, especially if she's feeling sad.

— What are you lovebugs doing? Mom asks if we're hanging around like that. Like if I have my arm around Lanlan, or if I'm playing with her hair. Or if we're just sitting doing nothing, letting the day come, or the night.

— Lovebugs, enough! she says. And I mean enough!

BLONDIE / I always thought the Chinese so industrious. And yet how lazy they could be—how many corners they could cut. For example, was it really necessary to pin a handkerchief to Bailey's shirt to wipe his nose with? Was it really too much work to get a Kleenex? Did we really need to see this snotty cloth hanging from his shoulder?

WENDY / — How about making something with paper, says Mom. You haven't done that in a while.

And so we do, while Bailey's still napping. We make stuff for the millennium, poppers and hats and window decorations, and funny-looking glasses where you look out of the middle two o's of 2000. Lanlan tries to pronounce 'millennium,' and I try to explain why everybody's storing up food and stuff.

— It's because of the computers, I explain. Dad says a lot of the computers go to 1999 and that's it. They think after that comes nothing.

Lanlan shakes her head, and when I say 'Y2K' she repeats 'Y2K.' I'm not exactly sure what the Y means, or the K, but it's computer talk, I tell her, for the whole mess.

— People are worried our lights are going to go out and nothing is going to work, and it will be like a disaster, I say.

Lanlan listens. Then she has to go get Bailey, who we can hear on the monitor is definitely awake, in fact jumping up and down in his crib like it's a trampoline.

— It's not fair, says Lizzy. It's not fair that Wendy's adopted from China and speaks Chinese, while nobody even knows what I am or where I came from. I hate being soup du jour.

And one day when she's picking cookie crumbs out of the family-room rug, she suddenly looks up and says: — It's probably how come my real mother abandoned me, don't you think it's how come?

— No, says Mom. I think she left you at the church because she loved you and knew she couldn't parent you.

LIZZY / It was like some present she popped out of her pocket all wrapped up but that you know she didn't wrap herself. It was like something she picked up prewrapped, like some bottle of perfume she was going to give to the school principal at Christmas.

— You're just saying that! I said. How do you know? You're just saying what it says in the adoption books you should say.

— You asked me what I thought, not what I knew.

— I could tell by the way you said 'parent' like that. That is like straight out of a book.

— And what should I have said?

— 'Take care of.' That's what normal people say. My real mother knew she 'couldn't take care of me.'

— We try to say 'birth mother.' Because I'm your real mother too. Both your mothers are real mothers.

— That's like out of a book too!

— It is not out of a book, said Dad, walking by. — It's out of the adoption video.

Then he left.

— Carnegie Wong! said Mom. Please come back here!

But he had something to do in the basement. It was like the basement was his burrow, and he was a burrower, which he would actually admit if you asked him. I knew that because once I did, and he said he was by nature and long practice, like most men, shameless in this regard.

WENDY / Anyway, he's calmed Lizzy down a little, Mom just wishes she could talk like Dad sometimes. But she can't, it's like her mouth just doesn't move that way, I know because in that way I'm just like Mom. Even if she isn't my birth mother, I'm like her anyway.

LIZZY / — And why should I learn Chinese when I might not even be Chinese? I said.

— You're right, it's not fair, Mom said, chopping up carrots for Bailey; she was always making these little containers of chopped vegetables and fruit and cheese. — You're right, and you don't have to learn Chinese if you don't want to. Although it's hard for a lot of people to say where they came from, they come from so many different places. Like me, I come from a lot of different countries. I don't have a simple label, like German American or Scotch-Irish American. I'm soup du jour, too.

— Yeah, but it doesn't matter as much because you're white and not adopted. Nobody wonders where you're from, nobody asks you.

— Well, I wonder myself.

— It's different, I said. Because if you don't want to wonder, you don't have to.

— Do people ask you where you're from?

WENDY / Mom means well when she says that, I can tell. She really does. Like she stops her chopping and looks at Lizzy and her whole face is so sorry, if I had any stones in my pocket, I would give her some.

But Lizzy doesn't get whether people mean well, she just hears their words.

LIZZY / — What do you think! I said. I'm like the only kid in my class who's soup du jour, do you realize that? The only one.

— Don't let them get to you, Liz, Mom said. Do you see that you let them get to you? You just have to ignore them. And what about that Monique Watson? Isn't she from someplace?

— Ignore them! I said. You have no idea what you're talking about. And why do you have to talk like everything is my own fault? Plus Monique has nothing to do with it. I'm not, like, from someplace. I'm from America, remember? Whereas she is French or something. She has this accent.

— So she has an accent. You're beautiful and articulate and courageous. Doesn't that count for something?

I so hated these questions she asked, not one of which was ever a real question. Like every single one of them led somewhere she wanted to go.

— You completely don't get anything, I said.

— I guess I don't, said Mom, moving on to cheese chopping. —But I'm sorry that I don't. Honestly.

— You are not sorry! You're sick of me!

— I didn't mean to upset you, she said, stopping again, but not until she had gotten to the end of that piece of cheese. Which was so typical of her—acting like she cared so much she couldn't go on, while the cheese all sat there in these perfect cubes. As if I might not notice.

— If you were my real mother, you would understand! If you were my real mother, you wouldn't be this brick wall! If you were my real mother, you'd be like Lanlan!

WENDY / That's when I start to hear her in Chinese. *Ni bu shi wode mama, ni bu shi zhende, ni shi jiade.*

— I am your real mother, says Mom, sighing. — And you are my honest-to-god fifteen-year-old.

I can hear a lot of things in Chinese if I want, things Lizzy says and other people too, and sometimes I do that with Elaine and she doesn't seem as scary. And sometimes I do that with Miss Tobey even though she is trying to be nice.

— She's a sensitive young lady, and that's wonderful, says Miss Tobey. We like to see that. And we respect everyone's feelings and support diversity, but we can't change the curriculum every time someone feels bad. We have to keep everybody on grade. And now there are state tests too, you can't believe what we're expected to do.

BLONDIE / Lizzy did have those outbursts. By the time the new millennium began, though, she was trying to learn Chinese anyway. And she was not blond anymore. Now she dyed her hair black, so she could look like Lan. Of course, because of the sort of dye she used, her hair came out flat black, like stove paint. It didn't shine like Lan's.

WENDY / Lanlan's hair is shiny. Like mine, Lanlan says. Lanlan says my hair is naturally shiny too, I just can't see it.

— I love China, Lizzy says now. China has issues, but America has issues too, and the Chinese economy is growing every day. It's a shame you can't say whatever you want in China, but in truth you can say a great deal and at least people don't get shot on the streets the way they do here.

BLONDIE / — Oh, really, I said. And what about Tiananmen Square?

— Or at least when they do, they get shot by soldiers and not by just anybody. And at least not in high schools, Lizzy said. They don't have, like, metal detectors. It happens seldomly.

She went on: — Someday the Chinese are going to stand up again, and then the whole world will shake. The Chinese have five thousand years of history, after all, compared to America, which is only two hundred years old but thinks it can bully everybody.

— Oh, really.

— That's why America is afraid. Because it knows it is—wait, Lanlan told me. I forget the saying. But it means strong on the outside, while actually weak inside.

— Oh, really.

— On the other hand, there is no place like America, this is the second-greatest country in history. China is the oldest, but America is the most successful today. The CIA controls everything. Everybody has to do what America likes, because if you don't, the CIA will bomb your embassy.

— Oh, really.

WENDY / Lanlan says America is very Chinese, really. The Chinese invented everything and now Americans invent everything, China used to be the Middle Kingdom, and now America is the Middle Kingdom, that's why everyone has to learn English.

— Oh, really, says Mom.

LIZZY / Russell was thinking about becoming a Communist. In fact he got this Communist tattoo to express his total disgust with capitalism. But Lanlan said no no no, he definitely should not become Communist.

— Have you ever heard of the Cultural Revolution? she said. The Red Guards killed my father.

WENDY / She's changing Bailey's diaper while she talks, which she has to do with him standing up these days because he completely won't lie down. Also she has to wrap tape around his diaper so he can't just take it off. Because he loves to take it off.

LIZZY / — They sent me to the North to the countryside, do you know how cold it is there? said Lanlan. All day long you want to cry. Except you cannot cry, because someone will report you. You do not know who will make a report about you, practically a goat can decide whether you will go home someday or never go home.

LAN / *How to convey the insanity of that era? The blind devotion of the Red Guards, and other people too. How they believed Mao was the sun, bringing us into the day. How people would work for days to buy a Mao badge, even if they had hundreds already. How they pinned them all over their army fatigues. One of my classmates pinned them to the skin of his chest. A neighbor in our courtyard was struggled against by his own daughter for putting a cup of tea down on a newspaper. Because the picture on the front page was a picture of Mao, she said. He failed to respect Mao.*

Of course the badges were beautiful, everyone thought that. Even I thought that until the Red Guards killed my father.

It was crazy, and yet in some ways life was better then. People were more equal. You didn't feel looked down on because you didn't have a college degree. We had less, but we didn't feel poor because no one was rich.

LIZZY / — Even China has market economy now, said Lanlan. Even China is Communist with Chinese characteristics.

— What does that mean? I asked.

— It means no one really believe in Communism anymore, said Lanlan.

— Not even the Communists? Then how can they be Communist?

— Still Communist, she explained. They are Party members.

— You mean they're phonies? said Russell.

Phonies were a big thing for Russell, because his mother died when he was little, and then he had three stepmothers, all phonies.

WENDY / So that's like the thing he and Lizzy agree about most, that mothers come and mothers go.

LIZZY / If you asked Russell, he'd say the problem is that no one's honest, no one can say things like, *This is just not my child.* Or, *I can't love this child as if he were my own because he isn't.*

As for my not feeling like I belonged to this family, he'd say probably I never would, but who would admit it?

Which was, like, so true.

My old boyfriend Derek was really smart, but he never got stuff like that. On the other hand, there was stuff Derek got that Russell didn't.

I hated having a special problem that other people didn't get.

WENDY / — But we know like so many people who are adopted, I say.

— You know all these people, says Lizzy. But I don't. I'm not like you, adopted from China. I'm plain adopted from nowhere, I'm soup du jour, it's completely different. Everybody wants to talk about where you're from. It's different to possibly be the grandchild of a Japanese soldier, which nobody wants to talk about.

— Japanese soldier? I say. What Japanese soldier?

— Some Japanese soldier.

— Are you sure? Says who?

— Says Lanlan, she says.

BLONDIE / How to explain about Mama Wong? The way she talked? The way she looked at Lizzy?

— We did wonder such things, I said. And we did indeed decide not to mention them. Because who knew what the truth was? How would we ever know? And what good would come of such talk?

Carnegie, strolling into the kitchen, tossed a cherry tomato up in the air and caught it in his mouth.

— We thought it would only hurt your self-esteem, I went on, glowering at Carnegie. — Please act your age.

— This is worse, sobbed Lizzy. This is way worse. To have people thinking things all along and not saying them.

— We're talking about whether Lizzy might have some Japanese blood, I told Carnegie. We're talking about whether she might be the grandchild of, say, a Japanese soldier.

He gulped down his tomato.

— And who says this? he asked. Pray tell?

— Lan, I said. But you know how Mama Wong always . . .

— Your not saying it all this time makes it seem like it must be true! cried Lizzy.

— That may be, said Carnegie. But the fact is, we don't know, and can't know, barring a fact-finding mission.

— We were just trying to protect you, I said.

— And so what if it is true, anyway? said Carnegie. What does it matter? Aren't you still our Lizzy? Growing up here, where, let's face it, most people can't tell Chinese from Japanese anyway.

— You lied to me! she cried.

— You know, mixed kids are going to be in the majority before you know it, said Carnegie. It's going to be such an asset. You're going to be able to move in all kinds of worlds. And it's going to be cool; in fact, I was reading about that just the other day. How cool it's getting to be already.

— It is not cool, she said. Maybe in the city it is, but here, in our town, it is not cool.

— Well, from the city to the suburbs, said Carnegie. Believe you me, ambiguity is in.

— But why did you lie to me? she cried. You lied. You lied.

Wrote Gabriela:

> i would definitely say something to lan if i were you. talk about inappropriate! to be telling lizzy stuff like that!

But how to explain what was inappropriate about it?

CARNEGIE / How was Lan supposed to know we'd carefully never discussed this? Thanks to the boundless love and exquisite tact with which dear Mama Wong broached the subject.

BLONDIE / In the end, we didn't say anything. In the end, I chose to focus on improving my relationship with Lan. For while Lan talked to the girls more and more all the time, she barely talked to me. It was strange. And always in English—she always spoke to me in English, though I'd tried, a few times, to speak Chinese.

Wasn't I a person people talked to?

it's her inner child, wrote Gabriela. it has nothing to do with you. you're a good egg to try to connect with her, given the situation.

It wasn't a matter of being good, though. I would have wanted to be friends with anyone living in my house. And I felt sorry for her—fellow pawn of Mama Wong's that she was.

what a great idea, to try and make common cause!

Lan, though, was not interested in making common cause. Indeed, I could not even get her to talk to me in a regular way. If I asked, Are you hot? Lan would answer, Not too hot. If I asked, Do you have something you need to do? Lan would answer, I can do it now or do it later. If I asked, Would you like to go shopping? Lan would answer, If you are go out shopping, I am happy to accompany you.

— She treats you like her superior, in other words, said Carnegie. Which, dearest, you are. And think how the Chinese write, traditionally: top to bottom. Think how they talk about time, even time runs top to bottom, with events above or below each other. Lan has that ladder-like outlook.

— You're defending her, I said.

WENDY / Lanlan knows her way to the video store. She's surprised we don't have a DVD player, not that she and her great-aunt did, they didn't have anything. But in China even their neighbor had one. First he had a VCR, and then he got a DVD player he let her use.

LIZZY / Never mind that the neighbor was this old geezer who used to paw at her while she watched. I was, like, how could you put up with that? But she said she used to just ignore him. She said probably she should have married him. Probably she shouldn't have cared he was so short. Of course I asked, like, how short? Which is how we found out that he came up to her shoulder.

WENDY / She says that in China people have these things called VCDs of every single movie we have here. And not like months later, they get them right away, and for really cheap. But anyway, the VCR is okay, and it is okay it is not Sony.

LAN / *In China, people buy* Sony. *Of course,* Panasonic *is okay too.*

WENDY / Because she hates America, but she loves American movies, and on the VCR she can watch all the same stuff she used to watch in China. Stuff like *Mulan* and *Titanic* and *The Matrix*. And this old stuff too, anything really famous. Like *Gone With the Wind,* she watches that a million times, even though she doesn't like it when Clark Gable says, Frankly, my dear, I don't give a damn.

— That is one hundred percent rude, she says.

And how terrible that Scarlett O'Hara! Talk about spiritual pollution!

But then she rewinds the tape and watches it again. She loves the remote control, when she first got it she spent hours just playing with it. Practicing, sort of. It's like the one thing she won't let Bailey touch.

LAN / *In China, I used to see people with calculators, with mobile phones, with electronic dictionaries. I loved to watch their thumbs fly. I always wanted my thumbs to fly like that too.*

WENDY / Sometimes she watches this guy Charlie Chaplin, she really likes Charlie Chaplin. And if she could get them, she would watch these movies her father used to talk about, stuff like *Waterloo Bridge* and *An Affair to Remember.* She tells us how much she'd like to see them as if everybody wants to see stuff their father used to see, while Lizzy and me are like, wow. Who knows if Dad even ever watched movies when he was young.

Some of the movies aren't even in color.

Russell tells her what to see, but she doesn't like what he likes, like she doesn't get this movie *Dirty Harry* at all.

LAN / *I thought that* Harry *very strange. What kind of hero was that? So rude. But sexy, it was true. I thought that* Clint Eastwood *almost as handsome as* Gregory Peck.

WENDY / She's more interested when Russell gets hold of some Hong Kong kung fu movies, and then some new movies from the Mainland. Some of them she saw in China, but some of them she didn't. A lot of them she says don't have anything to do with any Chinese she knows. Why do they have to make movies about such strange places, places nobody ever even heard of? But of course she watches them anyway, even though she says she would rather watch James Bond. She likes James Bond even though the British are the good guys.

— Of all things! she says.

And the way she says it we know it's like a practice phrase from school.

LIZZY / She hated the British because of the Opium War and gunships, which her father used to talk about all the time. Apparently he used to talk about this humiliation and that humiliation, so that 'humiliation' became, like, this big word for her.

WENDY / I'm not even sure what it means exactly, but when she says, *They humiliated us,* I can feel how *us* doesn't mean her and me and Lizzy. *Us* means her and people in China, which makes me sad. She says the American government is different than the American people, but when she says *they,* I still hear *you.* Very soft, it's like when you stare at something red for a long time and then look up and see green. *You humiliated us.*

But she still loves James Bond one hundred percent.

— Bond, she says, in that James Bond voice. — James Bond.

The way she does it, even Bailey thinks it's funny.

— Bon! he says, with like this little bounce up and down. He does that without holding on to anything, like he's dancing. — Bon! Bon! he yells, and then falls down *bump* on his bottom. His diaper makes this crinkly sound when he does that, and his cheeks jiggle up and down. Because he is like really really fat, Mom says he has the most chipmunk cheeks of all the kids.

LIZZY / Lanlan went around humming the tune to *Goldfinger.* And talking about who was sexier, Sean Connery or Roger Moore. She was fascinated by their chest hair.

LAN / *In China, we feel foreign men are very sexy. People say they can make love ten times a night, but I don't know if that's true.*

LIZZY / Also we talked about whether the later movies were as good as the old ones. I said they weren't, there being too much of a formula. But Lanlan said she loved the formula.

WENDY / Why does she still watch sad movies by herself when we're not there? Outside it snows and snows, it's so beautiful, but she doesn't go out, she just stays at home and watches those movies.

She likes us to visit her. Like she never shoos us out if we go bother her, even if she's off duty and not supposed to be taking care of us. Her studying is important, but if we knock on her door, she always opens it up with a big surprised noise, as if no one has ever visited her before.

— Hello! she says. Come in, come in! Then she says: — What's this?

And from behind her back come all kinds of treats.

Some of the stuff we've had before, Mom's always made us eat rice cakes and melon cakes and noodle cakes and red bean everything. But it tastes better when Lanlan gives it to us, who knows why, maybe we like it more because we eat it all the time now, maybe we've *xiguan le,* gotten used to it. Or maybe we like it because liking it is liking Lanlan. Also she gives it to us right out of her hand with a napkin, and maybe breaks it in half for us to share, and lets us walk around with it. She's not like Mom, who takes it out of the refrigerator and then checks it to make sure there's no mold or anything on it, and then puts it on a plate. One lump for me and one for Lizzy and none for her because they use lard. And then she watches to see our reaction, smiling like she smiles at assemblies even if we've totally messed up. Encouraging like. Lanlan is completely different, she brightens up as if she has this whole net of lights in her skin. Also she makes treats herself, after a while, using stuff we can get right in our grocery store, or from this Japanese market. Suzhou specialties like *qing tuanzi,* meaning green rice balls, or these itty bitty *zhongzi tang,* which are these candies you can pop into your mouth, and that have pine nuts in them, or mint.

In the beginning she gives us different things to choose from, in the beginning she asks, Do you like try this one or this one? But after a while she says she knows what we will like. And we do like it, she's right, she knows our mind.

— You are become like Chinese, she says, and her face is so happy her smile isn't even lopsided.

And when one day Lizzy says Mom never cared about us enough to bake brownies, these are our first brownies, that's what it means to have a mother who works, Lanlan says: — I am like you, have no real mother. Have no real family.

Sometimes she lets Bailey cruise around by himself in his play area while she tells us stories. Or play with the vacuum, he's like in love with the vacuum. She tells us famous stories about things we never heard of but that she thinks we should if we're not going to be one hundred percent American. Like filial piety. What's filial piety? we say. We have no idea, she's right, we're like *xiao ba wang,* the little emperors you see all over China these days, completely spoiled, which is why she tells us this story about some sixty-year-old man who played on the floor pretending to be a baby so his parents wouldn't feel old.

— That is filial child, children are supposed to do anything for their parents, she says.

— For our parents? says Lizzy. Our parents?

— To make them worry less, to make them feel better, anything, says Lanlan. Children are supposed to sacrifice themselves.

— But what if they aren't even our parents? says Lizzy.

— Yeah, and like what does that mean, sacrifice? I say.

LAN / *Of course, I am amazed. What kind of human doesn't know what sacrifice means?*

LIZZY / We tried to picture this old guy, like our dad's age, but crawling on the floor like Bailey. Would he drool? Would he put stuff in his mouth and get his food all over?

WENDY / Would he say, Da! like Bailey, for door and Daddy and dog and some other stuff too?

LIZZY / It was weird, but we listened anyway, if only because we knew how much Mom especially would hate these stories. Even if the crawling around was for the benefit of her and Dad, she would hate the crawling part. And what about the stories about taking care of your mother-in-law? Like the one about a woman who breastfed her sick mother-in-law, to give her strength. Could you imagine Mom breastfeeding Mama Wong? Even I hated that one.

— I can tell you one thing, I said. I am never ever going to breastfeed my husband's mother. I mean, if I even get married. And I am never going to China again if that's what you're supposed to do. And I am so glad that if I have any Chinese in me, at least it's not one hundred percent.

— Even in China nobody do that anymore, said Lanlan then. That is just old story.

— Whew, we said.

— China is very nice place, she said. But in China, that is the kind of story people all know. If you do not know that kind of story, you are not real Chinese.

— Hmm, we said.

— Or Japanese either, she added. Because Japanese way of thinking is very like Chinese way. Everything they have is come from China.

WENDY / And the way she looks at us you get the feeling that she doesn't think we are real anything except American.

She tells us stories about relatives of hers, which I guess makes them relatives of ours, sort of. So that we're interested in them even though they make us sad in a way, Lizzy says she just wishes she knew one single person who was related to her by blood, and as soon as she says that I wish it too.

Some of the stories are normal, but a lot of them are weird. Like one day during Bailey's nap, Lanlan tells us this story about a baby girl.

LAN / — So the baby is born, a girl, and when the mother found out, she know the father would be very mad at her for give birth to another girl. So she tell the servant to take that baby away. Throw out. So the servant leave the baby to cry cry cry. Nobody wash the baby, nobody wrap the baby in blanket, nobody give the baby milk. But still the baby cry. Even after all the blood become dry and brown all over, that baby is still cry cry cry until finally the *ayi* feel sorry for the baby. So she wash the baby, take the brown off. She wrap the baby in some newspaper, even find somebody to nurse the baby. And the baby grow up big and strong, and so beautiful the father mother are so surprise, they just love that baby. The way she smile and sing, everybody love her so much.

LIZZY / — Wow, we said. But that's an old story too, right? Like from a long long time ago?

— That story is—how do you say? My great-aunt, she said. My father's mother's sister.

— You know her? You know that baby?

— Not when she was a baby. When she was grow up.

— Wow, we said.

CARNEGIE / The video watching segued into, what else, stock watching. That all-American activity that, sad to say, felt far more immediately Chinese than studying Chinese characters or reading Chinese poetry. Every time I brought a stock site up on my screen I could hear Mama Wong's approval. *That's how family go up.*

Yet let me say here, for all time: I in no way instigated this new interest of Lan's. It's true that I had thought to ask her to tutor me in Chinese, my self-study program having predictably petered out. Why not a conversation class? In fact Blondie had entertained the self-same idea. With a certain wistfulness; how hard, after all, to imagine that Lan, who barely spoke to her, would agree to any such thing.

Post–kitchen incident, though—no. Post–kitchen incident I too regarded the idea with more wistfulness than hope. Was it not better to avoid Lan as best I could? Seeing as how sharp-eyed Blondie noticed even that.

— You have feelings for her, she said.

— Do I?

— If you didn't have feelings you wouldn't have to avoid her.

— Is that so.

So I said. Yet could I really deny that Lan had appeared in my dreams? That in my dreams I did kiss her, once—just once—but over and over, saying all the time, *It's impossible.* As she understood; that being the tenderest part of the dream, that she understood. *Of course, it's impossible,* she said; her blouse grazing her pubic hair. *Of course. And this, is this impossible too? And this? And how do you call this? Ah, this also—such a big big impossible.* Having never had children, she was tighter than Blondie, also easier. It was natural. She was 24/7. She never had a meeting in the morning; I was her morning meeting. There we were, our coffee all made. Ah, PowerPoint! Better, yes, to close the conference-room door.

Which in truth, as fantasies go, wasn't much. So missionary, to begin with; and how close its pleasures to those of good takeout. Still, I did not share it with Blondie.

Let me say again how Lan became interested in stocks on her lonesome. I would not have started anything.

But there was a sign posted outside the door of her ESL class, which she might never have noticed, except that one day an Asian person stopped smack in front of it; and as it happened, Lan had the habit—Mama Wong had had it too—of taking special note of other people of Asian descent. She thought nothing of squinting at them, in fact, as if at a vision chart. Taiwanese? Japanese? Malaysian? And of course she had heard so much about stocks in China without understanding the first thing about them.

LAN / *I went to a meeting, and was surprised. So many overseas Chinese—from Canada, Macao, Vietnam. And people from other places too. Russia. Brazil. South Africa. Some of them were from my program. But how friendly they were, here! Everyone was friendly. Even the black people. It seemed the friendliest place in America.*

Hello, *and* Welcome, *and* You need a blue sheet, *people kept say-*

ing. Do you have the blue sheet? Will someone please get her a blue sheet?

And so I left with a blue sheet.

CARNEGIE / The very sheet—'Getting Started'—that she presented to me in my study one snowy day.

— Carnegie?

I looked up casually, as if she just entered my consciousness. As if I had not been aware of her whereabouts, not only before she appeared in my doorway, but long before. As if I had not heard her leave the kitchen, then stop by the playroom, then rummage for something in the front hall. I looked up as if I did not know whose light step that could be, as if it did not quicken my own step to think of it.

There she stood. Lan! Bearing her blue sheet.

Outside, the trees shone. They had been sheathed in thick ice for days, but a recent warm spell was making them snap and shift as if shaking their stiff coats off. Tinkling, crackling, pattering, they sounded, oddly, like spring rain.

— Come in, I said.

— I, she began; then jumped.

An avalanche—the gutter ice dam having given way. I laughed to have had the ice broken by breaking ice. How sweet, as Lizzy would say.

— Come in, I said. It's nothing. Just the snow. Come in.

My study, being of new construction, was the only carpeted part of the house besides Bailey's nursery. Lan's footsteps fell silent as she crossed into the room. I did not know if Blondie monitored the meanderings of the household as I did; most probably my better half did not. Still I registered, *outside her radar.* I reached for the sheet of paper. Lan placed it, with solemnity, in my hand. Then, at my indication, she alighted on a chair.

All this in silence. We understood each other.

I reviewed the sheet with gravitas.

Had she forgotten our kitchen encounter? *Impossible, impossible.* Still I wondered, and was gratified to see how her gaze seemed to visit all manner of objects I did not believe of true compelling interest.

Practice account. Web address. Opening balance. I tried to focus, glad for the shelter of my desk. Feeling, already, my growing embarrassment. What with all the light bouncing up from the snow outside, the ceiling shone brilliant—so brilliant that a great light cascaded down, in turn, on us. That light was too bright; the room felt like a tanning parlor. How exposed I felt, and yet still I sat. Spoke. Swiveled.

Had she never tried to imagine me, under my clothes and manners, a man? Having imagined so much about her, I could not quite believe it. Guessing even now at her feel, her smell, her laugh. There she was, lovely, serious—Lan!—not five feet in front of me, the top of her head glowing almost white. She did not sink back into her chair, or even perch on it, exactly. Rather, what with her back a few inches forward of, and exactly parallel to, the chair back, she seemed to have stacked herself on top of it. Afraid of me then, still. Or was she afraid of herself? And how to put her at her ease? I explained the American Stock Exchange, wondering where she liked to begin. Whether she liked games; music; the morning. I guessed: passionate or shy, athletic or soulful, noisy or quiet. How long before she would lose herself with me? And how long before I lost myself with her? I was not self-conscious about my body, but wondered if she had it in her to make me so—even as I felt her breathing hard; beheld her jaw slack, her face unfocused, her hair everywhere. Her self-possession returned only in the moments after, in that sober, happy, half-embarrassed collecting—the combobulating, Blondie and I called it. I described the floor of the New York Stock Exchange, wondering whether she minded the floor. What her rhythm was. I hoped she was not bouncy; I did not like bouncy. I wondered whether we would prove a fit. Also what sorts of things she would divulge, come pillow time. What her regrets were, her dreams, her hopes.

You, I imagined her saying. *My dreams are about you.*

Though I could also imagine, *I dreamed the Dow Jones jump forty points.*

I explained what a stock was. A bond. A commodity.

Blondie was full of projects I could not take seriously. How often my love consisted, not of a feigning per se, but of a distinct getting up of support. Would that be true with any woman? And would I be able to forget Blondie while with someone else? Ah, marriage. Even as I dreamed of sin I involuntarily and to my own annoyance answered every question re: Lan with Blondie's response; indeed, framed the questions based on her. How I had wondered, once, at all the places Blondie had light coverings of barely perceptible hair—fuzz. How I had marveled at her many shades of whiteness. She was so blue-white in some places, so pink-white in others. And the curly paleness of her pubic hair—I had wondered at that, once, as at her blue eyes and translucent lids. Once upon a time I could have spent days watching the kick kick kick of her pulse. Her inner truth, it seemed, trying to get out.

But now, of course, I no longer watched. Now I beheld, simply, *wife.* Wife with worries, wife with plans, wife with issues. Wife who now required a certain expertise, from time to time. There were still nights of tumble and come; but other nights where judiciousness was called for. Much depended, now, on the time of month. It was possible, now, to miscalculate. Blondie, in short, required a consciousness I imagined smooth Lan did not. I had no data to support this. And Lan was, not to forget, a year older than Blondie. Probably this notion was racist. Behold, after all, the human stacking chair.

Still, I imagined her hungry, quick; her mouth warm and intuitive. I imagined our selves no selves, all sweet spring melt.

The Dow Jones Industrial Index. The SEC. The NASDAQ composite index, such a source of joy these days.

LAN / *Of course, I knew what was on his mind. Men are men. Zui weng zhi yi bu zai jiu—an old drunk's interest isn't in the wine.*

CARNEGIE / I convinced her to sit at my desk. To use my computer. She logged in successfully. She opened her account of five thousand dollars. The idea was to buy and sell for a semester; the club member who made the most money got one real share of stock in Amazon.com. I showed her how to place orders. I showed her how to read the stock pages of the newspaper.

Lan nodded and nodded, her forehead tensed. Trying to catch my words, it seemed, with her eyebrows.

— Do you understand?

She never tried to get me to say things in a way she could get. Nod after nod after nod, but each nod was more about appreciation than comprehension. It was what my mother would have wanted, had she been the explainer. Each nod saying, not 'I get it, I get it,' but 'You are so kind, you are so kind.'

Lan asked no questions.

My mother: *That is right way to listen! Keep mouth shut! If student has so much to say, he should be teacher.*

But what if the student just doesn't understand? What if the teacher isn't getting through?

Then student should study harder.

Mutual funds, earnings reports. SEC filings. I feelingly explained that 'P/E ratio' meant profits-to-earnings, or the number of shares you had to purchase in order to have bought one dollar's worth of actual profit from a company. Passionately I defined 'profits' for her, 'earnings'; lovingly I pointed out that a high P/E ratio typically meant that a company was overvalued, although investors had ignored such traditional measures in the case of companies like Amazon. I inquired tentatively about the Internet. Did she know what the Internet was?

LAN / *How could I be so ignorant? Just because I didn't go to college didn't mean I was a frog at the bottom of a well.*

— Of course, *I told him.* In China, Internet Café very popular. Spreading like hotcakes.

CARNEGIE / — In certain companies, I said, people begin to buy, not what the company is, but what it could be. What makes the market so interesting is that it is so much about perception.

Lan nodded.

I waited.

— Of all things! she said finally.

I linked from her class website to other visuals. She nodded a bit slower, her brow opening. Overtaken, it seemed, with helpless wonder. Partly this might have been the color screen; the color on my computer was truly miraculous. But also she seemed to see herself as entering some inner sanctum. She had that reverence.

LAN / *Finally I was watching the show that real Americans watch.*

CARNEGIE / It was as if she'd made her way from the outer courtyard of a Chinese house to the inner courtyard, and from there to the inmost chambers; even into the curtained room within a room that was a Chinese bed.

We were getting somewhere.

I showed her how to pull up a stock-advice site. Then, another. I showed her how different the advice could be, with one adviser bearish where another was bullish. That could be true at any time, but was especially so these days, what with the NASDAQ decline slowing. Some people thought the NASDAQ would rise again, I explained, others that they had better move to limit their losses. I backed up to explain what 'bearish' meant. 'Bullish.' Also how people kept tabs on the market while they were working, how they placed orders to buy or sell on their lunch breaks. Between meetings.

— Not everybody, I said. Some people. As many people as, say, keep birds in China.

The nodding stopped. She looked at me quizzically.

— Don't people keep birds in China?

— Of course, she said.

She looked at me thoughtfully, as if trying to make out the true meaning of my question, even as I made out the play of her breasts against her loose-knit sweater. The sweet bulge of the former, the obliging give of the latter. The barely perceptible enlargement of the knit loops that made for the give, each loop a peephole to the bra below. And of course I did peek, although each hole was too small to show anything more than the slightly shiny knit cloth of what I guessed to be a soft-cup bra. Ah, assimilation—good-bye cold war armor! As she inhaled, the peepholes along the top slope of her breast ever so slightly enlarged. As she exhaled, they ever so slightly shrank. The peepholes close by her nipples seemed to enlarge and shrink most; those closer to her shoulder, least. The difference was negligible, and what could one really tell through a sweater and bra? Yet her nipples did seem to protrude a bit more happily than might be warranted by an introduction to the stock market.

She tucked an errant hair behind her ear; her hand hesitating as it grazed her lobe, which she caught, momentarily, between her bent fingers. Tugging it down gently before her hand fell away.

She returned her attention to the screen. I made a mental icon of my wayward thoughts and dragged it into the trash.

Still rearrangement was in order.

— Here, you try it, I said. This is an icon. You click on it to select it.

She placed her hand on the mouse willingly enough, but did not click.

— Click, I said.

I reached down and gently depressed her soft-skinned fingers.

— Click, I said once more, then lifted my hand and drew back. My other hand gripped the molded-plastic back of the chair. How easily that chair swiveled! With the lightest touch I could turn her—just like that—to face me.

— Click?

I was about to show her again when she clicked herself.

My heart bumped hard.

She is good student. That is because she is Chinese girl. She is not like Blondie, think the sun shine every day. Lan understand in this world, all kind of way to fall down. As long as you have money, you have cushion. No money, your pee-pee will be so black and blue you cannot stand up.

—Now this is a critical graph, I said. Click again. Here.

I pointed to the screen, leaning carefully over her. I hoped I was not panting.

— You'll be a power user before you know it, I said.

The trees outside crackled.

— This end point, of course, is today, I said.

— This dot here? she asked.

I scrolled back horizontally, over the miles of data that preceded that dot.

— All this tells you something, I said. It tells you a lot. And yet we still don't know what happens next. Anything could happen.

She nodded.

— You can make a lot of money through the stock market, I went on lamely. Of course, you can lose a lot too.

I found myself lowering my voice as I spoke.

— Do you make money? she asked, lowering her voice to match mine.

We were not whispering per se; and yet we could have been construed to be murmuring, our talk assuming the low-toned back-and-forth of private exchange as we discussed how, just as in China, people here could start companies and became millionaires. How anyone could do it, even immigrants. Even people without connections.

— Not everyone in China who start company is Party member, she said, bristling.

— Did I say that?

— That is American propaganda, she continued; but her tone had a shrug in it.

— You could start a company. A dot-com, I said. Even without a college degree. Anyone could start one.

— No no no no, she replied, waving her hand like a shield. — Of all things!

— I'm not saying you shouldn't get a degree.

Still she was adamant; people like her could not start companies. On this matter we had no understanding.

Yet the underpart of her wrist thrust forward as she waved, like an eagerness belying her words.

I showed her how to position her hands on the keyboard. I explained that she was going to have to learn how to type.

Later that week I dug up an old Macintosh for her. This was an SE, one of the sand-tone small-screened boxes that had once seemed so eminently portable, slipping so niftily into its padded Cordura case. Now it seemed quaintly pre-laptop, antique-shop material. It had sixty-four megabytes of memory and no color and could only be hooked up to the Internet via the most creative finagling. Still Lan seemed transfixed by the idea that it was hers to use. I was in fact trying to give the thing to her, but she resisted so energetically that I finally allowed her to insist the computer was on loan.

I lugged it into her kitchen and made her sit down.

— This cable goes here, I explained. See this symbol? That's for the universal port.

— Universal port, she repeated. Thank you.

— This is your floppy drive, I said. This is your diskette.

— Floppy drive. Thank you. Diskette. Thank you.

She nodded, nodded. From downstairs came the surprisingly clear *naa*-ing of the goat.

— On, she said. Off.

She tried the switch. The first time tentatively, but the second time with matter-of-fact expertise.

— You plug the mouse in here, I said.

She peered around the computer. Her breasts did not quite clear the wood-look tabletop, but rather roosted on top, like a pair of pigeons. Above them, her scoop-neck sweater gapped. I could see her bra strap, narrow and white, slack, and under it an expanse of sweet, smooth flesh. All of her fine left collarbone, the beginning swell of her breast, and beyond it, at the tunnel of her sleeve, the tuck and turn of her entering arm. All was lit rose pink by her sweater, but not evenly. The pink was barely perceptible by the sweater's neck, deeper and deeper farther in.

I helpfully showed Lan how to access certain programs besides her stock-club site. The word processor, for example.

— Click on this icon here.

From below us came the sound of the van crunching up the driveway; then of car doors detonating, one after another. So loudly! Far more loudly than when you were downstairs, maybe because down there the noise was simply volume, whereas up here it was intrusion as well. So too the screeching of the children, returned from a shopping expedition. Bailey particularly was shockingly loud, his shrieks filling the apartment to the rafters.

Why had she never complained? I glanced at her, half expecting to be met with *You see? What I put up with, you scurrilous landlord.* But she did not look up. Back straight, she addressed the computer with her whole being: her eyes, her nose, her mouth, her ears, her clavicles, her breasts. Her fingers hunted and pecked, pinkies aloft like the oars of a rowboat, levered out of the water. Her feet were planted on the floor as if to launch her directly into the program if necessary.

So this was Lan concentrating. She furrowed her brow, glancing up to the screen and back down to the keyboard. Up and down, up and down. She bit her lip. She itched her nose with the back of her hand. She tucked her hair behind her ear.

And again: that catching of her earlobe between her knuckles.

Just an odd habit, then.

Thinking thus, I almost missed how straightening her back, she continued the motion up through her smooth, long neck—a time-lapse film of a fiddlehead fern, she seemed, every moment less fiddle-head and more fern—until suddenly she seemed, impossibly, to be raising her head, turning and tilting it toward me; and still the motion upward; until her face was lifted too, and her eyebrows, and her gaze.

LAN / *He was rich. American. Sexy. He seemed gentle, and perhaps loving. I had never had a man who was loving. Who made you shiver. And look how he had helped me already. He was kind. He was not short.*

CARNEGIE / — Thank you, she said.

Her gaze was shiny and honest and slightly cross-eyed, her pupils black and enormous.

I could not speak.

— You do so much for me, she said. You should not.

LAN / *I felt so grateful, in my heart, for his help.*

CARNEGIE / She glanced down; then with a lyric lurch lifted her head once more, gaze lowered, as if to be kissed. Her throat pushed forward, long and vulnerable. I leaned down; tucked her hair behind her ear; traced the line of her jaw with my fingertips. She shivered. Then I put a finger on that soft lopsided smile, coaxed the laggard side up, and kissed her.

Just once.

Impossible, impossible.

If only I had not caught, in the white blank of a newly created file, our reflection.

These girls, you do not know.

Are they not beautiful?

I kid you not.

I drew back.

You have not lived.

My chest was so tight, I could hardly retrieve my left arm from her chin. Nor could I breathe.

They will do anything.

LAN / ***He looked so strange.***

CARNEGIE / — Is this how things work in China? I asked finally. I had reclaimed my arm, but still my chest locked solid.

My nitroglycerin.

— Here too, I managed to say. Of course. Sometimes.

I rummaged in my pocket with my right hand as she searched my face furtively, quickly sweeping my eyes. One, the other, back. The computer screen lighting the corners of her eyes in one direction, but not the other.

— You don't have to thank me, I said.

— I thank you one hundred percent, she insisted—so sincerely, I lost all desire to touch her, for shame.

— You deserve a different story, I said. I want you to have a different story.

She smiled uncertainly. Lopsidedly. Pressed her fingers together.

— Do you understand?

— No, she said.

— Could I have a glass of water?

LAN / ***Such a strange, kind man.***

I thought perhaps he did not like me. I thought perhaps I was too old. Or perhaps he was afraid of Blondie.

CARNEGIE / — Thank you, I said, sweating.

With some effort, I reached out and took her wrist a moment, turning it to check the time on her watch.

— Time for me to go, I said.

— Of course, she said simply. You're very busy.

The next week, she made a confession.

— I dream last night I am millionaire, she said, blinking a little.

We were in the kitchen, waiting for a delivery; Blondie had ordered a massage table for our bedroom.

— You haven't even bought your first stock, I said.

— That was my dream.

— A millionaire, I mused. I'm trying to imagine you a millionaire. What about having plenty of nothing?

— It was a nightmare, she said. I woke up feel very afraid.

— Because?

— I was millionaire in America, she said. Not in China, I was millionaire in America.

— And could never go back.

She nodded.

— Why would you even want to go back? I asked. After all you've been through? People hated you in Shandong. Or would you try to settle in Suzhou?

She looked out the window.

— There's opportunity here, you know, I said.

I expected her to ask what I meant by that. If I was suggesting that she might stay.

Instead she nodded obligingly, but then said: — In Shanghai, there is big opportunity now too. They say many Chinese people, even they are born here, now they are move to China because the opportunity is much better. And no racism.

— Racism, I said. Where did you hear about racism?

— Lizzy tell me. Also people at school say so.

— Well, it's true. Though, you know, there's racism in China too. It's just not aimed at Han Chinese.

— So it is not such big problem then.

What to say to that? I cracked my knuckles, pondering.

— Americans believe all racism is a problem, I said finally. Or at least a lot of Americans. Some, obviously, don't. Seeing as how they're racist.

She seemed unperturbed by this news.

— Anyway, I have no green card, nothing to discuss, she said.

— It doesn't sound like you would even want a green card.

She half smiled. I heard the delivery truck pull into the driveway.

— Or would a green card still be nice?

— There is no green card for me.

— But if there were?

— Of course, she said.

It was not clear she even knew what a millionaire was, exactly.

A few days later, though, in response to a new printer, she explained what being a millionaire meant to her.

— Everywhere you go, people treat you like big shot, she said. Instead of everybody make fun of my beautiful bicycle, and make me fix it at night, they come help me with their special tools. Look like I go to university, and have a degree.

She stopped. I thought she might begin to cry then, but she didn't.

— Nobody, she said, treat you like a servant.

II

A Happy Family

BLONDIE / Her real eating began at McDonald's. We rarely ate fast food, but one day our heat went out—old house, old heat—and we found ourselves there.

Lan ordered a Big Mac.

— Make me miss home, she said.

— We love Mickey D's, said Wendy. We hate eating healthy.

WENDY / Lanlan eats the fries, and three of my McNuggets, and then drinks a big Coke. She has a whole apple turnover for dessert, and burps.

BLONDIE / After that we arranged takeout from McDonald's once a week.

WENDY / She likes the Quarter Pounder with Cheese and the Filet-O-Fish sandwich too, but Big Macs are her favorite because of the special sauce.

BLONDIE / She began to eat other things. Puréed vegetables. Mashed potatoes. Ice cream. For a while she was eating much the way Bailey used to, before he got teeth. But then suddenly she was eating everything, so that it almost did not seem strange when, in April, about the time the late daffodils came out—we had a huge bank of white thalias—Lan announced she'd like to try cooking.

Might we yet bloom into one big happy family? Might we yet prove late bloomers? I did hope so.

CARNEGIE / Blondie took notes in a special notebook she had bought, whilst I stalked bugs with Bailey. The paper in the notebook was handmade, with ragged edges and flecks of dried vegetation. It looked like something produced by nomads on the steppe, but actually emanated from an atelier in New Jersey.

— What's that? What's that?

Blondie seemed bent on normalizing her relationship with Lan through foodstuffs. Her enthusiasm was real—Blondie was never not real—and yet she seemed to have turned herself up, as if on a cooking show. You half expected subtitling for the hearing-impaired to begin scrolling across the lower reaches of her sweater. It was never enough to write down the name of the ingredient in the notebook. First she had to pinch it and lift it to her nose, or prod it and roll it, or snap it and sniff it again, or dab it on her tongue. Five-spice powder, hmm. Dried shrimp, hmm. Tianjin vegetables. Mustard greens. She asked if the item was yin or yang. If it was smoked or pickled, she asked what it was like fresh. She asked where it came from, and how you knew best-quality from second-best.

LAN / *I tried to teach her all kinds of dishes, but some Suzhou specialties too. Different kinds of shrimp, and cabbage hearts in chicken fat. Also* xian cai rou si mian*—noodles with pickled vegetables and pork. Once we managed to find mandarin fish, in Chinatown, for* songshu guiyu*; also eel for* xiangyou shanhu*—a kind of stewed shredded eel. But the family did not like the dishes with special ingredients. They liked dishes made with things they already knew. For example* xigua ji*—a kind of chicken steamed with watermelon rind.*

Of course, they would not say what they did or did not like. Still, I could guess. It was hard in the beginning, but little by little I began to understand American taste.

BLONDIE / She put sugar in everything. Lan said people in Suzhou liked sugar, in that way they were like people from Shanghai.

Probably she would have put sugar in Bailey's milk if I'd let her.

I tried not to say anything. I tried to simply use a little less sugar myself—set a good example.

LAN / *In Chinese we have a saying,* Ye Gong hao long. *Meaning a person like* Ye Gong, *who makes a big fuss about how much he loves dragons, but does not actually love dragons at all.*

LIZZY / That was so true about Mom. Like you could give her the ugliest thing for Mother's Day, and she would still say she loved it. She would still wear it all the time, and tell her friends how you gave it to her.

CARNEGIE / Blondie accompanied Lan to various grocery stores in Chinatown, returning with bag upon bag of food. There wasn't enough room in the cupboards for everything they bought; they had to store cans on the ledge by the basement stairs. Of course, when moving coolers and patio furniture and whatnot, everyone tried to be cognizant of the danger of avalanche. Still cans cascaded down, causing near injury.

I watched Blondie hover over the stove as if over a newborn. I watched her do the rice the way Lan did, not measuring the water, but eyeballing it, and stirring it with her hand before putting it in the rice cooker. I watched her slice things with a butcher knife, her fingers curled under. I watched her tease the fat away from the meat, half frozen to make it easier to slice. She did not complain about how cold her hands got working with the frigid meat, though she did blow on her fingers every now and then, to warm them up. Across the grain, across the grain. Probably I could have helped her with that; my mother had taught me to chop in my urchin years.

Chinese people can always become cook. Never mind you know anything or not, you say you like to cook they say OK! But of course if you become cook, your mother will commit suicide. Even I am dead I will rise up out of my grave to kill myself.

Blondie peeled the broccoli stalks. Typically, we bought broccoli florets; Blondie had always felt vegetable preparation a waste of time. Why not steal those precious moments for the family? Bailey especially needed attention; he needed his mommy to chase him and make sure he didn't hit anything, toddling around as he did with no brakes and no steering. He needed his mommy to take baths with him, and dance with him, and extract pesky foreign objects from his nose.

But cooking with Lan, she did things Lan's way; and Lan's way was to waste no food, no matter how much labor was involved. So Blondie gamely peeled not only broccoli stalks, but things like chestnuts too. The chestnuts involved dissecting out veins of brownish membrane from the little, ivory, brain-like nuts.

—*Heave-ho, yo ho ho,* I hummed as I passed. A tune from *In the Hall of the Mountain King.*

Blondie turned red.

—*Heave-ho, yo ho ho.*

— Chicken with chestnuts is worth it, she insisted.

After the chestnuts came chicken. For all her farm roots, Blondie seemed reluctant to actually lay her hands in full, committed contact with the meat. She lacked too the brute butcher confidence needed to swing the big cleaver high enough in the air that she might whack down—*aiya!*—with the requisite murderousness.

— Think guillotine, I told her, passing by again. — Think decapitation.

I carried wriggling Bailey upside-down in my arms.

— Hello, Bailey, she cooed, buzzing his exposed belly. — He needs a sweater.

— Think so?

— Feel the back of his neck, she said. In the hall.

Whack. Whack.

The sweater was not in the hall, but in the mudroom. Still she insisted, upon our return, on asking: — Was it there in the hall?

BLONDIE / I thought it was in the hall.

CARNEGIE / Her chicken looked like something prepared by zoo interns for their midsized carnivores.

BLONDIE / Lan was an exacting master. As time went on, she seemed to expect the meat sliced thinner and thinner. Faster, too. Not that she ever said so. She simply took over the meat slicing if necessary and, in her elegant way, finished up in short order. Her slices were perfect. Even her discard heap of fat and gristle was humiliatingly exquisite, a shame to simply throw out.

CARNEGIE / Over time Blondie began sneakily angling her butcher block away from the kitchen. Partly so that she could look out at the yard as she worked, and partly to evade Lan's scrutiny.

BLONDIE / There were still pockets of unmelted snow down by the woods, but the days were bright and warm, and the trees were in bud. The lawn, too, was strewn with petals from our early tulips. Some of these lay on their sides, but many had filled with the morning rain, so that they glimmered like miniature lakes. Each captured a bit of the sky; each reflected its partial truth about the heavens. Some were imbued with implacable blue, others with the restless white clouds.

And of course the tulip beds were all exposed pistils now, glistening and wanton, their pale parts lifted, skirtless, to the sky.

CARNEGIE / Lan produced heaps—of bamboo shoots, of ham cubes, of scallions. So unrelenting was her focus that though she was wearing an apron, it never got dirty. Her soy sauce never splashed, her cornstarch never rose in a pouf; to every step was meted the exact amount of energy required, no more. It wasn't until she got close to needing Blondie's meat that she stopped to study her apprentice, just at the moment that fluttery Blondie started talking, with a certain over-ardor, about feng shui. Her knife work slowed to a halt as she described the workshop she and Gabriela had gone to. How she didn't really have the time for such things. But, well, how Gabriela had talked her into it, a half-day deal, and how glad she was, in the end, that she had gone if only because she had come to realize that the feng shui of Lan's apartment was awful.

BLONDIE / —To be over a garage to begin with, I said. All that bad-luck empty space below you. I'm so sorry we didn't look into this earlier. And how terrible those spiral stairs! The *qi* just spills right down them.

Lan set a duck to marinate in Coca-Cola—not my favorite recipe for Peking duck, but it did work.

— We used your apartment as a case study, I said. It has too many windows, doesn't it? The instructor suggested we hang a crystal in some of them.

— That is feudal superstition, said Lan sweetly.

CARNEGIE / She turned to do something else, then paused to watch Blondie again, a frown rucking her forehead.

Blondie blushed.

Lan immediately smiled her half smile, and said: —Very good! You are my number-one student.

Still Blondie managed, with the next whack of her butcher knife, to slice neatly into her left thumb.

— Omigod, omigod! she cried. Omigod!

I rushed into the room even as Lan brought Blondie's bleeding hand to the sink and washed the finger under the faucet. A flap of flesh was hanging completely loose; you could open and shut it like one of the new flip tops that had recently become de rigueur for everything from toothpaste to shampoo.

— Oh, Blondie, I said. Are you okay? Omigod is right. And here I thought tourniquets were mostly for Girl Scout badges. Are you okay? I do think they'll be able to sew that back on. I mean if they can reconnect men's penises in Thailand, right? After their wives have taken the butcher knife to them. Really, those cleavers are dangerous. Are you okay?

— You will be okay, said Lan decisively. And with surprising authority: — Don't cry.

LAN / *The finger was bleeding and bleeding, but I bandaged it up. Of course, the children were frightened, especially Bailey.*

CARNEGIE / —If I hadn't married you, it would be perfectly all right to be a fork, cried Blondie on the way to the hospital.

She held her hand up in the air, elevating it above her heart, as per the instructions in our medical-emergency handbook. Still blood soaked through the massive bandage, dyeing it red-brown.

— If I hadn't married you, she cried, I'd be considered perfectly good-hearted just the way I am.

BLONDIE / We had for some time been trying to hold dinner conversations in Chinese. Generally we did this in the kitchen, but more recently we had moved to the dining room, which the girls found fun. Even Lizzy liked setting the table with place mats, and good chopsticks, and real silver. They liked lighting candles. And they liked thinking up little Chinese centerpieces—an arrangement of origami animals, a bouquet of colored incense sticks. A yin-yang design made of green and black tea leaves.

For Carnegie's fortieth birthday, Wendy and Lizzy did an especially elaborate job, with place cards and napkin rings, and family pictures hanging from the chandelier. There were balloons and streamers, and party favors on each seat—the effect so lovely that I was sorry I had scheduled a surprise party of friends and neighbors for later in the evening. What an anticlimax that party was going to be, after this.

How happy Carnegie was! Sitting there at the head of the table, without one wrinkle or gray hair. I sat at the foot, from which spot I alone faced the big mirror that covered the wall behind him. We had inherited that mirror with the house; but it had always seemed out of keeping with everything else, saying 'town' the way it did, instead of 'country.' Of course, there had been other details like it, originally. But we had removed the fancy column casings that surrounded the rough-hewn posts. We had pulled up the wall-to-wall carpet blanketing the wide plank floors. As for the mirror, we'd always intended to take that down too, and probably would have, if we had known an original feature to lie beneath it.

But here it was still, and how odd our family looked in it—all those heads of black hair, with just two heads of blond.

The Wongs and the Baileys.

Any passerby would have thought that Lan and Carnegie were the husband and wife of the family, and that I was visiting with my son, Bailey. Was it true, too, that the Wongs moved their heads more, and that we Baileys, being less at home, moved them less? It did seem so to me, watching in the mirror. Watching in the mirror, it seemed to me that the Wongs owned the space, and that you could see it in the way they gestured back and forth to one another. Lizzy, of course, the most flamboyant member of the family, was the one most likely to lift and wave her hennaed arms in emphasis. Carnegie was the one most likely to lean in and make a funny face, or to stop midsentence, jaw agape, or to burst out into loud song. Tonight he was teaching the girls Beatles songs—Lan, too. 'Nowhere Man,' 'Blackbird,' 'Yesterday.' But even Wendy gestured freely, jabbering back and forth across the table with Lan. And how Lan had relaxed! She did not throw her arms about, but she did have a subtly seesaw way of sitting forward, interested, then straightening up and drawing her head back, her whole body lifting with delight or surprise.

For my part, I encouraged and encouraged. Turning and nodding, turning and nodding, like a mechanical bear in a toy store. How awkward I was. Banging things with my big bandaged thumb—my plate, my bowl. Once I knocked my chopsticks to the floor. In all this I was not unlike Bailey, who alternated between listening with much excited banging and focusing intently on his peas. Taking a break from the stimulation, I suppose. Bailey was my good eater. He was a good sleeper, too—a solid child.

What did it matter, how a family looked?

Beholding my daughters, I did not see Asians. I saw persons I knew better than I had known my parents. I knew what it had taken to potty-train them. I knew how they reacted to being scolded, to being held, to being sung to. I knew how stubborn they were, how ingenious, how dreamy. How verbal, how physical, how dramatic. (*I need to wipe my tears before I can speak again,* Lizzy used to say.) I knew their earliest heartaches. (*Those kids are biting my feelings,* Wendy once sobbed.)

In a tape recording, too, I might have seemed more part of the family than Carnegie, whose Chinese was improving so slowly. For most of the times I turned and nodded, I did speak. I supplied a word someone needed. I supplied the correct tone. I was surprised, in truth, by how much I remembered; it seemed my college Chinese teacher was right. I could feel it myself—I was a natural.

Yet our reflection seemed to say something willful to deny.

Would I have felt this so strongly if I had not spent years in design?

How large my body! An inflatable compared with everyone else's.

I had not felt this way when the family was just Carnegie and Lizzy and Wendy and me. But Bailey had changed things a little, and Lan—I thought this even as I brought out the cake, and started the singing, and laughed at the trick candles—Lan had changed things more.

Carnegie, when we married, married more into my family than I into his. I am embarrassed to admit that I did not think much then about what it meant to be surrounded—what it meant to be outnumbered. I did notice that people did not talk about his nobility in marrying me. And I did correct them when they talked about my nobility in marrying him, especially since he came with Lizzy. *How open to difference!* they said all the same. *How loving! How willing to take risks!*

I wish I could say I did not fluff up my feathers a little, after a while.

Numbers matter, Carnegie used to say. He used to shake his head in that son-of-an-immigrant way and point out the painfully obvious. *Life is not about poetry.*

How different it would feel—I could not help but feel how different— to be, say, a white couple with one Asian child.

Was there such a thing as being too open?

You could not help but wonder when you walked certain streets now, in certain cities and towns. What would even my mother say if she realized that there were parts of Los Angeles that felt like Mexico City—that there were towns in the Midwest swamped with Hmong?

Probably my mother would still say, with satisfaction, *Ah, the family of man.* Probably she would still be a person to drive the newcomers to church or to the library or to the hospital. Probably she would be disappointed in me. *Plain Jane, runt of the litter.* Of course, I would feel overrun; all my life, I had felt overrun.

But maybe even she would say, *I feel invaded.* Maybe even she would wonder, *Is this still my home?*

Possibly—probably—she would say nothing. Unlike Mama Wong, who would certainly say, *Too many outside people here,* even if they were Chinese people.

In my shoes, Mama Wong would certainly have asked, *Whose family is this?*

If I had beheld our family's reflection from the doorway, I would have thought it a testament to human possibility. If my mother had beheld it, she would have felt me to be her own true daughter.

But if I thought about this being the group that would gather around my deathbed; if I pictured myself lying, as my mother had, with tubes snaking everywhere and everything on a monitor, I thought of myself as dying abroad—in the friendly bosom of some foreign outpost.

I decided to take that mirror down. I found a crowbar in the basement the next morning, and Carnegie's ancient safety goggles—from his high school days, these were. I smiled as I lifted them off their hook, envisioning my husband hunched over a Bunsen burner. I could see him surrounded by beakers he was trying to take seriously; I felt sorry for his lab partner. I found too the Shop-Vac Carnegie had asked for one Christmas, back when he had thought woodworking might be good therapy for Lizzy—never mind that he did not know a ripsaw from a jigsaw. I lugged my equipment up the stairs. Not so easy with my thumb. I upset some cans.

Once in the dining room, though, I paused in front of the mirror and laughed at my reflection. Had I come to resemble Carnegie over the long years of our marriage? Carnegie, not I, was the type to be discovered, first thing in the morning, with safety goggles on. Waving that big white thumb.

I was about to ask him for help. I was about to ask, too, whether a crowbar was the right tool for the task—shouldn't there be screws somewhere, holding the mirror up?—when the doorbell rang.

— *Buon giorno!*

12

Blondie Takes a Day Off

BLONDIE / The storm door was off having a screen made for it, so she wasn't even behind glass. There was simply a ring and—Gabriela! In enormous rhinestone sunglasses.

CARNEGIE / A guide to sacred places. I asked her what she was working on in Italy, and that's what she said. First she had to find the places, and then she had to write sections on their mystical significance. Then suggest rituals.

— The rituals are hard, she said. You can't just meditate everywhere. Neither can you howl.

— How true, I said.

— But that's what my editor wants, she said. So rituals there will be.

— Naturally, I said. One must consider one's editor.

— Of course there's always candles, she said. And incense. And it's not too inconvenient for most people to pack some rattles or a small drum.

BLONDIE / She twirled in the kitchen that I might see that she had not been 'abusing food,' as she put it. Not that she was interested in cutting a *bella figura,* either. She had, in fact, thrown out her mirror and her scale. Her frizzy hair, formerly tamed, was now an enormous radiant mass, with the front third tied into five or six knots such as one found at the ends of lightbulb pull strings; the knots dotted her head. Her fingernails, too, were not shiny with polish, as on her last visit, but simply themselves. And though she had yet to replace her sunglasses, she had given up her Eurotrash jeans and leather jacket. In place of stiletto heels, she wore running sandals.

— And-a guess-a what-a? she cried. I-a found-a myself a house-a!

CARNEGIE / For all her time in Italy, her Italian manner was exactly that of Bobby the Greek in the local pizza parlor.

BLONDIE / She had not e-mailed her big news, wanting to tell me in person. First, that she had practically bought an Umbrian farmhouse—old, of course, they were all old—a ruin, with the idea that she and Giorgio would fix it up themselves. Of course, there was a lot of red tape. But he had connections, and they knew a retired English couple willing to live in an outbuilding, as caretakers. And the beams! The floors! The courtyard! There were open showers, and half-moon windows, and a walk-in fireplace . . .

— Giorgio? I said.

— A surprise-a! cried Gabriela. We've-a been together for-a four weeks-a!

He was a puppeteer from Sicily, a genius, in the process of leaving Palermo and his wife, and moving his theater north to Umbria. She'd met him on the steps of the Duomo—a warm, earthy man, not at all sneaky as some people said people from the *Mezzogiorno* could be, although something of a mama's boy, that was true, and not sure why a man shouldn't have a lover or two. Or so he said, anyway; who knew what Italians actually did besides talk—mostly, it seemed to her, about how Americans did not know how to relax, witness how uptight they were about drinking, smoking, everything. And working all the time! He didn't know how anybody could think of America as free, he thought it was like a prison. The only words he knew in English were 'politi-cal-ly correct-a.'

But there was no time to talk. There was barely time even to say hello to her goat—though we did do that, of course, quickly—Tommy! Tommy! she cried. Do you recognize me?—before we jumped in the car. For we were late, it turned out, for the shower.

— Shower?

The brunch baby shower of a good friend of hers, what else, who lived in the next town, and who she wanted me to meet—or no, two towns over—which was great since it gave us time to talk about Giorgio—who for all his talk had never actually had an affair before and luckily had only one child, a girl, one-quarter Algerian, which mattered more than you'd think; but first what had happened to my thumb?

The rest emerged as we bumped down roads I had not known existed, even though I'd lived in this area for years. Beginning with how this Giorgio had been living at home with his mother even though he was married. But recently she had died, and now he was getting divorced—how interesting, I said—an old story, said Gabriela, and yet in this case true. He really was leaving his wife; they would talk about it every day during the *passagiata.* She was still convincing me how true when suddenly we had arrived at a strange house in the woods—an octagonal house, a hippie house. It had the air of a ruin, or a folly—maybe because it sat on the edge of a swamp, covered with leaves even now; and because it had an associated tower, also octagonal, containing at its top a homemade sauna. This was fired with wood, and entered through a trapdoor in its floor. We undressed and ascended into a cloud—the heavens, it seemed—where we were welcomed by ten or so pink and brown archangels, all naked, like the shower honoree, Rain, who was, of course, pregnant.

The women, sitting or reclining on the half circle of tiled benches, were of varying races, ages, body types. They were variously marked and pierced, but it was my thumb that provoked comment. I explained. Murmurs of sympathy. I was neither the fattest nor the slimmest; neither the oldest nor the youngest; neither the fairest nor the darkest; neither the lumpiest nor the smoothest. Neither was I the only one who did not know Rain—who could only poke her interested head in from the window of the adjacent shower stall every so often. Extreme heat being a hazard, of course, to the fetus. All those pregnancy precautions; I had forgotten how many there were. Another newcomer was being introduced; then Gabriela was saying hello. I breathed deeply—one breath, the next—while Gabriela introduced me as Shine. Shine! Gabriela did this sort of thing from time to time; I laughed and leaned back, stretching my back. My skin was becoming slick—I was shining. People reminisced about their pregnancies. I added something; several people turned out to have had the same midwife, and to have chosen home births; two hospital-goers turned out to have delivered in the same wing. There was a comparing of C-section scars; and a frank admiration of the pristine bodies of the two women who had never been pregnant. These were Gabriela and a woman with a series of Chinese characters tattooed up her spine.

— You can see they've never breastfed, said one woman. Oh, to be pert!

Gabriela pushed her chest forward, military-style; everyone laughed.

— Oh, not to be stretched out, said another woman. You don't know how lucky you C-section people are.

More laughter.

— Oh, not to leak when I leap, said a third.

Rain poked her head in repeatedly; her various friends took turns visiting with her. I visited only at the end, after showering and changing my dressing.

A large woman, expecting twins, Rain seemed monumental, especially semicloaked in a beach towel as she was. Her belly was alive, yet she reported that activity had slowed. The babies had gotten so big—they had no room to move. I had seen other people feel her belly on their way in or out of the shower, some with two hands; one woman kissed it, as if it was the Blarney stone. But I hesitated to touch her at all until she smiled and took my hand and placed it on her belly herself.

— My name's not Shine, I said.

— But of course it is, she said, winking; and from the depths of her drum of a striated belly I felt a knobby something that took me back to the feeling of Bailey in utero. That enormous creaturely mystery, surfacing.

— You have a child, said Rain. No, more than one.

— Three, I said. Two adopted.

— And one natural.

— Biological, we say.

— Of course, she said. Three natural.

— Exactly.

— I'm having two girls, she said. I'm so glad they're girls.

— A son's a son until he finds a wife, I said. A daughter's a daughter all her life.

— It's true, isn't it.

— I haven't gotten there yet. I don't know.

— Tell me when you find out, she said. Shine.

— I'll send you a postcard.

— Don't you wish someone would send us a postcard now? she said. To tell us everything else we should know?

— I do wish it, I said. Then I said: — You must have lost your mother.

— Yes, she said. You too.

— Me too.

— I could see it a mile away, she said.

Later there was an outdoor brunch, and a rose-petal foot bath for Rain—this last a ritual involving not only petals, but lavender oil as well. Clothed, wet-haired, cross-legged, we sat on boulders, in a natural circle formed by the arms of a pair of enormous fir trees. Marry-me trees, Rain called them. The trees towered up and up and up, and seemed to touch at the top—a giant's teepee. It was cool enough out that we probably ought to have moved into the sun, except that here in the light shade grew an entire forest of ladies' slippers. It was like being surrounded by fairies, a bevy of puff-bellied fairies, who swayed—look!—like Rain. Pregnant too. We held hands and sang a song. We had stoked the sauna fire before we left, anticipating that some of us might like a warm-up after sitting outside. Now a big whiteness billowed beyond the trees; you might almost have thought the tower on fire. But no—I squinted. Happily, it was not.

The idea of washing the feet of a woman I'd only just met made me feel awkward; indeed, washing anyone's feet seemed kooky. Not that I hadn't heard, of course, about the New Age rituals so popular these days. Renata and Ariela had lots of friends given to drummings and howlings and placenta burials. And of course, Gabriela had always loved workshops. Even in college she had done jewelry making and glassblowing and journaling.

But now here I was. Each member of the group, in turn, poured warm oil over Rain's bare feet, and sprinkled them with rose petals—then expressed a wish.

— I wish for you an easy labor.

— I wish for you sleep.

— I wish for you real support.

— I wish for you a way of taking it all in, and keeping it, and not losing it.

— I wish for you the courage to ask for an epidural if you need one. And dammit, may the drug thing work.

Soon it was my turn, and how lovely the liquid sound of the pouring—that *drip, pip pip pip.* The scent of the oil floated up to me—lavender, yes. I immersed my right hand and most of my left—all but my thumb. The dressing got a little wet at one edge, but never mind. It was good to be small, to be folded up humbly, to kneel before Rain, our madonna of the hiked skirt, who was sitting on a stump. Though I was wishing I had a sweater, she was perfectly comfortable, even without shoes; her body was running hot. She beamed down with such genuine kindness that I felt it as a shock. Her belly hung between her spread legs; she had no lap. She had no dignity. And yet her face, her kindly face, was the face of a saint.

Other women have wished to look like models; I have always wished to radiate that sort of kindliness. You had to have a wide, slightly plain face, and laugh lines. You had to have soft eyes and a bit of dough to your nose; and you had to have a slowness of glance, a way of turning your head as your eyes moved, as if your eyeballs did not rotate as easily as they might. The quick glance, the darting, roving glance belonged to someone else—the city person, the savvy person. The kindly person lifts her face in slow joy when she sees someone she loves, like someone half blind.

— Shine, Rain said. That suits you.

— I wish for you daughters who will appreciate you, I said.

— Better pour some extra oil on my feet, she laughed.

A number of the guests were neighbors who lived in an intentional community built along the edges of the swamp. After the foot bathing, a woman named Angela took Gabriela and me on a tour.

A thin woman with long braids, Angela was almost painfully informative.

— You can see it all online, she began. On our website.

But the pictures, she went on to explain, didn't do justice to the land, which had long been regarded as unbuildable, and which only the community founders had seen as one of the last unspoiled tracts in this region—beautiful and rich with wildlife. It was, in fact, home to a blue heron, and a host of smaller birds. In the summer there were acres of water lilies. Of course, there was the inevitable purple loosestrife, but they had managed to keep it back.

Gabriela and I nodded our approval.

Now, happily, Angela went on, the area was protected wetlands. How satisfied the community had been to know that this swamp and others like it would be left pristine, that no one would be allowed to build even what they had—plumbing-free stilt houses, each comprising three units. These had been grandfathered into the new legislation, partly because they had been shown to have so little impact on the land.

— Really, said Gabriela.

There was a series of boardwalks, for example, to keep people from trampling anything. They used composting toilets, and biodegradable everything; and of course, cohousing in general was so much more efficient than the single-family house, which was in truth as great a scourge to the earth as the automobile.

— How true, I said.

Angela explained how the community members had meddled with the swamp in only two ways. One being the loosestrife control, the other being the introduction of bats to keep the mosquitoes down. She showed us the community house, where they held yoga and meditation, dances and potlucks and seminars. It was where some people did their homeschooling; where they had seminars on Buddhism; and where they held their annual New Year's Day lantern ceremony. Beside it lay the community garden—they were committed to living closer to their food sources. In this and in other ways, they took their inspiration from communities in Denmark.

Gabriela and I nodded, nodded.

— A lot of people think it's going to be hard work to live in a community like this, said Angela. They think they're going to have to be 'on' all the time. But actually no one is expected to be on best behavior. No one is expected to be a saint.

— Really, we said.

— We are about tolerance, continued Angela. This is a place where people feel comfortable living off-grid.

Their mailman, it seemed, was a former law-school professor. She herself was dating a PE teacher she had met at a literacy center—a lovely man who could not read when she met him but was now halfway through *The Brothers Karamazov.*

— Should I move here? wondered Gabriela as we tromped back the short path to Rain's house. All along the way were happy trillium—hundreds, thousands of trillium.

— What about Giorgio?

— Giorgio, she sighed. Then she winked. — Maybe I'll move anyway.

— I'll move with you, I said. You know what this is? It's Independence Island.

— Your Grandma What's-Her-Name would've loved it.

In the car Gabriela resumed her analysis of Italy and Giorgio.

— I tell you what I think sometimes, she said. Sometimes I think it's Tommy I love most of all. Someday I want to have sheep too, and chickens.

— Too bad you never knew my Grandma Dotie. You could've moved back to Wisconsin with her.

Gabriela laughed.

— We could have grown ginseng. Gotten into the yogurt boom.

She was still interested in massage, and aromatherapy. In fact, once she was done with her guidebook and her renovation, she thought she might open a wellness center, with different kinds of yoga. And as soon as that got going, she was going to bring Tommy over.

— When do you guess that would be?

I hated to ask, but, well, it was illegal to keep him in our town, I explained. I explained, too, how Carnegie resented him, as did Lan.

— Lan resents Tommy? Gabriela looked distraught. — I thought the Chinese were so good with animals.

Should I have told her how Lan threw a pail at his head?

— Don't worry, I kept saying. I'll make sure it doesn't happen again. Don't worry. Tommy will be fine.

Still she was upset.

Later, though, she was back to Giorgio.

— It's too bad he's married, she sighed. He says he's going to leave her. But in his heart of hearts he thinks a man is entitled to two wives. He thinks it's only natural.

— I'm afraid Carnegie thinks that too, I laughed.

Gabriela shook her head.

— But where you're the first wife, I'm the whaddyacall it. The love wife, she said.

WENDY / We all smell when Mom comes home, I think like soy sauce and sesame oil, because we made dumplings in the kitchen. Dad and Lanlan chopped, me and Lizzy helped fold, and mine all stayed together in one piece, the ones that came apart in the water were Lizzy's. She says they weren't, but they were.

BLONDIE / Thanks to the short hall between the front door and the dining room, they did not see me right away. But I knew how things would happen, in another half moment—how Bailey would sense my presence and yell, *Mama!* How he would scramble down from his Tripp Trapp chair and come trundling headlong down the hall, calling, *Mam! Mam! Mam!* I knew how he would feel, solid and gymnastic, as I swung him up onto my hip. I knew how he would grip my waist with his knees, and how he would snuggle his head in toward my neck—how I would feel the small pant of his humid breath under my chin, even as I worked my purse off my shoulder, down onto a chair.

But for this half moment, for a half moment more, I saw them—Carnegie at the head of the table, in a baseball cap; Lan at its foot, in my seat. She sat the way she stood and walked—regally. Her hair shone.

All were quiet and absorbed.

How much more natural this scene than the one that included me. How natural, and how quiet it was—the quiet was almost the worst part. They were eating little snacks, in bowls. No one was eating out of a bag—even Carnegie was eating Chee-tos out of a pair of blue-and-white rice bowls. Carnegie and Lizzy and Wendy had in front of them lidded cups, such as I'd seen in China and

Chinatown; Bailey had his sippy cup, which I saw now was also a lidded cup. Everyone was wearing slippers. Lan's were blue, and perfectly plain.

The love wife.

I had seen those slippers many times—she was a slipper wearer. And of course, Carnegie had owned his fuzzy slippers for years. Lizzy, too, had fuzzy slippers, with a cuff; Wendy and Bailey had animal slippers—pandas and lions, respectively. I knew this. But never before had I ever seen them all wear slippers together.

Lizzy got up to do something, shuffling.

Lizzy, shuffling!

They were all working, of course.

Outside was an afternoon meant for ecstasy. The sun was high and soft—you could already smell the lilacs. The redbuds were out, and the dogwoods in the woods, and our circle of old apple trees was starting. It was time to lie under our trees and gaze up at the ceiling of bloom; had I been home, I would have insisted that everyone go roll down the hill. We would have climbed trees and picked bouquets and woven garlands and had a picnic.

Instead, everyone had a computer on.

Carnegie was working on a spreadsheet. Lan, I guessed, was working at a typing program. More surprisingly, Lizzy, it seemed, was writing a paper, while Wendy jabbed at the keyboard—Math Blasters, I guessed. Bailey, seated next to Lan, was playing with a pile of old floppies. Except that our whole beautiful yard languished outside, empty, the scene was sweet.

Everyone looked happy.

What was that smell?

The screens glowed, alive with color. The girls had their sound on. At low volume, it seemed innocuous, like the noise of a pet. Even the tangle of cords seemed a happy tangle, connecting the people as much as the computers. Carnegie, relaxed, had stretched his legs out full-length under the table, while Lan drew her crossed ankles back under her chair. This was apparently to avoid contact with his enormous slippers, which loomed big as snowshoes. For all her effort, though, their toes did seem to be ruffling the bells of her blue jeans the moment Gabriela and I finally announced our arrival.

— Oh, hi, said Carnegie, sitting up immediately and drawing his feet back.

— Mam!

Bailey scrambled down off his Tripp Trapp chair. The girls looked up.

— Hi, Mom. Gabbie!

The girls jumped up to greet Gabriela. Lan stood too, blushing. Carnegie had a sip of tea—since when did he drink tea?—replacing the lid of his cup before saving his work. Then, finally, he pushed his chair back, and stood up. He stretched dramatically, reaching for the ceiling with one hand—almost touching it. His gaze wandered somewhere over my left shoulder. He massaged his neck. Straightened his baseball cap.

— Mam! Mam! Bailey's arms were up.

I swung him onto my hip; he nuzzled while I maneuvered to put my bag down.

— How're you doing, cutie? What happened to your hair?

So absorbing had been the slippers that I had almost missed Bailey's bangs, which featured a big jagged gap.

— He cut by himself, said Lan.

— What was he doing with a pair of scissors?

Nobody answered.

— Mam! Mam! said Bailey proudly.

— Good for you, I said automatically. But next time how about letting Mom do it, okay?

I put him down.

— Mam!

He pulled me by the hand, putting his whole body weight into the effort.

— Pay me! Pay me! he said, meaning 'play with me.'

I drew him to me and kissed him; he pouted, knowing what that meant.

— Lizzy, I said.

And for once, she obediently took charge of her brother, who—still pouting—allowed this substitution. Surprising us all.

I ordered Wendy to follow them; she, too, for once, listened.

We four adults then just stood there, awkwardly. Like a group moderately acquainted but trying to recall how. Finally Gabriela, her hand on the back of a chair, began to stretch her hamstrings. Her legs were tan but freckly.

My thumb itched.

— You can work some more, if you like, I told Carnegie and Lan. I'm going to roll down the hill with the children.

CARNEGIE / Blondie did not in fact leave then as promised, but rather stood there menacingly, with her thumb in a wad and her hair gone flat.

— I rolled around with them yesterday, I said.

— Was it fun? asked Gabriela.

— Maybe I go see the children outside, said Lan.

— Of course, said Blondie. Don't forget your umbrella.

— Ah, said Gabriela, stretching some more. — That's tight.

Blondie opened a window.

BLONDIE / — There's nothing the matter with hard work, said Carnegie.

— Did someone say there was something the matter with work? I said.

— I was brought up to believe in work, said Carnegie. It's my religion.

— And why shouldn't you be a workaholic if you want to, it's a free country, said Gabriela, switching legs.

Carnegie sat down, turning his cap around backward.

— Thank you, and don't forget your goat, he said. If you leave him any longer, we're going to eat him.

He began typing an e-mail.

13

Blondie Quits

BLONDIE / I should have put my foot down then and there. But what was their offense, exactly? Sharing a table? Getting along? How was I excluded from their chumminess except in my own mind?

— No one has done anything, said Carnegie. You're too possessive.

— This is not in your mind, said Gabriela. You have to do something.

But based on what? What proof did I have?

Said Gabriela: — This isn't a court case. You have to trust your gut.

I could hear my mother, though, too. *In this family, we give others the benefit of the doubt.*

And so, for a while yet, I hesitated.

By late May, the girls were disappearing most nights after supper to go hang out with Lan. Theoretically she wasn't even on duty. But she insisted she didn't mind, and the girls begged. Carnegie pointed out, too, that this could only go on for a few weeks. Would it not naturally end with the end of Lan's intersession?

— Think how very much worse it could be, he said. Given that adolescents will hang out. The girls could be hanging with our own Dreaded Dreadlocks.

'Dreaded Dreadlocks' was Russell.

— You're right, I said.

A form of agreement, Carnegie would say later. Did I agree for Carnegie to disappear too?

— Got to go save my job, he'd say after the dishes. Should you suspect me of chatting on the Internet, you're wrong.

Or: — I'm actually in dire circumstances, you know. Dire, dire circumstances.

— Well then, go save yourself, I'd laugh. Got your bailer?

Honestly, I didn't know whether to be worried for him or not.

In any case, it was a treat to have forty-five to fifty-five minutes of precious one-on-one with Bailey before his bedtime. We made breadsticks and block towers; we played ring-around-the-rosy and airplane. We read books; we banged on the piano. Then there was floor time; I tried to spend at least fifteen minutes a day doing whatever Bailey wanted to do, following his lead.

For a good ten days I did not check to see what the girls were up to over there at Lan's.

But one night Bailey and I put some peanut butter banana crisp in the oven. Bailey had loved shmushing the bananas. I had loved helping shmush, and using up some brown bananas besides. What wonderful things Bailey had done! Threatening to touch the oven, but then pulling his hand back and saying *ssss*. And sitting on the potty by himself—not really doing anything, just trying it out with the door closed.

— Dtuck! he cried from behind the door. Dtuck!

— *Ss*tuck, I said to him, amazed and amused, as I pushed on the door. Gently, giving him time to back up as the door swung in. — *Ss*tuck.

Later, though—destabilized, it seemed, by his own new tricks—he threw a wooden spoon across the room.

In an effort to distract him I gathered him up into my arms, and carried him outside. This worked; he quieted, burrowing against me. It wouldn't be much longer before I wouldn't be carrying him at all, I knew—how much heavier he was than the girls at his age. Also he clung less, leaving me to support more of his weight. And I was older—creakier. Still I lugged him astride my hip.

He lifted his head wonderingly. — Go? he asked.

— Where are we going? We're going to Lan's apartment, to visit the girls. Doesn't that sound like fun?

He kicked his feet.

We went to go say hello to Tommy first. Why was his water pail empty? Anyway, I filled it while Bailey petted the goat, whom he loved; we used to feel we had to protect him from Tommy but, honestly, he got along better with Tommy than anyone else in the family did. Also I closed the toolshed door, so squirrels wouldn't get at the birdseed.

Up the spiral steps; Lan's door was open. Still I knocked as we entered, calling, Hello!—my heart thumping from the climb.

Lan was in the kitchen, at her computer. The girls were doing their homework in front of the TV.

— Hello, Lan. Hello, girls.

— Hello, said Lan.

— Hmm, said Wendy.

— Hmm, said Lizzy.

The TV was just inside the door, across from the kitchen. It sat right on the floor, the VCR beside it; the girls were splayed on their stomachs on the carpet, not more than two feet away from the screen. Though some parts of Lan's apartment were lit, the girls appeared to be reading by the light of the TV screen. Their faces flickered with the reflected colors—pale blue, pale yellow, streak red.

I set Bailey on his feet, then crouched down to shut off the TV. The girls' faces went suddenly dark, their eyes suddenly bright—gleaming now with reflected light from the kitchen.

Bailey started crying.

— Dee vee! Dee vee! he demanded.

He glared, solid with fury, his two feet planted for a moment in a stance that reminded me of my father. Then he began to stomp and bawl like the toddler that he was; I picked him back up.

— Lan, I said. Do you let Bailey watch TV?

Lan stood to answer, peering over the top of her computer. Her hair was in pigtails.

— Only once a great great while.

— I told you no TV for Bailey.

— Just once or twice.

He thrashed in my arms—the tantrum I had avoided in the house was upon us.

— Dee vee! he demanded, outrage in his cry. — Dee vee!

I switched on a floor lamp. The girls blinked—caught, it seemed, in the circle of yellow light. They were still lying on their stomachs. They had been banging their feet together in the air when I entered; now they toed the mauve carpet. Wendy wore her panda slippers; Lizzy was barefoot. I jostled Bailey, leaning back away from him, trying to pin his legs so he couldn't kick. Lizzy had drawn doodles all down the margins of her math sheet. She was, what's more, doing her problems in fluorescent marker.

Not the best approach, perhaps, for someone who despite a gift for math had managed to get a C in trigonometry last semester.

Bailey was kicking me now—hard, he had gotten strong. Lowering him to the floor, I knelt beside him.

— Lan, I said, my hand on Bailey's tummy. — Homework comes first in this house.

— Of course, she agreed, crossing the room. — That is why, even though they are watch TV, I say better do homework.

— Lan. The girls can't work with the TV on.

— Of course not. That's why I tell them shut TV off. But you know, they love TV on. They say that way they work better.

I knew this argument. Lizzy claimed TV relaxed her and helped her focus. She claimed she wouldn't have gotten that C in math if I'd let her watch TV while she did her homework.

— Lizzy, I said. Honestly. Do you honestly think this the best strategy? With finals coming up?

She touched her feet together. Wendy sat up.

Bailey struggled and wailed, rolling away from me.

— Lan, I said. You have to tell them no TV until they are done with their homework.

— You do not like TV, there is no TV, she said finally.

— This is just so typical, said Lizzy then, capping her marker. —Typical! You can't let us have one thing of our own. You have to ruin everything!

In an effort to calm Bailey, Lan offered him a piece of candy from her candy bowl, which sat on a small side table. He quieted and began to unwrap it, expertly.

— Lan, I said. I told you no candy.

In a voice I could hardly hear, she said: — That is date candy, kind of like fruit. Not the real candy.

Bailey wailed louder than ever when the candy was withdrawn.

— Can-dee! he cried. Can-dee!

— If you do not like candy, there is no candy, said Lan.

She stood outside the light circle. Her voice was perfectly flat.

Behind us, the door opened. Russell sauntered in, unannounced.

— Hey, man, he said. What's happening?

Russell had blond dreadlocks and an aggressive unflappability I recognized from the corporate world—the mark of someone for whom everything was a showdown. He wore bleach-splotched blue jeans, and a shirt with its sleeves ripped out.

— May I ask what you are doing here? I said.

— I'm here to get Lizzy.

— What on earth could you be talking about? I said. Elizabeth Bailey Wong, you know you are not allowed to go out on weeknights.

— This is what I mean, said Lizzy, finally sitting up. Her marker rolled across her math sheet but was stopped by the carpet nub. — Weren't we all happy until she walked in? And will you listen to her voice? *Elizabeth Bailey Wong, you know you are not allowed to go out on weeknights.* Can you hear how fake it is? Why don't you just yell? That's what I want to know. In fact, that's what we all want to know around here. Why do you have to talk in that fake voice?

— In this family, we—

— Then who even wants to be in this family! yelled Lizzy. Because I do raise my voice! Because I do yell! Because I am not fake like you, as everyone can totally see!

Bailey froze in alarm.

— Come here, cutie, I said. It's okay.

I reached for him, but Bailey sidestepped my embrace, stomped over to the side table, and grabbed a piece of candy.

CARNEGIE / — Lan loves them, I said.

— She'll do anything to win them, said Blondie. She never says no.

— How can we expect her to micromanage the girls when she isn't even supposed to be on in the evening?

— She encourages them. Don't you see? How she encourages them? Do you know what Lizzy said to me? *Why do you have to talk in that fake voice. That's what we all want to know around here.* We all. We all. You tell me who she means.

— Blondie. Think about what we tell her to do at school. Ignore people, right? You should practice what we preach and forget about what she says. Put that aging memory to work for you.

— Forget about what she says? Ignore her? She's my daughter.

— She's fifteen.

— And what about Lan? How old is she, please tell me. How old is she?

BLONDIE / I quit my job a week later.

CARNEGIE / — You don't have to do this to get the family back, I said.

And: — Can we really afford for you to do this?

A minor matter of mutual interest that I did think we should discuss.

— I can't afford not to, she said.

BLONDIE / Porter, my boss, was no more enthusiastic. He worked over a paper clip, bending and unbending it, then placing it on a pad of yellow paper to contemplate.

— Do we mind your deserting us? he said. Absolutely we mind.

Creatively, he offered me stock. Reduced hours, too—he knew this was a beef. More flex. More support. Even a company garden. There was a little south-facing plot that had apparently been double-dug then abandoned, over by the foundation of the main building. I did not know it had been double-dug, and was surprised that Porter knew. But I had noticed it, too. A plot right next to the foundation, the heat of the concrete bumping it up a whole growing zone, I guessed.

I would never have had the time, though, to actually work that garden. Porter had no idea how long things took, and never had.

Once upon a time a socially conscious money-market fund had seemed a thing to embrace. Not only because I had discovered it on my own, independent of Carnegie, but because I believed it. Would not such investing make a difference? It was easy to make the brochures beautiful, sick as I was—as we all were—of the Reagan go-go years. All that memememe. At the same time we founders were realists—realist idealists, I suppose.

Back then, the men in the company all had beards. The women wore their hair loose.

CARNEGIE / Hair. Everyone had hair.

BLONDIE / We all had the same size office.

CARNEGIE / There were quarters where the secretaries brought home more money than the CEO. Quarters where the managers barely eked out a living on their performance-linked compensation.

Then the nineties took off, and the same managers started taking safaris in the Serengeti. When their kids did Eygpt, they went boating on the Nile; they brought back papyrus for class projects. Their kitchens sprouted six-burner professional stoves, and Sub-Zero refrigerators. One-of-a-kind casseroles with whimsical handles and unusual glazes.

BLONDIE / In time, we founders all became wealthy—wealthy enough to live on one income with some belt tightening. Wealthy enough to live without any income, even, for a while, if Carnegie were really to lose his job.

Always we had talked in the office about what we meant by the word 'good'—what it meant to do good, and whether that made you a good person. How you knew you had done enough good. Now we asked different questions. Was it okay to live the good life, for example, and Could we do more good if we felt good.

I worried the scar on my thumb as Porter appealed to me to reconsider.

— I'd be happy to up your profit sharing if you'd like, he said.

— We were making a difference, I said.

— We're still making a difference.

— It used to be I was too busy to have lunch, I said. Now I'm so busy, I don't always have lunch.

Porter frowned at his yellow pad. He never sat down without a yellow pad in front of him; however, he rarely wrote on it. Mostly he pushed it away, as he did now, like linear thinking itself.

— No one wants you to skip lunch, he said.

The first day of my new life I woke, as usual, at six-thirty. Carnegie reached out to hit the radio snooze bar, then he swung that same arm like a bat to tap me on the shoulder. Grunting.

— I don't have to get up, remember? I said. You're the one who has to get up.

To this he said something about cavemen and animals and at what point people began to force themselves awake when they really wanted to sleep and whether man was not truly a sick animal who had trouble taking even occasional days off until their mothers died. Then suddenly he had spirited himself out of bed; I could feel my body cool with the absence of his.

Of course, he sang while in the shower, sang and sang. He sometimes said that the reason he didn't need to take a normal vacation was because he took a daily vacation. And indeed, the water flew. He was like a new-model garden sprinkler—the frenzied sort that spouted in all directions at once. He held the shampoo bottle high over his head so that the shampoo cascaded onto his scalp, then parked the bottle, uncapped, on a nearby shelf. The bottle would remain uncapped; he liked to throw the cap away first thing. Unlike me—why did I slavishly uncap my shampoo, use a bit of it, then cap it securely back up? I was a folder of towels as well, and of laundry, including underwear, before Lan came. Now she did it. But I used to do the folding, a load every other day. Carnegie, in contrast, threw his underwear into his dresser drawer in a heap.

— What difference does it make? he said. Folding underwear has no marginal utility, and may I make a similar case for socks.

Might I also, in my new life, become a tosser of underwear?

The children were stirring; the hubbub began. I could hear it before they were up, even as they turned under the tangle of their blankets and began to realize that they'd been sleeping with one foot uncovered, or that their hand had somehow come to nestle inside their pillowcase—conditions Carnegie and I often discovered in the course of checking on them at night. Still I lay in bed—feeling how one of my toes had not yet woken up. This was my fourth toe, a toe in which I had mysteriously never enjoyed as much sensation as in the others. I wiggled it and felt the wiggle more than the toe itself. Then I stretched my arms over my head. Would I find in another year that I had stopped shaving my underarms, like my sisters? I felt the heaviness of my cheeks, the tensing of certain muscles at the corners of my mouth. My mother had tensed those same muscles—the line between her smile and her grimace could be hard to discern. She was the type, after all, to smile even as she expressed her displeasure.

She was not like Mama Wong, who just let you have it.

Usually I sprang out of bed organizing—planning and noting, my options laid out. When, today, I finally opened my eyes it was to admire a shaft of light emanating from the side of the blind. It formed a narrow bright hallway that extended clear across the room, disappearing into the opposite wall—a shortcut for spirits, it appeared. A few minutes later, another such passageway appeared; I could actually see the passages begin and grow with the minutes, magically elongating. How could I never have realized our room so gloriously banded, floor to ceiling, by the morning light? I traversed the bands, arms out to either side. Light, dark, light, dark, light, dark. How could I have thought myself living?

The girls crashed into the room, yelling, What are you doing? I showed them. Lizzy and Wendy tried it too, then, in their nightshirts.

Prancing, whirling, tilting, giggling. Even Lizzy was giggling—how long since I'd seen her giggle like that! Bailey toddled in and began to jump too, but with a diaper so wet from the night I had to stop him and take it off. Should I have let him jump without a diaper? I did, with predictable results. But what fun to hear him shriek, and to see him run run run—as he had started to, all of a sudden, just this week—nonstop, his legs flashing, his body seeming to weigh nothing at all. How slow his sisters, in comparison. How already slowed by their years.

Lizzy lay down on the massage table for a massage, but it was time for those ancient ladies to get going if they weren't going to be late for school. I shoved everyone out, and opened the blinds, feeling the force of the light—like something that could tumble you back, knock you over and drown you.

We were washed happy down to breakfast. How long the day already!

It stayed that way, all day.

For years my days had been about running late. A little late, fashionably late, inexcusably late. Now there was morning, and then afternoon, and then evening. There was even early morning, and late morning. Early afternoon. Late afternoon. Twilight. Who needed to live to a hundred when every day was a year? I saw how the sun moved, and how the moon moved; how the far corner of the yard roiled with earthworms. How the fine white mushrooms lifting clear from the soft ground left craters in the earth at the base of their stems, and—look—sported little soil hats.

My father had cataract surgery. I was able, for once, to fly home and help out. My father could not bend down, because of the pressure this would exert on his eyeballs; it was good to be able to help him get things, and send e-mails, and cook, and not leave all the nursing to my sisters. It was good, too, to see my father enjoying his vision. In just one eye—he was going to have the other one done soon. It was good to laugh with him; he saw like a teenager now! I got more exercise keeping up with him than I had gotten for a long time, a turn around the block quickly stretching into five miles of walking a day.

WENDY / Mom quits her job and in the beginning it's like, Oh I love having time. She loves it that she has the time to walk places. She loves finding out things she didn't know, like that I love grilled cheese. Somehow she missed that, she says, she doesn't know how she could have missed that.

BLONDIE / I took the kids to the beach several times a week. We caught hermit crabs, and a real crab. We buried one another in the sand. We made drip sculptures—a family of hoary creatures with elaborate sea-grass hula skirts.

I took the girls on city expeditions, too—playgoing, museum-going, concertgoing.

— Guilt tripping, said Carnegie.

I didn't care. I could not believe my good luck—that I could stop whenever I wanted—that I could pause. That I could examine, for no good reason, a dragonfly—its stick-pin eyes, its stretch-net wings. And that gray-green skeleton pattern that traversed the length of its back; it seemed to be wearing its X-ray. I could stop to watch the throttle of a bird's throat as it warbled—to note how the bird tucked its tail under its body with the effort. One day I saw a snapping turtle. Probably there were always snapping turtles in our yard; there was a pond not far from us. But this one! An enormous prehistoric-looking creature with a great leathery dewlap. He looked like the march of time personified—determined, serious, inexorable.

How sufficient life seemed, for once. Every day I felt satisfaction. Every day I saw the birch trees in the yard anew. I saw them as protected, beclouded, wind-fluttered, earthbound—and in the now blowing, now settling, now alighting of my mind, felt rapture.

What a lovely community I belonged to now! Margie, Lindsay, Jaime, Cindee. Over the years I had lost friends, one by one, for lack of time. Now the world of friendship sprang effortlessly back to life. Soon I was joining friends at the park at nine, in running sneakers; I was joining them at the Tuesday farmer's market at ten. A book club formed around us—a reincarnation, apparently, of an earlier group. We read clusters of books—about blindness, about Australia. About religion, death, daughters.

I gardened as I had not gardened in years—truly tending to my plants.

Bailey and I spent hours in worm play now. We also did water play, sand play, pebble play. We walked funny. Talked funny. Took two baths a day. The girls and I slipcovered some furniture in natural muslin. How serene our new living room!

— Like a spa, said Lizzy.

— Like heaven, said Wendy.

We made cloud pillows, sky afghans. We admired our work—patted ourselves loudly on the back. And then sitting there, ensconced in it all, the too-warm afghans spread at our feet, we began to talk—Wendy especially, but Lizzy too. They began to tell me things in a way they hadn't since they were toddlers. There was a boy in love with her, Wendy said. He turned red whenever he saw her; his name was Lionel. She beat him at chess, but he beat her at Scrabble. And there were girls in her grade wearing real bras, with cups, she said, not trainers. They had to buy their bathing suits in the grown-up department, otherwise their nipples would show.

Lizzy announced that she was going to become a journalist when she grew up, seeing as how she was good at giving people a hard time and could always tell when people were lying. Also she asked me if you really always had to make the guy wear a rubber—a baggy, she called it.

— Oh, Lizzy, please yes, I said. Will you promise me you will? Will you promise?

— I promise, she said solemnly, her head to one side. — I'm not saying it's an issue. Just that it would be so stupid to get AIDS.

— It would, it would be stupid, I said. It would be very very stupid.

It was worth having quit just to have that conversation.

Other conversations, too. For example, the conversation about whether she could go camping with Russell, even if a whole bunch of other people came along. The conversation about seeing Dr. Mark—my friend, yes, but a wonderful gynecologist to boot, I assured her. The conversation about permanent tattoos; we agreed she could do what she liked once she was eighteen. The conversation about whether she was allowed to turn her cell phone off when she was out with Russell—the upshot being no.

And what about expensive gifts? We had a conversation about what Russell was and was not allowed to give her.

— In this family, we don't accept electronics, I said. In this family, we recognize that no gifts come free.

— That is, like, so cynical, said Lizzy. Why shouldn't he give me stuff his family has extra of?

Still, she returned to Russell the CD Walkman he wanted to give to her—a good thing since it turned out to belong to his stepmother.

— She would never have missed it, Lizzy declared at one point.

But another day, she said: — I can't believe Russell thought that was okay.

Both girls had programs for the summer. Wendy was in arts camp and Lizzy in a drama workshop. But while Wendy could take days off whenever, Lizzy had rehearsal to think about. For guess what—she was going to be Maria in *The Sound of Music*!

— The director thinks I have a voice, she reported, dazed.

Maria! A voice!

— He doesn't think anyone will care that I don't look Austrian, she said. I told him two of my great-grandparents were German. He said that must be why it seems so natural.

Carnegie rehearsed almost as much as Lizzy:

> How do you make her stay
> And listen to all we say?

But Lizzy sang, too:

> Ed-el-weiss, ed-el-weiss . . .

Only in her room, of course. Here she was, preparing to sing for an auditorium full of people, and yet she still wouldn't sing in front of us. Out in the hall, though, we could hear her; I spent whole evenings in the hall, listening.

Her play was a success. Was this our Lizzy? In a dirndl? Jittery the first night, but in finer and finer voice every night after that, until by the end of the run she filled the whole stage, the whole auditorium. We clapped and clapped, crying.

— Lizzy is going to be okay, said Carnegie later. We can stop worrying. She's going to be able to support us in our old age after all.

In August, I set up a crafts room, hoping to try some of the sorts of projects my sisters had done with their children. Scrapbooks, découpage, twig stools—sweet ideas involving homey materials. It was a beautiful room the girls helped design, with lots of built-ins, and a skylight right over a big table.

— Oh, sweet! said Lizzy when it was done.

Then suddenly, like a desert djinn, resistance arose.

— Découpage? No way, they said.

— How about twig stools? I said. Or what if we did a wall mirror with a shelf with a hole for a hair dryer? We have little shelves like that at the yoga studio; they're handy.

— No twig anything, Lizzy said. Twigs are boring.

— And who uses a hair dryer, said Wendy. Except like in the winter.

I took Bailey, that evening, on a long walk—the last walk of summer, you could feel it. How languorous the air—how humid. It was the sort of air you were more conscious of than you were of your clothes; you knew rain was on its way.

And sure enough, the next day the heat broke dramatically.

— It's the space, said Gabriela, watching the storm.

We were downtown, wearing sweaters, warming up over lattes.

Said Gabriela: — The space makes them feel that they're choosing.

Choosing, of course, being on Gabriela's mind, as Giorgio had gone back to his wife.

— It's like Palermo versus Umbria, she continued. It makes the decision more either/or. Also it means that there's a program, it's not all about freedom. It makes them feel that they're signing up for something. Committing themselves. I read an article about this somewhere.

— Of course there's a program, I started to say. Of course they're committing themselves. I'm their mother.

But Gabriela looked as though she was going to cry, and so I pushed a biscotto toward her instead.

— He's a jerk, I said.

— He is, she agreed. Just like Lan. What do the kids even see in her?

WENDY / Lanlan isn't in charge of us as much now that Mom's home more, but we go visit her anyway, and listen to her stories. Like she tells us this story about some great-aunt and how she was an opium smoker, which her great-uncle didn't know until they got married.

— How could he not know she was an opium smoker? says Lizzy.

Lanlan says because the husband didn't even meet the wife until they were married, that used to happen a lot in China. Also a lot of people were addicted to opium, it wasn't just a few, and because the mother was addicted, when the child was born it was addicted too.

LAN / —Baby like that you have to blow the opium smoke on it, otherwise the baby will die. You can blow less smoke every day so the baby can get rid of the addiction, but you must go slowly, slowly. So she is try to go slowly, slowly, but when the baby is one month old there is a big big party to celebrate, because he is a boy. Here come many many visitors. Mother try to blow smoke on the baby, but there are so many visitors she cannot take the baby away so often. And so not enough smoke, and the baby die.

LIZZY / — Wow, I said.

— What exactly is opium, anyway? said Wendy.

— A kind of drug, said Lanlan. Kind of like what Lizzy smoke.

— Weed, I said, is completely different. And at least I'm not doing Ecstasy or raiding my kid brother's Ritalin like some people.

— Drug is drug, said Lanlan. You should stop. Period.

WENDY / She says it in that soft Lanlan voice, as if she is telling Lizzy what color shirt she has on.

— You're as bad as my parents, says Lizzy.

But she says it in a soft voice too, as if she knows her shirt is black, that's just what color it is. Anyway, she says, she only does a little, to be social, she's not like her stoner friend Xanadu.

LIZZY / Lanlan said I shouldn't sleep with Russell either, or he would never marry me. But I told her if I didn't, he wouldn't even be my boyfriend. I told that, in fact, I'm lucky. In fact, some people sleep with guys and don't even get to be their girlfriends. They're just 'friends with benefits'—that's what the guys call them.

— Anyway, I don't care about getting married, I said.

But she said I should care, and one day would care.

— You will see, she said. Getting married is very important.

— But you're not married, I said. Right? You never got married.

— That is why I know what is important, she said. I have that experience.

WENDY / We love the strange stories even though they're sad, they're kind of like those opera videos Lanlan used to watch, except that these don't make her cry, in fact she doesn't even look upset. She just tells them in this plain old way. Lizzy likes them because they're real, she says they're not all dripping with syrup like the stories Mom tells.

LIZZY / You had to watch those farm stories—too many, and your cheeks turned pink.

WENDY / Lanlan thinks we have too many stories, we should *talk something nice* instead. But if she says that Lizzy gets almost as mad at her as she does at Mom.

— Come on, tell us a strange story, she says.

And after a while, if Lizzy goes on long enough, Lanlan will tell another story. She has this stool she sits on, it's this stool me and Lizzy used to stand on to brush our teeth when we were little. She sits up on it while we sit at her feet, and she likes that. She likes us screeching when her stories are scary and groaning when they're gross.

LAN / *My old ayi used to tell me these stories all the time, when I was little.*

One day the story is about a baby girl.

—That baby, when she was born, her father not happy. Her father wanted a baby boy, have two girls already. So he take that baby, and he hold her by the feet like a chicken. Then he swing her and just like that, smash her against wall. And of course that baby die.

WENDY / — He smashed it against the wall? I say.

— And the baby died? says Lizzy, picking at the carpet.

— Of all things, says Lanlan.

Nobody says anything for a long time.

— That one is too gross, says Lizzy finally.

— Too gross, agrees Lanlan. Of course, that kind of thing happen in the countryside. How about next time I tell a story, not so strange?

— Okay, we say.

But the next time Lizzy asks for a strange story just the same.

BLONDIE / I would talk to Carnegie. Carnegie would talk to Lan. Lan would promise to stop. But a week or so later, the girls would report back with another charming tale.

The new stories were mostly about the Cultural Revolution. It was as if they were done with the baby horror unit, and now were doing this one.

— Last night we heard how the Red Guards made this guy stand for hours and hours in front of thousands of people, with a big tall dunce's cap on, said Lizzy. It was like this rally. And then after he confessed to everything, they killed him anyway.

And: — Last night we heard how Lanlan's father got killed. She said they slit his throat and then threw him out the window to make it look like he committed suicide. But he didn't commit suicide. She knows because they killed him right in front of her, she saw it happen. She was a witness. In fact, they had to tie her to a chair to keep her from attacking the people who did it. They tied her to a chair and left her in front of a window, so she could see her father's body lying down there on the ground in the courtyard, with nothing to even cover it. Only someone did cover it, finally, with a straw mat. No one was allowed to move it, but someone did cover it, she never knew who. Can you imagine?

What to say?

— No, I said. I can't imagine. No.

— That happened to Lanlan, said Lizzy. To Lanlan. It really happened.

— Poor Lan, I said. I am so sorry. Poor Lan.

— And that's the real truth, said Lizzy. People suffer, it's just not something we like to talk about in our comfortable American suburb.

WENDY / We listen and listen to Lanlan, the person who doesn't listen is Bailey, in fact everybody has to listen to him. Like when he wakes up Bailey wants to be carried downstairs with his blankie and his animals, he won't walk down the stairs and he gets really mad if anyone puts him down, even if it's because one of the animals fell, which happens all the time, seeing as how there are so many of them. Like Big Pooh, and Medium Pooh, and Little Pooh, and Piglet, and Tigger, and sometimes Baby Beluga. Then he decides what to have for breakfast, like maybe a waffle that he wants cut up into pieces, but Lanlan can't just cut it right up into pieces. Not right away. She has to wait until he tells her to, otherwise he throws a big fit. Or if she puts the wrong thing on the waffle, like raspberry jam instead of blueberry, he throws a fit. Then he decides what to have to drink, orange juice or milk, and which cup to have it in. Lanlan holds up all the cups.

— This one? This one? Blue one? Yellow one?

Of course he wants the one that's in the dishwasher, so Lanlan has to get that out, and wash it, and bring it over with the juice if that's what he pointed to. If she opens the carton before he points to it he has a fit, and if she pours the juice before he points to it he has a fit, and sometimes he wants to put the sippy-cup cap on himself, which of course he can't, so then he spills the juice and has a fit.

It's like this really terrible computer game.

Sometimes Lanlan doesn't mind. Sometimes she just says, A child cannot understand things like a grown-up. Or else she just shrugs and says in Chinese, *Little Yellow Hair.* And then we all sigh and say, *Xiao Huang Mao* and feel better.

But one morning he doesn't want the cup he had before or the blue cup or the yellow cup or the Tigger cup, he wants the dog-and-fire-truck cup that's out in the car. Or that's what we guess at least seeing as how he doesn't want any of the other cups. So Lanlan has to put on her coat and go outside while I go to the bathroom, and when she comes back Mom is in the kitchen wanting to know why Lanlan left Bailey alone. And when Lanlan says because Bailey wanted the cup with the dog and the fire truck, Mom says Lanlan has to learn to say no to him.

— That's what love is, Mom says. Doing the best thing for the child, not just the thing that will make the child love you.

Says Lanlan then: — If you want me say no, I say no.

And she does. When Bailey wants this, wants that, she says: — Your mother said no. You cannot have it, no.

So there are fits all the time now.

One day he is throwing a fit because he doesn't want his dirty diaper changed, and finally she holds him over the toilet and says: — In China, no diaper. In China, parents hold baby and baby goes *xuxu, eheh,* how about you? Just because you have yellow hair, you think you are better than those other babies? Yellow hair, black hair, make no difference, you understand me?

Za zhong, she calls him. Meaning soup du jour, like Lizzy.

Then she shakes him. And he is so scared he cries even more and right then Mom walks in.

It's just lucky Mom didn't see the shake, even so she's really mad.

— We don't talk like that in this house, she says. Do you hear me?

But the way she says it, mad like that, she's even scarier than Lanlan, who at least didn't yell.

BLONDIE / He didn't come to me. He clung to Lan and would not come to me.

And the next day, I understood why.

LAN / *If Blondie would let someone sleep with the baby, he wouldn't be so fussy. He wouldn't act so spoiled. I told her that one day. But Blondie believed Bailey should be independent, and sleep by himself. Independent! A baby! Sometimes when I looked at Bailey, I could feel how lonely he was. I could feel how small he was too, much too small to sleep by himself. Lately they put him in a* big-boy bed *because he was climbing out of his crib. They thought that was dangerous. But that bed! I felt so sorry for him. I could feel how it was too big for just him and his blankie. Too big and too cold. No wonder he never wanted to go to sleep. Sometimes I lay down with him to help him fall asleep. Of course he loved it. And sometimes I fell asleep too, it was only natural.*

BLONDIE / — Get up! I said when I found them. — Get up. Get up!

I had expected to have to unsettle a couple in bed one day, but honestly had expected it to be Lizzy and Dreaded Dreadlocks.

— Get up! Get up!

CARNEGIE / What was the matter with their napping together? I failed to see the crime in this.

— She already has the girls, she cannot have Bailey too, said Blondie. Bailey who she does not even love. Yellow Hair, she calls him. Yellow Hair! What kind of way is that to talk? Even the girls call him Yellow Hair sometimes. And when I say, We don't talk that way in this family, guess what they say? But Daddy calls you Blondie.

— How egregious.

— I want my home back, she went on. Where this is my house, and these are my children, I get to decide what the rules are. I get to decide who sleeps with who.

— And I? Do I get to decide too?

— I want my home back.

— Just asking, I said.

— Do you understand me? Carnegie?

I allowed silence its eloquence.

She glowered in reply, the corners of her mouth drawn tight, the asterisk on her nose much in evidence. I had never seen her eyes so hard. The house was perfectly still; the air around her seemed to be crystallizing.

Finally I said: — You want your home back.

And: — I beg your patience.

And with that I took her hand and walked her to my office, where I sat her down in my infinitely adjustable chair and swiveled her toward my computer. Together we e-mailed our infamous Hong Kong relative. In the subject window we wrote: Returning Lan Now.

The reply read:

> Your mother's mind was clear as a bell when she wrote the will. I have no choice but to honor her dying wishes. She wrote years, plural. In my mind that means at least two.

— Please, I begged Blondie then.

— Does she even want to stay? Blondie asked.

LAN / *A good question, which no one did ask me.*

CARNEGIE / — Only twelve more lousy months, I said. Just let her live here; we can find someone else to do the child care. We can even ask Lizzy to do some. Isn't Lizzy old enough?

— Lizzy! said Blondie.

WENDY / — Think if there was a sinking ship and only one life ring, says Lizzy. Who would you throw it to, Lanlan or Mom?

— To both of them, I say. They could share.

— But say they were on different sides of the boat, so you had to choose.

— Dad would not choose Lanlan, I say. He would definitely choose Mom. And so would I, I would throw the life ring to Mom and then jump in to go save Lanlan.

— What if you couldn't save Lanlan?

Lizzy is doing her hair while we talk, making these two little high pigtails, like rocket engines.

— I would still try, I say.

— Well, Dad would try too, and that's why Mom is mad.

— But wouldn't she try, if she was on the ship?

— It's one thing for her to try, and another thing for Dad.

— Why?

— Because she's jealous, says Lizzy, looking at me and, before I even ask her, starting to do my hair too. — That's what I'm trying to explain to you.

CARNEGIE / I strolled over to Lan's apartment one Saturday afternoon; the refrigerator was reportedly making noise. She was not home. I thought to come back later, but then—seizing this golden opportunity to avoid her—I let myself in.

As I had not been in her apartment for a while, and had in any case rarely ventured past the kitchen, I was startled to stand in her space and realize how much it had come to resemble my mother's. Recall: she had started out with my mother's massive furniture. But over time, other things of my mother's had been ferreted out of the attic for Lan as well. For example, my mother's bedding. Come last winter, we had liberated my mother's quilt from its storage box; also my mother's blankets. No one wanted to see these things go to waste.

While rummaging around, we came upon my mother's red corduroy reading pillow too, with its stuffed arms and pockets.

— Your mother liked to read in bed, Lan observed.

I said yes, and then insisted that she try this wonderful pillow. Now it loudly presided over Lan's boat of a bed. And under it, my mother's flannel sheets. Blondie and I had bought Lan new sheets, but she was happy to replace them with these—so soft, and practically new.

— Your mother liked soft things, Lan said.

Something I had not particularly noticed, but now saw to be true. Corduroy, cashmere, flannel. Did she find such fabrics comforting? Did she like them because she was lonely? Lan didn't mind putting this and that to use again, in any case. Nor did she mind using up various toiletries my mother had never even opened—her toothpaste, her lotions. The thought of using a dead woman's toiletries gave Blondie the heebie-jeebies; she did not use the same products Mama Wong had anyway, and thought I should've tossed them. Lan, though, had no product preferences. Neither did she have a decorating style to speak of; she cheerfully pulled out of retirement many items Blondie would have felt beyond the pale. My mother's Venetian glass candy dish and Wedgwood vase, for example. Her monkey-head flowerpot. Also, now that Lan had started cooking, she had my mother's everyday pots and pans. My mother's miscellaneous flatware, and chopsticks. Her footed Chinese rice bowls. Our ancient melamine plates.

Mere ownership of these things could not have influenced the way Lan stored her fungus and dried mushrooms, or arranged her jars in the fridge—the buzzing fridge. Yet, eerily, she did these things much as my mother had—filling, for example, the largest of her countertop canisters, the one clearly marked FLOUR, with rice. She had a blackboard in the kitchen, like my mother. And there, center stage on the kitchen table—the computer. My mother had only had an adding machine, but it had occupied that very spot.

Of course, I was the person who had set the computer up there. I was the person who had somehow, on autopilot, picked that place. But Lan left it there; that was true too.

I shivered as I worked the fridge out from its under-the-counter alcove, seeing all the while my mother, young and struggling. I saw her energy and drive; I imagined her exhaustion. I felt what it must have meant to her to be making it, on her own, in a strange country, her child in tow.

The compressor.

And in a way I had never been able to love her when she was alive, I found that I loved her now.

14

Shang

BLONDIE / Carnegie spent almost his whole career at Document Management Systems—fifteen years, anyway.

CARNEGIE / Our offices were a tribute to the half-round bull nose, an enshrinement of real-wood veneer. The newer armchairs were gray, but the older chairs were dark green, holdovers from the company's golden granola days—the days when, fresh out of the garage, early tech types could believe beards and jeans and Birkenstocks were forever. Dark green hadn't yet become the color of the decade, the color that would herald a new interest in our planet Earth. Back then it was still a forester's color, a half-preppy, half-sixties-lives-on color. It was an alternative color perfect for people who had attended alternative high schools and sought alternative careers. People who repaired, on the weekends, not to the golf course but to the woods. It was anti-maroon and anti–powder blue. It was anti-peach. It went with almost nothing except wood tones and Ping-Pong tables.

Also plants. For a while our office might have passed for a greenhouse, except that the plants were so well browned at the edges; they seemed required by some unwritten code to have lost the majority of their major fronds. But what matter? We were revolutionaries. We were beyond office décor.

BLONDIE / Were they not, after all, the firm that had reinvented document management?

CARNEGIE / Where did the dot-coms come from?

There had always been young MBAs, hungry to make their mark—to accrete some of my power, such as it was, to themselves. Then suddenly the kids didn't want jobs; suddenly what they wanted was for me to plunge with them into this venture or that, as messianically described in their quarter-baked business plans. Who would have said yes? Should I have given up my VP-of-development job, representing fifteen years of zigzagging ascent, for a fly-by-night gig with a bunch of twenty-somethings?

How mildly vindicating when their tide finally went out.

BLONDIE / If only they had not brought all of high tech down with them.

CARNEGIE / The dot-com air was our air; we all of us breathed it. Telecom, for example. All that cable they laid down! For the new age to come. But it wasn't just telecom; everyone spent and spent. There were people, yes, who knew Time Warner would one day rue its wooing of AOL, that AOL would one day come to mean Albatross Online. But real-time employment lay in keeping your edge—in being considered a company of the future. Who dared defend old-economy thinking?

The tone, then, with which one uttered the words 'in the past'; and how the past seemed to nip at your heels, the enemy. How quickly things became old technology, old economy, old old old—quick as a wink, you might say, except how slow a thing, how pathetically slow, a wink had become. No one could afford to move that slow. How you had to whir to stay new!

Until, of course, you didn't.

BLONDIE / Once he was a star.

CARNEGIE / I was the crack strategist; I was the deep analyst. Once I divined the inchoate needs of the market. I drafted, forecasted, recruited. Acquired, jettisoned, revamped. Every year ended with a bang and a bonus.

Then consultants arrived, dropping names. They made eye contact; they offered new paradigms. They wore expensive ties. When they departed, it was more in person than in fact, leaving behind as they did their fat reports and fatter bills.

Maybe I was from the start, as my mother claimed, a sap. Maybe once the environment grew tougher it wasn't enough to be someone who did his best and let the chips fall. Or maybe that faint aloneness I'd always felt—a vague vertigo, a feeling that I had to take extra care not to fall out of synch—did matter in the end. Or was it my true level of commitment?

Maybe.

Though how many men, in truth, don't kick one back some days and think, *I am a fucking slave*?

More likely I'd been called a good guy a few too many times. How much better to have had coworkers report, *He's a ballbuster.*

Instead, what? I could only imagine. *You can really talk to him.*

He gave me extra leave.

He made sure the insurance got backdated.

He believed in diversity.

A counterpart called me insufficiently crisp.

— If only my feet had been held to the fire a bit longer, I said.

— I'm only trying to help, said said counterpart. You're a good guy.

Of course, said counterpart was himself laid off shortly thereafter.

— What did you expect? people said. The guy read novels during lunch.

How can you be my son? I tell you honest way, I don't know who you are.

I was reorganized, in any event, first from my line job to a staff position, with no bottom-line responsibility, and then to a non-position, where I was given an office but nothing to do. Put out to pasture. Once upon a time I had complained about my e-mail; I could get upward of two hundred messages a day. Now I dreaded my in-box still.

How thoroughly I read every companywide announcement.

At least Blondie, bless her, sent me little notes. Forwarded jokes and weblinks. Who had time for weblinks? That's what I used to think. Now I happily perused whole blogs.

Shame me into resigning. That seemed to be the plan, so as to avoid paying severance. The desperate strategy of a desperate company. No one could look me in the eye. People I had promoted, people I had aided and abetted, people I had gone to the mat for, now glanced away when they saw me, as though they had developed this inexplicable neurological tic. Or else they crossed the hall to greet me—*great to see you, man!*—slapped my back heartily, then conveniently broke away.

How I had worried about being laid off! Now I dreamed of it.

I dreamed of telling them the truth as I left:

One day, you too will not matter.

One day, you too will think, I used to matter.

How they would writhe with self-knowledge!

If only Blondie would go back to work, I thought sometimes. Then I could afford to quit.

Though—to be saved by Blondie! That would have been worse.

BLONDIE / I didn't see why.

CARNEGIE / Mother of all ironies: over the years Blondie did far more of the juggling—far more of the feeding and picking up and temperature taking—than I; she arranged more play dates, drove more car pool, did more open houses, field trips, potlucks, bake sales. And yet still she managed, inexplicably, not only to avoid the demotion most moms took, but to substantively advance in her work. Was this because she had not particularly tried to advance? Because she believed in her cause? Was she right to credit, as she did, dumb luck? She depressed many a fellow mother, in any case. A fact that depressed her.

— As if things aren't difficult enough for everyone already, she'd say.

As for yours truly—I can still see there, on our kitchen desk, Blondie's pink, oversized paycheck. This was for many years larger than mine in every dimension, thanks to her fee-based compensation. Tied as it was to a percentage of the fund.

I freely admit that I was in full support, when the opportunity arose, of her signing up for direct deposit. Call me pathethic: at least I tell, here, the truth.

— My contract is for another twenty years, I told Lan, one afternoon in the kitchen. — Get Bailey through college, then I'm done.

— Contract? said Lan, putting down her marker.

Lan was studying at the kitchen table, baby monitor at her elbow, her homework in piles. She was happier these days, having scored high enough on the TOEFL for us to enroll her in an undergrad program in August. As for whether she would be able to complete that degree—well, we vaguely hoped things would work out somehow.

In the meanwhile she was majoring in business, minoring in color coding. Different-colored stick-its bristled from every book. Beside the books lay pens in an array of colors too—also highlighters, which I could see she liked to use. The pages before her pulsed with color. There could not have been more than a paragraph left in its original naked state.

— Sometimes I think I should have done something different, I said. Of course, we have this saying, 'The grass is always greener on the other side.'

— The grass is always greener on the other side, repeated Lan.

Contemplating a green marker as she spoke. Was she inspired by that aphorism toward a coding-scheme refinement? She stood when the kettle shrieked, to get my coffee; I waved to her to sit back down. Thinking, *How nice a roll in the hay after a day in the pasture,* but maturely managing a just-friends smile.

LAN / *You will rise again from the East Mountain, I told him. Dong shan zai qi. Don't worry. Right now your doorway is so empty you could catch sparrows in it. But ku jing gang lai—after bitterness comes sweetness.*

CARNEGIE / It was a great day for wisdom.

I made my coffee. Considering, as it dripped, the kitchen floor, which layers of wax had restored only to a wan version of its former glory.

How happy I was, in any case, to see Lan bright with hope.

LAN / *Carnegie had some relatives living in Beijing, one of whom he thought had married a woman from Suzhou. Of course, who knew what connection there really was. Still, it was worth looking into. And while I was too old for a regular job, I was beginning to think maybe I could help some foreign company do business. Maybe translate for an American company, Carnegie said. Who knew? Maybe someone could arrange something.*

If not Carnegie, then maybe someone else.

CARNEGIE / With what authority she chatted, now, on the miracle of microlending in Bangladesh; the rationale for outsourcing software programming to India; the importance of thinking new economy. I applauded her disquisitions as I drank.

— After just four weeks! I said.

She paused at this. Rearranged her markers.

It went almost without saying that she adored her professors, especially one Woody Something—business development—and that Professor Woody adored her.

— Be careful, I told her.

But who was I to tell her anything? Having had to ask her to define 'microlending.'

I did not, she suggested, know everything.

And later, when I continued to press her: she hoped I was not jealous.

— Of course not, I said, stung. And yet noting, such non-contact contact. It was like talking to a former lover. — I wish you well, that's all. I will always be interested in your plans.

She laughed a little, pressing her fingers together.

— Plans, she said musingly.

LAN / *I had known so few good men in my life. He was like a father. Younger than me, and yet like a father, or a brother.*

CARNEGIE / A few weeks later I once again found her in the kitchen—still surrounded by piles of books, but looking pensive. She did not greet me in her usual way when I walked in; instead she glanced up, then back down. Around her, that color-coding paradise, that rapture of highlighters. But the marker in her hand remained capped, and how disconcertingly black and white the pages before her.

— Is something the matter? I asked.

— Nothing the matter.

She pulled her sleeves down. She was wearing a droopy men's sweater, cardinal red. With the sleeves pulled down, she appeared to have no hands.

— How are your classes?

— What classes?

Across the street, Mitchell unloaded a bassinet from his new station wagon; the minx was, unexpectedly, expecting. Next came a changing table, a swing, a car seat still in its box.

— Let me guess. I took a breath, then said: — Woody.

The sun slanted diagonally across her sweater like a sash.

— Are you in love with him?

— Which him?

— Are there two hims? I joked.

She did not laugh. — You know, I am Chinese age almost fifty.

— American age only forty-seven, I said.

— With no job. No family.

— And no green card, right?

Next to her, the baby monitor lit up. A spike of red lights. Was that a cry? She drew her sweater sleeve back to turn the sound on, only to have the red dots go out. Crackling. She turned the sound off, rolled her sleeve down.

— I'd be happy to sponsor you, you know, I said. If I can get Blondie to agree. And if we can do it.

The dimensions of these largish ifs would have seemed to me of interest, but Lan did not appear to find them so.

— You are very kind, she said. At school they say there are three million people on waiting list for the green card.

— Nevertheless, people do get them.

— People say the big opportunity is not in America anymore.

— Hong Kong. Shenzhen. Shanghai. Is that what Woody says?

— Not just Woody. And Hong Kong look like not so great these days. Too much risky.

At least she was talking. I put a kettle of water on.

— America is no longer America, I said.

— Still America, she said. Just not the only one.

— Here we have freedom. Don't people care about freedom?

— Freedom? Individualism? She laughed, touching her hair with her sleeve. — Too much individualism. Too much argue here. Chinese people love peace.

— What about freedom? Is there too much freedom?

— Freedom is not always so good, she said. Look at Russia. Anyway, other problems too. Too much violence.

— At school they say this?

She nodded.

— Why do I bet that even if they're doing business abroad, they're hanging on to their U.S. citizenship.

— Of course. U.S. citizenship very useful. Don't even need citizenship. Just a green card.

The kettle whistled.

— Coffee? I offered. Tea?

She shook her head, but began to push her sleeves back. Uncovering her hands, long and pale and elegant.

— That's what they say at school? That a green card's enough?

A half nod.

— Someone in particular too says this, I guessed.

A second half nod.

— Woody.

— Not Woody, she said.

— Not Woody? Then someone with a green card. Who could use a Chinese-speaking partner.

She blushed.

— I'm sure it's way too early to be thinking about marrying, I said, pressing on. Guessing wildly, boldly, but lo! She rolled the sleeves of her sweater back down. — Marry for love, I told her. Pouring my coffee, trying to keep my voice light, but hearing urgency in it all the same. — You can, you know. This is America.

— Of course, marry for love very nice, she said. Her return voice was at first very low, like a cell phone signal I was about to lose. But then it grew stronger. — In China, by the way, we have love too. Though sometimes not right away. Sometimes the man and woman learn to love each other after they are married a long time.

— Is he married already?

— He is supposed to divorce his wife, she said.

— Oh, Lan, I said.

LAN / *What was so terrible? If he didn't want me, shouldn't he at least let someone else try?*

CARNEGIE / — And how did you meet this guy?

— Blondie made arrangement, she said.

— Blondie?

— She met him in that feng shui class.

— Blondie?

— Gabriela dated him once.

BLONDIE / It was Gabriela's idea.

CARNEGIE / *You can't trust that Blondie.*

BLONDIE / I just sort of went along.

CARNEGIE / Being an agreeable person.

WENDY / His name is Shang. He shaves his head bald like a monk and Lanlan is not sure about him. Too short, she says. But she smiles when she says it and starts looking at nothing, which Lizzy says means the guy knows a way to make money in China.

— How do you know? I say.

But she just says: — Watch.

And the next time this guy Shang comes up, she says: — Don't sell your soul. You can make money in China yourself, you don't need this guy.

— Not so easy, says Lanlan.

LIZZY / — You just have to set your mind to it, I told her. You make your own luck. Have you heard the expression, 'Where there's a will, there's a way'?

— Where there's a will there's a way, repeated Lan. Where there's a will there's a way.

But then she said: — In China, relationships are very important.

— Women don't need men, I said. We are perfectly capable of standing on our own two feet.

— You are too young to understand, she said. Someday you will understand.

LAN / *He was a little older than me—in his fifties—and called himself Shang, after his grandfather, who came from Fujian. I think his real name was* Brian. *He did not look Chinese at all. Not even as Chinese as* Bailey, *just like any* lao wai, *brown hair all over. Everywhere but on his head. He was not handsome. But he was interested in China, more interested than* Carnegie. *He had lived in Taiwan and studied a lot about it. His Chinese was rusty, but he still spoke some. He had visited the Mainland several times. And of all the places he visited, he said he loved Suzhou best. He liked Lijiang also, and Hangzhou, and Guilin. But nothing was like Suzhou, he said. He said that before he even knew my* laojia *was Suzhou.*

Of course a lot of people from Taiwan liked Suzhou, so many that people said there were Taiwan-style tea shops all over Suzhou now. Taiwanese people liked to invest money in Suzhou too. That's what people said. They were like Singaporeans that way. Probably Shang just learned to love Suzhou from living in Taiwan.

Still, it made me want to see him again.

I hadn't talked to anyone who even knew where Suzhou was in a long long time. It meant so much to me, I was embarrassed. Probably that looked like love. But really, I just wanted to talk to him.

He wasn't as kind as Carnegie. *But I thought maybe he would see, someday, that I was* Suzhouren. *I had that hope—that he would see how I should have grown up there, in my family's garden. That I should have grown up writing poetry and practicing calligraphy by the pond. That our pavilion should have been full of musicians and opera singers instead of laundry. That I should have had a cook to cook all the Suzhou specialties. That I should have hardly known what the kitchen looked like. That I should have been married to someone very rich. Not necessarily so handsome; I should have been married to one of those old bespectacled scholars in a gown who went to the teahouse in the morning, and to the bath at night—who wrapped water in skin in the morning, and skin in water in the evening, as we used to say. I should have had a mother; my father should have lived a long and peaceful life. I should have had children. My children should have had cousins. I should have had sisters-in-law to gossip with, and a mother-in-law to complain about.*

Later people said Shang was my ticket to a better life. That was true too. But in the beginning I mostly wanted to talk to him.

I was embarrassed.

CARNEGIE / This guy was from the beginning the wrong story. I knew it from Google-ing him; also from someone who had once worked for him but now, it turned out, worked for one of my erstwhile direct-reports. Hazel Riley, her name was, a big-haired software engineer and PTA president who also ran kids' soccer for her county.

The scoop from Hazel being: not only bald, but frighteningly thin. Drank lots of water. One of the first to predict, in fact, that there were big bucks in bottled water. That people would actually pay for it, and walk around with it. He made a lot of money investing on that hunch. Sushi too. Back when no one thought Americans would eat the stuff, he bought stock in a company that wanted, of all things, to sell sushi in airports.

The height verdict: not short exactly. However, on the short side and unpleasantly relational. The sort of man who felt a need to put his hands everywhere. Hazel said that if he entered your office, he was sure to pick something up off your desk. He could not pass a pregnant employee without putting a hand on her belly. And then, of course, there were other body parts with which to make contact.

The most generous view of this: that for all his money he was hungry for connection.

The dominant view: if he were a dog, he would have peed on absolutely everything.

Hazel said Shang was always borrowing things. Pens, calculators, pads of paper. Vacation ideas. Mannerisms. She said that before he put his hands on things, he put them up things; apparently, as a boy, what with those long, thin arms, he had worked as an inseminator of prize mares. But he lost that job, Hazel said, because he killed a horse once. Or at least that's what people in the office said; and people believed it because of his temper. He threw things across the room. He tore things up. He once threw a computer out the window. That was after he smashed its screen with a marble-based Frisbee trophy. It shook Shang himself up, people said, that he had done that.

He took up yoga for stress reduction. However, he complained it was not competitive enough, and thought there might be money in yoga tournaments. He took many herbs. Also he tried feng shui—jumbling the office furniture so thoroughly that people barely knew where to sit. He was a crazy man to work for, Hazel said, a walking soap opera.

On the other hand, what companies the man came up with, you had to give him credit. The most recent featuring a stadium seat pad with reusable freezer packs, sold via CoolYourBuns.com. When the company went public, said Hazel, even the secretaries made a mint.

The dominant view: all that craziness just went with genius.

He viewed everything as a proposition, a stock in which he would or would not invest. For example, if you said to him, School committees, he'd say, Sell. School vouchers: Buy. Rent control: Sell. Campaign finance reform: Buy.

As for where he was putting his money now, the answer was China. He had always loved China; he loved it still. The women of China. The food of China. The sounds of China. He loved the *erhu,* he said. Such a planetary sound.

— Whatever the hell a whatever-it-was was, said Hazel.

But that had impressed Lan, that Shang knew what an *erhu* was. He said his Chinese driver played it for him regularly.

The most generous view: he was interested in other cultures, attuned as he was to the limits of Western civilization and the enlightenment tradition.

An alternate view: his real interest lay like a big dog at his feet, you couldn't miss it even if it mostly just panted.

LAN / *I first saw him on a panel on* viral marketing. *I did not ask any questions but only listened and took notes, and so was surprised when he came up to me afterward and introduced himself. He gave me his card with two hands, Chinese-style. I did not have a card, so I gave him my number.*

He took me out for a drink the next week. At such a fancy place!

That was when he told me he loved Suzhou. Even before he knew I was from Suzhou, he told me that, and in Chinese! Apologizing for his accent, which was indeed terrible.

And so of course, yes. When he asked me out to dinner, I said yes.

A most beautiful dinner! With an ice sculpture indoors, right in the middle of the restaurant. A pair of swans—how they reminded me of China, they were carved almost as beautifully as ice sculptures in China. There were little vegetable flowers too on the dishes. Those were nowhere near as fancy as vegetable carvings in China. But still the food was delicious—French. The tablecloths were pink. There were candles. And so many glasses! I was surprised how many glasses there were, and with what slender, slender stems.

I could not believe anyone would treat me so well. At my age! I thought I must be in a dream.

He had brought pictures of all the gardens he visited. Some of them were very famous, of course—the Humble Administrator's Garden. The Garden of the Master of the Fishing Nets. But also he had visited many smaller gardens, gardens more like my family's. We looked at the pictures for a long time. I was impressed that he had taken so many, and of all sorts of things. The different-shaped windows, and the patterns of the tiles in the paths. The color of the roof tiles. The fish. The view before you turned a corner and the view after—the surprise. He had even photographed Baodai Qiao, *a famous ancient bridge, at night, so you could see how on certain nights each of its many arches held a moon of its own—how the moon threw a string of reflections across the water, like a necklace of pearls, stretching from one shore to the other.*

— To think you might have grown up there, *he said finally.* Unbelievable.

I almost cried then.

There was a dance floor; he asked me to dance. I said I didn't know how, but he said it didn't matter, and it didn't. He taught me. And for dessert he ordered the special warm chocolate soufflé for two. *He looked at me while we were eating; I thought I must be doing something wrong. That maybe there was something else he wanted to teach me. But still he looked, and finally he touched my arm. Not even my hand—just my arm. As if he did not dare touch my hand.*

Then he told me he wanted me to go back to China with him. The big opportunities, he said, were in China. Not that every company succeeded. Of course not. But while in America only one in twenty start-ups *made it, in China the odds were one in three.*

— You just have to try and try, *he said.* People say if you last five years, you are going to survive. So if you try one company at a time, in fifteen years you should have something to show, right? And if you try more than one at a time, just think. But of course you have to know how to handle the Chinese. That's where you come in. I need somebody to soften them up. Speak their language.

— I understand your meaning, *I said.*

— Everything is a joint venture over there. Say that in the U.S., a certain company does sales and only sales, no service, right? Well, they get to China, and what happens? They find themselves in a nice joint venture with the government, doing service. And then in another joint venture, doing investment. Until there are four companies doing something for the government, and only one company doing sales. I need somebody to handle all that. Keep the Chinese happy.

— I understand, *I said.*

— You do, *he said, looking at me.* I see that. You understand China. And you're a nice woman. Of course, if all goes well, one day you will not have to be so nice.

That surprised me.

— I don't understand your meaning, *I said.*

He laughed.

— Don't worry, I'll teach you. For now, just imagine it. What we could do with a good idea. Which I have. *He leaned back in his chair.* — Online gambling. Think about it .

He had it all worked out. How people would use prepaid phone cards to place their bets, and to collect if they won. How they could bet on all sorts of things. Wimbledon*—that was a tennis tournament. Or the* World Cup*—that was soccer. Anything on TV. Or else they could play card games online. A game called* blackjack, *for example. Or something more traditionally Chinese. Mahjong. We could find out what they used to do in Shanghai in the olden days,* *he said. We could call it* LasVegas.com. *Or what was Chinese for* Get Rich?

— Eventually we would want to get away from the phone cards, *he said.* Do our own cards. And then! Do you realize how much money we could make in breakage alone?

He explained breakage *to me, and how he was shopping his business plan with venture capitalists right now. But he wanted me to be in on this from the start. He wanted me to be a* cofounder.

— You know what I thought when I first saw you? *he asked me.*

I shook my head.

—Buy, *he said.* Buy and hold.

—Where will the business headquarters be? *I asked him.*

—Suzhou, *he said.* Of course. We're going to set up shop in Suzhou like all the Taiwanese businessmen.

When he reached for my hand, I gave it to him gratefully, with all my heart.

CARNEGIE / It was like a grade-B movie: he never picked her up at the house. Because of his wife and kids, he always picked her up behind the post office downtown, a five-minute walk away. Never mind that he lived three towns over; he wanted to be careful. And in a way his trepidation about our neighborhood was justified: everyone knew everyone else's cars, and took keen notice of anything untoward, it was true. A hedge flopped over, a flag left out in the rain, a tricycle gone loose. Stray pets. Dandelion proliferation, especially if said dandelions were allowed to advance to the puff state so tempting to children and so threatening to the neighborhood.

In town there was less apparent surveillance. Actually, though, I did occasionally catch his comings and goings, because the temple to health I had recently joined was located on the second floor of a building facing the post office parking lot. Always I had wondered why the floor-to-ceiling windows in clubs like this—such a magnificent view of the parking meters, after all. And where was it written that treadmills must needs face big glass? I had personally never yearned to exercise with the world as my witness, and had long ago predicted the demise of this particular trend. Who really wanted to watch humans in the throes of their will-to-fitness?

Everyone, it seemed.

Now I too exercised in the display window Saturday mornings. Jogging, not running, as per my cardiologist's orders. My heart on a monitor.

This is how I knew Shang drove a black BMW convertible, and that when Lan got into the car, she did it quickly, with a furtive air. She liked black cars, I knew; in China the power elite all drove black cars. She had in fact once wondered aloud why Blondie and I didn't drive black cars with tinted windows too. How passionately we avowed, then, our undying love of our van! But I digress. She in any case had barely enough time to close the door before the car zoomed off. Once her scarf got caught in the door. She was able to disengage herself; Shang stopped more or less immediately. Still my heart rate spiked so alarmingly that the treadmill flashed and beeped, and I was automatically eased into a cooldown.

Once too from an Exercycle at the far side of the gym, I saw them enter the diner across the way, or thought I did; I biked a good quarter mile squinting in disbelief. Was that really Lan? Wearing skin-tight jeans, and where did that blouse come from? A deeply V'd affair with a ruffle like a bed skirt, perfect for showing off some cleavage and a carnelian necklace I could have sworn to be my mother's.

It was as if, through some strange computer cut and paste, a bit of Shanghai had ended up downtown. For there, sure enough, despite my best efforts, was one of those desperate Chinese women Mitchell's brother Nick had described, on the make.

LAN / *Probably it did not look so nice. But in fact Shang was unhappy with his wife long before he met me. The only reason they had children was thanks to test tubes. He was a lonely man. I felt sorry for him.*

Sometimes I wondered about our business plan. Could we really yi bu deng tian*—reach heaven in one step? I did wonder.*

But still I felt hope. For the first time in my life, I felt real hope.

CARNEGIE / When Lan spoke to me now, it was with minimal eye engagement. If I asked, Are you going out again? she would say, If you like me to I stay home, I stay home.

One morning I discovered a white sweater soaking in the laundry sink. There appeared to be a large red ring on it, as though someone had used it for a wine coaster. The room stank of bleach.

Also she carried a beautiful leather backpack now. A tailored, polished half-moon this was, with thin straps and a zipper that ran across its knife-edged top.

WENDY / If you knock on her door, she still says, You! and, Come in! But she doesn't make snacks anymore, and it's like she wouldn't exactly mind if you left. Before if you tried to leave she'd think of something to try and make you stay. But now if you try to leave, she just says bye-bye. And she still asks you how things are going at school, but if you tell her about something that happened at recess she might ask you about recess five minutes later. And if you tell her what happened again she'll say, Oh! That's so funny! again or, Oh no, that's terrible! And if you say to her, You just said that, she'll say, Did I? And look genuinely sad and sorry.

Sometimes she cooks and says it makes her feel better. But sometimes she cooks and it just makes her cry.

— Cooking is for families, she says one day in her room.

She has her books all around her but they're on the floor like Lizzy's, and if you look at her notebook you can see how she doodles in the margins like Lizzy too. But anyway, she's not studying right now, right now she's trying to play chess with me.

— I have no family, she says.

She says: — Even if I get married tomorrow, probably it is too late.

— What do you mean? I ask her.

And when she says she's too old to have children, I tell her that's not true, she can always adopt.

— Adopt what? she says.

And she makes such a bad move, hanging her queen, that I have to tell her she can take it back. But of course she doesn't want to and so what should I do? Take her queen?

— A girl like me, I say. I'm adopted, remember? In fact you could probably adopt me.

She just laughs though and says in Chinese: — *I meant a real family but okay. I'll take you.*

I look and look at the board.

— *I'm not a bad second choice*, I tell her. *I was my parents' second choice.*

And finally I do it, I take her queen. Leaving her in this awful position.

She doesn't even care.

— *No no*, she says. *You were their number-one choice, and would be my number-one choice too.*

— *I wasn't*, I say. *But second choice doesn't mean second-best. That's what they say.*

Lanlan looks at me funny then.

— Of course you were born in China, she says in English, but practically you are born here.

— Practically but not exactly, I say. Check.

— Ah! she says. You are too good for me.

— If you use your knight you can block me, I say.

She uses her knight.

— Checkmate, I say.

— Ah! she says again. But then suddenly in Chinese she says: — *That kind of thing doesn't matter. I can understand you no matter where you come from. No matter what, you are my number-one choice and my number-two choice too. You are my good friend.*

Then she looks at her toes—not that she can actually see them, seeing as she has her blue slippers on.

— *Lanlan*, I say, *what do they say?*

— *They say they are old but maybe all right still*, she answers, sort of smiling but sort of not. *Though who knows. Maybe they will someday look like my great-aunt's toes, and my skin will look like her skin. I have hope these days. But maybe in the end I will still die in house full of flies.*

— *That's not going to happen*, I say, putting the chess pieces away.

But she just says: — *Who knows?*

CARNEGIE / More scenes from the grade-B movie: Lan comes home with a gift box in hand. The night of her next date she appears in a new sweater or skirt or jacket. A number of items are leather. No more V-necks with ruffles; these clothes are up to the minute, with features. The cut is unusual; it ties up the back; the color appears black or blue depending on the light. It shimmers, it zips, it comes with a carrying pouch.

WENDY / — I thought you didn't need clothes, I say.

— I need nothing, she agrees. But look, so beautiful.

She holds up a dress.

LAN / *These were not Hong Kong-style—more American. But I liked them, I did. And I had to think what a* cofounder *should wear.*

LIZZY / — Use your brain, I told her. No gifts come free.

But she just laughed.

— Look at these, she said, showing me some shoes.

LAN / *Ah, but the shoes were something! I had never seen such shoes. Maybe in Shanghai, they had them, but not in Jinan. I thought they were so so beautiful. Such colors! Not just bright red, for example, but dark red too, and persimmon. Some were suede. Some were patent, or embossed to look like snakeskin. One pair had a T-strap. One had straps that wound around the ankle.*

WENDY / She puts them on for me, and walks around in these bitsy steps.

— You look like you can barely walk, I say.

— Rich people do not need to walk, she says.

BLONDIE / She experimented with her hair. One day she gelled it, another day cut her bangs so that they hung down into her eyes. The bottom edge grew fringed. More wisps appeared all the time.

She wore more makeup too—foundation, blush. Eyeshadow. Pale lipstick some days, other days a diva red. She used a lipstick pencil for better lip definition. She tweezed her eyebrows and curled her eyelashes. Another woman might have looked ridiculous. Lan looked like a movie star.

How could we ever have thought her plain?

Of course, as Lan changed her look, so did Lizzy and Wendy. Lizzy took up a baby-girl style of dress—lots and lots of pink.

LIZZY / Worn ironically.

BLONDIE / Then came a style that shunned commercial purchases. Lizzy asked me to teach her to sew—delighting me—and began to make her own clothes. Her once-empty room was now full of scraps. She allowed me to teach her to knit too, and to crochet. Sometimes I thought she was turning into my sisters—she had that utopian aesthetic. She liked to make little crochet squares, the kind other people turned into potholders and afghans. She turned them into tops.

From the crochet tops she went on to bandanna tops, then to cropped tops made from old Boy Scout uniforms, or gas station uniforms, or bowling shirts. All her material came from used-clothes stores. Nothing matched—that was part of the aesthetic.

She made quilts too, in unconventional shapes. Star-shaped quilts and oval quilts and amoeba quilts. She made a quilt that looked like a giant Citgo sign, and sold it.

LIZZY / For two hundred dollars! I gave the money to Russell's band.

BLONDIE / Like Lizzy, Wendy wore skirts and pants together, and shirts over sweaters. She copied Lizzy's color combinations—pink with burnt orange, black with pastels. She wore Lizzy's hand-me-downs, blouses with Peter Pan collars or puffed sleeves. Which at first Wendy's classmates thought weird. But then Elaine started copying Wendy, and pretty soon everyone else was copying her too.

CARNEGIE / Wendy Bailey Wong, trendsetter.

BLONDIE / Lan thought all this very strange.

LIZZY / — You don't like anything in the store? said Lanlan.

— Everything these days has a logo on it, I said.

— And we hate logos, said Wendy.

— Logos just make you feel like you're owned by corporate America, I said.

— Of course American corporations very bad, said Lanlan.

— We hate fashion, said Wendy.

CARNEGIE / The grade-B movie: sometimes Lan came to breakfast with eyes so puffy she looked like a *National Geographic* photo, you could actually see the caption. *By puffing up her eyes, this creature is able to avoid prying conversation.*

But invariably flowers arrived before noon. She was such a regular stop that the delivery boy did not even ring her doorbell, but simply shouted, Yo! Lani! up to her window.

BLONDIE / She began to stay out overnight.

CARNEGIE / We knew this because on the advice of some fellow parents we were spot-checking Lizzy's whereabouts in the wee hours. Not that we didn't trust her, we did, yada yada. But what e-mails we were receiving these days; ominous as something from the FBI.

> Some things going on. You might keep an eye out. Also do not leave your house empty on weekends. And if we all lock our liquor cabinets, well they'll be locked, and please let's keep a lid on the instant messaging.

It was no big deal to add Lan to the security tour. Harder was adding her to the sex-talk list. Not that we had to do birth control; she had to know about birth control, she was from China for chrissakes. But AIDS was not the subject in the East it might be.

BLONDIE / We tried to get her to see the same gynecologist, Dr. Mark, to whom we'd sent Lizzy.

— It won't cost anything, we assured her. It's completely covered by that health policy we bought you.

CARNEGIE / We thought she might go because such a visit would be preventative; she had the idea that American doctors did nothing to strengthen you. That they preferred to see people get sick, so they could charge big fees to cure them.

Her interest in Dr. Mark, all the same: zilch.

BLONDIE / — Isn't that Dr. Mark your friend? she asked.

As if we were trying to trick her somehow.

CARNEGIE / And what to do now about her coming home with her clothes torn? A torn blouse. A torn skirt. Her beautiful new backpack had to go to the shoemaker to have its strap fixed. No sign of bodily harm, though, besides, one day, a red ear.

And one day, a bruise on her forearm.

— I bang myself somewhere, she said. Maybe on the door. Maybe on a chair.

— Which was it? we asked. The door or a chair?

— I don't pay attention to such things, she said. No marginal utility.

And another day: — No big deal. I bang my arm all the time.

And another: — This is America. I do not have to make report to you.

LAN / *I didn't mind Shang's fits. His secretary said she'd never seen anyone more able to calm him down. I suppose because he did not shock me. Shang was terrible, but I knew how to handle him.*

It was Carnegie *I found strange. Such a nice man, such a kind man, but I could not understand him. For some other story, he kept saying. I was meant for some other story. But what other story?*

Shang and I were working on the business plan. Tweaking it, *he said. We had one investor already, but our second guy dropped out.*

We needed to replace him. That was our next step.

WENDY / Sometimes Shang doesn't pick her up himself. Sometimes he sends his driver, who is Chinese Chinese, like from China, and tallish, with this carefully combed hair. He drives the black car but the top is never down, and he drives extra slow, like he's giving this zoo tour. It's like there are no animals so he has to drive slow, slow, slow, hoping to find some. Then the car stops and the driver gets out and opens the door for Lanlan. He waits for her to climb in and like arrange herself. Then he closes the door after her, and taps on the window, and gives her this smile. He has a wide mouth like a frog's, and these beautiful eyes with a soft glance, once it landed on me and it was like a butterfly you didn't want to disturb. It was like something you wanted to stay on your shoulder for a while even if it only picked you because it matched your shirt.

Sometimes he drives her home too, he brings her all the way home instead of leaving her at the post office. You get the feeling he isn't supposed to do this. He looks both ways, then taps on her door and opens it slowly. He gives her his hand to help her out, and sometimes he helps her up the walk. They walk slow, slow, like old people. Sometimes he carries her coat for her, or her shoes. Or her purse. He hangs her purse around his neck, not to be funny but just to carry it, like it's convenient and he doesn't care if he looks like a Saint Bernard. Once she shuffles up the walk in a pair of men's slippers, who knows what they were doing in the car. Anyway she doesn't give them back. For the next couple of weeks we see her in those men's slippers, which are cracked brown leather and way too big for her.

So that now Lizzy says he's the one Lanlan really loves.

— Not that she would admit it, she says.

— Why not? I say.

— Because it's hard, she says. Sometimes you don't even want to admit it to yourself.

— Does that mean you miss Derek? I say. But won't admit it?

— What about Lionel? she says. Do you love him?

— I think we're just friends.

— You can think whatever you want, she says. That doesn't make it true.

BLONDIE / One day Lan forgot to put a diaper on Bailey.

Another day she complained he did nothing but cry, only to discover—that is, we discovered together—that a child at the playground had put seeds in his ears.

— She's in love, said Gabriela. People in love are psychotic. They have no judgment and cannot be relied on, as I remember all too well.

Yet another day Lan scolded Bailey for getting paint on his

clothes: — *Do you know what I wore when I was your age? Do you?*

— It's her inner child, said Gabriela. Inside she is still a motherless girl without enough food, clothes, heat, anything. It's hard for her to see your children grow up with so much. You can't blame her, in a way.

— You're right, I really can't blame her, I said.

But yet another day I found Bailey crying, and Lan holding a spoonful of soup to his lips.

— You eat, she said. Good soup!

— Hot! he cried, his face turned away. Hot!

— You know, one day I will not feed you anymore, she said. And under her breath she muttered: — *Xiao Huang Mao.*

Little Yellow Hair.

— Is it hot?

I picked Bailey up and tested the soup. If Lan was surprised by my appearance, she didn't let on.

— Ow! I cried.

Lan dumped a sippy cup out in the sink.

— The potatoes, I said calmly. Potatoes really hold heat, you know.

— If you like it cooler, I will make it cooler.

— Please do, I said. Because potatoes are not like rice. You may not have realized. Rice doesn't hold heat the way potatoes do.

— Potatoes hold heat, said Lan. They are not like rice.

— Please be more careful.

— If you like me be more careful, I will be more careful.

CARNEGIE / Then came The Bathwater Incident.

— Bailey was crying, reported Blondie. That water was just too hot.

— Are you sure he wasn't throwing a tantrum?

— The water was too hot. I felt it.

— Did you tell her not to use such hot water?

— I told her.

— And?

LAN / *I said:* — If you like the water colder, I will make the water colder.

CARNEGIE / For what it's worth: I did not sneak up on anyone. Yet as I ascended the textured steps of Lan's spiral staircase to have a word with her, it is conceivably true that I did not announce myself as unmistakably as I might have. An easy matter, in running shoes.

And so it was that, her door being ajar, I came upon Lan visiting with a man not Shang. They were sitting at her kitchen table, talking earnestly, then laughing, then talking earnestly again, in a dialect I did not recognize.

LAN / *Shandongnese.*

CARNEGIE / She was not wearing Shang's fancy clothes. She was wearing her own clothes, and no makeup.

LAN / *Why should I dress up for the driver?*

CARNEGIE / Her hair was braided, in pigtails; the ends bristled, brush-like. How girlish she looked! How utterly unself-conscious and animated and beautiful. I watched as she unwrapped a bunch of flowers—they were bundled in paper towels—then began to work a rubber band off their stems.

— No no, said the man, producing a pocketknife.

But as it happened the rubber band stretched and stretched against the knife blade and would not cut. Lan wanted to take over; the man insisted the knife would work; still the band stretched; until finally he tried the blade against his finger, and sure enough drew blood. *Aiya!* They laughed and laughed, barraging each other with gay heckling foolery.

How I wished I could make her laugh like that.

And yet—to witness, for once, such rightness. To be so happily jealous! How natural she and this man seemed together; how right, and how lucky. They seemed the start of a happy story whose denouement featured baby carriages and PTAs.

WENDY / He carries a cricket in a cricket gourd inside his coat, so that you hear this chirp as he walks by. And he lets us see it if we want. He puts it under a lightbulb to warm it up if it's cold, so it sings.

LAN / *He was like my father that way. My father used to carry a cricket in a gourd sometimes. Just like that, in his coat pocket.*

WENDY / Also Uncle Su plays the violin.

LAN / *His English name was* Jeb. Jeb Su. *His Chinese name was Su Jiabao.*

WENDY / One day he brings his violin to show us. Lanlan won't play even though she says she knows how, but she cries and cries when he plays, maybe because he does like the sappiest things. Another day he brings an *erhu,* and that makes her cry even more, it reminds her so much of her father she says, even though the songs Uncle Su plays are all northern. It is hard to explain how she knows that but she says she does, right away, from the sound. The Suzhou songs being like everything else from Suzhou, more delicate and refined. And his technique—well, he isn't exactly Ah Bin, she says. Ah Bin being this famous *erhu* player who was like this blind beggar or something, and not exactly from Suzhou but almost.

LAN / *He was from Wuxi, a town not far away.*

WENDY / Uncle Su comes by on his bicycle and rides Lanlan around, she sits on the back rack with no hands. Just balances there, comfortable as can be, leaning back with her feet crossed while he pedals. She says it's easy, in China everyone can do it.

— You're in love with Uncle Su! says Lizzy. Face facts, you are!

But Lanlan says she isn't. Because he is a citizen but has no future, she says. Because he has *old way of thinking.*

BLONDIE / I had so enthused about quitting and my new life that I was embarrassed to admit now how the days had begun—when did this start?—to drag on. I began buying books on self-esteem—itself a sign of low self-esteem, according to Gabriela.

One failed to work out; one failed to keep one's endorphins high. One failed to arrange for the child care required for one's self-care.

One failed to raise happy children. How much more upset I felt now about, say, Wendy's having to eat lunch alone, or Bailey's licking everything. How much more defeated by Lizzy's refusing to have anything more to do with drama.

— You have a gift, we told her. You need to honor that. Don't you see?

But she said no, she didn't see.

And what about singing? Wouldn't she like to try singing lessons?

— If I sing at all, she said, it will be with Russell's band.

— Do they need a vocalist?

— No, and I'm not going to ask them to ask me, if that's what you're thinking.

All kids have issues. That's what my book group said.

Still, there were days when I could not get out of bed. Days when the light bars of the morning imprisoned me.

When I was working, all I heard were the voices of women who had chosen to *focus on what really mattered.* Now all I heard were the voices of people who went back to work.

I would have had a nervous breakdown if I had stayed home.

You can only drive so much car pool.

How many times can you answer What's happening? with Nothing much—?

I wondered if what I had really needed was a sabbatical. Why hadn't Porter offered me a sabbatical?

I thought I might do something volunteer. Then maybe something more—if I could. What with the weak economy, I'd heard a lot of women were having trouble getting their old jobs back.

So there I was, being interviewed by someone I had hired. Being told by someone I had hired that I just wasn't what they were looking for.

Would that happen to me? I never would have thought so, but when I heard Porter had replaced me, I did wonder.

I was surprised that I didn't want to garden all the time; I'd always thought I could've gardened night and day. I was surprised, too, that I hadn't fallen into something else—riding, or potting, or painting. I was surprised that my deepened perceptions of the world hadn't coalesced into a passion.

How I had wanted—longed—to be swept away. But whatever notes it was that passion played, I had to conclude that they were not mine.

Though whose idea was it, that one should be passionate? Interesting? Full of the sort of idiosyncrasy that made one feel—and others believe—that one had bravely flouted society and stayed true to one's inner self?

Gabriela thought I should give myself more time.

— A couple of months, she said. What's a couple of months? You're still slowing down. You're still unwinding.

But I did not believe it was a matter of time.

Janie, runt of the litter.

I found myself curious about things Zen—all that emptying. A perfect passion for the passionless. And in any case, I was still doing yoga during Bailey's nap. I didn't feel I could use Lan to baby-sit when he was awake anymore. But when he was asleep, I liked to try and sneak in a class. For fashionable or not, it was something I could say that I loved—that peace. It was a touchstone.

WENDY / Mom is at yoga and Lanlan is outside doing the goat when he comes so that the first thing he does is get butted by Tommy. Lanlan laughs with her hand up to her mouth and her shoulders scrunched up, and for a minute it almost seems like maybe he's going to laugh too. Because it's funny, the way that goat sneaks up and gets him right in the behind. You can see how surprised he is because he never comes to the house and maybe didn't realize we had a goat until ouch! it got him, I know how it feels, like you got poked with a broom handle only sharper. I'm in one of the apple trees, the one with the big long limb that goes right down to the ground, you can walk up the whole thing like an entrance ramp to the upstairs of the tree if you don't lose your balance on any of the knobbies. So I can watch him do what Dad calls the That Damned Goat Dance. He kind of hops and trips away and reaches back with his hand and arches and twists, trying to look at his own rear end which makes him look like a person turned into a cartoon, you can practically hear people laughing, and if it was Dad he'd be making a big snorty noise and shaking his fist and laughing too. And probably singing, this is exactly the sort of time when Dad sings something like:

There was a goat lived on a farm
and dinner was his name, oh!

T-O-M-M-Y
T-O-M-M-Y
T-O-M-M-Y
and dinner was his name, oh—

in a funny voice that he makes funnier and funnier if we don't laugh until finally we can't help it. But Shang isn't singing, he looks back at his own behind with a face so dark red it's like his skin isn't strong enough to keep the blood inside. Then you realize how mad he is, which is mad enough to pick up the pitchfork Lanlan uses for Tommy's hay. Lanlan screams No No No No and tries to pull him away by the waist or grab one of his arms to stop him, but his arms go up and down hard, with her hands wrapped around them like she's teaching him how to use a Chinese butcher knife. Then Tommy isn't even standing up he's just lying there first bleating and panting and bleeding, and then just making a gurgly sound with his head in a funny position and blood coming out of his ears. That's when you realize how bony his backside is, and how his tail used to point straight up. Because it's just lying there now not pointing at anything. But here's the weird thing. Lanlan's trying to stop that Shang but she looks like she's hugging him. It's like what Lizzy says. Lanlan should hate Shang but she doesn't. She doesn't hate him.

It's Tommy she hates.

Then Shang stops and wipes his forehead with his arm and puts the pitchfork back in the toolshed next to the garage while Lanlan wails and wails, you would swear she actually loved that goat, we just couldn't tell. Except that she looks up while she's wailing and watches Shang put the pitchfork away, and then it's more like a story she's telling. It's more like one of her strange stories, only she's telling it and in it at the same time, some story about this girl and the goat she loved, she just wants Shang to sit down and listen and feel what a terrible man he is, like an emperor who killed this girl's heart. It's like one of her strange stories, only here in America when it should have stayed in China, what is it doing here? And what is she doing in it, and how can Shang understand it? When Shang has probably never heard one single other story like that. How can he feel bad when he's like children who have never heard of sacrifice? When he's not even Chinese?

It's too strange for a yard like our yard full of squirrels and apple trees and a play structure. A squirrel jumps from one branch to another, rustle rustle right over my head as if I'm part of the tree or maybe it's not afraid of me because it can see I'm so paralyzed. My arms and legs feel tingly and full of sap, I'm surrounded by leaves, it's amazing how many of them there are left, considering how many have fallen off, like a ton. Also how much blood there is even in a small goat. It's all coming out of his ears. So it's mostly in one place, all around his head, which is good. Does it stain driveways or just wash off? Across the street is the buzz of Mitchell's ride-on lawn mower, going like for one last time before the grass stops growing. And another noise—the squirrels on the roof of the barn that scratch scratch scramble, they're always losing their footing, Lizzy says Russell says these are like the most uncoordinated squirrels he's ever seen. And the mockingbirds, they're making noise too up on the telephone wire, except it sounds like it's being vacuumed up by the sky today. It's those clouds hanging down like the insides of an old couch if you crawl under it, you know how you can't hear practically anything down there. Everything is going, the mower and the squirrels and the birds just like usual, except that Tommy is lying there and even with the blood I think he's sure to get up and start tracking it all over except that he's like this animal in a museum now, you know how they don't even blink if a fly lands on them. He doesn't and doesn't and doesn't. And that's when I realize the soundproofing isn't in the sky, it's in Tommy. It's so weird he can do that, you just can't believe it, but Tommy is soaking up the noise, he's soaking it all up and turning it into blood. So that all that's left is words, I hear them like they're in tree talk. *It's dead.*

— You killed him! He's dead! Lanlan cries and cries and cries and cries. She's kneeling next to Tommy and bending over him so her hair is practically in his blood but not quite, she flings it back behind her shoulders and kneels in a place too where his blood won't get on her knees. But mostly she's crying and crying, even when she stands up and kind of steps over and around Tommy's body, closing the toolshed door so the pitchfork is inside. You can still get to the toolshed from the garage door which is open, but at least you have to go around a little corner, and you can see Lanlan thinking that.

Because Shang is still mad.

He's the kind of guy who wears Lycra everything. These shiny black bicycle shorts with a padded seat and a matching black shirt with a zipper at the neck and a yellow stripe across the shoulders to be snazzy. It's the kind of clothes that make him look even hairier than he probably is, because it's so smooth and he's so hairy everywhere except his head. And red, his face is red like one giant birthmark. He's full of new words for Lanlan, words I'm not sure I exactly know either like what does 'two-timing' mean, and 'whore'? He's yelling so loud I can't understand everything he says, I have to keep closing my eyes. What Lanlan says, in a lower voice—I can't hear all of that either, I just want to flutter like a leaf and not hear anything. Lanlan says she understands the goat now, she sees it could not help what it did, it had no choice, but he says to leave the goat out of it, she was no goat and did what she wanted. She says she's sorry, she doesn't know what he's talking about, she was just optimizing, isn't that what he told her to do? She was keeping her options open just like him, wasn't that what he was doing? Staying married to his wife?

— That is not the same thing, Shang says, but when Lanlan asks him to explain, he doesn't.

The sky is getting heavier and heavier.

T-O-M-M-Y.

Lanlan kicks the goat. It's exactly like what people do with Elaine sometimes, they make fun of other people so they'll be on her team and she won't make fun of them. Except the first kick isn't much. It's sort of experimental, she does it in his back, in a dry spot. But then she kicks him again and again and knots her hands up into fists, and it works. Shang laughs.

— You hated that goat, he says. Who wouldn't.

She kicks the goat again and I'm surprised at the look on her face, it's not like any look I ever saw. She looks like she could be one of the Red Guards she told us about, or like one of the guys outside the car when I was adopted in China, Lizzy said they looked like they were never ever going to get what they wanted their whole entire lives and had to watch on TV while other people did.

— Options! says Shang suddenly, it's as if somebody woke him up in the middle of a dream. — What a joke.

— Not a joke, says Lanlan. This is America, right? Land of the free. I think free means you have options.

— I see law school in your future, he says.

— I give all your clothes back, she says.

— Good, says Shang, and starts to pull her skirt off.

— Take your hands off! she screams.

The lawn mower stops. Did Mitch maybe hear her? But no, he is wearing a Walkman and bouncing while he loads up his leaf bag with grass. And now the wind picks up so that the leaves are flapping and flying off, like all at once, pretty soon everyone's going to be able to see me.

— I was going to marry you, Shang says, still grabbing. — I was going to leave Vicky for you. What a joke.

— As if I would marry you!

— Now that's a real joke, he laughs. Anything else funny, Miss Show Me What Is Sex Slave? Miss Tell Me What You Like?

He pulls the rest of the skirt down so she is standing there in her underpants. She has some bikini underwear for dress-up, but right now she is wearing plain underpants like mine, only rattier. She is struggling so hard she steps into Tommy's blood once, twice, three times, she's stepping in it and stepping in it until her sandals are all splattered and her skirt around her ankles too. They're not her fancy sandals and it's not her best skirt, but still I know she's upset about them.

— Stop, she begs. Stop.

It starts to rain these huge drops, every one of them splats really loud. Tommy's blood begins to run and Lanlan is leaving huge pink red footprints all over the place including right on her skirt, which is still caught around one foot.

— Stop! I yell then too, even louder than the rain. — Leave her alone.

I jump out of the tree like a squirrel, landing on the driveway. I'm shaking like a squirrel too but it works! He stops.

— What are you doing back there, he says, and his look is suddenly friendly, like this uncle I barely know but who knows my mom and my dad and how I was adopted and everything.

— Not in front of Wendy, says Lanlan. And to me she says: — It's a game. I like it.

She smiles this completely crooked smile at me.

— Really. You don't have to worry.

— A game, he echoes. She likes it. And then he says: — I see it's raining out.

— It's pouring, I say.

Because it is, the wind is suddenly blowing and the rain is coming down harder and louder, and far away you can hear there's thunder then that *shhhh* of the rain really starting to drench everything.

— Excuse us, says Shang. We're going to step in out of the rain and you should too young lady. Why don't you run inside and get yourself some dry clothes before you catch pneumonia.

Then he grabs Lanlan in her underpants and drags her into the garage. Her skirt stays outside.

— Mitchell! I yell, starting to run down the driveway. Mitchell!

But then I remember the pitchfork. I run back to the garage door and go in the toolshed, and there is Lanlan with no clothes on except the blood and her bra and her shoes and Shang is holding her arms behind her back.

— I have a new word for you, he's saying. The new word is—

— Not in front of Wendy, says Lanlan. Stop. Stop!

He does stop then, and turns and looks at me while I hit him with the pitchfork, which is when Lanlan gets away and attacks him too, and I swing and hit him again, as hard as I can. It's sort of scary hitting someone, I've never hit anybody before. I just hope I didn't hurt him, I'm not like Lanlan who is kneeing him and kicking him like she wants to kill him.

He crumples up on the floor, right on the concrete floor, in his nice shiny black outfit.

It is raining and raining. I think I hear Tommy but I guess I don't.

Lanlan is pulling her underwear back on. Shang moans. His face is like something you made up on a computer program, it's like you hit the command *shmush,* except that he's crying.

That means he's alive.

Lan doesn't look at him or say anything either.

I think maybe we should get him some water or something.

I'm still holding on to the pitchfork but it's getting heavier and heavier. The handle rust is scratchy, and there's like this nail head sticking right into my hand.

Tommy, I hear. I swear I hear Tommy.

Where's Tommy?

15

Independence Island

CARNEGIE / The first rule for noncitizens being to avoid the law, we did not press charges against Shang, but instead dispatched Lan to Maine. The plan being for her to live for a while on Independence Island with her friend the driver. Let the goat affair cool down, and who-knew-what heat up. Predictably, Jeb Su—a former professor, it turned out—leapt at his chance. What with his wide mouth, he grinned literally from ear to ear as, sitting in my study, he heard out our proposal. He thanked us profusely and eloquently for our help, in flawless English; among other things I was happy to see that Lan had gained a great tutor. I tried to impress upon him that November wasn't exactly honeymoon season in Maine. That there would probably be snow, and that the heat in the main cabin consisted of a woodstove. But the stove was at least new and large and efficient, I told him. If you stoked it right, it would burn all night.

— Don't worry, I'm sure we will manage, he said.

— We'd be happy to lend you a car, I said. We have an old Jeep we were going to give Lizzy when she got her license. Please use it as long as you like.

— Oh, no, he said. We can't take a car from Lizzy.

— We've recently realized we don't want her to have her own car anyway. This is the perfect excuse to keep it away from her.

— You are very generous, he said then. Thank you.

— It has four-wheel drive, I said. Which you are going to need.

— Thank you, he said again.

A solid man, he filled his chair perfectly. Its armrests seemed designed to support his arms; his feet reached exactly to the carpet.

— Life may be difficult there, he continued, but it is a long way from Heilongjiang. Coincidentally, you know, I was also sent north to the countryside, way back when. Lan and I have that experience in common.

— I didn't know that, I said.

— I bring it up, he said, as a way of saying I have relevant experience for this challenge. You don't have to worry. I'll take good care of her.

As if to underscore his qualifications for his new role, he wore a red plaid lumberjack shirt, apparently just off a shirt cardboard. Fold marks divvied his torso into rectangles.

— How wonderful, I said. I'm so glad.

— She is well worth the trouble, he said. His hands lifted from his armrests with enthusiasm. — A wonderful girl.

Blondie and I agreed.

— Please let us know if there's anything you need, she added, leaning forward in her chair.

— I'm so happy for you, I said. Lan too.

And so I was.

Lan, though, when I visited her apartment, seemed on edge.

— It's cold, but it's not Heilongjiang, I said.

She packed.

— He loves you, you know. Blondie and I are so happy for you.

She packed.

— Do you not love him?

— If you like me to love him, I will love him, she said finally.

Her windows rattled.

— Are you not happy about this? I saw you laughing with him.

— If you like me to be happy, I will be happy.

— He seems like such a nice man. So well-spoken. So educated.

— He used to write propaganda for the Chinese government, she said.

— He used to write propaganda?

She softened.

— He didn't want to, he had to do it.

— And this, we have to do this, I said. Do you see that? Who knows what Shang might do if you stay. He's a dangerous man.

She packed.

— Do you not want to go?

— If you like me to go, I will go.

— Please stop it, I said.

However she felt about Shang, she was packing the fancy sweaters, the leather pants. The fancy shoes, in different colors, with high heels and pointy toes. Just the ticket for Maine. She was wrapping these in tissue paper, and arranging them just so—her manicured pinkies sticking up higher, it seemed, than ever.

— If you like me to stop, I will stop.

LAN / *Even now I sometimes think I could have worked things out.*

No one could handle Shang like I could. Yes, he lost control. But later—how sweet he could be! After the rain, the sun.

Besides, we had one investor already, and two meetings set for next week.

BLONDIE / How to explain to Gabriela about Tommy? I brought her chicken soup, but she would not, could not eat.

— You and Lan, I sighed, on day three.

— It's your fate, said Gabriela. Trying to get people to eat.

— It is. How did this happen?

— You agreed to it, said Gabriela, tasting a spoonful at last. — That's how.

WENDY / One thing about Lanlan finally being gone is that Mom can start looking for a new baby-sitter. She hangs up signs, she runs ads in the paper so that the phone rings and rings, but she says it's not so bad screening the calls because half the people don't speak English and she definitely wants an English speaker because of Bailey. Plus she has a form she got from a friend, she just asks the questions on the form and checks boxes. Do they drive? Smoke? Drink? Have experience? Have they ever been in a car accident? What would they do if a child in their care started choking? She's in no hurry, she says if no one clicks, no one clicks. After her last experience all she wants is to get the right person.

Then there's stuff to think about like finding me a therapist, she says she really wants me to see someone about what I've been through.

— I'm so proud of you, she says. But it's too awful. And to think you never cried. I think you need to cry.

— Okay, I say.

She hugs me.

— Here we spent your whole babyhood trying to get you to stop crying, and now we have to get you to start.

We laugh. But then I tell her it's true, I have bad dreams about Shang and Tommy and Lanlan, bad bad dreams where Shang gets back up and attacks me with the pitchfork, or grabs me the way he grabbed Lanlan.

— He was scary, I say.

— I bet he was, says Mom. You have to stay away from people like that. Then she hugs me again, saying: — If I could, I would vacuum it—*pfft!*—right out of your head.

And when she says that I start to cry a little, because of there being no vacuum, I just wish there was a vacuum.

— I like hugging you, you know, she says. And: — Picture Lionel. When you start to think of that Shang, think of Lionel.

So I try that and find that it works pretty much.

That's one thing.

Also there's Russell's band getting busted for breaking into a school to borrow something, I think maybe an amplifier and they were going to put it back, but they got in trouble just the same, so that now Mom wants Lizzy and Russell to break up. She doesn't call him Dreaded Dreadlocks anymore, now she calls him Mr. Wrong.

— If you learn anything from Lan, she tells Lizzy, it should be that Mr. Wrong is Mr. Wrong. You can follow your heart right into trouble.

LIZZY / But I was not interested in learning from Lanlan. First of all Lanlan wasn't following her heart, and second of all Russell wasn't even one of the ones who broke into the school.

— He's not his friends, I said. He's an independent mind. You should hear what he writes, it is so much his own sound. It has like totally nothing to do with his friends or anybody else. Including his parents, who can't even sing on tune.

— Is that so, said Mom.

— He's not like you, I said. Reading what your friends read and running because your friends run and doing yoga because everyone in the world is doing yoga. Russell says gardening is the number-one hobby in America besides, you are such a follower.

WENDY / Russell wants Lizzy to live with him, that's the new thing. Mom and Dad say absolutely positively no, but Lizzy wants to try it.

— It's not like I'd stop going to high school, she says. Or like I wouldn't apply to college.

— So you're planning on going to college, says Dad.

LIZZY / —What you really mean is, You must be kidding, I said.

— You're sixteen, said Dad. One-six.

— Sixteen may be a baby to you but it's old enough to get a job, I said. It's old enough to drive. It's old enough for a lot of things.

— Do tell, said Dad.

He wanted to call Russell's parents, but couldn't remember Russell's stepmother's name. He said he could only remember the names of wife one, who was friends with a neighbor of ours, and wife three, who he knew some other way. Wife four he could not remember for the life of him.

— The question is, If I give Russell's dad the pop quiz, think he'll know?

— Dad, I said, you can't manage me the way you managed Lanlan. You don't get to decide who lives with who, I have news for you.

— I did not manage Lan, he said.

WENDY / Lanlan and Uncle Su get married almost right away but nobody goes to their wedding because they don't even call first. Also it's not really a wedding, they just go to some office, there's no dress or cake or anything, it's just to solve the visa problem because Lanlan was on this J-1 and had to be in school, and now she's not in school. Lizzy says maybe she's pregnant but I say remember how she thought she was getting too old?

— She gets her period, says Lizzy.

— Still, I say.

And sure enough instead of having a baby they have a shop where they sell Chinese food.

— Remember all the food she cooked for us? Mom says. Now she's cooking it for other people. She says she's so lucky she learned American taste.

Nobody can sit down in the shop, it's like so small they can only do takeout. But it's doing well, that's what Dad says, it's the immigrant success story all over again. He says they work all the time, it's hard hard work, much more work than homework, which we shouldn't complain about, as long as we think homework is work we will never get anywhere in life. He says that in this big pleased way, as if he's finally found something he can vote for in the world. It's like things are going terrible for him at work but at least this one thing is going great.

LIZZY / As if there was somewhere to get to.

All grown-ups cared about was houses and cars and sending the kids to college. As if we even wanted to go.

WENDY / Dad says Lanlan is an inspiration to us all, but Lizzy says Lanlan is practically the same as Mom and Dad now, doesn't that kill you?

— Like she had an affair with Shang and with Uncle Su both, figuring one or the other of them was bound to marry her, says Lizzy.

— That's not why, she was in love with Uncle Su! You said so yourself, I say.

But now Lizzy says Lanlan was just using her brain.

— Uncle Su wasn't married, she says. Shang was. But Shang had a great plan for making money in China. Remember how he was going to make her a cofounder of his company? Uncle Su just meant a green card and a job who knew where. McDonald's.

Lizzy says this while putting these little braids in her hair, like all over.

LIZZY / Lanlan was like that. Like when I asked her should I live with Russell, she said I should think about how much money a musician was going to make. And how I was going to make him marry me. And whether anyone else was going to marry me either, after I lived with him. I tried to tell her how living with someone didn't make you, like, ruined. It wasn't like I was headed for some seconds bin in some bargain basement.

— You are still young, Lanlan told me. Don't sell short.

WENDY / Whatever, I still think she's great. Like she told me that I shouldn't worry so much about Elaine, that no matter how bright a sun, in the end it goes down. And she was right. Like it turns out Elaine's father is going to jail for stock fraud, which Dad says is a fancy way of saying cheating, everyone is so depressed at her house people say they're not even going skiing over Thanksgiving. Now when anyone sees Elaine, all they have to do is put their fingers up in front of their face like bars and she runs away crying. She wrote a whole essay for the class magazine called 'Kids Can Be Mean,' which just made everybody laugh more. Then she wrote one called 'You're Not Anything, You're Just You' and one called 'People Just Need to Pick On Somebody.' I feel sorry for her but Lizzy says I have to learn to tell people to go to hell.

— You think Elaine would feel sorry for you if you wrote an essay and everybody laughed? she says.

And she makes me practice saying it: — Go to hell! she says.

— Go to hell! Go to hell! Go to hell! I say.

One day I even say it to Elaine's face: — Go to hell! I say.

But the way she turns away I feel sorry for her, I can't help it, which the therapist says is all right.

Her name is Mary Kay, and she has an iguana in her office.

LAN / *Our storefront was the smallest one on* Main Street. *The store was like a tunnel. But sometimes there was a line all the way out the door to the street, even in the snow. People came from the next town over, even from the next county. And guess what our most popular dish was? Dumplings! The same dumplings I used to make for the family.*

The line outside was better than any advertisement, in fact we moved the register even closer to the door to make the line longer. That was my idea, just like the window into the kitchen so people could watch the cooking, and the free dumplings we gave to the first ten customers of the day. Of course we didn't say why we were moving the register. We said we needed more room in back, for the kitchen, because of the increased volume. Which was true too.

Already people were talking about us. There was an article in the newspaper. Because so many people had tried to open businesses on Main Street, *and so many had failed. If you walked down the street all you saw were half-empty stores, with too many shelves.*

What was our secret? the reporter wanted to know.

LIZZY / Of course the answer was work. The answer to questions like that was always work.

BLONDIE / We returned to the center of our lives. Bailey settled into day care. Lizzy moved in with Russell, then—thankfully—moved back home when she realized he was eavesdropping on her phone calls.

— I wasn't allowed to go out without his permission, she said. That was another thing. I swear, he was worse than you guys.

Meanwhile, Wendy made a new friend, Mya, who was smart, and sweet, and good at chess.

CARNEGIE / Suddenly all three kids had new modes of transportation. Lizzy, unfortunately, got her driver's license; how we worried and worried, though not any more, as Blondie pointed out, than we had worried about Russell driving. At least Lizzy didn't say anything, to our surprise, about the Jeep.

More happily, Wendy claimed Lizzy's Rollerblades and learned to do tricks. And Bailey became so enamored of a hopalong ball that he stopped walking entirely, that he might hop everywhere like a kangaroo.

This precipitated a conference at day care.

BLONDIE / Carnegie got a new job—chief technology officer of an educational nonprofit dedicated to supporting teachers in rural areas. It was hardly cutting-edge, and who could get over how he had been treated at DMS? *In this family, we do not speak of DMS.* But he liked the people at his new job, and supported their mission, and found that in this outfit, he could take days off every so often. Even a week here and there.

CARNEGIE / I took up sailing. Thinking, as I tacked hither and thither in the sun, how healthy this was. How balanced. How sane.

But was it me?

BLONDIE / All fall and winter and spring our house seemed filled with our own music. There will be no nickel eating in this family. Of course we can get a new chess clock. A new way of defending against the Grunfeld, that's terrific. There will be no licking Mom and Dad in this family. In this family, we do not tackle. In this family, the weekend curfew is eleven o'clock. Lollipops do not count as dinner in this family.

We had stopped looking for a sitter, not feeling that we needed one for more than an occasional Saturday night. And I was finding myself less depressed with less free time—in fact, happy—realizing, I suppose, that I needed to keep busy. This was hardly the deep revelation I had hoped for. But there it was.

In the meanwhile, I performed culinary experiments. One week was packet week—fish in parchment, chicken in foil, beef *en croute.* Next came a run of chutneys, followed by fun soups—tuber soup, pink soup, spider soup.

And celebration soup!—when Lizzy started seeing her old boyfriend Derek again.

WENDY / Derek the Normal.

CARNEGIE / How sweetly obsessed Bailey was with trains then, just like Lizzy, when she was little. Every day it was *Choo choo! Choo choo!* Then, *Crash!*—there was always plenty of crashing. And then, *Break train!*—meaning that he needed the breakdown train to come set things right. And of course the breakdown train did always come when he needed it.

Where did his sense of humor come from? He would call himself Juice and laugh; he gave his bears names like Butter. And when he discovered Blondie sleeping in one day, what did he say? But *Oink oink, Mama! Oink oink!*

It did not mean anything exactly, this sort of thing. And yet it did make you feel as though you had sat on banks such as you wouldn't want to have missed. That you'd seen rivers.

BLONDIE / Then came the first news of trouble.

WENDY / — You're kidding, says Mom. You're kidding.

She has this look like something just ran over her face, everything is flattened out, and her voice is funny too, quick and kind of skipping around. Hyper and then quiet. The quiet is like this big box you know has something in it.

BLONDIE / The takeout business was a success. But when it was time to move into a bigger space, they found that there was only one landlord in town. And that landlord was set on a certain rent not only for a new space, but for their old space. He maneuvered and argued— I knew this man, he collected fire insurance on a building every other year. So in the end they moved into the new space—they had no choice. But really it was too expensive for them.

CARNEGIE / Did not people still swear by their dumplings, though? Which they offered in four scrumptious flavors, including All-American. (We didn't dare ask what that meant; it came, they said, with special sauce.)

As for their landlord laments, what else was new? That landlord was a greedy bastard, everybody knew it. In fact some people said he was one reason the town was depressed, that he destroyed every business this way. The mayor himself, that great man, encouraged Lan and Jeb to stay.

LAN / *The mayor himself had lunch with us and told us how he didn't want us forced into another town. He said what the landlord was doing wasn't right, and that a store like ours brought all kinds of foot traffic into town. It was stimulating for the economy. It was good for everyone.*

And so we promised him we'd stay. We shook hands with the mayor and had our picture taken with him. We told him that for the good of the town, we'd stay.

CARNEGIE / To bring down their labor costs, they replaced some of their help with Chinese immigrants like themselves—one legal and one not—whom they found through a community bulletin board on the Internet. As for how to explain this change:

Friends of the family, we have an obligation, they said.

We are very sorry, but you understand.

Mr. Su has these friends.

Most people called him Mr. Su. For example, the employees, at least until they were fired. Then they called him 'that asshole Su.'

Those Chinese stick together, the only people they trust are their friends.

Jeb tried to suggest that there was a skills issue also, that the new help had more experience cooking authentic Chinese food. (Of course, here he glossed over the All-American dumpling.) Not long after that, though, it came out that the new help were not even friends, as they had been presented.

These guys do nothing but lie! I'm telling you.

Lan finally came clean and admitted the new help was just cheaper, but to no avail.

They pay these people nothing.

LAN / *Finally we fired our immmigrants and replaced them with local help, at far higher rates. But even so the help believed themselves underpaid.*

What the hell can we do? We could be replaced by immigrants anytime.

BLONDIE / We tried to tell Lan and Jeb to ignore what people said. It was just envy and resentment, we said.

CARNEGIE / —Red-eye disease, we said. You'll be all right in the end. You have the support of the mayor.

And was not the mayor a great guy? O'Reilly, his name was, an Irishman, he knew how things could be. How long ago was it really that being Irish meant fighting with somebody over something all the time?

— People were having you left and right, he said.

LAN / *Shu da chao feng—the tallest tree catches all the wind.*

BLONDIE / The PR problem grew when the help started filling some bags fuller than others. In theory, they used scoops, and all the portions were the same. But in practice, there was variation. People started comparing what was in their bags, and the blacks in town—all six of them—claimed that they were routinely shorted.

Then there were claims that the shop used peanut oil in everything. Three children in town had peanut allergies; their parents always asked before ordering whether such-and-such dish had been made with peanut oil. And Lan was always careful to ask the cooks. But the cooks were perhaps not always honest in their answers—or perhaps they were. The fact that a child got sent to the hospital and that the mother blamed the shop was perhaps not even fair.

Still the rumor flew that Lan's Chinese food had almost killed a child.

LAN / *There was another rumor too—that in the interview we'd given to the newspaper we'd said that the reason we'd succeeded was not that we worked hard but that we worked harder than anyone else. Now there were people in the bar down the street asking, What's the matter, don't you work? To which their friends answered, No sir, I do not. I mean, not as hard as some, that's why you see me in the very same fashion garments I've been wearing for ten years.*

Of course, Jiabao and I never hung out at the bar ourselves, being too busy. That was a source of joking too. Our prep chef told us what people said.

What are you doing here, you lout? Loafing around again.

If you worked harder, you wouldn't be living in a double-wide.

If you worked harder, you wouldn't be hanging around here.

The way you work, pretty soon they'll be needing you down in Mexico.

Of course, Jiabao thought it was true, that some of the townspeople were lazy. San tian diao yu, liang tian shai wang, *he said—Fish for three days, take two days to dry the nets. The way they worked, he said, they could be Chinese government officials.*

CARNEGIE / Then there was the house.

16

Sue's Beach

CARNEGIE / Last backtrack—to just after Bailey was born.

Recall: I went up to the house alone, taking the day off, to see what manner of intruder was setting off our alarm.

That long, long drive.

Those rude, lewd beach bums.

Then turning on the cabin lights: only to discover empty cans, dirty plates, sippy cups. Unpopped popcorn. Someone having expected a microwave, it seemed, not realizing that the Baileys were diehard Luddites who popped their popcorn in long-handled baskets over a campfire. Also I found diapers, wipes. Toys.

The woman had set up camp in the library building next door—the coolest of the outbuildings in the summer, thanks to the willows. I had never been met with someone so magnificently unkempt. A mountainous woman with felted hair, she did not stand when I came in, but only opened her eyes and glared glazedly at me as if to impress upon me my rudeness. I might as well have walked in on a séance. The corners of her mouth drew down in annoyance; she so pointedly closed her eyes again that they seemed to recede, as if hauled in, under her jutting brow. Her speckled bosom heaved and fell.

— Hello? I said. Hello?

She did not respond. Instead response came—startlingly—from a baby, emerging from under its mother's wraps as if in a school play about Mother Hubbard.

I was not an infallible judge of children's ages, but I guessed the baby (on closer inspection, a her) to be around eighteen months old or so. She was wearing a yellow T-shirt with a ruffled edge, and a heavy diaper. In her condition of hair and shelf-like brow she resembled her mother, but she could not have been less mountain-like. On the contrary, she toddled and tumbled, rolled and plunked, nonstop.

— Hello, I said.

She scurried back into her mother's skirt.

Probably I should have had them both summarily removed for trespassing. Instead I impulsively invited the woman to dinner in the main house. It was dinnertime, and how were they going to cook, if I was using the kitchen? So I offered.

— Thank you, said the woman, rousing herself.

Her eyes—an unsettlingly clear blue, now that she'd woken up—seemed to scan me for hidden intentions. She was like a child herself in that she did not hesitate to look and look and look if she liked.

— We would be happy to dine with you, she concluded.

Grandly, astoundingly, she rose.

— Did you mean just now? she asked, once she was fully risen. — Or did you mean later?

She took a step; it was like watching an Egyptian temple being wheeled off an opera set. She was lighter in motion than I would have expected; her feet, improbably small. Her child too seemed somehow out of scale beside her, like a miniature child.

— Just now, I answered, mentally reviewing the contents of a cooler I'd brought.

— Very well then, she said.

And so we proceeded, the three of us, to the main house.

She was, as Blondie could have told me, Mr. Buck's great-granddaughter. Her name was Sue. Her daughter was Ashley.

— And who are you? she asked.

I explained as I cleared the big table and set the food out.

— I remember your wedding, said Sue. You had a little girl.

— Yes, I said. Like yours.

— This is my girl, she said then. Don't get any ideas.

— Oh, no, I said, setting out some stuffed grape leaves in a pickle dish. — Of course she's yours.

Ashley sat on her mother's lap. From across the table, I could see all the better now how overgrown and broken her small nails were, and how beyond detangler her hair. Her eyes too—a beautiful blue, like her mother's—were crusted in the corners, her lips and cheeks chapped. Her arms and neck and face were bumpy with bug bites and scabs; she scratched so constantly that my skin itched in sympathy.

We ate. Sue's pace was not abnormal, only the placid way she kept at it, eating and eating and eating. Ashley was less restrained; she stuffed things in her mouth, cramming and cramming.

How many times we had had to coax our girls to eat! Singing to them as they ate, reading to them. Cutting the sandwiches into bird shapes and heart shapes, cooling off too-hot foods in the freezer.

In contrast, Ashley. And how strange the woman and child looked, both eating at once, one above the other, in a bilevel arrangement.

I obligingly put out all the food I had brought. Food from the cooler—fish, shrimp, chicken. Lentil salad, orzo salad, tofu salad. Pad thai. Carrots. Kale. I had not wanted to bring so much food; but what if the situation took a few days to straighten out? So had asked Blondie. There was a greasy spoon in town, but it was anti–heart-healthy. Hence: broccoli soup. Tomato soup. Carrot soup. Salsa. Yogurt. And from my grocery bags, bagels. Crackers. Bread. Veggie chips. Tortilla chips. Rice cakes. Nuts. Fruit. Though I had brought beer, I left that in the bag.

Outside the window, the lake shone and shone, innocence itself. Every so often the surface stippled, then calmed. Tied up to the dock—a surprise—the bicycle ferry bobbed gently. It was missing, interestingly, its handlebars.

Sue and I talked. About the weather, the motorboats, the harbormaster, the town. But also about the house, which Sue believed belonged to her.

— Don't go getting ideas, she said.

I assured her I would not.

— My family owned this island before the Baileys, she told me. My family owned this island before it became a school. My great-grandfather built this cabin. He built all these cabins. We gave the island to the school. Not to the Baileys, to the school.

— The school sold it to the Baileys, I said. Or not even to the Baileys, right? To my wife's grandparents, who passed it on to my wife's mother, who married a Bailey.

— Now you are living here.

— Just visiting, I said.

— You may, she said. So long as you don't go getting ideas.

I passed her some veggie chips.

Across the way, the setting sun bisected the hills—the top half bright with sun, the bottom dark with shadow.

— We are going to take it back, she said.

— How very interesting, I said.

She lowered her protuberant brow.

— Not that I'm getting ideas, I said.

— Don't be fresh, she said.

Ashley, finally full, wriggled off her mommy's lap. Hovering by the edge of the table, she picked up a bagel and looked at me through the hole. I waved, then picked up a bagel too, and squinted through it. She smiled and threw her monocle on the floor, where upon I threw mine on the floor, like the monkeys in *Caps for Sale*—a book I hoped someone would someday read to her. She giggled.

— You're getting ideas, said Sue.

— And here I'm not even a Bailey, I said.

— I can see that, she said. Don't be obvious.

— I don't know if it's so obvious, I said. I could be a Bailey. I mean, someone who looked like me could.

— Don't go getting ideas, she said.

The sun began to go down; the lake turned orange-pink. Rummaging for some candles, I asked Sue how long she had been living in the library.

— Forever, she said, pointing out the drawer with the matches.

And how long was she planning on staying?

— Forever, she said. This is our home.

— Not to be fresh, I said. But I believe the Baileys think this their home.

— They may think what they like, she said.

— Of course, I said.

That seemed the most acceptable thing I had said so far.

— This isn't a great place for a child, I said, lighting a candle. —Where do you live when you don't live in the library?

— Elsewhere, she said. Don't be stupid.

— Of course, I said.

I tried to ascertain whether she had a job, or health insurance, or a partner. Zero for three.

— Does Ashley have a doctor? I asked.

— Everything would be fine, said Sue suddenly, if we could stay here.

— Of course, I said.

— May I smoke?

— Of course, I said again, though the Baileys hated smoke and did not allow smoking indoors.

Sue produced a pack of Marlboros. Ashley and I were eating apples, crunching loudly at each other.

— I'll make you a deal, I said. You can work as our caretaker if you bring your child into the clinic in town. I'll arrange everything.

— Then we can stay here, she said.

— You should be seeing someone too, I said. Are there social workers up here?

— Don't be ridiculous, she said.

Ashley cuddled in her lap, sleepy; I produced a bowl for an ashtray, half afraid Sue was going to drop burning ash on her child's face. I offered her and Ashley beds in the main cabin too, but she said I was welcome to use them.

— I just had a baby myself, I said as she left. — That is, my wife did. Just have a baby. His name is Ellison Bailey Wong.

— Of course, she said.

— He's so beautiful, I said. You should see how beautiful.

She threw her cigarette butt onto the ground outside the door when she left. The ground in that spot was perennially damp, as she maybe knew; condensation collected under the shingles in that corner. Still, when she turned the corner, I stomped on the butt to put it out.

BLONDIE / Carnegie did call the department of social services, and the local clinic, and the police when he got back. But by that time Sue and her child had left.

Carnegie began using the alarm again.

No one was breaking in anymore.

CARNEGIE / Now it was almost summer. Having survived the trial by white of winter, and the trial by brown of mud season, Lan and Jeb were now enduring the trial by blackflies and Sue; for Sue was back. By their account, she was more solidly of this world than when I made her surreal acquaintance. Her hair was cut, and her clothes clean, and she seemed largely awake. Still, they were more afraid of her than they were of the bear family that regularly outwitted even their most ingenious garbage enclosures.

— The bears are not crazy, they said. Sue is crazy.

LAN / *One day when we were sleeping* Sue *walked right into the house. That was how we first realized there even was such a person. That was how we first realized that she was living in the library, right next door to us. Jian guai bu guai, Jiabao told me—Do not be afraid of the strange. Still, I was scared.*

CARNEGIE / We told Lan and Jeb not to kick her out. We told them that Sue was harmless, that she had a daughter. That if anything they might try to establish a relationship with Sue, so we could get her and Ashley some help. Lan said all right, but in a few days called again and said that there was no daughter.

— The daughter might come back, we told her. Keep an eye out. Sue is harmless.

LAN / *After that we locked the door, but sometimes she came and stood outside the window. Of course we slept with the windows closed. Still we could hear her saying,* This is my home. This is my home. *We drew the curtains, but still could see her silhouette. And through those old windows, we could hear her. A man had come, she said. A man had brought her heavenly food, and told her to take care of this island.* You are its caretaker, *he told her.* To you is given the care of all its buildings and all its plants, for as long as you walk on its ground. *Or so she claimed. Sometimes she claimed too,* My family owned this island. My family owned this island before it became a school. My family built the buildings that sit on this land. My family gave the island to the school. No one ever thought the school would sell it. To a family that did not even come! Who gave it away to foreigners! Where did they go getting such ideas? *She said her great-grandfather had come to her in a dream.* Check the contract, *he said.* The contract says we give this island to the school, a place for children to learn. If it is no longer a school, we take it back.

Now she chanted outside our window.

— We take it back, *she said.* Check the contract. We take it back.

— What contract? *Jiabao said one night. He pulled aside the curtains and opened the window. I tried to stop him, but could not. He said:* — If there is a contract you should Xerox a copy for everyone to see.

She did not seem surprised that he had opened the window and was talking to her. She just looked at him and said: — You are not even a Bailey.

— The Baileys sent us here, *said Jiabao.* This is their house and we are their guests. We plan to buy this house from them one day.

— Don't go getting ideas, *she said.*

CARNEGIE / That was news to me. Jeb and Lan thinking to buy the house? But when I asked Blondie, she said she had indeed said they might. That she would talk it over with her father, yes. Seeing as she didn't feel we could just up and sell it, even if it did belong to us.

— Most certainly not, I said.

LAN / *After a while we weren't so afraid. We felt sorry for* Sue, *especially when we found out her child had been taken away by the government. But why didn't she find a way to help herself? Like Jiabao and me.* Have you never heard of bootstraps? *Jiabao asked her. We told her if she worked hard, she could have her child back.*

If she worked hard, she and her child could have a house, and food, and new clothes. Jiabao said she was mentally ill, but I thought she was lazy. I told her how Jiabao and I had winterized the main house with our own two hands. I explained to her how warm we were after we put the insulation in. We told her that any night she felt cold, she was welcome to stay with us. Because even in early summer, it could still be quite cold at night. Sometimes we saw frost on the ferns in the morning.

But Sue refused our offer, just as she refused, later, a job in the kitchen.

—Don't be ridiculous, she said. How can I hold a job?

She was waiting, she said, for her daughter to come back.

Then the warm weather came, and with it, no daughter, but many friends.

Not only did people use the beach around the bend, they used the beach right in front of the house. And they stared at us, brazenly. Me especially, because I was a woman. Every time I stepped outside the house people stared and stared. As if I was on their property. Sometimes I hid behind the big pine tree that grew right beside the house. Of course, that just made people laugh. I was glad there were so many bugs; for a while, when the sun went down, the bugs drove the people away.

But when it got hotter, the people ignored the bugs.

By July there were more and more people. They began to make campfires in the evening, so they could have dinner on the beach. They liked to barbecue things. We could smell the barbecue from the house. Also the smoke, people said, drove the bugs away. Sometimes it seemed they were never going to leave at all. Jiabao and I could come home from the store at eleven at night and still find people sitting around their beach fires.

— That's dangerous, I told them. You are too close to those willow trees. Those pine needles too are very dry.

But they just laughed.

It seemed that there were more fires all the time, and closer to the house too. Sometimes we would look out and feel as if we were si mian chu ge—hearing Chu songs on four sides. It was as if we were being held captive in the camp of a barbarian army.

We felt we could not leave our house. How endless, already, the summer seemed!

BLONDIE / I wished they had called us.

LAN / *We did not think* Carnegie *and* Blondie *could help us anymore. Too busy with the baby, we thought. So we called the police. And when the police didn't come we went to the mayor, who shook his head but then explained he was only the mayor. He said we should call the police.*

CARNEGIE / If only the police did not themselves use the beach for their annual All You Can Eat pancake fund-raiser.

BLONDIE / The locals called it Sue's Beach. They called the island Buck's Island, and the beach, Sue's Beach.

LAN / *Sometimes Jiabao would yell at the intruders from the screened porch overlooking the best strip of beach. Sometimes he yelled:* — Get off this property! Go away!

Sometimes he yelled: — This is not your beach!

One day he stormed out of the porch and down the front steps. I begged him to please stop, to please come back in.

— Ignore them, I said, in Shandongnese. Better to do nothing than to overdo.

But he didn't listen.

Of course, the people answered: — Fuck you. This ain't your beach either.

One of them was particularly loud, a big man with tattoos all over his body. Big ears too, like the Buddha. He walked over with a towel around his neck.

BLONDIE / Billy.

LAN / *I begged Jiabao once more to come inside.*

— Please, I said. I'll rip up my green card. *Please.*

I said that because sometimes he believed I had married him to get a green card. *Sometimes he believed I was going to divorce him as soon as I could say we had been married for two years, and have the conditions on my* green card *removed. It made him crazy, made him do crazy things.*

— Come back in, I said.

— This beach is the town beach, *said the tattoo man.* It belonged to Sue's family originally, and now she's taken it back and given it to the town.

— This beach, *said Jiabao,* belongs to the Bailey family. According to the law. And America is a land ruled by law.

— Oh yeah? And what does that have to do with you?

— They gave it to us to live here.

— Oh yeah?

— Of course, we plan to one day buy it from them.

— Fucking foreigners, *said somebody.* Fucking foreigners are going to own our beach.

— Can you fucking believe it? *said some other people.* Fucking foreigners.

Most people went back to sunbathing then. They rolled over on their towels and went back to sleeping or smoking or talking or drinking. Some people went in the water, or played with their kids. There were a lot of rafts in the water. People liked those rafts you could lie on, especially the ones with cup holders for their beer. Only a few people sat up. Still the tattoo man stood there.

— This is not your beach, *said Jiabao.* This is the Bailey family's beach.

— This beach belongs to the earth, and the earth belongs to no man, *said the tattoo man.*

— You heard him, *said some of the people watching. The tattoo man put up his hand, meaning 'quiet.' Then he went on:* — Now, reasonably speaking, you must admit there is something wrong with the one beach on the whole lake, the one beach in the whole town, belonging to a family who doesn't even come for the weekend. Who has their house all opened up but then decides they're not sure if it's worth the drive to come lie on their beach. You must admit there's something wrong with their giving it to foreigners to use when the people who live here have no beach whatsoever. And you must admit there's something wrong with its being offered to foreigners to buy without one person in town even knowing it's for sale. Do you follow my drift?

— No, *said Jiabao.*

— It is plain unnatural, *said the tattoo man.* Because like I said, the earth belongs to no man.

— I thought you said it belongs to Sue.

— Sue's family gave it to the children of the town. They never meant for it to belong to foreigners, *said somebody else.*

— Nobody, nobody ever intended it to belong to fucking foreigners, *said a third person.* That's clear. The earth or the Bucks either.

— It was perhaps rude and unnatural of the Baileys not to think more of their neighbors from the beginning, *said Jiabao.* Perhaps there were laws beyond the law they might have considered. As for the earth, however, I must tell you: I do not believe the earth has an opinion.

At this, a boy on the beach laughed: — How could the earth have an opinion?

Others shushed him.

— Further, *said Jiabao,* if the earth does have an opinion, then no one can say, This piece of land is mine. No one at all. Neither the Baileys, nor anyone else. Does anyone here own land?

No answer.

— Perhaps we may agree that the earth agrees to the principle of private ownership in capitalist countries, *said Jiabao.* Or at least has no way to object. Do you agree?

No answer.

— And one more thing, *said Jiabao.*

— Aw, shut up already, *said someone.* Will you just shut up!

Some people turned their radios up.

— I am not a foreigner, *said Jiabao.*

— How now? *said the tattoo man.*

— I am a U.S. citizen.

— You're a citizen? How could you be a citizen? *said somebody.*

— Idiot, *said somebody else.* He's whaddyacallit. Neutralized. Naturalized.

— I passed the test, *said Jiabao.*

— You passed the test, *said the tattoo man.*

— The citizenship test.

— The citizenship test! *People laughed.*

— My uncle took that test, *said someone.*

But still people laughed and laughed.

— Let me ask you, *said Jiabao.* How about if you tell me how many branches of government there are.

No one said anything.

— Three, *said Jiabao.* The executive, the judicial, and the legislative.

— Yeah, and how about you tell us how many ways you can be fucked, *said somebody.*

Everyone laughed.

— In any case, the fact that you're a citizen doesn't make you an American, *said the tattoo man.*

— Oh, really, *said Jiabao.* And how is that?

— A citizen thinks this country is about law. But an American knows it is about who is really American.

— Please leave this beach, *said Jiabao.*

— This land does not belong to you and, trust me, never will.

— You're right, *said Jiabao.* It belongs to the Baileys. Please leave.

— Please leave, *people echoed.* Please leave.

— Why should we listen to you? *said the tattoo man.* You piece of shit.

— Because in China I was a professor, *said Jiabao.*

— A professor! Professor of what? Professor of Shit? With a B.S. degree?

I went out onto the steps.

— Come in, *I told Jiabao, in English.* Time to eat. Come in. Food is getting cold.

He looked up. People were still laughing.

— Please come. Please.

He hesitated but did come in, finally, shouting: — You people are crazy!

— You are crazy too, to talk to those people, I said. Those people will kill you.

— Let them kill me, said Jiabao. You know, I look at the beach and I see it is beautiful. And the pond, look how beautiful it is. Like something in a painting, a place for scholars to go fishing. And this

house is beautiful too, and my wife—look—you are the most beautiful of all. If I had not left China, I would never know how much happiness could never be mine.

— It will, it will be yours, I said. Our shop is doing very well. Probably we will start making money again soon.

But he kept saying: — I wish I did not know. I wish I did not know. We can buy the Baileys' house, but we cannot own it.

He laughed and laughed.

— Sue's beach can never become Mr. Su's beach, he said. You cannot add one word, no matter how much money you have. A joke! It is truly a joke!

And later: — Someday I will go back to China and help our country rise again. You watch. I will help the Chinese people stand up to these ignorant American bullies.

— Maybe I'll come with you, I said.

— You! he said. Who can depend on a woman like you? I know your type all too well. In the morning you say three, in the afternoon you say four.

— I would definitely come with you, I said. If you invited me.

— You mean, so long as Mr. Shang did not invite you to be his cofounder, *right? No more dumplings for you then.* Mrs. Cofounder!

I tried to tell him that I had always wanted to go back to China, that Shang would have helped me go back to China. But he would not hear me.

He loved me but did not hear me.

Later he was more himself.

— Nao xiu cheng nu, *he said—constant shame becomes rage.*

He said: — I understand the townspeople. What their life is.

He said: — Maybe I should not have become a U.S. citizen. *I should have just taken a* green card *like you. Forget about citizenship. Then I could go back and forth freely. Make a living in America, retire in Shandong. Though of course, you would never come with me to Shandong.*

I could not say that I would. I could say it with my mouth but not with my heart. And so I said nothing. Which he understood.

— Anyway, he said, it is too cold here.

He went to sleep early, with a headache. I stayed up much later.

Yet, having a doctor's appointment, I got up earlier than he all the same.

Of course, even then it was quite windy. It had been a calm evening, but the morning was windy.

Why did I not wake Jiabao?

I let him sleep. It was so early. I had to start out early because I did not know how to drive the car, and was planning to walk. Not *that it was so far, a couple of miles.*

Jiabao needed sleep.

How windy it was! Like Shandong in the spring.

BLONDIE / I knew that wind—how it roused the water, making the whitecaps rise. We used to shut the windows when the wind came up like that. My mother would tell us kids to quick go make sure the boats were tied up. If the boats weren't tied up, we would be sure to hear about it from my father.

CARNEGIE / I remembered that wind too. How could I forget? How suddenly it came up. How it turned the pond against me.

LAN / *Some people said the fire was malicious, an answer to Jiabao's insults. Others said the fire was the result of carelessness—a smoldering beach fire that would have normally gone out. Yet others said* Sue *set the fire. They said* Sue *thought that it was winter and that she was shut out of the house again, her house. They said she made the fire to keep her child warm.*

We had never shut Sue *out, but that's what people said. Perhaps she had come other winters, and found herself locked out. That was possible.*

In any case, a tree caught fire, and then others. The willows. Then the big pine nearest the main house fell over as if someone had pushed it. It fell over, burning, onto the roof. Which needed work badly—Jiabao had noticed that when we put in the insulation.

One day, he said, the rain would pour right in.

CARNEGIE / The roof beam had apparently snapped when the burning tree fell on it. Even if Jeb had woken up, he probably could not have escaped, people said. The whole island was burning. The smoke reached the sky.

LAN / *There was so much smoke that even from town I smelled something. As I came out of the doctor's office, I stopped in front of his flower bed, thinking about what to do. Then I looked up. At first I did not realize what the smell was. Or why the sky was so dark. All I could think then was what a surprise it was—at my age!—to have gotten pregnant. I was old enough to be a grandmother; and indeed the doctor had said that I should not get my hopes up. That I might well miscarry. But still, he said, I could try. And who knew? Look at Blondie, after all. I was older, even, than Blondie had been, when Blondie had Bailey. But hadn't she thought herself too old too? And I was already three months along—past the most dangerous time. The doctor asked me why I didn't come in right away, but I had just thought my period was stopping. That I was in menopause.*

I was going to tell Jiabao, of course. I knew how surprised and excited he would be. How nervous I was! But how happy.

How I wished, in a way, that I were in China, where I could take herbs for the pregnancy, and eat all the special foods that made a baby strong. If I were in China, though, who knew if I would be allowed to keep the pregnancy? Who knew what my unit leader would say? Or what the quotas were for the year. I could have begged him, Please. At my age, my only chance. I'll do anything. Pay anything. And maybe it would have worked. But maybe he would have just laughed.

How lucky to be pregnant here! And with Jiabao, who loved me.

So I was thinking—so many things, that I did not realize right away that the sky was black with smoke, and that the smoke was from a fire. That the smell was from a fire.

It was all my fault, I see that now. Jiabao always believed I had married him to get a green card, *and that ate at him. That made him do crazy things.*

BLONDIE / It was my fault. How could I have allowed Lan to be introduced to that Shang? What kind of a person did such things?

CARNEGIE / How could I have sent them to Maine? How could I not have seen how unwelcome they would be?

The cinders rained and rained into the lake, people said. It was apparently quite a show, better even than the town groundworks on the Fourth of July.

The funeral home had discreetly covered the more fragmentary parts of Jeb's body with a sheet, but we were allowed to view his less disturbing parts, including his charred but mostly intact upper body and neck and face. We were not long in our viewing, thanks to the smell. A sickening barbecue-like stench; we fought our stomachs every moment of our visit.

He lay on a metal table, a heavyset man, built a little like myself, with a knob of some sort on his collarbone. His hair was burnt off, as were most of his eyebrows and eyelashes. You could see he had not woken; that he was asleep when he died. There was that relief, to see peace on his face, and his eyes closed. It seemed the smoke had gotten to him before the flames. But how gaunt he was; and with his face gone dead, you could no longer see the kindliness of his expression, the intelligence of his eyes. His gumption. I envisioned him helping Lan, as he had so many times. I envisioned him at the front of a classroom, his sweater powdered with chalk dust. I envisioned him pondering a book, having a laugh with friends, burping after a good meal. What if he had never left China? What if he had never met Shang?

How much he had loved Lan! Had he minded that she didn't love him as much as he loved her? Did he hope she would someday?

What a wonderful father he would have made.

That smell.

LAN / *I told him in his next life, he can live on a pond. In his next life, he can have a hundred ponds, and fish there like the scholars in olden days. In his next life, he can fish and write poetry all day, he can live in the land of peach blossoms and have so, so many wives, if he wants, every one of them more beautiful and capable and loving than I.*

In his next life, he can blow up the trailer park too. I told him in his next life, he can blow up the tattoo man, or Shang, or me, if he wants. In his next life, he can blow up America.

BLONDIE / How black he looked under the fluorescent lights—a flat black, like Lizzy's dyed hair. What sorrow to think he would never again see daylight. That he would never again feel the sun. That he would never again close his eyes to see how his eyelids glowed red. And what was the sky, or the water, or the summer lupine to him now? Had he ever even had the time to go see the lupine, over there on the far side of the island?

CARNEGIE / I made myself touch him. I made myself place my hand on his cold, black, stiff chest. He was not as baggy as my mother, being younger, but even so—how sunken.

I could not bring myself to look at the rest of him, but could see how the sheet lay, in places, oddly. That there were strange suspensions in the cloth, sudden hanging valleys.

— I do beg your forgiveness, I said.

— Please, if you can, forgive us all, I said.

BLONDIE / My family came to Maine for the funeral. Not my brothers-in-law; they stayed home with the kids. But my siblings all came. The service was simple and beautiful. We bought Jeb a grave plot in an evergreen grove, with a view of the water. We took pictures—hoping to send these to his relatives in China, someday. This was not going to be simple, as all his papers had burned. Lan knew only that like her great-aunt he came from Shandong, where he was the fourth or fifth child of a coal miner. He would never have gotten an education except for the Communists, she said. But he joined the army, and was sent to school. He was grateful for this until he discovered, during the Cultural Revolution, that he had become intelligentsia—a social element to be struggled against.

LAN / *A drowning dog, he was. There were many hard years. But in the end he was lucky. By writing propaganda, he was able to rehabilitate himself. Though there were people who said he wasn't a real rebel, his chief accuser was himself shot in the head before he could complete the procedures against Jiabao.*

He liked mantou*—those steamed buns Northerners ate instead of rice. And he spoke that awful Mandarin that hurt your ears, the way people in Shandong did.*

BLONDIE / Somehow he ended up Shang's interpreter, when Shang visited China. And Shang liked him—sponsored him, later, to come to the U.S.

Jeb came hoping to someday teach again. He hoped not to have to write propaganda forever. Shang promised him that he would drive for a while, translate for a while, but eventually go back to school. And then teach.

CARNEGIE / I did try giving Shang a ring, to see if he knew anything about Jeb's family. His secretary blocked my call.

The INS was similarly forthcoming and friendly.

BLONDIE / We buried him.

CARNEGIE / The mayor did not attend the service. He did, however, send a midsized floral wreath.

Doc Bailey beheld this in silence. A squirrel scampered up to the edge of the grave, looked in, and scampered away; Doc Bailey did not notice. His large body, which, like Blondie's, normally boasted a certain lightness, was today immobile and hulk-like. He clenched his jaw.

— Couldn't have said it better myself, I said.

— No doubt he's tied up having drinks with that landlord, said Doc Bailey.

— Renegotiating the kickback, I said.

— The question is, What was this man doing here? That's what I want to know. And in our house.

— I suppose, I said, that it was my idea. Lan being a relative from China, as you know. Who lived with us.

— Of course. And the man—her boyfriend?

— Her husband. They got married up here. Opened a shop together.

— As you encouraged them to do.

— I did.

— Thinking?

— Thinking that there was something wonderful about their having that chance. You know, to do the immigrant thing. Work hard, get ahead. It gave one faith in America to see them do well.

— Does one need faith in America?

— Faith in something.

— And why is that?

— There must have been some evolutionary advantage to it at some point.

— To being oriented to something out there, you mean?

— I'm only guessing.

Doc Bailey nodded. Only slightly; still, the motion made him seem a bit more himself.

— Your parents did that, he went on. The immigrant thing.

— My mother did.

— So why shouldn't these people. Was that your thinking? Keep the tradition.

— I was glad to see someone have a shore to swim for. That wasn't, you know, a joke.

We eyed the mayor's carnations, so nicely wired together.

— Well, said Doc Bailey finally, stretching his hands. — I suppose there's no point in blaming yourself.

Gregory peered into the grave.

— A masterpiece of excavation, he said.

BLONDIE / — A professor, said Peter later. Of what?

He looked at me.

— I'm embarrassed to say I don't even know, I said.

LAN / — Of Russian history, *I said.* He specialized in Russian history.

BLONDIE / Gregory was going to ask something too, but Renata stopped him.

— This is not a time for fact finding, she said.

— Did I say something? said Gregory.

— She's a sad woman, that Sue, said Renata. I vote we give the island back to her. Unless Lan would like to stay here.

Lan shook her head no.

— If only it hadn't gotten burned down first, said Ariela.

— Sue may not even want it, in its present condition, said Peter.

— I'd sooner die than give her anything, I said.

— You don't think she had anything to do with the fire, do you? said Peter.

LAN / *I wanted to kill myself.*

Still Doc Bailey talked to me.

— What are your plans? Are you going to keep the baby?

He told me that it might be healthy, who knew. It could be healthy.

— Do you understand?

I nodded.

— I'm sure you realize you might not have another chance.

I nodded again.

— I'd like to say that we'll support you in every way we can. If you decide to go ahead. I don't mean to pressure you.

— Thank you. I'll think about it, *I said finally.* In just a few days I give you an answer.

— Take your time, *he said then.* It's your life.

— What do you mean? *I said.*

— I mean that it's yours, *he said, giving me a funny look. Not to make me feel uncomfortable; he didn't mean to embarrass me. But I was embarrassed.* — Has no one ever said that to you before?

— Chinese people don't talk that way, *I said.*

CARNEGIE / The next day the Baileys and I walked Independence Island one last time. It was surprisingly gray for July—the sort of Maine day when the sky and water and land all seem ingeniously derived from one bargain-basement material. How much smaller the island seemed, leveled! Not all the cabins were burnt flat to the ground. Here and there parts of walls still poked up. The Jeep was still recognizable, and the bicycle ferry. Yet like an unfurnished apartment, the peninsula seemed too small to have held everything we remembered it to have held. The footprints of the buildings, likewise, seemed unexpectedly miniscule.

What grew was the sky. Legrandin's patch of blue, said Peter, is much enlarged; and how newly enormous it did seem, its grand belly stretching on and on. The peninsula sat unmistakably high relative to its surroundings, but how infinitesimally so compared to the sky to which it aspired. And how much closer it seemed now to the trailer park—so short a stone's throw that the peninsula almost seemed an extension of the park, awaiting trailers. Trailer residents watched us as we circumambulated on our plane, slightly above them, hands in our pockets. They were trying not to bother us. Still we could hear the more projective of their voices providing avid commentary on our progress, against a background murmur: *Such a shame, such a shame.* Every comment was, to our surprise, compassionate. We'd noticed on the way in that several people had tucked flowers into our gate. Now we beheld, on a large rock, a heart drawn in charcoal. In its center was scrawled, *Mr. Su.*

No one knew what to say.

Around us the ground felt rockier than before. Black fallen logs, stumps. Pockets of ash. There was no green, but here and there a squirrel appeared. A bird.

We'd seen all there was to see. Still the Baileys tromped around. When they stopped to view a particular aspect of the devastation, it was now with their hands behind their backs and a way of opening and shutting those hands—stretching them—as if saddened, indeed appalled, by this particular loss; and yet slightly fatigued by matters, generally, of the world.

We gazed out, finally, at the water, which seemed strangely unchanged. The sun had come out; how the pond sparkled! There was an enlivening breeze. In a circle, we talked about the weeds threatening the pond now. Millefoil.

— The seeds come in on the bottoms of boats, Peter said.

The geese. We talked about how the geese didn't migrate anymore, but just hung around all winter. Native geese, people called them. There were golf courses using Border collies to chase them away; people were buying up bottles of fox urine. Searching out goose nests in the spring, and dipping the eggs in oil.

Doc Bailey cried.

— Your mother, he said. You can't imagine what this place meant to her. I just pray there is no way for her to see down from heaven to what's happened. It would kill her all over again.

Blondie and Ariela and Renata tried to comfort him. I was surprised and touched to see him plant his large head, for a moment, on Blondie's shoulder.

— This world can disappear like any other, said Blondie later.

Ariela nodded: — Grandma Dotie used to say that.

Everyone was quiet for a while.

Said Renata finally: — It's amazing the fire didn't spread.

Everyone agreed.

— Though it does make you feel a bit singled out, as it were, said Gregory.

— For misfortune? I said.

— What else, said Gregory.

But Peter disagreed: — Nothing like this has ever happened to us before. Do you realize that? How disgustingly lucky we've been?

— It's globalization, said Gregory. Sooner or later we were bound to get caught in someone else's mess.

— That trailer park, countered Peter. With no beach. Sooner or later there was going to be trouble.

— What are you saying? said Gregory.

— Are you suggesting, I said, that the beach should have been given to the town?

— You could've done that, said Renata. You could've given it to the town. It was your house.

But Blondie demurred: — It was and it wasn't. The only person who could've done that, really, was Dad.

Doc Bailey, thankfully, appeared not to have heard. But Blondie's sisters did, and her brothers, and no one disagreed.

Said Peter, returning doggedly to his point: — I'm just saying maybe we didn't get caught in their mess. Maybe they got caught in ours.

More quiet.

The water lit up for a few moments, but beyond it, the woods held their dark.

— Was there insurance on the place? asked Gregory finally; and when I replied yes, he said: — Brilliant! Brilliant! I always told Peter you were brilliant!

— Where is the woman now? Renata wanted to know. That Sue?

— She's in a center of some sort, Blondie said. Her child is in a foster home. They're trying her on antidepressants.

— And what about poor pregnant Lan? asked Ariela. What's going to happen to her?

— Now there's a question, said Renata.

17

The Waiting Room

WENDY / Lanlan is back but Mom is leaving, as we know because of Mom and Dad's talk. Honestly. Absolutely. Truthfully, they say.

Honestly. Honestly.

Lizzy imitates them: — Honestly, I never say anything honest. Honestly, I have no idea what I even mean.

— Lizzy, says Mom. Please. You are making a difficult situation even more difficult.

— Honestly, says Lizzy. I have never said one real thing in my entire life.

— Where did you learn to talk like that? says Mom. You know, sometimes I just wonder.

— Honestly, I learned it from you, says Lizzy. Honestly, listening to you say nothing my whole life just made me hear every single thing you weren't saying.

— Great, says Dad. And what does Brazelton say to do now?

His cell phone rings, the tune this week is 'When the Saints Come Marching In.'

— If you answer that thing, says Mom.

He opens the fridge door and puts his phone in the vegetable drawer.

— There, he says, shutting the door. — Are you happy?

She's leaving. For another house, for a while, she says, just for a while. She is still going to take care of the garden here, and us too, of course, she's never going to forget about us. We will always be her Wendy and her Lizzy, she says, we're going to live with her half-time, she wishes she could stay.

If it's just for a while, though, how come she says stuff like never and always? That's what I want to know. And where is she going, and how long is a while, and what does that mean, 'half-time'? But I don't get to ask, thanks to Lizzy.

— You're abandoning us, says Lizzy. Honestly, I always knew you would.

— I'm not abandoning anyone, says Mom.

— Honestly, that's what mothers do, says Lizzy. They quit. First they try really really hard, and then they just quit.

— I'm so sorry you feel that way about mothers, says Mom. But it's not true.

— I'm so sorry you're my mother, says Lizzy. Honestly, I wish I'd gotten a different mother.

— Well, I'm glad I'm your mother anyway, says Mom, crying. — And, as my mother used to say, Be careful what you wish.

— I'm glad I got you for a mother, I say then. I don't want Lanlan for a mother, I want you.

— That's not true, says Lizzy. Honestly, you completely wish Lanlan was your mother.

— I used to wish it, sometimes, I say. But I'm sorry I did.

Says Mom: — It's okay to wish things like that. I've wished all kinds of things too. We all have.

— Like that you had different children, right? says Lizzy. That I wasn't so out there and that Wendy wasn't so shy, that we were all more like Bailey. Isn't that what you wished? Honestly?

— Honestly, begins Mom.

But then she doesn't finish, she just starts crying all over again so that her face is pinker even than when she's running and out of breath, and her eyes are bloodshot and swollen up and red-rimmed all around. You're just surprised in a way that her eyelashes look pretty much like normal, only wetter, and that her hair does too, and her teeth.

BLONDIE / Honestly, I just wasn't brought up to talk that way.

Honestly, to talk that way was to be a completely different person than I was.

Honestly, I needed to not think about anything for a while.

— Wendy, I said. I'm not quitting, do you hear me? I'm only going for a while, to try and figure things out. And even while I'm doing that you'll come live with me three and a half days every week.

WENDY / — Is that what 'half-time' means? I ask.

— That's what 'half-time' means.

— What are you trying to figure out?

— About Lanlan, stupid, says Lizzy. Honestly! Use your brain!

Lizzy says all this is happening because Dad wants Lanlan to move into the house now. He doesn't want her to live in the barn anymore, like a servant.

BLONDIE / — This poor woman, he said.

— Think what your mother would say, he said.

— Think what she's been through, and where she is now. All alone in a foreign country, and knocked up besides, he said.

CARNEGIE / For the record, I also said: — If you want her to stay in the barn, we can do that. Lan can absolutely stay in the barn.

I did say that in the end. I did give in.

BLONDIE / I said: — Honestly, she might as well move into the house.

I said: — To be honest, I am no longer playing.

I said: — Mama Wong won, that's all there is to it. I quit. End of game.

WENDY / Mom is taking Bailey with her, that's another thing.

— Bailey is too little for joint custody, says Mom. He can't possibly understand what's happening. Do you understand? It's not that I love him more than you and Lizzy. He's just littler.

— I understand, I say.

CARNEGIE / I could see that he was too little to shuttle between households, even for a while. I could see that a real father—like the real mother before King Solomon—would refuse to have his child split in two.

But where was King Solomon to award Bailey, therefore, to me?

— You always wanted him to be a Bailey, I said. More Bailey than Wong.

— And is that a surprise? she said. When not even you wanted to be a Wong?

I had to chew on that one for a while.

— If that meant being like Mama Wong, you mean? I said finally.

— What else could it mean?

— It could mean being like me, I said. Aren't I a Wong? Or a reasonable facsimile thereof. Am I not as much a Wong as my mother?

WENDY / Lizzy says first Lanlan burned down the other house and now she's burning down this one too.

— I thought you liked Lanlan, I say.

— I do, I'm just saying, says Lizzy. Plus it's not her fault the houses were ready to burn.

Gabriela had a breast cancer scare, that's another reason all this is happening, Dad says. Gabriela's going to be all right, she had a lump but they cut it out, the only thing is it's reminding Mom how no one lives forever.

— Not that Mom is going to die anytime soon, don't worry, he says. And neither am I, even if the doctor does see a bypass in my not-too-distant future.

— Hmm, says Lizzy.

What I can't believe is that he said 'breast.' But maybe that isn't even what he said, because Lizzy didn't laugh or anything.

— I thought cancer was from smoking, I say.

— That's lung cancer, says Lizzy.

— And what's a bypass?

— Everybody old has that, says Lizzy. Practically.

— Not everybody, and you don't even have to be old exactly, says Dad. But yes, a lot of people do have it, and the point is that Mom wants to feel she lived the life it was given to her to lead. That's why she quit her job. That's why she wants to feel like her house and family are her own.

— So what is Lanlan now? I ask. Is she still our nanny? Is she going to live with us forever?

Dad furrows his eyebrows so hard they look as though they might crash into each other, if Bailey was here he could call for the breakdown train.

— We can't send her back, he says. Not while she's in the process of having the conditions on her green card removed. As she can now that she's a widow. Plus she has no job and no home and a baby on the way.

— What I mean is, Is she the love wife?

LIZZY / She heard that from Gabriela, there's no way she figured that out herself.

WENDY / Our house is like so quiet in the afternoons now. Lanlan is there, but she's quiet, almost like the way she was when she first came, only even sadder.

— It was all my fault, she says. It was all my fault.

She says that and everything about her is just hanging. Her hair is hanging, and her head, and her shoulders, and her hands, and her legs and feet too, she's not even interested in what they have to say, seeing as how they're obviously saying nothing.

— *Where's your qi*? I say—your life spirit.

She used to always like it when I talked to her in Chinese, and even now it makes her smile a little. But she doesn't answer.

She only eats because of the baby, and she refuses to move into the house even though she can now. We try to bring her to go see Mitchell and Sonja's girl across the street—she's starting to walk, we say, you should go see!—but Lanlan hardly goes out, and when she does, she doesn't even use an umbrella, she lets the sun shine right on her face. The only normal thing is that she cooks a little, still. Sort of in slow-mo, but at least she does it.

We don't need a baby-sitter exactly, with Bailey gone most of the time and Daddy wanting to take care of Bailey himself when he comes, you've never seen him sit on the floor so much. But Lizzy and me hang out with Lanlan still, and fan her, and talk about America—stuff like how her child is going to be American, but she hopes not too American. We talk about what that means, 'single mother,' and how she is going to support the child. What kind of job she can get at her age, and whether Grandpa Bailey is really going to pay for everything.

Sometimes she's afraid Shang will come get her.

Sometimes she wishes Shang would.

Sometimes she misses Uncle Su. She can't see a single musical instrument without crying.

LAN / *Ren qin ju wang*—Both man and music have died.

WENDY / Sometimes she talks about how things were her fault, but also Dad's and Mom's.

LIZZY / And not to forget Mom's family, with that beach they let sit there until the whole town went ballistic. Dad said they should have sold it.

— So why didn't they? asked Wendy.

— Because Mom and Dad couldn't sell it, and the Baileys couldn't get around to it.

— I think they loved that house, and that's why, said Wendy. I mean, they talked about it all the time, even if they hardly ever went there.

— They had their pictures all over the walls, I said. And no place else to put them.

— Hmm, said Wendy.

— Probably they could have found some other place, but it wasn't going to be as great as what they remembered.

— Hmm, said Wendy again. So I guess they didn't.

— Exactly.

— Meaning that they did love it? Sort of?

— Meaning that they weren't exactly paying attention to anything else. Like to the town and the trailer park and everything.

— You mean, they were in their own little world?

WENDY / Lizzy looks surprised.

— Exactly, she says.

— That's like me, I say. That's how I know, because it's like me sometimes. Which is okay, that's what Mary Kay says.

Lizzy looks at me as if looking at me is finally as interesting as looking out the window.

— You're not as bad as you used to be, she says.

Lizzy is sounding more like her old self these days, maybe because of Derek but maybe not.

— A boyfriend is just a boyfriend, she says. They can make you miserable, but they don't turn you into a completely different person. You are who you are, you just talk about different stuff. And that makes you different in a way, but not completely different.

— Hmm, I say.

That same day Lanlan suddenly starts this program to think calm and happy thoughts. Because she thinks a calm and happy mother will make a calm and happy baby, she says, it's very important. Also she looks at a picture of Sean Connery every day, so that her child will be handsome.

LIZZY / We were, like, seriously? But she believed it was going to work. She really did.

— And what if it's a girl? I said.

But she said she knew it was a boy, because her tummy was pointy.

— What tummy, I said. You can barely see your tummy.

Also she craved sour foods, not spicy, she said, and could we tell she was pregnant from the back?

— No, we said.

— You see, she said. It's a boy.

WENDY / — This is a great country, your kid is going to have so much opportunity, I tell her one day.

— Opportunity for what? says Lanlan.

But another day I find her sitting in a little patch of sun, like a cat.

— Who knows, maybe my baby will grow up and be a millionaire, she says. You know, some of my classmates from school have got some really good jobs already. So who knows what will happen, as long as Uncle Su doesn't whisper in the baby's ear. Tell him go back to China, help China become strong again. Tell him go back help China stand up to the U.S.

— Do you think he really might do that? I say.

— Yes, she says. Of course, either way, I would be very proud.

Lizzy says Lanlan is in love with Dad, maybe she wouldn't mind becoming our real mother.

— Except that she's not our real mother, I say. Mom's our real mother.

— Obviously, says Lizzy.

CARNEGIE / One day I came in to find Lan in the kitchen, making eggs with soy sauce for breakfast. This was something we did all love but probably would not have picked; probably, given the heat, we'd have picked ice cream. Full fat, we were eating these days—half hoping, I suppose, that Blondie would discover this and move back expressly to stop us. Still, there, this morning, stood Lan, wet-haired, in shorts and a T-shirt, cooking. Her belly was swelling, of course, yet I could not help but notice that the greatest growth had taken place in her breasts. From over her shoulder, I expressed hearty enthusiasm for her eggs; and then finally, against my better judgment, kissed her. For how natural it did seem, there in the soft summer sun, to part her cool hair and lightly touch my lips to a triangle of her wet neck.

I stopped. From my new, closer vantage point, I could see an enormous blue vein, big as a pipe, branching down her neck and chest; I could see too her sweetly burgeoning ovoid. Giving evidence of reasonable adult impulse control, I contemplated these things.

She put her hands to her lower back, stretching a little. Her elbows flared. She turned the heat off.

Something between us relaxed.

But then to my surprise and confusion, she turned to me. There was a new sluggishness to her grace; you could see how soon she'd be moving like a largish piece of low-gear construction machinery. Still, we kissed.

We cooled down later with ice cream.

LAN / *It was like a* grade-B movie. *I could see that, how my life was like a* grade-B movie. *I wanted my life to be like a* grade-A movie *now, but I wasn't sure what that meant. I thought I should watch some* grade-A movies *and find out, but when I went to the video store and asked for a* grade-A movie, *that* Eileen *behind the counter just laughed.*

— You were on the right track in Maine, *Carnegie told me.* You were working hard and making things happen. You were the immigrant success story.

— But everybody just hate us, *I said.* Is that part of the story?

CARNEGIE / — Let me ask you, I said. Could you really not afford to use local help? Did you really need to import immigrant labor?

— Not clear, she said. With the high rent price we were not sure we could make money or not.

— And did you give the black customers smaller portions?

— We didn't like it, she said. But we heard too many black customers can kill your business. So we feel we have to be careful.

— And did you check about the peanut oil? When you knew the kids had allergies?

— That we were very careful, she said. Children health very important. Then she asked again:—Why everybody hate us?

—Red-eye disease, I said.

You don't know what America is.

LAN / *So so much trouble over an* old-economy business.

WENDY / Mom stays and stays in her new house. Her new house is a cottage, not a house exactly, and she likes that. It's not so full of stuff, she says she feels free there, she's buying her new furniture one piece at a time. So far she has a green loveseat, and a green reading chair, and a bookshelf. She's trying different colors on the wall, and for Bailey she has a small sunny playroom, all carpeted, with built-in shelves. She's bringing stuff from home little by little, to fill them up. Not a lot of stuff, but some, so the shelves won't look so empty. And for me and Lizzy she has a bunk bed in a special room that opens right onto a porch with a hammock. A long time ago the porch was for hanging laundry, but now it's full of flowers.

She has a little yard with a new garden, and she likes that too. She likes it that the garden is small but big enough for sunflowers, in fact it was already planted with sunflowers when she moved in, that's how she knew this place was for her. They weren't blooming yet, but they were there, and now they're going to bloom any day. She says the other garden was too big, she felt behind all the time, and she likes it that this neighborhood is full of children. She likes it that she and Bailey can walk down the street to the park where there are lots of other mothers and other kids. Of course she has her friends from our neighborhood too, it's not as if she is really so far away, but her new place makes her feel like she never has to leave her block.

— I don't even subscribe to the newspaper anymore, she says. Why take all of that in? I feel like a clamshell these days. You know—

She makes this closing motion with her hands.

It's weird going to visit. Mom's so happy and glad to see us, and has so much time. She makes special treats for us—roll cookies and teacakes and even plain brownies when Lizzy complains she never made us plain brownies—and she listens to everything we say. She loves us and loves us.

Lizzy's upset but she eats Mom's treats anyway, even if the brownies make her cry. And she only comments every now and then about how the rest of the world is like starving, and how if Mom has so much energy she should volunteer in a soup kitchen.

Says Mom: — I'm done feeding the world.

— Of course. Why feed the world, says Lizzy.

— I am exhausted, says Mom, a word you will understand someday.

And she goes on to talk instead about how she's going to force some bulbs over the winter. She doesn't say anything about coming home to live, and we don't ask, not even Lizzy asks.

We play with Bailey more than we used to, first of all because when we go to Mom's house there's not a lot else to do. Besides doing homework and talking on the cell phone all the time, like Lizzy does, she talks so much to Derek she has to get one of those headsets like telephone operators wear, and carry her cell phone on a belt clip.

But also we play with Bailey because otherwise we're going to have to talk to Mom the whole time, she just wants to talk and talk and talk. She's kind of like Bailey, in a way, except that his questions aren't all about you. Like he wants to know what bites. If you show him a bug, he asks, Dat bite? And if you see a kitty cat, he says, Dat bite? And even butterflies, if you see a butterfly, he asks, Dat bite? He likes to pretend he's a bird, or a cat, or that he's spitting, which he isn't supposed to do.

Of course when Mom sees me playing with Bailey, she's happy.

— What a good sister you are! she says.

She says playing with Bailey is keeping me in touch with my childhood, it's a wonderful thing.

But Lizzy says Mom just wants us not to hate Bailey, since we do.

— I don't, I say.

She says I do, though. She says that I might not realize it, but that I hate him for being bio and a boy and a Bailey, not like us, the one child Mom took with her from the house.

— He isn't a Bailey exactly, I say, he's soup du jour, like you. He's just been like more adopted by Mom than by Dad.

Lizzy laughs when I say that.

— How can he be adopted, she says, he's natural.

— He is, I say. You're just jealous because you think he's more adopted than you.

CARNEGIE / Blondie promised to keep up the garden at the house, but in the end it grew so jungly that I mowed the thing down with Mitchell's weed whacker. I mowed down her out-of-control goats-beard. I mowed down her yellow-leaved ligularia. I mowed down her overgrown malva and her ratty, ratty beebalm. And everything else too—more plants than I could name—I terminated them all. I did it all in an hour, with the sun beating on my back; and when I was done, I looked at my work and wept.

Of course it gave me hives.

To Blondie, apparently, it gave nothing.

— I thought I loved that garden, she said, looking around. — But now I have a new garden.

BLONDIE / Perhaps I was becoming a little like Bailey, from being around Bailey. From seeing how he could love something so so so much one day—his Pooh bear, or his train set—but the next day move on.

CARNEGIE / The more Lan thought about Blondie, the more she hated her.

LAN / Blondie *was fake. From the very first moment, I felt she was fake.* Lizzy *said it too, how fake she was. From the very first moment she wanted me to go home.*

CARNEGIE / I tried to convince Lan that wanting someone to go home was not the same thing as not liking them, exactly.

It was tough going.

Neither was talking to Blondie a walk in the park.

— Lan will never take your place, I said. We all say that, you know. The girls too. How you're their real mother, their one and only mother.

To which she answered: — Of course I'm still their mother. I am simply no longer your wife.

Sometimes I argued on Bailey's behalf. How could I not? When every night I dreamed of my serious-faced boy—felt him on my knee, tense with worry. I heard him asking for his room, with the sand, and ocean, and blue sky. Heard him asking for Lanlan. Asking for Tommy.

— How can you do this to him? I said. Do you know what he asked me today? He asked me if daddies bite. And what's a fire? he wanted to know. Do fires bite? This is his childhood. Do you see how you're robbing him of his happy childhood?

That at least made her cry, when I said those things. She did cry.

But other days she returned to her mantra: — Mama Wong won. End of game. I quit.

One day, I read her a poem:

Short and tall, spring grasses lavish
our gate with green, as if passion-driven,

everything returned from death to life.
My burr-weed heart—it alone is bitter.

You'll know that in these things I see
you here again, planting our gardens

behind the house, and us lazily gathering
what we've grown. It's no small thing.

That day she listened, and bowed her head, and closed her eyes; and when I said that I thought these Chinese poems had more to do with her, in the end, than with my mother, she cried. She cried and allowed me to take her in my arms, but later gathered up her bags just the same. How those bags bulged! Mostly with Bailey's stuff, but with other stuff too—all being removed, mini-load after mini-load, to her house. Which I had never seen; which she did not want me to see. As if I were so full of cooties that my very gaze would cooty-ize anything on which it fell.

— You are becoming like Lizzy, I told her.

For Lizzy had had phases where we were not allowed to touch certain things, see certain things, even speak of the certain things we had not touched or seen.

— She just wants her privacy, Lizzy explained now.

And: — You give her the creeps. Leave her alone.

I was trying to leave her alone. But each time she came, she left with more bits of our old lives.

— I'll thank you not to look through the bags this time, she said pleasantly. — I'm not stealing anything.

— I don't look through the bags, I claimed.

— How interesting, she said.

— Stay home! Stay home! cried Bailey one day as they left. — Stay home!

But still she took him, openly—the greatest theft of all, for which she did not even need a bag. Bailey cried and cried, bereft, as she hauled him down the walk and strapped him into his car seat; but as soon as she put on *Baby Beluga*, he stopped. How blond he looked in the car; as one would expect, it being the end of the summer. And why shouldn't he be? Blonder and blonder. If I weren't myself—if I were Blondie—why would I want him to be Chinese in the least?

Lan came up behind me as I waved to Bailey, in case he looked up. Which he did not.

— Blondie looks so happy, she said. Maybe she already found new boyfriend.

— Not that fast, I said.

Still I punched a door so hard that day, I almost broke my hand.

BLONDIE / My new sunflowers were not as tall as the flowers I once had. Their glory, too, seemed somehow less glorious.

Still they brought me joy—the flowers growing so thickly that I could cut them for bouquets. Indeed, had to cut some. How to describe the pleasure in this duty? In crunch-clipping, if not sawing, those coarse, hairy stalks—in felling the flowers. The stalks were so substantial and yet hollow, some of them—quite wonderfully so. I could have spent an afternoon face-to-face with the pebbly plates of the flowers, but I could have lived in the glow of light inside the stalks. The larger stalks especially seemed to emit their own light; their green was peace; if there were a place I'd want to go in my next life, it would be there, into that pure light. I imagined it, sometimes, in my dreams. I pictured myself surrounded by green light—turned into light. I was happy. I was on a happy adventure—the light was glad—but I was alone. Where was Carnegie?

Once upon a time—how long ago it seemed—we had bought resting places together, he and I, in the same cemetery. Not grave plots exactly, like Mama Wong's. Instead we'd chosen a new fashion—spots just adequate for an ash urn and, above it, a modest commemorative stone. The latter, if we liked, could be set in the ground, like a stepping-stone, in a path. The spots were beautiful, on a piney trail, flanked on one side by azalea bushes, the deciduous kind. The bushes were mature and pruned to show their lovely tiered branching; in the summer they were densely leafy.

Ours was a beautiful spot.

But would I see, from heaven, for all eternity, how Mama Wong's plot overlooked ours in the winter?

Honestly, I thought that even then.

Honestly, even before Lan, I went down the green hall alone.

WENDY / Mom comes for my eleventh birthday. My class party won't be for another week, around Labor Day, when everybody's back, but we have a family celebration on the day itself. And even though my birthday is so close to Bailey's, I have my own party like always, Mom has always made sure I had my own birthday. She makes my favorite dinner, ham and creamed onions, and she decorates the dining room with a chess theme. She makes a chess cake, and for a present gives me a book of certificates, every one of them good for something I love—chess lessons, chess books, a promise to bring me to a tournament if I want. My friend Mya brings her new Siamese kitten named Pad Thai, and I am so so happy except at the end.

— Will you stay? I say. Just this one night? For my birthday? Please?

I am crying so hard asking that when she says yes she will, I don't even hear her, she has to say it again. And then yes! She does stay! For a whole night she stays, Bailey too. Bailey stays in his old room, on some blankets on the floor. Mom stays in the guest room.

But in the morning it's not my birthday anymore. Dad comes out of the guest room looking like he's been crying, and Bailey really is crying. Still Mom packs up a couple of more bags of stuff—fall clothes, she says, time for long pants.

BLONDIE / Perhaps it was selfish. I asked myself, sometimes, if my actions were selfish.

But then I would see Lan, or hear Lan. I would see her set a dish in front of Carnegie in so familiar a way I could cry. The girls said she knew all his favorite dishes now, that she made him something special every night, and just the way he liked it. I myself witnessed, one evening, how she stood at his elbow, her little belly bulging forward—waiting to see whether he liked some new fish.

Of course he loved it.

— You see, I know your taste now, she said, with that crooked smile of hers. — I can do everything the way you like. I know your taste.

LAN / *In one way, yes. I knew his taste, yes. In one way, I could do everything he liked.*

But in another way, zhi ren zhi du bu zhi xin—you can know a person, and know his stomach, but not know his heart.

I felt that.

CARNEGIE / So there we were: split, on most days, into two natural-looking households, but feeling distinctly halved. Missing quite keenly our true motley splendor.

My wife informed me I was not to call her Blondie anymore. From here on out, she said, she was Janie.

— You like me to say Janie, I say Janie, I said at first.

But then I said: — Blondie! Blondie, you are Blondie, dammit!

WENDY / It comes on a Friday afternoon right after school starts, a mailman brings it to the door himself. Or not a mailman exactly, this is a man with very short hair and what looks like a fish shaved into the back of his head. When I was younger, I probably would've asked him if it really was a fish, but now I know that even though people have things like that on their heads, you're supposed to act like you don't notice. In fact Lizzy would say that's exactly why they have it, because they like making you uncomfortable, and I know she should know in a way. But still I think maybe he just likes fish. Because how do we really know? Lizzy would say she knows because she's older, she just has that confidence. She says she knows all kinds of things now, pretty soon nothing will surprise her and then she'll be an adult.

Says Dad when I tell him that: — I myself still hope to be surprised every once in a while, if only to keep me alive.

He is signing the fish man's special electronic pad while he talks, he is saying, *if only to keep me alive.* Will I have to be kept alive one day? I am trying to figure out what that means when Dad says, Hong Kong!

That's because the package was sent FedEx from Hong Kong. In the beginning Dad doesn't know what it is, but then he finds it positively funny, he says, that this relative of Mama Wong's who has held on to this thing for years suddenly had to send it rush.

— A piece of work, that one, he says. No doubt some deathbed request got him in gear.

He unwraps the book, which inside all the bubble wrap turns out to be three books, actually, with soft covers, all navy blue. They're bound in thread along the side, and have these tall skinny labels stuck on what we would think of as the back, except that it's the front, with these black Chinese characters going from top to bottom. Dad flips through the books looking at all the Chinese—there's like no English anywhere. He looks at the way the pages work, it's like each page is actually a sheet of paper twice as big, folded in half, so that the edge of each page is not an edge at all, but a fold.

And inside one book there's a note sure enough, that says this guy the Hong Kong relative just finished promising some dying friend not to get caught with like debts or something.

CARNEGIE / 'With debts unpaid and promises unkept.' The note went on:

> And so here is your family book. It is the story of your mother's family, going back 17 generations in Sichuan. Of course, she is the first generation where we write down the girls, lucky she is in it. Unfortunately, you are not in it, because you were adopted in the United States. Anyway you were not born yet when the book was updated. However your older sister will be happy to see her name, the only child in her whole generation.

WENDY / Dad puts that letter down and turns pale and sort of sweaty. Of course it is kind of hot out for September, we're all hot, but he has little beads of water on him, as if he's a car window and it is drizzling out.

LAN / *Was something the matter? I came in to see.*

WENDY / He hands her the letter, which she reads over and over, her whole forehead is like a lake full of frowns.

— Did you know? he asks her.

— My father said my mother ran away and then died, she says in this low voice, sort of between regular and a whisper. — Of, how do you say. Brain tumor. Long long time ago.

She's pretty pale too, they're like a perfect match.

— She swam to Hong Kong, says Dad. With a basketball under

each arm. And from there this relative helped her. The same one who sent this book.

— Basketball?

— Two, says Dad. Two basketballs. One under each arm.

Nobody says anything for a while, and so I say: — Wow.

— And so what happened to the number-two husband? says Lanlan. Did she leave him too?

You can hear everything in the house that hums then. Like the fridge, and the radiators, and the timer that turns the living room light on.

— No, he died in an accident, says Dad. I always just assumed he was my father.

He cracks his knuckles.

— Adopted! he says.

— Who's adopted? I say.

— Me, he says. How do you like them apples.

He looks strange, like one corner of his face got caught on a fish hook.

— How lucky! I say.

The sweat beads are getting bigger.

— Second choice doesn't mean second-best, I say. It's just how things happened.

— A joke, he says. Haha. A joke. Why didn't my mother tell me? How could she not have told me?

LAN / *He kept saying that. But doesn't everyone have things they want to forget? It's only natural.*

WENDY / — And why did your father never tell you? he asks Lanlan. — Why did he tell you she was dead?

— Maybe he did not want to talk about such unhappy things, says Lanlan. We had so much unhappiness already. Maybe he thought I was not strong enough to know. And anyway, what use was it?

LAN / *I said that because my family was from Suzhou, we were still* Suzhouren. *Even if my mother was from Sichuan, we were still from Suzhou. A very nice place.*

We looked for my name at the end of the book, just to see it. And sure enough, there it was. Lin Lan.

Then I began to feel strange too.

WENDY / Lizzy comes in so we have to explain the whole thing all over again, it's like we have to convince her, she just can't believe it. Meanwhile Lanlan stares and stares at the book like she sort of gets the characters but not what they mean exactly.

LIZZY / Dad was like the opposite. Shocked, but then inspecting the book. Asking for translation. Pointing things out.

— Is that where my name would be? he asked Lanlan. Right next to yours?

— Of course, we do not even know that everything in the book is true, said Lanlan.

— You are in denial, I said.

— Denial? she said. What means 'denial'?

She put her hand on her potbelly. Her nails shone.

LAN / — Younger brother, *I said. Then I said it in Chinese.* Di di.

He put his head in his hands.

— At least you are not my real brother, *I said.* At least we are not like brother and sister, grew up together. It is just our names put together in the book.

CARNEGIE / And yet how much more natural, in the end, to be married to Blondie.

A joke!

WENDY / — I think it's great you were adopted, I say again.

But no one says anything back, Lizzy is looking at the two of them and thinking who knows what.

— Don't think anything, Lanlan says to Lizzy. Nothing to think about.

And she starts flipping through the book, reading all the characters like it's the easiest thing now.

— Look how many sons were give away to other families to carry on their line, she says. Look! In this generation, only one family had sons, all the rest had to adopt a son from somewhere else. Maybe your mother didn't tell you because so many families are adopt sons all the time. Who is going to carry on the family name if she does not adopt you, right? Really, she has no choice. Nothing to discuss.

—Maybe your mother didn't tell you because she thought it would make you feel bad, I say.

LAN / —Chinese people try not to make people feel bad, *I said.* We try to talk about something nice.

CARNEGIE / —That was Mama Wong all right. Never one to say something that might make someone feel bad, I said.

WENDY / The sweat beads are like running down in little streams now. He's this weird color I've never seen him turn before, and his face has that hooked look again and he sounds like he can't talk.

LAN / *My mother! I asked if I could see a picture of her, but no one answered, that's how strange* Carnegie *looked. That's how pale.*

LIZZY / —Are you okay, Dad? I asked. Dad! Are you okay?

WENDY / Mom used to say that once when I was little I sat on the stairs with her and asked if she would die, and when she said that she would, I cried and cried and said I didn't like dying and that if she died I would come and shake her and make her wake up. And when she said that might not work, but that there might be a heaven, she wasn't sure, some people thought so, I said I would go and find her there, but how could I find her? And she said it would be easy because she would stand in the very most obvious place, all I had to do was think what the most obvious place would be. And I said, in the garden, and she said okay, it was a deal, she would meet me in the garden.

But now I look at Dad and think where am I going to meet him? We never said where we were going to meet, and so I shake him and shake him and say, Dad! You have to wake up! You have to wake up! You have to wake up! Dad! Dad! And his eyes do open but they look so weird especially compared to his eyebrows which look the same. And when he says, My medicine, it's as if he is making his voice funny for fun, except that he's not joking when he says, Call 911. Although he does also tell us to tell the ambulance not to stop at Dunkin' Donuts.

— Tell them this time of day there are no more Munchkins anyway, he says.

And: — Don't shake me please, can't you see I'm already shaken?

And: — You'll always be my peanut. Don't forget. Don't forget.

CARNEGIE / They say you can't remember open-heart surgery, how could I possibly remember a thing? Maybe the ambulance ride, so much bumpier than you'd expect, and everything rattles, and it's amazing how slow cars are to get out of the way, apparently, because what you feel is not how fast the ambulance is going but how often the driver hits the brakes, again and again and again, thank god the EMT is there to protect you, where did they get this driver? And how many unconscious patients must be jolted back awake by the noise of the siren! You know you're still alive because it's giving you a headache, and besides, you feel the urge to drive yourself. At least tell them the best way to go. *This time of day I wouldn't take Route 2,* I say. Everything happening so fast and so slow, the snapshots already out of order: the face of the EMT, so much more interested than you'd expect, given how many emergencies he saw a day, I'd guess four or five, or was that wildly off? And Lizzy's round face when they slid me like a pizza into a pizza oven. Lan's thinner face and great posture. And Wendy's face, the thinnest, how hard it was to believe she had been such a fat baby. How teeny she seemed, disappearing behind my huge feet, my enormous feet, teenier even than Bailey would've seemed, if Bailey were there, because Bailey would've been held up by someone, whereas there was Wendy on her own feet. Teeny. Though that wasn't why soccer wasn't her sport, it just wasn't. Where was Blondie? I thought. Blondie. Bailey. All I could hear was Wendy's child-sized voice, dwarfed by my sheet-draped feet. Asking, Should I tell Mom?

— Tell Mom, yes! I shout, as best I can with the oxygen mask already over my mouth. The rubble of an earthquake mounded on my chest. — Tell Mom to take care of you! I try to tell the EMT, in case she can't hear me. — Tell her to tell her mom. Take care of her. Tell her.

— Relax, he says. Relax. Is this your first heart attack? Don't try to talk. Just nod or shake your head.

I nod.

— Good, he says.

— I want to go back, I tell him. My son. I need to call my wife.

But he just says: — Try to enjoy the ride; I'm giving you a little something.

Maybe I really did remember all that, but could I have remembered the emergency room, people pounding on my chest and yelling yelling and more people running in and yes the decision yes to open my chest and yes massage my heart yes? Of course I was under, and yet I have an impression of it all the same, no doubt from movies and *M*A*S*H:* the klieg lights, the veins found, the sensors stuck on, and not to forget the dozens of extras, all crowding around, squeezing your hand, delivering their big line. *Okay, we're moving you onto the table now. Just a pinch. This will be cold. You're going to be okay. How's the weather out there? You got to love the new tunnel.* A warm blanket; the cold cold O.R. The lights, the radio, the surgeon's eyes behind his glasses, and everyone splattered by the end like a butcher.

Of course I didn't see it, and yet I knew it later, vividly, the surprise was what my body knew—things it had never known before, my bruised and broken body, my pried-apart limbs; how punctured and be-tubed. Fluids in, fluids out, intake, outtake, meds and nurses, meds and doctors, visitors and dreams, all I could think was, I suppose I really am no longer young, to which Mama Wong said, Young! Of course not young, how could you be young! But you never grow up either! That's how I know I brought you up Chinese and still you grow up American.

Mom! I said. You're better.

Of course I'm better, what did you think? I was going to stay like an idiot forever?

Mom, I said. I had my heart attack. I got attacked by my heart.

Your heart was always problem, she said. From the beginning I say so—no drive, number one. Number two, have to rescue everyone. Even I am dead, look how you try to rescue me. For what? What kind of joke is that?

Mom, I said. Do you know this poem?

> We the living, we're passing travelers:
> It's in death alone that we return home.

Of course I know it, you think I have no culture? she said. You will never know how much I know.

I was going to be okay, but they were sending me back to the O.R., why were they were sending me back to the O.R.? Suddenly there was Lizzy saying they had to leave Bailey, Bailey wasn't allowed to come, good luck though, we all love you, and then there was Lan's voice, I thought, saying what? Was she whispering? And Wendy saying, We hope you live, then Blondie telling her not to say that, she shouldn't say that, and Wendy crying and saying I couldn't hear her anyway and what did that mean, 'unconscious'? Did that mean I was being kept alive? And was that Blondie's voice then telling her it was okay, even if I could hear I wouldn't mind? I hoped it was Blondie's, but then it was Lan's, and then they were all gone, and I couldn't say good-bye, I just wanted to remember what I could remember while I could. Why did everything hurt? Bailey's first full sentence—Dad go away. Followed by Mommy mine! Mommy mine! How Lizzy's arm hung stiff beside her after her tetanus shot, how she wouldn't let anyone even see it, and yet how she played still with her dolls and blocks and shopping cart. Played and played, with one arm. How old was she then? And Wendy, demanding Read book! I want Lizzy read book! Insisting, when we couldn't see the moon, Lizzy find! Lizzy find moon! Telling us, I don't like dying. Asking, What will happen when everyone on the earth is dead? And, When I have babies, will you be my grandpa? And there was Lan at her computer; and there, Blondie dividing perennials in the garden. Now who can I give this to?

And there I stood at the kitchen sink, licking the peach juice off my hands before washing them, of course I had to wash them, but first I had to get all the juice. It was a beautiful afternoon.

We were lucky! Now you think so. All that time you act like you want to be something else; now you wish you were FOB. That is because you know the end of the story. At the beginning of the story, you do not know what is happen, you don't feel so happy, believe me.

On the other hand, sometimes we get up early in the morning, just me and my small son, and I feel this is a big life. Sometimes I think how many people are bored, and how we are not bored. We are going somewhere; we are going, going. I made up my mind about it already, and I know. We are going up. You can be rich in money, and of course, this is good. But you can be rich in story, and this is good too. Sometimes I think people just want to be rich in money because money make their life a story.

Ma, I say. I got the book, and it turns out I'm not even your son.

Only an American boy would read something and think, Oh, that must be true. As if true is that simple!

So what is the truth? I say. Tell me before I go back to my family.

Your so-called family, she says, with a laugh.

My family, I insist.

She laughs again.

Lan is your daughter.

My long-lost daughter.

And I?

She laughs. Who you are if you are not my son?

I love Blondie, you know, I say. That's another joke. I married the love wife.

Then how can she be the love wife? Tell me.

And what about Lan? I might have married her, you know. If Blondie divorced me.

Another wrong wife!

Ma. Weren't you the one who sent her to me, from your grave? A second wife? A love wife?

Laughter.

It seemed natural enough, I say.

Natural! she exclaims. On the other hand, marry Blondie not so natural either.

What is, then?

Nothing is natural, she laughs. Nothing.

This is a joke, I say.

She laughs and laughs. No one is so easy to surprise as an American, she says. Let me ask you, now, honest way. How can you be my son?

How can I not be? I say, after a moment. After all, you wrecked my life.

Ah! Now you are like real Chinese! See some big joke.

Stay, I say. Mom. Don't go. Stay.

But she does not answer.

Come back, I say. How can I wreck my life by myself?

You doing fine by yourself, she says. Anyway, I am not your mother, talk to you. Of course not.

What do you mean?

Look how you love me, she says. How can I be your mother, you love me like that?

But I do, I say. I do.

Then I am not Mama Wong, she says. Do you see?

I see and I don't see, I say. I see and I don't.

Good! See and don't see, say and don't say, know and don't know. That is the natural way.

What do you mean?

Listen, she says. I was not your mother. You were not my son.

But that's not true.

Okay then. I was your mother. You were my son.

That's not—

Exactly!

I thought you said, A child should say this is my mother, period. This is my father, period.

Otherwise family look like not real, I said.

I thought you said—

Since when do you listen to me anyway?

Since—

What you listen is your own fault! I am dead! Don't blame on me!

But—

I am dead! I am dead! I am dead! Do you hear me? Dead!

But—

Shut up, she says. Go! No but.

But—

Two wives are always trouble, I can tell you that.

But—

Go, she says. The way you hang around, looks like I am the love wife. Go!

But—

What's the matter with Lily Lee? That's what I want to know.

Ma—
Go! Go!

WENDY / The waiting room is full of people waiting and waiting. Nobody says live or die, everybody talks about making it. *Did he make it? Did he make it?* And we talk that way too. *We hope he makes it. We hope he makes it.*

We talk about the other people.

We talk about the cafeteria.

We talk about the shop downstairs.

But mostly we don't say much. Mostly we hope, and wait for when we'll know what we'll know. And I guess that will be it. This world can disappear like any other, that's what Great-grandma Dotie used to say, but anyway, right now, here we are. Bailey and Lizzy and Lanlan and Mom and me. We're eating chips, we're watching TV, we're taking Bailey to the bathroom. We're doing somersaults, and shooting fire, and playing birthday party.

— I am three! Bailey tells us. Not two! Three!

Nobody stares at us, I guess it's obvious we're together.

Waiting.

One corner of the waiting room is ours because that's where we put our stuff, by the window. We take up five seats, but Bailey just uses his to jump off of. Mom sits across from Lanlan and her tummy. They both have snacks for Bailey, and Bailey takes snacks from them both. They both play with Bailey, and Bailey plays with them both. But it's like they're on opposite sides of the earth instead of in the same little corner, if one of them walks in front of the other, the other looks down. Mom's eyes barely even look blue anymore.

It's hard to believe you could ever call either one of them a love anything.

But these are our seats, there are no other seats, the waiting room is crowded. On the other hand, if we leave, no one takes them, I notice. Because they're our family's.

Mostly we don't leave anyway. Mostly we sit, minute after minute, watching the same clock, here in the corner of the waiting room that is where our family sits. Soon we will know, soon we will know, soon we will know something.

In the meantime, the family book is mine, I think. Does anyone even remember that? Mama Wong left it to me. Though of course I'm going to share it.

When the sun gets too bright, we pull the shade.

And just that second the surgeon appears, a silhouette in the doorway.

— Well, we went into extra innings, he says. But we made it.

We made it! How we cheer and cheer then, wildly, all of us—cheer and cheer, our whole family, together. Hooray! We made it! We went into extra innings, but we made it!

It's happy, so happy, and who knows?—just might stay happy. Look at us all hugging, after all, Lizzy and Bailey and Mom and Lanlan and me, and look now! How Lanlan grasps Mom's hand, and Mom grasps hers. That's happy!

But then they let go, and look away, blinking.

We made it! And yet we know now, too, what we know.

This world can disappear like any other.

It's amazing how dark a room can suddenly get.

Acknowledgments

Eternal thanks to the American Academy of Arts and Letters, the Lannan Foundation, the Radcliffe Institute for Advanced Study, and the Fulbright commission for their timely and critical support.

I thank too, for their endless good nature and inexplicable faith, my agent, Maxine Groffsky; my editor, Ann Close; and my husband, David O'Connor.

This book draws to an unusual degree on the stories and perceptions of a large number of people. I thank you all for your patience and candor and enormous generosity.

PERMISSIONS ACKNOWLEDGMENTS

A NOTE ABOUT THE AUTHOR

Gish Jen grew up in Scarsdale, New York. Her work has appeared in *The New Yorker, The Atlantic Monthly,* and *The Best American Short Stories of the Century.* The author of three novels and one book of short stories, she lives in Massachusetts with her husband and two children.

A NOTE ON THE TYPE

The text of this book was set in Bembo, a facsimile of a typeface cut by Francesco Griffo for Aldus Manutius, the celebrated Venetian printer, in 1495. The face was named for Pietro Cardinal Bembo, the author of the small treatise entitled *De Aetna* in which it first appeared. Through the research of Stanley Morison, it is now generally acknowledged that all old-style type designs up to the time of William Caslon can be traced to the Bembo cut.

The present-day version of Bembo was introduced by the Monotype Corporation of London in 1929. Sturdy, well-balanced, and finely proportioned, Bembo is a face of rare beauty and great legibility in all of its sizes.

Composed by Stratford Publishing Services,
Brattleboro, Vermont

Printed and bound by Berryville Graphics,
Berryville, Virginia

Designed by Soonyoung Kwon